HUNTER

Hunter by name Hunter by nature

Zom Lee

Thanks for reading!

Zom ☆

Print ISBN: 9798453484690

Dedicated to my darlings Voz and Frey for your endless energy, cuddles and memes.

To Ugz, thank you for everything else.

PROLOGUE

Beginnings

This Friday the thirteenth is turning into a monumental nightmare. A thin layer of sweat clings to my skin and clothes, every person sitting here in this warm, air less and crowded departure lounge, is hot and sticky. This so-called life changing, backpacking around the world trip is already beginning to feel like a big mistake, and I have not left the country yet.

"Check him out." Chloe points excitedly at the guy she spotted coming out of the toilets this morning. I sigh, bored with waiting for this fiasco to be sorted out and listening to the ever-constant ramblings of Chloe is not helping matters. I glance towards the toilets, looking at the mass of bags, miniature suitcases and rucksacks that litter the floor of the departure lounge. Who would have thought that the weather would be so hot in England, that the tarmac on the runway of the largest UK airport would melt, causing the cancellation of all outgoing flights from airports up and down the country. Our gap year travelling the world has not started well in this stagnant hell.

"Did you see that? He just smiled at me." I glance at the bubble head next to me, her mascara smeared around her eyes, her usual long and sleek hair is now a blonde ball of fuzz framing her sweaty pink face. There is a clatter of feet and suddenly like the arrival of a swarm of bees, there is movement around us. People begin to walk and jostle towards what has become the makeshift information desk. We were told we could leave the airport but if we do, it would be at least a two week wait before we could be re-scheduled onto other flights. Most of us have decided to stay and wait it out.

"Any flights going out at all today love?" Shouts an angry man with a moustache.

"Come on just give us a time frame." Shouts a mother with a sleeping baby wearing only a nappy strapped to her sweaty body. The flustered woman behind the information desk is beginning to shake with nerves. She has a sheet of paper and is attempting to reel off flight numbers that are cancelled today but are hoping to leave early tomorrow. The shouting from the crowd grows louder, forcing a security guard to move closer to the desk with nervous anticipation. After a visibly deep breath, four expected times of departure for flights today have been announced. Sadly, none of them apply to Chloe and me. I walk back to my make-shift bed and ignore the childish behaviour of families desperate to get to their two weeks, all inclusive, package holiday abroad.

I lie down on the cool tiled floor, my hands behind my head and attempt to enjoy five minutes of peace, in front of the in-dustrial sized fan closest to me. On thinking about it, if there is no announcement by eight tonight, I am going home and will just drag Chloe with me. We can start our gap year in a couple of weeks, when British summer time returns to its usual cold, grey drizzle. Time moves slowly. I survey my surroundings and watch the family opposite. Two parents with two children; a boy and a girl. The kids are sitting cross legged on the floor reading their books, their mother sits reading her magazine, but it is the father who has caught my attention. He cannot stop fidgeting. I reckon he has Tourette's or something. Considering the noise, heat and general chaos in this place, his family sit sedately in their own little bubble, while their dad stares into space one minute and then starts his ritual of moving around the next whilst tapping his head in an almost painful rhythmical motion.

I watch as he crosses his legs then uncrosses them, he stands up and paces, then sits back down, then moments of silence as he seems to zone out, with just an odd jerky movement. I observe his behaviour, it's odd the way he taps his head, not quite in a soothing way more like he is trying to dislodge something.

I roll over on to my side, take a deep breath of warm humid air and slowly breathe out, my moment of relative calm disturbed by the audible grunting of the man opposite. I take another deep breath before I roll back. The head tapping frenzied. I can't tell if he is in pain? Everyone glances over in his direction and his wife looks at him from over the top of her magazine. His head tips backwards and his eyes stare unblinkingly at the ceiling, his left leg twitches in an odd way. His behaviour has become less annoying and more unnerving as the minutes tick by.

I decided to go in search for that wayward sister of mine. She has made friends with the bloke from earlier and I am thankful that he is with a group of people. I do not disturb them, they seem to be enjoying themselves despite the heat, instead I choose to use the toilet before heading back to my makeshift bed on the floor. Two hours pass and we are none the wiser on whether we will travel tonight. I hang up from a brief call with dad. He has the right idea, we should go home and let the insurance deal with our cancelled flights. According to the weather report, we are expecting some cooler weather early next week. I promise to keep my folks updated as my eyes are drawn to the behaviour of my neighbour. The father is talking loudly to himself now, his children are completely ignoring him, but his wife is beginning to look worried. The couple who was sitting next to the family have moved away and no one comes to replace them and take the space closest to the industrial sized fan, clearly the public prefer to sweat and swelter then put up with the ramblings of a nervously agitated man.

Chloe comes back with water and a warm cheese sandwich for lunch. She even managed to bring me an iced coffee. I smile up at her with gratitude. We sit together, crossed legged on our towels eating. She tells me about the group of people she has been hanging out with, Chloe wants to swap numbers with them so they can contact us when they get to Australia.

"Sure, we can do that." I reply, half thinking that even if the dates are right and we are all in Sydney at the same time, the likelihood of seeing them again is slim at best.

The man opposite shouts out in what sounds like pain. I look over, wondering what is going on with him. Chloe is still nattering away, completely oblivious to what is happening around us. The wife is looking panicked, this unnerves me. Her husband is gripping his head with both hands as she rubs his back, speaking to him in whispered tones. Their children have disappeared, and the couple are alone. He rocks gently backwards and forwards, clearly whatever she is saying is having no effect on him. He pulls at his hair and thumps at his head between his eyes, his shirt is absolutely soaked through with sweat his skin is flushed.

Chloe and I discuss the possibility of us packing up and going home, she is against the idea of course, unaware of what is going on opposite and how uncomfortable that man's behaviour is making me feel. She wants to stay and hang out with the cool group, I should not complain as it is her holiday too, so we compromise. If our flight is not called by eight, we will leave and go back home. I glance over as the foursome who were set up on the other side of the family opposite, begin moving away from them.

Now this looks odd. The family are sitting in the middle of a large space with a huge gap around them. The children are back, and their mother is trying to reassure them as she lays her husband down on the floor, propping his head with one of the children's rucksacks.

Chloe, having done her sisterly duties leaves me to go back to her new friends. I am grateful that she has a distraction. I pick up the remnants of our lunch and pop it back in the bag ready to discard, which I then drop as the man opposite lets out a blood

VIII

curdling scream. I see security getting closer. One guard on his radio and four others are watching from a distance. People on the floor are all looking at him, a couple of people shout out for him to go home. His wife looks horrified, and I cannot help but feel sorry for her. I get up to go for another walk, giving the poor family a break from my prying eyes.

I stop at the shop for more water, a bottle of Coke Cola and a John Grisham novel they had on offer, then check on Chloe, she is having a great time socialising, so I leave her to it. I walk back to our stuff and into pandemonium central, the wife is in tears, one of the security guards has her children and is moving them away from their father. Another guard is attempting to comfort the wife, who is now sobbing uncontrollably. She has no idea what is wrong with her husband who is now lying on the floor in the foetal position, wailing like a baby and shaking. I open my Coke and sip it slowly. Watching the scene unfold, a guard glares at me for staring, so I pick up my book and read for an hour, ignoring the hushed whispers, sobs, and muffled screams.

Pins and needles in my legs cause me to put the book down, I glance around, looking for my sister and spot her at the bar with one of the girls from the group. I'm brought back to the here and now as a team of people arrive to check on the man opposite. One has a first aid box, not that I think there will be anything in there that could help. In the last hour he has changed from a crying mess to a loud aggressive animal. His wife is desperately trying to calm him down with little success, he snarls at her, swatting her hands away as if he cannot bare her touch. He has been requested to move somewhere more comfortable for him and his family, but he will not leave the departure lounge in case his flight is called. The poor chap is delusional, no way are they going to let him on a plane in his current state. Suddenly he sits up, he does not look right, his eyes are bloodshot and wild looking, his skin is translucent, the pink flush from early now faded to a pallid grey, he stares into space as if he cannot see or hear, for a few minutes he is quiet and still, scarily still. Security is on the radio, quietly talking, monitoring him no doubt. A plan is being formulated and the emergency services called.

Twenty minutes later and he is back to fidgeting again, his legs jerk forwards like he has no control over them, he shouts out and looks wildly around while holding his hands over his ears. The staff shrug to one another. One thinks he is having some sort of panic attack and advises his wife to get him to put his head between his legs and breathe deeply, the other thinks he is having an episode, of what I cannot hear. I watch in stunned silence as the group of security guards leave, one on his phone describing the man's strange symptoms. Things quieten down for a few minutes; I am surprised the police haven't been called and he forcibly removed. I pack my book away and gather up our things, a horrible feeling in the pit of my stomach that things are only going to get worse confirms I am making the right decision. I am ready to move away, quickly if I need to.

He is back in his catatonic state but looks wrong. His wife is talking to him, audibly disturbed by his behaviour and is begging him to go home but with little success. I glance at my watch, it is coming up to six and in another couple of minutes, the airport representative will be back with an update. As if on cue, people start moving, running, and pushing to get to the front of the information desk. Out she comes, a different woman this time, all smiles with bright red lips and a sheet of paper in hand, flanked on both sides with two of the airport's security guards. I stand, ready to move and join the crowds when I am knocked to the ground. I am momentarily winded as I try to get my bearings and catch my breath. It takes a second to realise that the man from opposite is on my back. He is snarling and his drool is dripping onto my neck. Self-preservation kicks in, this guy is big, but I am bigger, and age is on my side. I do not want to hurt him as he clearly is not in charge of his faculties, but I don't want to be injured either. His wife is screaming and attempting to pull him off me, but he is not listening. All I can hear is his laboured breathing, grunts, and snarls.

"Get off me mate." I yell but he doesn't seem to hear. He is frantically grabbing at my head with both of his hands. The heat is radiating off him and he has an odd smell. We struggle on the floor, I can hear his wife shouting for help as I manage to finally push myself up, knocking him off my back. Rolling over onto my stomach and jumping to my feet. Years of competing in Judo competitions have kept me strong and agile. His feeble attempts to get to his feet are laughable. We are surrounded by people who stand open mouthed, not one of them is interested in tonight's flights anymore. Security makes their way through the crowd and scan the scene.

"Can someone please help this man." I shout, yet no one approaches us.

Everyone talks at once and the noise level increases tenfold. The man on the floor finally manages to stand, security look less than pleased about having to manhandle him. I look around for Chloe; I have had enough and now just want to leave and go home. The crowd continue to watch us as he sways but not like he is drunk. He looks like a boxer who has taken too many punches to the head in the twelfth round. His movement is odd as he attempts to walk forwards. I look to his wife who seems to be in terrified shock and then look back to the man standing before me. We are closed in by a wall of people all waiting for something to happen. No one is interested in the information desk now. Stepping back slowly, keeping my eyes on him, adrenaline kicking in and pulsing through my veins, he stands there blankly looking at me, through me. I now pray that the police have been called.

I scan the body of people, looking for Chloe and as I glance away from the drooling man to look behind me, a woman screams. In seconds, he has moved a good three meters, launching himself into the crowd. People are panicking and desperately trying to move away, stumbling as they attempt to flee. The screaming continues, he lands on one man, knocking him to the ground and taking a bite out of his shoulder, blood flowing freely as he yells in shock. The screams around the departure hall grow louder and panicked. This man is rampaging through the crowd, grabbing, and biting randomly as the public scatter in all directions.

My heart sinks as I realise my sister is frozen to the spot in fear and he is heading right for her. In that moment the need to protect my sister overwhelms me. I run into the crowd and pull the growling man off Chloe before he gets a chance to do any damage. Punching him twice in the back of the head to get him to let go. I have his attention, he turns his mouth open wide, blood and saliva dribbling down his chin. I punch him in the face, and he stumbles backward, I grab him and pull him with all my might away from my sister. In my adrenaline filled state I can hear his snarling, feel his hot hands attempt to grab my head so I do the only thing I can, throw a punch that lands at his chin, forcing him to turn away.

I take the opportunity to grab his right arm and then his left, putting him in an arm lock while kicking his legs from under him. Using my full body weight, I twist and slam him to the ground, he lands sprawling onto his stomach giving me the opportunity to sit on his back holding him down.

I struggle to keep a hold of him, his skin on his arms slippery from a mixture of blood and sweat. I can still hear screaming and panic as one security guard approaches and shouts if I'm okay to hold him like that until back up comes. I look at him in disbelief but nod yes, hot from the exertion of manhandling him and soaked to the skin with my own sweat. I scan the crowd and find my sister who looks shaken but unhurt, she gives me a sad smile as one of the girls from the group earlier puts her arm around her shoulders and a security guard ushers them away and out of sight. I close my eyes briefly, blinking out the sweat that is running down my brow from my forehead, heaving a sigh of relief that my sister is fine. Unbelievably, I have been forced to keep the man below me restrained for another half an hour at least, he is snarling and thrashing about to dislodge me from his back, not once does he waver or stop wriggling. He is strong, and from the look of him I would never have guessed just how strong. I have him face down on the floor and between my legs, my body weight is attempting to keep him in place. His head turns as he looks over his shoulder, jaws open and teeth displayed.

This monster would bite me if he had the chance. The departure lounge is evacuated. Only the people who were bitten and airport staff who are administering first aid remain. Eventually some handcuffs are found, and his hands are cuffed behind his back by two members of the security team. Yet apart from this one act, no one is willing to get close to us. A medical screen is moved around us, and I am left alone with this thrashing monster.

My arms ache and my lower back is killing me from the position I am in. Yet he does not give up trying to dislodge me and not once does he speak. He continues with his constant struggling and attempts to overthrow me. I have no idea where my sister is now, I cannot reach my mobile, so have no chance of contacting my parents. I have been left alone, completely cut off from the world around me. I hear the faint voices of airport staff whispering, no one comes to check on us, I have never felt so frightened and alone in my life.

After what feels like forever, I hear the footsteps of someone approaching us, the screen being moved. This causes the maniac below to snap his head up as he begins to oddly sniff the air. The thrashing begins in earnest again as I hold on tight, wishing that this nightmare would just end. A man appears, one that I have not seen here in the last twenty-four hours. Jet black hair swept off his face. Dressed in Jeans and a black t-shirt; black tattoos cover his arms. I look up at his face, relieved to have someone here to finally help but this guy does not look like a professional in any capacity.

"Well done for keeping him restrained." He says as he walks around us slowly.

"What's wrong with him?" I stammer, barely able to get the words out of my mouth. Finally, he stops and drops to his knees, his green eyes searching mine.

"I'm going to need you to hold him down for thirty more seconds than it is all over." I nod as panic fills me; this feels wrong. Calmly he reaches behind him and pulls out a weird gimp mask from his back pocket. I feel my own breathing increasing in panic. He straps the mask around the head of the still thrashing man, which muffles the sounds coming from his vocal cords. He then pulls out from his back pockets, two things; a filled syringe and needle and what looks like a pen. He unsheathes the needle and plunges it into the neck of the man beneath me. I look at this guy, he doesn't look much older than me, I stare in awe and disbelief. I'm not truly sure what he is doing as I watch him push the plunger and feel the thrashing body below begin to slow his movement.

"What's wrong with him?" I ask again hearing a new level of panic in my voice. I loosen my hold on his body a little and watch as he places the pen gadget into from what I can see, into the man's mouth, there is an audible click causing the man to fall still. Bile hits the back of my throat when I realise that the man beneath me is dead.

"You can stand now." The words are stern and sharp. I shift myself slightly and like a robot, stiffly move. My feet are rooted to the floor, and I hesitate as I watch the removal of the mask from the body that lies dead on the floor.

"What did you give him?" I stammer, my body beginning to shake, as shock begins to set in, he stands looking at me, like he deals with this every day.

"Just a sedative. Are you injured?"

We both look down at the floor as the body of the man makes one last gurgling sound. I am not injured, I force myself to face this unnamed killer with the mask and syringe.

"No. No. No, no I'm fine I think." My usually well-hidden stammer takes over. I swallow in a large gulp of air and attempt to continue to speak.

"What the fuck was wrong with him? Is he dead?" The words finally come out in a jumbled mess. I know he is dead, and it sends shivers down my spine. I am desperately trying to hold down my cheese sandwich. The man shrugs non-committal.

"He was just another DROM that needed to be dealt with. Do not worry about it. We'll take it from here."

"You go wait at the information desk and I'll have someone come to see you." I turn, willing my legs to move and step over the body that lies dead between my feet.

"Hey what's your name?" My body quivers from the stress my muscles were under.

"Cameron Peel." I stammer.

"Cameron Peel, you did really well and saved lives today." I take one last glance over my shoulder at the unnamed killer as I walk away shakily in horror. This end of the departures lounge has been cordoned off. A group of four men dressed in black wait patiently outside the screen, watching me as I walk slowly to the information point. I lean over and vomit on the floor.

A security guard and an airport official guide me out of the departure lounge. I am given a quick check up by a doctor who is looking for bites and scratches. I was very lucky to have escaped unscathed or, so I was told. My details are taken before I am reunited with my relieved and sobbing sibling and walked out of the airport to a waiting car. No one else stops to talk to us, no one requested I give a statement or an account of what happened, and no one mentioned the man with the syringe and mask. Chloe and I are driven back home in uncomfortable silence.

An hour later, the car pulls into our road, mum and dad are in the front garden waiting for us. We get out of the car and into the arms of our waiting parents, our luggage left on the kerb by the driver. Without a word the driver and car are gone. There is no mention of the police wanting to contact us later, no crime number given. The world is acting like nothing happened at that airport today. I am happy to be home, mum is fussing over Chloe and I. Dad has switched on the television, after I explained to my family what happened half a dozen times. We watch the twenty-four-hour news channel. There is no breaking news of a crazed man rampaging at an airport. There is no news of the death of a man at all. Then at eleven that evening, a small story of a fight breaking out over bottles of water in the airport is mentioned. We were at that airport and that is not what happened. My family look at me in disbelief. I am shocked. It seems that today did not happen. No mention at all on the news of me wrestling a crazed, rampaging man to the ground. There was no naming of the father who lay dead on that tiled airport floor and no mention of the tattooed killer wielding the syringe and mask. The incident today seems to have been complete erased.

CHAPTER ONE

The Return

A shiver runs down my spine whilst kneeling in the raised flower beds. I stop for a moment as a spider, black and hairy runs across my knee. I watch it scuttle lazily along the fabric of my trousers, keeping still so as not to disturb its path. I pull my eyes away from the humble arachnid and look up briefly, having the strange sensation that I am being watched. I decide to pack up and finish this flower bed first thing tomorrow morning when it is cooler, it is just too hot out here in the afternoon sun. I notice movement out of the corner of my eye, the shadow of someone approaching me, no doubt Andy my fellow gardener needs advice for the eighth time today, I wouldn't mind but he has worked here longer than I have. I lower my head and continue working, if I look busy perhaps, he won't bother me.

"Ellie, the manure has arrived. Where shall I put it?" I hold my breath for a second before I gaze up. I can't help but frown at Andy, who I am sure is on a mission to drive me crazy.

"Can you be a dear and chuck it behind the shed where we usually keep it." He smiles as he walks past, breaking into a tuneless whistle whilst pushing an empty wheelbarrow. I watch him as he walks away, shaking my head slightly at his nerve. Andy stops to look back, flashing me his usual surfer boy smile, then oddly glances up and over my head. His smile fades, replaced with a slight grimace.

"Hello Ellie." My head turns towards the sound of the deep yet friendly voice. I am greeted by a huge grin that reveals a small dimple to the right of two plump pink lips. A head of jet-black hair, swept back and out of control, frames the handsome face of its owner. I smile up at the familiar pair of bright green eyes which are attempting to search my squinting brown ones. I know exactly who has arrived at Hedge Hill for the summer, after all I have been dreaming about him, on and off for months.

"Julian Hunter." I reply a little too loudly, whilst standing. Julian is still grinning as I step over the wall to join him on the path. Feeling a moment of awkwardness, I remove my gloves and drop them to the floor, extending my sweaty hand out in a professional manner. Julian takes it firmly and we shake. I cannot drag my eyes away from his. My damp hand still in his.

"When did you arrive?" I ask, pulling my hand gently away to brush dirt off my green shirt. A little wave of nervousness sweeps over me as Julian's eyes follow the movement of my hands, he raises an eyebrow, a smile evident on his lips.

"You look beautiful." I instantly flush with embarrassment and begin to fiddle with my hair, my flustered brain trying to think of a meaningful reply. Thankfully my attention is momentarily drawn away from Julian, Andy comes into my field of vision, walking toward us with a raised eyebrow and a questioning look, his wheelbarrow piled high with horse manure.

"Behind the shed Andy." I shout over, thankful for this brief distraction and trying not to laugh at him struggling, he nods his head at me, but I can see he is dying to know who I am talking to.

"Sorry about that." I mumble. Julian smiles as he glances at Andy and then back to me. I can see Andy hovering out of the corner of my eye, Julian stands patiently putting his hands in his pockets, looking amused.

"I got here a couple of hours ago. I have unpacked, had lunch and am now ready to explore the gardens before settling back in my room with a good book."

"Are you staying with us for the usual four weeks?" The question is out of my mouth before I can censor myself. Julian gazes over at Andy and then the hotel grounds. I take a deep breath and use this moment to compose myself.

"The gardens look as lovely as ever." I smile at Julian with pride and nod in agreement.

"Thank you, we have tried to make the hotel look extra special this year. You will find a touch of the old English garden all around the grounds. Plenty of roses dotted about, a camomile lawn just over there, and we have a secret garden tucked away around the back that I highly recommend you explore, bring your book as there are areas perfect to sit and read." I realise I am rambling and look down at the floor, my mouth finally getting the message from my brain to shut up. I am positive he doesn't want to hear the verbal tour that I give our elderly guests. My legs feel like jelly as I look back up at Julian, taking in his attire. Julian smiles warmly, his eyes following mine as he folds his arms tightly over his chest. I notice the muscles of his upper arms bulge slightly through the material of his shirt and I can't help but swallow.

"I'm going to go for that walk now. It is lovely to see you, Ellie." I smile warmly at him, my eyes wandering over his strong chin and up to his lips briefly.

"Of course. It is nice to see you too. Enjoy your walk and enjoy your stay." I catch myself staring at Julian and turn my head away momentarily. My heart is thumping under my breastbone, and I feel flustered. Julian smiles, his eyes linger a moment longer than necessary before walking on. I need to get into the shade and have some water. I feel completely flushed and I am not entirely sure it is because of the heat. Reaching down I pick up my gloves from the floor, pulling them on and steadily climb back into the raised flower bed. I begin filling my sack with the freshly pulled weeds as I think happy thoughts about Julian's return for the summer season.

"Good afternoon, dear." I look up to see the friendly face of an elderly gentleman and his wife on their afternoon stroll.

"Good afternoon." I reply as they walk on. I pull at a large dandelion as my mind wanders back to all things Julian. He looked well but then he always does. His skin is sun kissed, face freshly shaven and framed perfectly by his messy mop of dark hair. The way he dresses makes me feel a little giddy. I tug hard on a weed, its roots firmly holding it in place before it uproots, and I place it in the sack. Julian's style reminds me of a librarian at a wedding, grey trousers, long sleeved navy shirt with a grey tie and a grey tank top. He must be absolutely baking in his outfit. I smile to myself, momentarily lost in thought, it appears I still have a small crush on him.

Last summer he stopped and said hello when our paths crossed one morning. Over the following days we got to know each other a little, he would stop to talk when he saw me working outside; rain or shine and I appreciated the company. I had been caught up in grief to really talk to anyone. One Tuesday last summer, I was having a particularly tough day. Nothing was going right that day, my orders had not been delivered, Andy was off sick and there was me holding the fort.

That was not the problem or the cause of my distress however, as I found myself in tears searching the shed for a trowel. I let myself cry that day and when I had finished, I left the shed to find Julian standing outside with two cups of black coffee in his hands. Julian stood leaning against the shed wall; no doubt having heard my sobs of utter distress. I emerged, flushed, puffy eyed and tear stained. Silently he handed me a cup, he did not say a word and neither did I, just a small smile when I accepted the cup of steaming liquid.

He never asked me what was wrong, choosing to walk me to the bench and sit me by the lavender. I never told him either. I couldn't talk about it being exactly six months to the day that my mother had died. My tears were triggered by one single happy memory that had my emotions spiral out of control. It certainly had not been the first bad day I have had to deal with and most definitely would not be the last, yet that simple act of kindness on that day pulled me out of my grief induced darkness.

That was the start of our friendly but sometimes awkward acquaintanceship and soon, coffee become a regular thing. Julian would turn up just as I was finishing work for the morning, sometimes with a coffee, sometimes with a smile and if I were lucky, both. Together we would sit outside by the lavender as I ate my sandwich. We chatted about anything and everything, it was pleasant, light-hearted and I looked forward to seeing him each day. I tug on another weed, deep in thought when a cough disturbs me, I gaze up into a pair of piercing green eyes and the handsome face of Julian Hunter once again.

"Pardon?" I look quizzically up at him, realising that he has just spoken, and I didn't hear a single word.

"I am here for my usual four weeks. I did not answer your question earlier. Are you free later?"

I drop my fistful of weeds into the burlap sack, glancing at the mess I have made. I stand and swipe at my forehead with the back of my gloved hand and climb as lady like as I can muster, back down to his level on the path.

"Yes, I am actually. Free that is. Free tonight." I am aware I am rambling like the village idiot and force myself to stop.

"Meet me at the bar for a drink?" For some reason I flutter my eyelashes instead of verbally answering yes to his invitation. Inside I cringe, this is such a face palm moment! I feel completely under dressed, have been talking like a crazy woman and now I have lost control of my eyelids. What is wrong with me?

"Yes." I mumble, my brain finally taking control of my body.

"Yes, that would be lovely".

"Great! Is seven good?" Julian asks returning my smile with a jaw dropping one of his own. I notice the sly way he looks me up and down, causing my cheeks to redden a little more.

"Seven is perfect, I'm really looking forward to seeing you then."
I reply, mortified at how desperate that just sounded. I send a
silent prayer to the gods to keep me quiet. Julian reaches his arm
out and very gently with his thumb rubs my forehead, I flinch
slightly at his unexpected touch. His brow furrows.

"Sorry, you have a little streak of dirt.... just there." He gives me
an embarrassed look as he slowly withdraws his hand from my
now blazing skin. I would bet fifty quid that I am as red as a
beetroot.

"Thank you." I reply timidly, taking my glove off and tenderly
rubbing the area he has just touched.

"Seven." He repeats nodding his head. I stand dazed for a second
as I watch him walk off. I touch my forehead again before pulling my glove back on. Reaching over to grab my burlap sack, I
decide to definitely call it a day out here. I look up to find Julian
has stopped. He smiles one last time, then is gone. I take in a
deep breath as I clear the pulled weeds from the flowerbed, place
them into the burlap sack and walk to the back of the sheds to
dispose of them on the compost heap. I head to my tiny office,
strategically placed by the shed, a portacabin that houses our
office equipment, my desk, computer, and a small fridge. I grab
my bottle of water and sit on the stool by the door to cool down.
Andy has his back to me as he walks quietly past. Suddenly it
dawns on me, what am I going to wear?

* * *

The countdown has begun. It has gone five and I have exactly
two whole hours to get myself ready. I leave the storage shed and
take my time as I walk back to the main building, entering the
hotel through the back doors and head up to my suite, well room
really. One of the benefits of working at the hotel is living on site.
I am one of four staff who lives on site at Hedge Hill hotel and living at your place of employment has its advantages. Breakfast,

lunch, and dinner are all provided which is handy, I no longer travel to work on public transport but most important of all, my best friend lives here too.

Once I entered my room, I change into a pair of shorts and an old t-shirt, then head down to the staff room to grab a snack. I managed to pick at some grapes, a digestive biscuit, and a stick of Cheddar, just enough to keep my blood sugar levels up for the evening ahead. At six, I head back to my room, nerves are starting to set in, and I must admit I am feeling just a little nervous. Last summer, the impression I had gotten from Julian was of an individual with no close family or friends. I sensed an element of loneliness in him, and I understood it, feeling the same. He never mentioned a significant other, I presumed he was single, not that I asked him outright, but I noticed he did not wear a wedding ring. I still do not understand why he chooses to save up his annual leave and take it in one, four-week block, at a hotel in West Sussex.

I head into my small bathroom, stripping out of my clothes before diving under the cool water. I give my long ginger hair a quick shampoo and apply some conditioner while I shave my legs and ex-foliate my entire body. After giving my head a good rinse, I wrap myself in my towel, as I contemplate what I am going to wear. Forty-five minutes to go and my hair is towel dried, I apply cocoa butter to my sun kissed skin, despite using sunscreen twenty times a day I have developed a tan which makes my brown eyes stand out and my red hair glow, not to mention causing a dusting of freckles across my nose and each cheek.

Grabbing a pale pink bra and matching knickers, I pull them on and rummage through my wardrobe needing something feminine but not sexy, something I can stay cool in and look half decent. As luck would have it, I find my cream-coloured linen dress, I pull it out and praise the gods for it being almost crease free, which is a miracle. I stare at my finished self in the mirror, I'm passable but I need a little something extra. I apply a smattering of mascara and a little pale pink lip gloss, and I am done. I glance at my clock again, willing the minutes to pass. I feel on edge, and I am having to tell myself that I am just catching up with a friend, nothing more. At the stroke of seven I enter the bar and spot Julian straight away. I stop and run my hands down my dress one last time, more out of nerves than anything else. I will my legs to move and begin to walk slowly towards him. He is sitting with his back to me, I give myself a moment to admire his strong shoulders and his mop of messy jet-black hair. Julian glances over his shoulder as if sensing my presence. He stands, his eyes not leaving mine. I give him an embarrassed smile and a small curtsey. In a quick and fluid movement, Julian is up returning my curtsey with a bow of his own. I stifle my laugh as he moves towards me, placing a strong hand around my waist and giving me a quick chaste kiss on my cheek.

"You look absolutely lovely Ellie." It occurs to me that this is the first time I have ever dressed up when meeting him for a drink.

"Thank you." I reply warmly, noticing that his hand is still resting lightly on my waist.

"Where are my manners?" Julian pulls out a chair inviting me to sit, which I do.

"What would you like to drink?" I smile and gaze into his lovely green eyes, I've never noticed how amazing they are before.

"Could I please have a sparkling water." Julian returns my smile and nods before heading to the bar, leaving me at the table to my thoughts for a few moments. Despite the heat this evening, Julian is overdressed. He appears to be wearing the same clothes he had on earlier, although his hair looks a little damp. I watch him move; my eyes wander over his fully clothed body as he stands politely at the bar waiting to order. He has the physique of a swimmer; strong upper arms and broad shoulders, I glance down and spot his muscular bottom as he leans over the bar. I am transfixed by it, and I chastise myself again. Thinking of him in that way is going to get me into lots of trouble if I am not careful.

"Here you go, one sparking water with a slice of lime and ice." He gives me a wink as he places both glasses on the table.

"Thank you." I reply, eagerly picking up my glass and taking a quick sip, the bubbles from the sparkling water tickling my tongue and the back of my throat. I am impressed that he remembered how I like my water as I take another cool sip. I glance out of the window casually, trying to gather my thoughts. Julian pulls his chair closer to me, his knee lightly brushes mine. I take another sip of water to give myself a second to think of something to say when I notice Julian is studying me. I put my glass back down on the table.

"So how has your year been?" I ask, Julian laughs lightly, leaning back in his chair, his arms folded over his chest.

"That is a pretty broad question." He glances at me, the tone of his voice and the expression on his face sends a shiver down my spine but not in a good way. I shrug off the sudden weird vibe I just got from him. I stay quiet, not quite sure what to say next.

"My year has been very busy work wise, travelling repeatedly around the country. I have certainly been looking forward to coming back here for my break that is for sure." Julian holds my gaze for a moment longer than necessary. I can't help but wonder why he was looking forward to coming back to Hedge Hill Hotel. This place is in deepest darkest Sussex and is hardly the most exciting hotel in the world. Julian reaches for his glass and takes a sip. I watch him closely as he swallows.

"How has your year been?" He returns my question. I momentarily think of my year so far, how every day is still heartbreakingly painful yet easier to manage, I feel like I have turned a corner and can see the light at the end of the tunnel.

"I have been busy here with work, planning those flower beds." I gesture with a nod of my head out of the large window. I smile, feeling more positive about my life then I have in months.

9

"Are you seeing anyone?" My eyes widen at the question. I glance nervously around the room before I answer his question, trying to think past my sudden mental block.

"No. I'm not seeing anyone." I stop, my stomach in knots but my head is determined.

"I haven't been in the right frame of mind for dating anyone, plus I have been relatively busy with work." I continue, gesturing to the gardens again. Julian smiles, keeping his green eyes on me.

"Good." He replies watching me. I smile and look away briefly, feeling my flush from earlier. I return my gaze back to Julian and decide to change the subject completely as we drink, keeping the conversation light-hearted. The bar begins to fill with patrons and with it the temperature rises. Julian places his empty glass on the table.

"Do you fancy accompanying me on a walk?" There is nothing I would like more than to walk but I hesitate, causing Julian to lean in towards me. He raises his eyebrow in expectation.

"I promise not to bite." I laugh nervously, what a strange thing for him to say!

"Yes, a walk would be nice, it is too hot in here." I mumble, gulping back my drink and placing my empty glass next to his. Julian stands, offering me his hand, which tentatively I take. I regret my decision to join him on a walk instantly.

CHAPTER TWO

Mine

We exit the bar together in silence. Julian walks beside me, his body guiding mine forward with his hand resting lightly on the small of my back. It may be the barest of touches, but it is enough to send a shiver down my spine at the unfamiliar contact. As we head out of the door and into the hallway, Julian removes his hand, the fabric on his upper arm brushes mine as he takes a hold of my hand firmly in his. He keeps his eyes forward despite my startled gaze up in his direction. His grip tightens a little, like he can sense that I want to pull my hand away. I glance at him again, wondering what is going on in that head of his. I decide to keep my sanity and leave my hand where it is for the time being. I am led out past main reception; an opulent room housing luxurious brown leather sofas and a whopping great oak desk, where our guests check in. Together we walk through the double doors and descend the steps out into the slightly cooler evening air. Julian's thumb skims over my knuckles lightly. I look down at his strong hand holding mine and it feels a little weird. I am clearly over thinking this. I glance left and right, not sure where we are headed but glad that I know the hotel and its grounds well.

I gently attempt to remove my hand from his, but Julian just squeezes tighter, holding on as if his life depended on it. I have no idea where we are going, and his quiet demeanour is leaving me feeling unsettled. I want to say something, not quite sure what just yet. I scan the path, looking for someone to stop and say hello to, of course we are the only ones out here. I keep up with his strides yet cannot find a single word to say to him. We walk on, I still have no idea where we are going, until I spot a car parked at the end of the driveway, which we are headed for. I breathe in deeply, keeping the pit of growing panic under control until I finally find my voice.

"What are your plans for the summer?" I tug my hand gently backwards trying to remove my hand from his, only his grip gets tighter as the words tumble out of my mouth.

"I came to spend my summer with you."

I stop dead in my tracks, the shock of his words jolting me back to reality where I can finally prise my hand from his with one strong tug. Julian stops too, thrusting his hands into his back pockets like a petulant teenage boy. I step forwards and turn so we are standing face to face.

"I really am not sure what is going on here Julian, but if you are trying to freak a girl out, you are going about it the right way." I stand firm with my back straight and my arms folded over my chest. I stare at him waiting for him to attempt to diffuse this tumbling situation.

"I am perfectly aware of that." Julian replies smugly. He sounds like he is talking to a naughty child, I do not particularly like the tone of his voice, in fact I'm finding it and him irritating. Julian removes one hand from his pocket and runs it through his messy hair, brushing the strands away from his forehead, his unblinking green eyes bore into mine. He is as still as a statue, and I am positive he is holding his breath. With a determined look on his face, his nostrils flare as he breathes, he is clearly mulling over something.

"Well, is that all you can say?" I wait for him to reply, becoming irritated by his stance as he watches me.

"Ellie, you are mine!" His words came out in a whisper. I stand firm waiting for him to elaborate or explain what he means. But he does not. Julian's words reverberate around my head, like he shouted them as though he bought me at auction. A feeling of disgust washes over me. I'm confused by his meaning and in urgent need of clarification. We stand staring at each other, I decide that Julian is delusional, and I am matching his madness because I am still here. I take a steadying breath while Julian studies me. I do not reply straight away, we stand face to face, our eyes locked in some secret, silent duel. But I cave first, the tension too much for me to handle.

"Julian, I am not interested in any kind of relationship with you. It is best if we don't see each other again. Enjoy your stay." I turn and head back to the hotel, adrenaline coursing through my veins. Without giving my body the chance to protest I walk quickly, willing myself not to look back at him.

I enter the large building I call home. A lot can happen to a person in a year and boy has Julian changed. Although, I did not really know him well to begin with. I jog up the stairs and decide to go and talk to Nicky. I feel deflated at how half an hour ago I was so excited to have a drink with Julian. I really do not want to find myself in some sort of oddball relationship, I live and work here, I am sure it would be unethical to engage in any activity with a hotel guest, no doubt there is a rule to stop staff fraternizing with the guests.

I rub my fingers, remembering how warm and strong Julian's hand felt holding mine and I almost feel sad walking out on him, almost. After three loud knocks causing my knuckles to sting, the door swings open revealing a man with a very wet and naked torso and a white towel wrapped loosely around the waist.

"Hey honey, you're just in time to scrub my back." Nicky says grinning. I air kiss his cheek as I brush past him and plonk myself on the edge of his messy, unmade bed.

"Go and dry yourself off, put some clothes on, I need to pick your brain."

"What's up?" He shouts at me as he disappears into his bathroom. I reach down and prise off my shoes before scooting backwards to sit in the middle of the mess.

"Make yourself at home." Nicky sneers, knowing full well that I already have. I wait for a minute, smoothing out the duvet around me. Nicky comes out wearing faded blue jeans and a tatty Kiss t-shirt that is now damp around the shoulders.

He dives onto the bed, manoeuvring himself opposite me, rubbing furiously at his wet hair with his towel.

"What is the matter with you?" He sings, attempting to look at me from under the towel. I sigh loudly and explain exactly what happened minutes earlier. Nicky looks me over and starts laughing.

"You are a fucking idiot, Ellie." He manages to get out between full belly laughs.

"I thought you were supposed to be my BFF dick head." I retort, folding my arms in mock annoyance which only makes him laugh harder.

"This is serious Nick; I'm going to have to see this guy around all month."

He stops laughing and looks thoughtful for a second. Nicky is devastatingly handsome, black hair and eyes to match, especially when he puts on his posh public school boy accent. Thankfully he is one of the good guys, although he does spend an enormous amount of time laughing at me. Nicky swears like a sailor and prances around almost naked without a care. But when he is in serious mode, he is desperately honest and insightful.

"Ellie I am not sure that what I have to say is what you want to hear. I would suggest you go with the flow. This guy has got under your skin from what you have said. You had a little crush on him last year, remember. What if he has been harbouring feelings for you too?" Nicky stops for a moment, choosing his words wisely.

"So, what if he is only here for a month, have a little fun with him, if he wants to hold your hand, let him." Nicky stops again, giving his head one last rub with his towel. He hasn't heard a single word about how Julian freaked me out.

"You did hear what I said about me being his and all that?" I ask fidgeting with my hair. Nicky nods and gives me a solemn look.

"He sounds as awkward as you are. Ellie, if you were really scared you could have removed your hand and asked him what exactly he was doing, you were in a public place. You did not. Sure, he appeared possessive, it was just nerves and as we speak, he could be sitting in his room crying into a cup of English tea and feeling stupid at what just happened. Granted, it was the wrong use of language, but you like him, you always have. He likes you, so put yourself out there." Nicky stops, his face solemn as his eyes search mine. I smile a little, mulling over Nicky's words.

"If you have completely gone off him, that's okay too. Do not give him a second thought. You know you are more than welcome to come party with me, I can hook you up with lashings of totty if you are ready for fun." I get a pearly white smile flashed at me, which I return with a well-aimed pillow to Nicky's head.

"Thank you. I better go." My hand is grasped for the second time tonight.

"Ellie you are allowed to have a little fun you know. If this guy is genuinely interested and I suspect, he is judging by the whole you are mine scenario." He stops and gazes at me, his expression becoming serious again for a moment.

"I can tell that you like him too, otherwise this wouldn't have bothered you. Give him a break. Take a chance and do not over think it. He did not ask for your hand in marriage, he just told you that you belong to him. He just might be lovely; he might be a clairvoyant. He may also be able to get into your knickers, dust you off and give you the best orgasm of your life." I pull my hands away and hit his arm.

"Thank you for that thought but it really doesn't help my situation." I get off the bed and scoop up my shoes from the floor.

"Will I see you for breakfast?" I ask.

"I am off to Brighton for some fun, I am hoping to get lucky so that will probably be a no. Do you want to come?" I laugh at Nicky's plan and shake my head.

"Thank you, not tonight. Play safe." I wave goodbye and leave, not wanting to hear any of the sordid details of his getting lucky plans tonight.

* * *

Up in my room I ponder my evening, lying on my bed with my feet up against the wall and hugging my pillow. I consider the options, Nicky does have a point, I do need to get out of my comfort zone more, I'll go and see Julian tomorrow, apologise for my hot headedness and walking away. I still feel agitated and have a desperate need to clear my head, I need to go out and walk off this excess nervous energy. I slip on a pair of plain black ballerina pumps and leave the hotel using the emergency exit at the side of the building. I head towards the great woods at the back of the building, which is now a local public nature reserve and my haven over the last few months. I breathe in the fresh, slightly damp air. I certainly was born an outdoor girl, just as well I chose a career in garden maintenance. I glance around making sure I am alone; I know the area well but am aware that it isn't the safest thing to be wondering around the woods at night.

"I was hoping I would find you here." My eyes find Julian's briefly, I freeze, glancing left and right realising we are most definitely alone but already having a route mapped back to the hotel.

"I was waiting for you over there." He points to an elder tree a few of meters away. I am positive that he wasn't there when I arrived moments ago, yet I glance to the area he points to.

"I was waiting, hoping you would come out, like you always do." Julian gives me an awkward smile. I stay mute momentarily lost for words.

"You know you shouldn't be out here by yourself in the dark, nasty things come out at night." Julian has a look of seriousness with a hint of warning.

"Why were you waiting for me? Are you my stalker now?" I finally ask, my fear overridden by sudden interest with a hint of anger. Julian takes a step forward and I step back, keeping my wits about me and ready to run if he gets too close.

"I'm sorry that I freaked you out earlier. That wasn't my intention." Julian's green eyes are on me. I stare back, searching his face for an explanation.

"I have a confession to make." He stops, taking a moment to run his hand through his hair.

"I come here every year to see you Elspeth." My heart thumps like crazy in my chest. How does he know my real name? I stare at him, watching him closely as he studies me. He wants a reaction and I need a second to figure this out. He takes a step towards me, this time I do not move away. He reaches out, gently lifting my chin so I have no choice but to look into his eyes.

"Speak to me Ellie." This is not a question but a demand that I hear in his voice. I splutter as I try to get the words out, I am momentarily tongue tied.

"How do you know my full name? Only my mother called me that." I finally manage to get the words out. Julian provides an embarrassed smile, his hand moving to my upper arm, touching me like an old friend.

"It is a very long story, one that I will explain. In time." My world spins. Absolutely no one except my mother and my head teacher in primary school has ever called me Elspeth. I am Ellie and no one has ever asked me my full name, not even Nicky. How did Julian know? Julian reaches down and takes my hand, brushing my fingers with his thumb.

"Ellie, I truly apologise. This appears creepy, I can see that. What

I am trying to say is that I need you to know that I could not wait to come back here. To see you." He stops again, a look of pain flashes across his strong masculine features for a split second. I on the other hand should be freaked, yet I feel it deep down in the pit of my stomach that he is not a threat. There is something about him that intrigues me regardless of his odd behaviour. I say nothing, my mind trying to convince me to walk away. I look down at my hand that he is still holding, with his odd classical bookish look to him, an almost hipster look but with muscle and I sigh. My brain as always is in self-preservation mode, but my body has other ideas. There is something about him that intrigues me, Nicky is right, why should not I have a little fun if I want to. I squeeze his fingers in return, my leap of faith is rewarded with a smile.

"Please realise that telling a girl something like that could really freak her out. Flowers and a card would have sufficed." Julian laughs, a look of awkward relief softening his features.

"I'll remember that in future."

"You do that." Suddenly I feel like the world is no longer on my shoulders. The man in front of me is as awkward as I, so we have something in common.

"Let us go and grab a drink." I state pulling him in the direction of the hotel, throwing my common sense and caution to the wind.

Julian goes and gets the drinks as I get comfortable on one of the bar's sofas. This time I ask for a whisky on the rocks, a little liquid courage is required after tonight's events. Julian raises an eyebrow at my order but says nothing as he heads to the bar. He comes back with a glass in each hand, he has opted for a glass of red wine, which really makes me laugh.

"What?"

"I saw you as a beer kind of guy." I reply with a straight face. He places his hand over his heart in dramatic fashion.

"I am wounded by your comment. I enjoy a good glass of red at the end of a busy day, sadly this isn't a good glass." I laugh and raise my glass.

"That is why I opted for the whisky."

"Whisky on the rocks is not really much of a feminine drink. I would have taken you as a gin kind of girl." I laugh, swirl my whisky once and take a swig.

"I'm not a big drinker but I do enjoy a gin." Julian studies me, his eyes search my face trying to read me. I maintain my composure as I stare back, at least now he knows that I am intrigued on this so-called research he has done. I will ask him about it at some point.

"If you are not much of a drinker, why the whisky?"

"Purely medicinal!" I reply, draining the rich amber liquid and clinking my glass on the table. Julian and I spend the rest of the evening talking. Our conversation is not forced and flows easily, considering the state I got myself into earlier. I notice that he hasn't drunk much of his wine and wonder why.

"Can I walk you home?" The hotel bar is closing, and we are the last here. I smile at him.

"Yes, I live upstairs." He takes me by the hand, guides me out of the bar, along the hallway, up the stairs and right to my door. Butterflies fill my stomach as I turn to face him.

"Thank you for an interesting evening." I whisper. Julian smiles, raises my arm, and kisses the back of my hand.

"See you tomorrow. Good night, Ellie." His eyes linger for a moment before he gives me one last smile. I stand with my back to the door and watch him go.

"Good night, Julian." I whisper to myself.

CHAPTER THREE

Dinner And Daisy Chains

Fumbling, I clumsily reach over and grab my phone nearly knocking over my lamp and glass of water that sit next to my bed. I press the on button and wait for a moment, it is just after eight in the morning when my phone finally springs to life and begins filling my ears with it's annoying sound. I have two text messages waiting for me in my inbox. The first is from Nicky who has managed to drag himself away from his party and can meet me at nine for a breakfast catch up. The second is from Julian. My stomach tightens then somersaults in delight.

Sleep well?

Julian x

Julian wants to know how I slept. I beam in dreamy happiness. I do not remember giving him my number, I contemplate this as I stretch and yawn in a very unladylike manner. Julian wants to know if I slept well, and I did. But it does not detract from the fact that he has my number. This research he has done on me seems to be crossing so many personal boundaries. I roll over, resting my cheek on the cooler part of my pillow. In the grand scheme of things, I am overjoyed that he contacted me. I choose to overlook it this once. I have an overwhelming urge to fire a text back straight away informing him that I slept well, but childishly decide to pull the duvet over my head instead. I remember Nicky's text and hear my stomach rumble, so I throw my phone down on the bed and decide to join Nicky for breakfast.

I enter the empty staff room and immediately set to work, switching on the kettle ready to make myself a cafetiere of extra strong coffee. The door opens and Nicky strolls casually in, looking fresh as a daisy despite being out to God knows what time. I smile as he brushes past me, despite all the space in the room. Nicky is very touchy feely and constantly has the urge to touch me, it is his thing, it is childish, I can only imagine how annoying he must have been as a child.

I fill Nicky's mug with boiling water and hand him a liquorice tea bag, how he drinks that stuff is beyond me. Still holding the kettle, I pour boiling water into my cafetiere and leave it to brew. Nicky pulls out two chairs side by side at the table and sits on one as I grab a couple of plates from the cupboard. I hand him a plate as he beams at me, the look of the dutiful husband waiting for his breakfast, the silence between us is golden. Grabbing my favourite bright orange cup and saucer from the shelf, I swipe the cafetiere of freshly brewing coffee, placing them next to my empty plate.

"So how was your night?" I enquire, breaking the comfortable silence. I know he is desperate to tell me. Reaching over the table I grab a freshly baked and still warm pain au chocolate from the stainless-steel tray that has been left on the staff room table. I start nibbling while waiting to plunge my coffee, I eye up the fruit bowl considering what to take.

Nicky flashes me a smile and as if reading my mind, he grabs a hulled strawberry and pops it in his mouth.

"Good thanks." I watch him as he swallows the ripe red berry, waiting for him to continue.

"You know the drill darling." He reaches over me, grabbing my pain au chocolate from my hand and takes a bite, practically eating half.

"Get your own." I protest crossing my arms like a child, he does this just to annoy me. With a mouth full of my breakfast, Nicky chews fast, throwing down what's left back onto my plate.

"Last night I met a cute girl at the club, a skater type, you know lashings of dark eye liner. She flirted with me something rotten until her boyfriend turned up. He didn't look so happy witnessing her behaviour, so she excused herself." Nicky shrugs his shoulders and I contemplate eating the last of the chocolate filled pastry sitting on my plate.

"Imagine, there I am left with her boyfriend, who I think is going to give me grief but as it turns out, he is bisexual and made a move on me as soon as she left." I smile as I pick up the remnants of the pastry, sounds like an average night out for Nicky.

"One thing led to another, we ended up in the couples room. I gave him a blowjob, then fucked him." Nicky looks off into the distance, a dirty smile plastered on his face. He is shameless. I drop the remnants of the pastry back onto my plate, my stomach rolling in disgust. Thank goodness I did not finish it. I reach over and grab a fresh one, pushing my used plate away. I hold on tightly to my fresh pastry whilst keeping an eye on Nicky, there is no way he is getting his grubby hands and mouth on this one.

"Sounds like your average night." I reply narrowing my eyes at him. I did not need to know every single sordid detail.

"Tell me darling, how was your evening with Julian, why didn't he sleep over?" Nicky raises an eyebrow and I shrug.

"I was really all over the place, completely out of my comfort zone to begin with. It got better and I did enjoy myself, the evening ended well. I got a kiss on my hand. Definitely gentlemanly and romantic but no sleep over." Nicky nods at me, I can see the cogs in his head turning. I shudder slightly at the sad thought that Nicky can get more action in his lunch break then I did in an entire evening with Julian. Then it dawns on me. How does he know Julian did not spend the night?

"Have you heard from him yet?" Nicky asks with a cheeky grin.

"It was you who gave him my number, when did you see him?" I reply accusingly, nudging his shoulder with mine.

"It was odd actually. When I got back here, I was telling Alice on reception about my night. Julian appears from nowhere and introduces himself. He just butted into our conversation and started talking to me. He knew who I was of course, and we chatted for a moment or two. Next thing I know he asks me outright for your number. He was on a mission. Alice's expression could have been framed. She was in shock at his forwardness." Nicky stops to put a fresh pain au chocolate on his plate before continuing.

"He seems nice. You have bagged yourself an eligible cutie Ellie! I didn't want to stand in the path of true love, so I handed it over." Nicky winks as he takes a bite, dropping flakes of buttery pastry down his shirt. I am happy that it was Nicky who passed on my number.

"Darling, you haven't answered my question, have you heard from him yet? And no, I did not want to build your hopes up, just in case he didn't contact you this morning. That could have been awkward." I let out a sigh.

"No, sadly I haven't heard from him." Nicky's face is ashen, he looks like he could be choking.

"Gotcha! Yes, I have heard from him as a matter of fact and thank you very much cupid. He sent a morning text." I stop to plunge my coffee, then pour the delightfully aromatic black liquid into my cup. I glance at the sugar bowl before deciding against adding any.

"And..." Nicky prompts.

"What did it say?" I smile, pull my phone out of my pocket, and show him the text.

"Sweet. You got a little kiss at the end; he is really into you!" How Nicky can decipher that is beyond me. Nicky finally takes his tea bag out of its little paper packet and pops it in his mug of hot water, swishing it around for a few seconds.

"Seriously, when he asked me about you, he was very attentive and a little intense, nothing I can put my finger on as such, but I got the impression that his feelings for you run deeper than you think. You know just from his body language. He digs you darling." I smile at Nicky as I watch him dunk his tea bag repeatedly in the mug, I can't help but hope that Nicky is right.

"Should I reply?" I ask innocently. Nicky splutters his foul tea over himself, some of which dribbles down his chin, joining the flakes of pastry on his shirt.

"You haven't replied yet. What are you fifteen? Text him now! Come on Ellie you are an adult so don't play games with him." I pick up my phone full of guilt. I do not know what to type so I just stare at the screen blankly.

"Just hit reply. Ellie, ask him to lunch or something, it is not rocket science." I roll my eyes at Nicky but give in and type out a brief message.

I slept well thank you.

How about you?

Ellie x

I hit send and place my phone back on the table. I find myself glancing at it constantly, willing it to buzz with an instant reply.

"Earth to Ellie." Nicky's long slender finger rudely taps my head.

"You have not heard a single word I have just said, have you?"

"Hey, I am listening, but I have heard it all before, you're boring me." I reply with an impish grin. Nicky gives me a look of mock hurt whilst clutching his heart.

"You wound me darling." Before glancing at his watch.

"Shit, I have to go and get ready, I'm taking Louis to football today. Judy is getting her hair done again, I think she might be shagging her hairdresser." I laugh, she is just like her older brother. Nicky stands and kisses me on the top of my head.

"Louis is a lucky boy to have you as his uncle. Give him a kiss from me." Nicky narrows his eyes at me in a dramatic fashion.

"Yes, I'm sure he would appreciate his camp uncle doing just that. I hope you hear from Julian soon, text me later." He calls out as he leaves the room. I'm left alone with my coffee and my thoughts. I finish the last of my coffee and rise from my chair, collecting all the mugs and plates dotted around the staff room and bunging them into the dishwasher before heading back to my room. When I arrive, there is a delicate daisy chain hanging on the handle of my door. I pick it up carefully, then glance up and down the hallway. I slip my key into the lock and let myself into my room stepping over a folded piece of paper that is lying on the floor.

The scrap of cream coloured paper had been torn out of a journal, an expensive looking one, judging on the thickness and quality of the paper. The handwriting on the note is beautiful, the calligraphy breath taking. I read the note whilst still holding the daisy chain.

I have taken your advice, flowers it is.

In answer to your question, I did not sleep well as you were on my mind.

Have dinner with me?

Julian x

I smile. How romantic. My heart is singing and beating frantically in my chest. I want to jump up and down and scream but Nicky is right, I am not a lovesick teenager. Still clutching the note and holding the daisy chain carefully, I sit on my bed, reading the note again. I grin to myself; I have never received a handmade daisy chain before. Without hesitation I type a quick reply on my phone.

Dinner would be lovely.

Thank you for the daisy chain, it is beautiful.

Daisies are my favourite.

Ellie x

* * *

I spend the rest of the day running errands, tidying my room, and taking my flower arranging class. I desperately tried not to think about Julian but that proved to be difficult. He was constantly in my thoughts, his smile, his eyes, his note. Goodness at one point I even broke out into a sweat and had palpitations when I thought I had seen him in the distance.

As I enter the hotel, Jamie gets my attention from behind the reception desk, waving me over with one hand and phone receiver tucked in the crook of her neck.

"Hey honey, there is an envelope here for you." She whispers, her hand covering the receiver as she takes a booking. Jamie smiles warmly at me, she is desperate to know what is inside, I can see it written on her face. As I never get internal messages. I take the envelope and tuck it under my arm waiting for her to finish. I do not want to open it down here. When she replaces the handset, I ask how her day has been?

"Not too bad. Do you fancy coming to the pub later? It is just me and Bob tonight, Nicky is at another one of his parties." She winks at me, code that Nicky is out on the pull again. I shake my head no.

"I can't go out tonight I have something on possibly, but do you fancy doing something tomorrow afternoon? It's your day off, right?" Jamie beams and claps her hands in glee, I know what is coming.

"Yes, that would be great. Do you fancy a trip into Brighton? I've fallen in love with a pair of red heels in a boutique down North Lane and as we have just gotten paid, I'm going to treat myself." Jamie loves her shoes.

"Sounds good to me, meet you here at eleven." She nods as she picks up the phone that has begun to ring and I head up the stairs giving her a little wave as I go. I enter the staff room, to find Nicky tucking into a chunk of cold chicken.

"Who won the game?" Mentally hoping it was Louis' team, the last time they lost, Louis would not leave his bedroom for a week.

"We won darling, Louis scored two goals, so was the hero of the match." I let out a gentle sigh of relief, Nicky's nephew really is the sweetest boy and is nothing like his uncle.

"Ellie you've dropped something." Nicky says with a mouthful of chicken while pointing to the floor. I look down and realise I've dropped my envelope.

"Didn't your mother teach you manners?" I ask as I crouch down and pick up the Hedge Hill Hotel embossed envelope.

"Nope. She taught me bugger all." He mumbles still chewing. I rip open the envelope and pull out another scrap of cream coloured paper with the same beautiful calligraphy that I had received this morning.

I'm hoping this evening ends with a bang.

Meet me in reception at seven.

Julian x

I read the note twice. Is this an offer of sex?

"Hey what's the matter? You look pale." Nicky asks looking worried. I say nothing, shoving the note into his face instead. He wipes his hand down the front of his jeans and then takes the note from me, he must go through masses of Vanish to get the food stains and God knows what else out from his clothes. The man clearly would never think to use a napkin.

Nicky raises both eyebrows and his mouth breaks out into a huge grin, chicken fat making his lips and chin all shiny.

"It appears you are in for a banging tonight darling." He hands the note back to me smiling. I pull out a chair and slump into it before reaching over the table, picking at some grapes. I pop one into my mouth and chew slowly, feeling the burst of sweetness cover my tongue.

"What are you going to wear to your hot banging date then?" Nicky breaks the silence with his question.

"I really don't know. I better go and start to get ready, I have just over an hour to look my best."

"Hey, calm it down sister, what about your summer dress, black ballerina pumps and wear your hair down." I give Nicky a small smile.

"I'll try it on and see how I feel before I decide." Nicky places his greasy hand on mine and looks into my eyes.

"Remember darling, you do not have to do anything you don't want to. I know how you feel about sex and all that jazz. Don't feel pressured into doing something you're not comfortable with, okay."

"I know and thank you." I blow him a kiss and get up and leave the table. The problem is I suddenly feel very nervous about going on a second date.

"Text me later so I know you are okay. And eat some chocolate before you go out, the sugar will help." Nicky shouts after me as I leave the room to go and get ready.

CHAPTER FOUR

Hysterical Confusion

The door flies open hitting the wall as I rush into my room in a blind panic. Seriously, what am I going to wear when I have no idea where I am going. A shiver runs down my spine, remembering the words written in that cryptic note. I head straight to my wardrobe and push hangers aside holding out various skirt, top and dress combinations. I feel a bout of good old-fashioned hysteria coming on. Surely Julian would not be so crass as to leave me a note indicating his intention to have sex? Shit as much as I would like to, I really do not think I am ready for such a giant leap so soon. I push the notion of all things sexual from my mind to concentrate on outfits, with difficulty. Pulling the current clothes off my body and throwing them on the bathroom floor like a slob. I climb into the shower. Thankfully the cool temperature of the water does the trick, jolting my brain out of panic mode for long enough to allow a couple of rational thoughts to filter through. What did his note mean?

I shampoo first and then rub conditioner into my hair, shave my legs and under my arms until I am completely de fuzzed. Twenty minutes later, my red hair is looking shiny, sleek, and most importantly under control, I am smooth, my skin moisturised. Now back to my original problem; clothes. I pull out my best undies, a delicate set that I shamefully have never worn. I run my fingers over the fabric of the cream balcony bra that is subtly trimmed with lace and matching knickers. These elegant undies are a million miles away from my usual Marks and Spencer's undergarments which were bought on a whim under the watchful eye of Jamie, who cunningly dragged me into the very posh Rigby and Peller shop in Knightsbridge on one of our day trips to London.

The memory of that day brings a smile to my face and finally, hopefully someone other than shopaholic Jamie will get to see them at some point. I slip on the knickers and bra, admiring the delicate fabric, they really are flattering, it is such a shame that Julian probably will never get to see them, at least not tonight. Glancing at the pile of dresses lying on my bed, I opt for the sleek corn blue one, completely disregarding Nicky's earlier suggestion. This dress is sensible, plain, and most importantly, knee length and nicely fitted, pulling me in at the waist and flaring slightly from hip to knee.

It reveals a hint of cleavage but not enough to scream harlot. I apply a little mascara and pale pink lip gloss to finish the look. I present myself to the mirror as I do a turn. Too late to change my mind now. Throwing the lip gloss, my purse, and keys into my little cream handbag, I pick up my phone and a cream cardigan. One missed text from Nicky wishing me luck tonight.

I slip my feet into a pair of cream ballet pumps and take one final look in the mirror before leaving. I look flushed, probably because nerves are getting the better of me. I walk down the stairs trying and failing to calm myself when I spot Julian, waiting in reception. My stomach somersaults at the sight of him, my heart pounding and my palms begin to sweat, Julian looks sexy, dressed in a black suit, he is pacing the reception floor and has his back to me, but I know it is him. The blue collar of his shirt is just barely visible under his jacket, I spot a brief glimpse of his neck as he cocks his head to one side. My eyes roam admiringly up and down his clothed body, his floppy black hair somewhat under control tonight, the long strands just skimming the base of his neck.

My eyes are drawn to his shoulders and back, his suit jacket is nicely fitted. Julian turns and begins slowing walking back in my direction. I feel like I am spying, he looks a little edgy as he glances at his watch. I thank the gods that I am not the only one who is nervous tonight. I stand on the last step and continue to watch him, Julian still hasn't noticed me, I can't help but wonder where the hell we are going because I suddenly feel very under dressed. I smooth my frock down for the millionth time when Julian's eyes finally find mine. He stops dead, breaking out into a grin. His eyes slowly work their way up from my legs and over my body. In three confident strides, Julian is in front of me, offering me his hand which I gingerly take.

"You look beautiful." He raises my hand and gently places his soft lips on my knuckles. The contact of warm lips to skin, however brief has my body feeling things it really should not. He looks handsome and is freshly shaven. His green eyes twinkle as he takes me in. I really need to get a hold of myself.

"Good evening, Julian." I answer feeling slightly embarrassed by the heat that is coursing through me.

"Shall we." He indicates towards the door of the hotel and grasping my hand firmly in his, leads me out. We exit Hedge Hill Hotel and down the steps to his waiting black car.

"Wow." I exclaim and it is, I have no idea what make or model this is but as cars go, this is cute. He opens the passenger door for me with a smile and I try to be as ladylike as I can getting in. Julian slides into the driver's seat beside me and I sneak a peek at his profile as he fiddles with his seatbelt. The smell of him is heavenly, hints of citrus and mint, fresh, clean, and only now do I realise his hair is damp. I sit quietly in my seat as the engine starts and the car purrs to life, Julian faces me and flashes me a sexy smile.

"Are you ready?" I nod my head and we set off. I still have no idea where we are going, he is yet to divulge that nugget of information.

"How fast does this baby go?" I tap the dashboard with interest, deciding to start the conversation on neutral ground. For me talking is a sure-fire way of getting over nerves and talking about cars will surely be a winning conversation starter.

"I have absolutely no idea, I stick to the speed limit." Julian's laugh is deadpan. I watch him, he is easy to watch, yet I have no idea if he is joking with me.

"What's so funny?" I ask, he is still laughing lightly to himself.

"I have a confession to make, I have no interest in cars whatsoever, I prefer motorbikes. My brother insisted I needed a car, recommended this and it looked good, so I treated myself." He continues to laugh.

"Fair enough, what make is it?" Genuinely interested and testing him. He owns the car, surely, he would know how fast it can go.

"This monstrosity is a Porsche." I give Julian a surprised look.

"Really a Porsche, I thought they were those little flat cars?"

"Flat cars...oh you mean a Lamborghini. I shrug my shoulders; I know nothing about cars.

"No this is a Porsche Cayenne Coupe, fast and good off road. Perfect for what I do." I glance at Julian.

"And what exactly is that?" Julian keeps his eyes on the road.

"I will get to that bit in time." Julian does not elaborate so; we sit in silence for a moment. It is a beautiful evening, not a single cloud can be seen in the blue sky above us. I glance shyly at Julian.

"How has your day been?" I ask. He glances over to me and gives me a little smile.

"My day was torturous." Looking his way waiting for him to continue but he doesn't. Julian's eyes are focused on the road ahead, his expression unreadable.

"How was your day, Ellie?" He enquires after a minute. It is like he has forgotten how to hold a conversation. Do I make him nervous?

"Are you okay?" His voice is deep, I am totally lost in his presence. I smile, catching myself and begin to speak. Desperately trying to keep my nerves under control.

"I'm fine thank you. My day has been busy. Where are we going?"

"You will soon see." Julian smiles, checking his mirrors as he answers.

I begin to relax a little into my seat. I still have no idea where we are heading, choosing to let this be a surprise. As we drive and chit chat, I do the only thing I can and inhale discreetly. I really am surprised by how good he smells. Glancing down and noting how my thigh is barely inches from his. The feeling of being so close to him is overwhelming, that I am faced with the realisation that I am attracted to him, this going beyond my previous crush. We leave the traffic behind us, as Julian pulls off the main road.

A private road sign welcomes us as we turn onto it, the road is narrow, lined with trees on both sides, sunlight casting eerie shadows around us. I try to keep an open mind and am thankful that the evening is still bright, the sun not due to set for another hour and a half at least. The silence between us broken by the shrill ringtone of Julian's mobile phone. He glances at it as it sits in a cradle on the dashboard but ignores it.

"Feel free to pull over and answer it." Julian shakes his head in annoyance and continues to ignore it. The phone stops ringing and there is an instant change in Julian's demeanour. He does not look happy. The phone's screen lights up and its ring tone fills the car once again. Julian thumps his hand on the steering wheel, which makes me jump. He reaches out and switches the phone off completely without saying a word or looking at me. Finally, we reach a clearing, Julian keeps his eyes focused on the road ahead and is lost in his thoughts. I, on the other hand have become uncomfortable with his silence. The private road begins to widen, the trees here cast dancing shadows over us. It is very picturesque and romantic, yet there is an element of creepy as I can see no large buildings, homes or hotels that would be suited for an area such as this.

"Where are we going?" I notice my voice rise slightly as I ask the question. I am downright nervous.

"You will soon see." Julian does not look at me as he answers, his expression is serious as he focuses on the road and his voice gives nothing away. His reply does not help to ease my rising worry. We carry on moving and, in the distance, stands a structure that looks like a small outbuilding with parking spaces marked out. Unease washes over me as we drive closer and the road ends.

I frantically scan the area only to find we are situated at the edge of a great field, panic floods my brain. This is easily the kind of place where a dead body could be buried, and no one would ever find it. Trees and bushes line the perimeter, they look dense, anything or anyone could be behind them. The field itself is flat with newly mown grass and there is not a single person here but us. Julian parks the car, gets out and comes around to my side, silently my door opens, he looks serious, deep in thought and I want to ask If he is okay, his answer may give something away. He continues to say nothing as he extends his hand, forever the gentleman, I reach out and take it. This is all very polite, sophisticated even but I don't know where we are and that has caused fear to bubble in the pit of my stomach, that feeling of hysteria surfacing again. The car door slams shut, causing me to jump at the sound echoing around me. Julian glances at me and then at the outhouse and gives me the strangest look, in that moment I feel utterly terrified.

CHAPTER FIVE

Shotguns And Fairy Rings

I stiffen as I feel Julian's hand move along my back, his fingers resting on my waist, I am awkwardly drawn closer to him as we walk towards a slightly bigger building that I didn't notice before.

"Come with me." Julian whispers. Alarm bells are going off in my head. I look left and right and conclude that if I wanted to run, it would be extremely difficult to do so. I have watched enough horror movies in my time to know how this evening could end. For now, we walk towards the building, I try to keep an open mind, but it is difficult, especially when you are convinced that you may have got yourself into a dangerous situation. I plan on what to do if the worst-case scenario were to happen, my only option would be to run and head for the dense woodland. A squeak comes from the direction of the building and door the opens. My attention is instantly dragged away from my thoughts and focuses on an older man wearing wellies and a green waxed jacket.

"Good evening Mr Hunter, Miss White." He nods his head at me, following it up with a genuinely warm smile that instantly puts me at ease, while extending his hand to Julian. The two men shake. This chap is much older and looks friendly in a grandfatherly way. I let out a small sigh of relief.

"Good evening Heston, is everything ready?"

"It is Mr Hunter, all ready when you are." He walks over to the building and disappears back inside, the door slamming closed behind him. Julian turns towards me; his chest is so close that I can feel his warm breath on my face. I am still at a loss as to why we are here but having Heston around makes me feel at ease. Julian gazes into my eyes, I stare back feeling like my knees are going to give way at any moment, the adrenaline that has been pumping through my veins for the last five minutes is now subsiding, being replaced by oxytocin.

"Do you shoot, Ellie?" The shocked expression on my face must have been evident and answered his question. Julian laughs gently whilst taking my hand. I do not know anyone who has a gun and I have certainly never been involved in gang warfare.

"No." I whisper feeling a little confused by his line of inquiry.

"Sorry, that came out wrong, it sounded so much better in my head." He says grinning and giving my hand a gentle squeeze. I give him a shy smile back and realise he probably has quite a few conversations in his head and forgets to say them aloud.

"No, I don't shoot. Guns scare me." I do not know what else to say, it's not a question a girl gets asked every day.

"Come." Julian commands. We walk towards the brick building and directly in front of it is a table I did not notice before, so much for my observation skills. The table holds two guns, two pairs of ear defenders, two pairs of protective eye wear and a brand-new pair of trainers. I should be shocked by what is in front of me but I'm not. I have never seen a real gun before, yet in the heat of the moment I am drawn to them, I have an overwhelming urge to pick one of them up and feel the metal in my hands.

"These are shotguns." Julian studies me closely as I gently run my fingers over the cold metal of the gun nearest to me.

"I thought we could try a hobby of mine if you are game? Clay pigeon shooting." I remove my hand from the gun and turn back to him.

"We can try that." Now I understand his cryptic note, the bang of a shotgun. In a way I am relieved. There is no expectation that

I shall be stepping out of my knickers any time tonight. Julian takes one of the guns, holds it firmly in his strong hands and walks me out into the field. He stops and I follow suit.

"Shooting a gun is pretty simple in principle." He takes my bag from my shoulder and places it gently on the grass behind us. He offers me a pair of ear defenders, which I put on before handing me the shotgun, I hesitate for a second, not knowing what to do with it. Julian smiles in encouragement.

"This is how you hold it." His hands manipulate mine, his touch ever so light. I can't concentrate on what he is saying in any great a depth because he is just too close. He almost whispers his instructions as his hands and arms touch mine. I am slowly manoeuvred into the correct stance for shooting, I gaze longingly at him as I stand like a posed mannequin.

"You are now ready to aim. Oh, but we need to get you into some decent foot ware." Julian walks me over to the table and effortlessly picks me up and sits me on it. He remains silent as he crouches down, removing my pumps ever so gently. He looks up at me, his face is hard to read, but I notice his nostrils flare. Julian's hands delicately replace the pumps with the trainers.

"Much better." He says whilst tying the laces. He stands and offers me his hand, helping me off the table. Together we walk back out to the field, I am shown how to hold the gun again. Julian corrects my posture and out of the corner of my eye I see Julian raise his right arm. I hear a loud noise as my eyes and then the gun I am holding look upwards, I see the clay pigeon fly high into the sky above us and instinct kicks in. Looking along the barrel of the gun, my eye lines up with my target as I softly squeeze the trigger and fire. Noise fills the air. Never have I heard a noise so loud in my life. The power of the shotgun has me gasping in shock and causes me to step back slightly. Julian grasps my upper arm to steady me, tilting the barrel of the gun to point down to the floor.

"Well done. You managed to hit the pigeon on your first shot!"

I feel exhilarated, that was exciting. Never in my life would I have guessed that I would spend an evening manhandling a gun. Nicky will die of shock when I tell him about this tomorrow. I smile, did I really hit the clay pigeon, because I didn't see that bit. I stupidly look up, raising the gun up with me. Julian tuts audibly, tapping his finger on the metal barrel, a smile dancing on his lips. I understand instantly and drop the gun, safely pointing it towards the floor where I can do little damage. Shyly I study his beautiful face, I notice he is gently chewing on his bottom lip, I cannot pull my eyes away.

"Again Ellie...Ready?" I nod. I want to try this again. This time I stand with my feet a little wider apart, my hips and knees are ready to absorb the power of the shot when I pull the trigger. With the shotgun in position, I wait to hear the noise of the clay pigeon's release. Julian raises his hand and in a split second I see my target fly high into the sky. My eyes follow the clay pigeon's movement as it soars into the air. I do the same as last time, lining up my eye with the end of the barrel, never taking my eye off the clay pigeon. I gently squeeze the trigger and the gun fires, this time I see the clay pigeon shatter in mid-air. The exhilaration of hitting the target is amazing, the adrenaline is back and is pumping through my veins in a good way, leaving me breathless and excited. If I weren't holding the gun, I would be clapping my hands right now. I feel so proud of myself, who would have thought playing with a gun could be so fun.

"You are a natural, like I knew you would be." Mutters Julian, I am caught in the moment too much to analyse his comment, let alone ask him what he means by it. We continue with the shooting for a little while. I seemed to have grasped the concept easily, as I have somehow managed to hit every clay pigeon, the exception being the second to last one. Julian takes the gun, reloads it, and takes a few shots himself. He is calm and collected as he aims and fires. He does not miss a single clay pigeon and he makes shooting look easy, too easy. It is clear to me he has shot a gun many times before. I stand and watch him move, causing a rush of heat to spread over my entire body. I am attracted to Julian and him shooting that gun confirms this. I want this man in my life.

The sun begins to make its descent. With the light fading Julian decides it is time to stop as it is no longer suitable to shoot safely. I smirk, it reminds me of tennis at Wimbledon before they built the new roof over centre court. Heston appears from nowhere and takes the shotgun from Julian.

"Everything is ready for you sir." He states solemnly. Julian nods in thanks.

"Thank you, Heston. Get yourself off home to Helen who has a single malt waiting for you. Goodnight." Julian takes my hand and leads me through the field where the remains of our clay pigeons lay shattered. We walk silently for a minute or two before I am steered towards the trees. This whole area is breath taking, the sound of the birds settling down for the night fill the air as they sing to us from their nests high in the trees above. I feel relaxed as the warm breeze rustles through the leaves in the trees. It is a far cry from the fear I felt earlier. In the distance I can see lights twinkling, becoming brighter the closer we get. As we approach, I notice the picnic blanket first and on closer inspection I realise it is set within a fairy ring.

 Mushrooms have grown in a circle and that circle is perfectly circular and is at least three metres wide. As natural phenomena go, this is spectacular. The trees directly around us have fairy lights scattered over their branches emanating a delicate twinkling light as they move with the breeze. Our picnic is lit by candles placed in old glass jam jars of varying sizes, which are scattered around the ground among the mushrooms. This is beautiful and utterly romantic.

"Julian this is amazing." Glancing from the fairy ring to him with wide astonished eyes. This is the most romantic place I have ever been to; made ever so special because of the fairy ring. Julian really has gone through an awful amount of trouble to organise all of this; I am touched and feel incredibly guilty that I doubted his intentions earlier. Julian who is still holding my hand leads me to the blanket and helps me sit. He takes off his jacket and places it behind him, joining me on the picnic rug that has been placed on the floor for us. In this light he is devastatingly handsome and for a fleeting moment I wonder why I am here at all with him.

"Thank you for all of this, it is truly beautiful." I feel myself flush as Julian reaches over and takes my hand, his lips brush over my knuckles for the second time tonight. I just wish those pink full lips of his would find mine. I hold my breath for a second, trying to control my racing heart and wayward thoughts.

"You are beautiful." Julian mutters more to himself then to me but I cannot help but smile at his comment. He returns my smile, revealing his perfect dimple that I just want to place my lips on.

"Are you hungry?" He asks and I must admit I am but only for him.

"Yes...a little." I reply still astonished at the beauty surrounding me and the man sat opposite.

"I wasn't sure what you would like so I got a range." I glance at the feast delicately laid out for us. I catch Julian staring at me, I look up and our eyes meet, I genuinely do not know what I am doing here. His dark brooding features captivate me, and I cannot pull my eyes away from his intense gaze. Julian reaches out and gently caresses my cheek with his thumb.

"Eat." I have lost my appetite, but I manage to try a little of everything. We tuck into tiny sandwiches, vegetable batons, roasted nuts and tasty dips, the food should have been a distraction, but it only adds to my growing frustration. I am sitting here in the great outdoors, watching Julian eat in the candlelight, my stomach is in knots, I am being swept away, getting lost in his company. Julian, as if on cue, pours us both a glass of sparking water.

I find it odd that there is no alcohol but then again, he is driving. When we have finished eating, he pulls out an ornate platter from the second picnic basket complete with tiny pastries, mini cupcakes, beautifully decorated chocolates, and plump berries. They all look too good to eat and sadly I am full. I stall for a moment, fingering the long stem of my glass, before taking another sip, the clean crisp bubbles cleansing my tongue as the cool sparkling water hydrates my parched mouth.

"I knew you would be a great shot." He tells me. My eyes flick to his, a small smile present on his lips.

"What made you think I would be any good at shooting?" I enquire curious.

"I mean, I have never held a gun in my life, so in theory I should really suck at it." I take a juicy raspberry and pop it into my mouth, chewing slowly, feeling the burst of flavour and sweetness explode on my tongue.

"You have the physical attributes of one who knows how to handle a gun." He replies with a smile.

"Are you telling me I have that whole gangster swagger going on?" Julian laughs at my ridiculous comment.

"Certainly not in those shoes, but I am glad the trainers fit." I laugh out loud.

"In answer to your question, you definitely don't have that gangster swagger.... But you do have a cute wiggle when you walk if that helps." Thank goodness it is very dark because I know I have just flushed scarlet from head to toe.

"Sorry, I hope I haven't embarrassed you." I am at a total loss for words. I have no come back from that and know if I open my mouth, I am going to get flustered, and tongue tied.

"Um no....I'm not embarrassed, not at all. Okay, cool. I can't believe you just said that." I babble. I grab another raspberry, popping it into my mouth quickly, deciding it's better to just shut up and eat. Julian watches me as I chew, he has a grin plastered across his face and now I am thinking all sorts of things that I really should not be thinking about. Suddenly his note pops into my head and before I can stop myself the words are out of my mouth.

"From your note, shooting was not the kind of banging I thought you had in mind tonight." I stop myself from uttering another word by clapping my hand over my mouth in mortified horror. I can't believe I just said that aloud. Julian's expression does not falter, he doesn't look shocked by the nonsense that has just passed my lips, which I am relieved to see.

"Well... I am sure what you are thinking about could happen in time." My eyes widen in response. Julian picks up his glass and takes a sip, I notice that this time he avoids my eyes completely. We sit in silence for a moment and as if on cue an owl hoots in the distance, our attention diverted to the direction of the treetops.

"Do you know the significance of a fairy ring?" I look back to Julian, considering my reply.

"Folklore significance or scientific?" I question.

"Folklore".

"Yes, I do a little. As a child I was obsessed with fairies, elves and goblins." I stop, I could imagine fairies dancing here, holding hands, and moving in circles to music played on little foxglove flutes. I smile at the thought and then realise that the sun has set, we are completely illuminated by twinkling lights and candles.

"I'll let you in on a little secret, I really love fairy folklore and the science behind magical creatures and the unexplained, I was a little obsessed with cryptozoology as a teen."

"How interested exactly?" He asks, taking a delicate bite from a luscious looking strawberry.

"You know, I like reading about weird creatures of the world, lore and what have you. I was obsessed with vampires and werewolves, I even visited Loch Ness once, sadly I never managed to spot Nessie in the flesh." Julian looks thoughtful.

"What are your interests?" I enquire instead. Julian licks strawberry juice off his delectable lower lip.

"I have many interests. Clay pigeon shooting, archery, fencing, and swimming being my main hobbies... I like the great outdoors; I love to read, I also hunt." I am not sure about hunting. Many of the hotel guests are keen hunters, some hunt foxes' others travel the world hunting larger game. Listening to their stories leaves me feeling uncomfortable and sorry for the animals they stalk and kill.

"Do you eat what you hunt or just mount it?" Before I can censor my brain, the words have tumbled out of my mouth again, do I even want to know the answer to that ridiculous question, no I do not.

"Neither." Julian leans back, placing the palms of his hands on the floor behind him.

"What I hunt are pests and need removing from the land they occupy. I do not hunt for sport but for work. I see it as the removal of a non-indigenous species before they cause damage." He stops and gazes into my eyes, his expression is solemn and sad. I sense there is more to his words, but I don't push for information. His hunting hobby I can overlook; I just hope he never wants me to tag along on one of his hunts. I jump at the high-pitched screech of foxes frolicking in the distance, Julian sits up looking alert. He turns his head and surveys the trees that surround us. Even in this light I notice his brow creasing, in that moment, I see the hunter in him. Hunter by name, hunter by nature. Looking back to me he gives me a warm smile, but it doesn't reach his eyes.

"I should be getting you back to Hedge Hill." I have no chance to protest, Julian is up on his feet extending his hand out to help me up. I accept and find myself standing very close to him, chest to chest with my hand still in his. Desperately I try to control my breathing as Julian's face moves in towards me but then he hesitates. His eyes search mine before he withdraws, letting go of me completely. I stand rooted to the ground, as he stoops down to pick up his jacket and my bag and cardigan from the floor. We have just had a moment and I am a little confused as to why he pulled away and did not just kiss me. Very carefully he reaches behind me and places his jacket over my shoulders.

"Let's get you home Ellie, where it is safe."

In no time at all we are back at Hedge Hill. My disappointment at being back so soon must be evident on my face. Julian parks the car and gets out, opening the door for me in a gentlemanly fashion. Without a word, he slips his arm around my waist and walks me back to the hotel whilst holding my pumps. We walk up the stairs and to my room where we stop outside my door. Julian lets go of my waist and reaches for my hand; he places a single kiss on my knuckles for the third time tonight.

"I had a wonderful evening, thank you." His words hang in the air.

"Thank you, I had the most perfect evening." I reply breathlessly. I observe his movement as he leans in. Finally, he is going to kiss me and then he does not, pulling back completely. Julian's nostrils flare and a look of irritation clouds his eyes briefly, I can hear the vibration of his phone in his pocket.

"Goodnight, Ellie." He plants a sweet and tender kiss on my lips, hands me my shoes then turns and walks down the hall. He does not look back.

CHAPTER SIX

Anger And Frustration

Pulling my phone out of my pocket in frustration, I hit redial as I take the stairs two at a time. "Sebastian, you dick, you fucked up my night." I yell, fully aware that I am walking through a hotel but not actually giving a fuck.

"Yeah. Yes. Whatever. They want only me, I get it. How much did you say they are paying? Fine. You owe me. You know I am working on something here. Text me the details." I hang up, make a fist, and almost punch a hole through the wall. Entering my room to change, I realise I am minus a jacket. Visions of Ellie haunt me. She looked amazing tonight.

I sit down on the bed as I pull off my shoes and socks. The look of complete confusion and disappointment on her face as I pulled away from what would have been our first kiss, left me feeling lower than low. Shitty does not even cover it. I wanted more! I glance at my door, the urge to run back down to her room overwhelms me. I rub my head in irritation, I am so angry that I could kill right now. I stand pulling my trousers off, then unbutton my shirt with one hand as I grab a change of clothes from the wardrobe with the other. Jeans, T-shirt and a black hooded top, my uniform for the want of a better word. I pull my jeans on, slipping the T-shirt and hoodie over my head and my feet into my Vans. I am ready for business. Distractedly, I walk around the room grabbing things and throwing them into my bag, still no ping from my phone. Why is it taking Seb so long to send me the details for tonight's hunt. Really it has been half an hour since we spoke, it does not take a genius to send a fucking text. I run my hands through my hair in frustration, I could be with Ellie right now, instead I walked away from her and what was meant to be a perfect night. I walked away with no explanation. She hates me right now. Christ, I hate myself! My phone vibrates and lights with a text message .

Sorry bro, major problem! Details vague. Had to cross reference.

All sorted now.

Shit! Again! I stare at the screen, wondering what in the actual fuck is going on? This is becoming ridiculous. Going out on a hunt with the wrong information is going to get me killed one of these days. I have been to a few dodgy hunts over the last few months, and I am starting to think that maybe someone out there does want me dead. Seb still has not given me an address and right now I just want to get out and do what I must. I shake my head in anger. What kind of man am I, contemplating bringing Ellie into this twisted world of mine? I am one selfish son of a bitch. Stooping I grab my bag and leave my room. Heading down to the car via the back staircase, my phone vibrates with the address I have been waiting for and head there straight away. Arriving at my destination in Lewes, I switch the ignition off and sit in the dark, surveying the vast land on the edge of the South Downs National Park. I contemplate what I am going to do as I morbidly enjoy the silence. My eyes scan the dark, watching and listening carefully to my surroundings. I can't seem to keep my mind on the job tonight.

I am beyond pissed that there is a mole in this whole operation. Someone is fucking us around and worse still, we do not know why. Incidence of DROMs have increased tenfold and the information about them is sketchy at best. Then there is Ellie. I have waited for her, for so long. Now that I have permission to be in her life, I am completely at a loss. Do I just ask Ellie to dinner? Sweep her off her feet? Follow her around like a lovesick puppy? Shit who am I kidding, I am doing the latter already.

I really want Ellie to be with me for me, not because of the history, not because I hunt. Yet I cannot help but feel at a loss in how to approach her. I am awkward at the best of times, trying to play down my life is hard. I should just tell her everything. Tell her about me.

I glance at the windscreen mirror, nothing. It is still and quiet out there with just the occasional sound of a sheep bleating in the distance. I am still pissed that I had to walk away from Ellie but as I am bloody here, I may as well get this started. I take a deep breath while reaching under the passenger seat to pull out the small case hidden there. I hear the click as I thumb the clasp and pull out my handgun and silencer, feeling its weight in my hand. I check the mirror again before switching on the headlights to wait. The steady beam of light in the dark gets their attention quickly and like a moth to a flame, entices them out from wherever they are hiding. It takes a good few minutes before I notice movement in the distance but then I see it. There is one on the move, making its way towards the car.

My eyes study the general size and gait of the DROM ambling towards me. I repeatedly look to all three mirrors of the car, checking to make sure that this one is very much alone. When I am happy that it is, I open the door and get out, slamming the door loudly behind me. That will get its undivided attention and announce my arrival, that, and my scent. I am still amazed by how good their sense of smell is considering rigor mortis has begun. In theory the stiffness begins to occur in the dead an hour or so after death, although it is different in DROMs, rigor mortis begins and then abruptly stops. It is why DROMs move in that rigid way. Yet they retain their hearing and sense of smell. It is fascinating in an absolutely fucked up way. Not that I have time to explore their physiology. I am just here to hunt. It is what I do best.

I stand and wait in the dark, I don't like to rush this part, because that is how mistakes happen. I quietly observe it as it gets closer, it moves noisily, they always do. I hear that unmistakable intake of air as it sniffs wildly and what's left of its brain registers it is not alone. It grows hungry, gearing up to tear at the flesh of the nearest living thing and tonight it is me. This beast begins to run. It has finally caught my scent; it knows I am here and bloody hell, it is moving faster than I expected for its size. I spread my legs and assume my stance, raising my arm to shoulder height. I wait, and when it is mere meters from me, I take pleasure in the gentle squeeze of the trigger, followed by the unmistakable thump as it falls to the floor. I stay still for a few seconds just in case it wasn't alone. When I am sure I am, I look down and there it is, dead with a single gunshot wound to the forehead. With my job here done and task complete, I look down at the sight I am leaving behind. I no longer feel anything when I see them dead, yet I remember every single one. I take the silencer off my gun and replace both silencer and handgun in their case. I look back at the DROM on the floor and can't believe I want to involve Ellie in all this. I place the case back under the front seat and lean against the car. Tonight's hunt was clean, quick, and easy, just the way I prefer. It was very easy money too, no wonder Seb called.

Over the last few months, the hunt has become a financial venture as much as a humanitarian one. Still, I would have rather been back at the hotel with Ellie. Despite the stench emanating from the floor, I can still smell her, the sweet scent of rose that lingered delicately on her skin. Being back here and so close to her is driving me insane. I pull my phone out of my pocket and make the necessary call for the clean-up team to come and do their thing. I text Seb, telling him the job has been completed with no hitches before throwing my phone on the passenger's seat and head back to the hotel for the night.

It is just after four in the morning when I finally arrive back, it is getting brighter, I'm wired from the adrenaline flooding my system. I contemplate knocking on Ellie's door and continuing where we left off last night, but I have no right to do so. I know I upset her leaving like I did, that was evident from the expression on her beautiful face, but duty called. Parking my car, I grab my bag and walk towards the hotel entrance, passing the lawn and the daisy's nestled amongst the grass. I stop, bending down to pick a few even though they are closed; nothing some water and light from my desk lamp won't fix. I will make Ellie another daisy chain to apologise for running out and ruining our perfect evening. I'm showered but still buzzing so I sit at my desk with tweezers and a Stanley knife in hand. I look at the daisy I am holding, remembering the daisy chains that were made for myself and Ellie as children. Does she remember that at all? It takes me just under an hour before the delicate chain is complete.

My mind wanders, thinking back to her mother's funeral, Ellie's strength blew me away. She spent that horrible day, thanking everyone for coming to pay their respects. She supported those in mourning despite being in mourning herself. I watched silently as she moved with grace and poise, dressed in black, her red hair neatly pulled back in a bun. She looked heartbroken. Hell, it broke my own heart to watch her greet each person. She had no one there to support her in the way she needed.

I begged my father to let me comfort her, but he was right, the funeral was not a good time to reveal who I really was. It would have only made matters worse. My life is fucked up at the best of times. Me confessing my love, would have been selfish and confusing. Instead, I watched as an outsider, silently observing. I watched how she went back to work and continued with her life, holding it together. She truly amazed me. Death is one serious head fuck and here I am right in the middle of hell surrounded by it and wanting to drag Ellie down with me.

Taking my journal, I rip out another page, I find my fountain pen and write my note, it is not much, I can hardly tell her why I had to leave, at least not yet. My note although brief, will hopefully convey my way of an apology and my wish to see her again. How I want to see her again, like right now. I rummage around my room looking for something to put the daisy chain in, finally finding a cuff link box that I didn't know I packed. I pull out the cuff links, discarding them on the desk and place the daisy chain inside, the note I manage to squeeze into the lid. That will have to do.

I find myself leaving my room and heading down to Ellie's, it is pure instinct. Since arriving here, I just want to be near her. The day I arrived, I dropped my bags by the bed and sat on the large sofa which I had instructed reception to move to the window before I arrived. I sat for an hour watching Ellie tend to the gardens while working up the courage to go down and speak to her. I watched her tug weeds, talk pleasantly with people out walking, watched her laugh. It was beautiful to finally see her happier.

I glance at my watch, it's six in the morning and my hair has finally dried after my shower. My nerves are getting the better of me as I walk down the stairs and down the corridor that leads to her room. Shall I knock? I am so tempted. I stop outside her door and listen, maybe she is up and about, an early riser. Nothing. Resting my forehead on the door I wait, for what I am not sure. Strength? Courage? A sign? I hear a click and an elderly man walks out into the hall from his room opposite. He gives me a funny look; I must look like a complete nut job standing outside the room of a single woman at this time of day. Right now, I do not need twenty questions.

"Good morning." The old man states, it is not a greeting but a silent question asking what I am doing here.

"Good morning." I reply, giving him a curt nod. Keep moving old man I think to myself. I take the blue box and put it on the floor, up against the door. I'm tempted to knock and walk away but I don't, it would probably freak her out to be woken at this hour. Reluctantly I retreat to my room, as I walk, I hear muffled snoring, televisions, voices talking in whispered tones. People locked away in the safety of their rooms, the safety of this hotel, living lives that they believe are safe. It is all a lie, no one is safe in this world anymore, the human body is more complex than we thought and the change that happens, can happen to any one of us, at any time. The sun continues to rise and set and her I am attempting to open a new chapter in my life, one where I hope Ellie will accept what I am and what I do. I reach my room and enter, closing the door on the bright world behind me. My room is dark like my soul, like the life I lead, kicking off my shoes, I fall into bed exhausted and sleep the day away.

CHAPTER SEVEN

Bloody Shopping

What just happened? I feel completely stupid as I realise, I am still wearing Julian's jacket. Gingerly I attempt to remove it, feeling a ridiculous wave of loss wash over me as I pull each arm out from the soft sleeves. Holding the jacket firmly in my hands and running my thumbs over the fabric, I stupidly bring it up to my face and inhale his scent, my stomach knots and I feel lost. A peck on the lips and not a full goodnight kiss, under other circumstances I would be the first to say he behaved like the perfect gentleman.

I wipe my tired and confused eyes with the back of my hand and inhale Julian's jacket one last time before hanging it on the back of my door. For a split second I am tempted to phone him and tell him I have it, he will come back to collect it. Thankfully the sensible part of my brain kicks in and decides against that idea, I will give it back the next time I see him. I head to the bathroom and look at myself in the mirror, studying my face. I have just returned from what is probably the most romantic evening I am ever likely to experience and rather than appreciating it for what it is, I am worried deep down that he doesn't want me. I am pretty sure tonight should have ended with a proper kiss, unless I completely got my wires crossed, it did look like we were heading in that direction.

I close my eyes for a moment, holding on to the sink to steady myself. Julian's attention to detail for a first date was incredible.

I open my eyes and stare back at my tired reflection. Julian impressed me tonight. His behaviour in the car was odd but I am just putting it down to nerves on his behalf, once the clay pigeon shooting began, our date was perfect. Unorthodox but perfect, nonetheless.

I take a deep cleansing breath, letting the final waves of disappointment and confusion dissolve. There is a tiny part of me that is annoyed. After spending the evening together, I am ashamed to admit that I wanted more. Then again, I did not have the nerve to ask him back to my room, so the idea of more was never going to happen. Shit, was that what he was expecting? I decide to put this down to experience and go to bed. Sleep will make me feel better or at least give me time to process tonight's events. I just need a little perspective and if that does not work, I'll have to give myself a mental slap in the morning. I remove my mascara before grabbing my toothbrush and wince when I start brushing, thinking of how soft Julian's lips were when they briefly touched mine. I splash water on my face, washing the last remaining traces of Julian from my skin

* * *

A noise rouses me from my slumber, I squint in the dark and reach for my phone, it is half past two in the morning and I have three missed calls from Nicky. I switch on my lamp and listen for the sound that woke me. A knock on the door has me up and out of bed, grabbing for my robe and swinging it over me as I reach for the handle.

"Hey darling, when you didn't answer your phone, I got worried." Whispers a stern looking Nicky. I squint at him as I step to one side, my heartbeat slowly returning to normal.

"Nicky, you didn't have to rush back for me. I am absolutely fine." I reply pulling him gently into my room and closing the door quietly behind him.

"What happened? Why did you get back so early?" I cover my mouth as I yawn.

"Who did you get to spy on me?" Nicky has the good grace to look embarrassed.

"Darling, I am only looking out for you, you know that. I asked Alice to phone me and let me know when you got back and here I am." Nicky grabs me in an embrace, holding me tightly against him. His concern is the comfort I need. I swallow hard trying to control my emotions.

"Sweetheart what happened?" I shrug my shoulders and shake my head, my sadness and stupidity at my probable over reaction to Julian's hands off policy resurfaces from my memory. I push away from Nicky slightly, noticing his worried expression.

"Nicky I'm not upset. We had a lovely evening. Julian took me clay pigeon shooting and then we had a picnic in a fairy ring. He took me home, walked me to my door, gave me a peck on the lips and left. I don't think he is interested in me in that way." I take a deep breath in, reliving that brief kiss. Nicky grasps my hand, the look of confusion on his face is evident.

"He took you shooting. What on earth is a fairy ring?" I take another deep breath and pull Nicky down to my bed, I scoot back a little and cross my legs, pulling my robe over me. I start at the beginning and tell Nicky every single detail of my date. It felt so good saying it out loud. When I finish, I glance at him who just so happens to be wearing a broad smile, he shakes his head at me and tenderly touches my shoulder.

"Ellie, you really are as dense as the woods you had your picnic in. Are you sure you are not blond under that red head of yours?" His hand moves and brushes a lock of my hair away from my face as I roll my eyes at his insult.

"Darling, that man is crazy about you. Believe me. Absolutely no man goes to the trouble of making daisy chains and setting up picnics in fairy rings for just anyone. It is too much like hard work for the average male. That was seriously romantic." Nicky stops and looks off into the distance for a moment, before breaking out into a huge grin.

"How in the hell do you find a bloody fairy ring anyway? He is just taking his time to get to know you in the old-fashioned way. Believe me, it does not happen very often and, it is good to know that there are a few guys out there who like to sweep a girl off her feet. Don't write him off just yet." I ponder Nicky's words. Looking at my situation from his point of view, I can see he is right. I guess I can give Julian the benefit of the doubt. I will give it another chance if one should arise.

"Right well now we have sorted out my love life what did you get up to tonight?" I ask feeling guilty but touched that Nicky blew off his evening because of his concern for me.

"To be honest I wasn't in the mood to party. I was actually worried about you." Nicky gives me a reassuring smile that I return.

"Nicky my love, you are the best friend a girl could have. Thank you." I try to stifle a yawn but don't quite manage it.

"I really need to get some sleep. Do you fancy spooning with me?" Before I have managed to crawl back into bed, Nicky has his shoes and socks off, he pulls his t-shirt over his head revealing his tight muscular torso, then pulls down his jeans discarding them on the floor. With an impish grin, he jumps into bed beside me and plants a noisy wet kiss on my cheek before reaching over and wrapping his arm around me, without hesitation he pulls me tightly to him.

"Darling I thought you'd never ask." He replies with a childish giggle. The sound of him being silly makes me smile, he really is a big kid at heart.

"Good night, Nicky, love you." I say, thankful that Nicky is wearing underwear.

"Sleep tight Ellie."

I wake with a thumping headache and parched mouth; I didn't

even have a sip of alcohol last night. Nicky is unconscious beside me, lying on his back, mouth open and breathing heavily. I watch him as he sleeps, I really am lucky to have him, he is my family and we have slept like this for years. I squint at my phone, it's after ten in the morning and I really need to pee. Quietly I get out of bed and head to the bathroom. I emerge twenty minutes later all showered to find Nicky getting dressed hastily.

"Why didn't you wake me?" I pinch his cheek as I move past him towards my wardrobe, one towel wrapped around me, the other balanced perfectly on my head.

"Because you looked too cute to disturb." I reply with a grin.

"I've got to go; I'm having lunch at Judy's today and she will kill me if I am late. Do you want to join us?"

"Thank you but I have plans with Jamie later." Nicky nods, knowing how I feel about his sister's terrible cooking. He leans over to kiss my forehead and opens the door.

"Ellie, hot stuff has left you something, see you later." Sitting on the floor outside my door is a little blue box. I pick it up, Nicky squeezes by me giving me a wink and a wave. I close my door and sit on my bed forgetting to reply to Nicky completely. I hold my breath as I tentatively open the box. Nestled inside is another daisy chain. Under the lid is a note written in the same beautiful handwriting.

I enjoyed my evening with you, I can't get you out of my mind.

Julian x

I clutch the cream piece of paper to my heart. Nicky was right he does like me.

* * *

My day passed in a blur of bargain hunting; Jamie purchased yet another pair of shoes from a little boutique down one of the lanes. Decorated in turquoise leather and completed with a bright red jewel that sits above the toe, they were cute but very over the top. I, on the other hand spotted a new shop with a beautiful window display of summer outfits. I was lucky to find a couple of new wrap dresses that although simple, looked too pretty, not to purchase in the sale. I was spoilt for choice with designs and in the end, I opted for an emerald, green dress, and a simple plain wrap, in duck egg blue.

"Oh my god you must buy them." Shouted Jamie when she saw them on me and it was all the convincing I needed to splash out and treat myself. I must admit, a little retail therapy felt good for the soul, I couldn't remember the last time I went on a shopping spree. Brighton was busy. The city centre packed as always with people out shopping, eating, and enjoying the weather. Jamie and I held hands as we weaved through the crowds, stopping to admire a very cute busker singing and playing his guitar. Jamie took photos of the chocolate shop window, telling me for the hundredth time they will be making her wedding cake one day before we finally stopped for an iced coffee in our favourite little coffee shop.

We sit, almost passed out on large brown armchairs, our bags of shopping at our feet. I slurp my iced coffee, enjoying the coolness over my tongue as I swallow but trying to ignore the couple arguing at the other end of the coffee shop. Jamie throws dirty looks in their direction as one of the baristas attempts to intervene and quieten them down.

"It is so sad." I mumble to myself gazing out of the large window that we have sat in front of, the street outside buzzing with shoppers.

"What's sad?" Jamie follows my gaze as I nod my head and point to the large notice board, which stands outside the Quaker building opposite us.

"Do you know anyone who has gone missing?" I ask, unable to prise my eyes away from the various missing posters that cover the board. Jamie shakes her head, whilst taking a noisy sip of her coffee.

"It's Brighton babe, people run away from their mundane lives all the time." A shiver runs down my spine, it must be awful to lose a loved one like that. Having someone just disappear into thin air. I had noticed over the last few months shop windows, notice boards and local newspapers have become inundated with posters of local people who have gone missing. The crazy thing is, with all the messages for loved ones who have run away and there are hundreds of notes, cards and posters, the amount of homeless people seen on the streets has significantly decreased. Gone are the days when shop doorways used to be filled with the sleeping homeless by night. They have simply all gone, and I have no idea where they have been moved on to. Put simply; the homeless themselves are missing.

"Don't worry about it. Those posters are old. Half of them have been found and are home safe. Now finish this with me." Jamie extends her hand and I take the large chunk of chocolate chip cookie she holds out to me, but I drop it when we hear a scream. The couple fighting has taken things a step too far. The woman has attacked the man she is with, everyone in the shop stops to watch them. The woman is animalistic, snarling and grunting and is practically sitting on the man's chest, who is now lying flat on the floor. We watch in horror as he apologises aloud while begging her to stop. He has a hold of her hands, which stops her from injuring him, yet it does not stop her behaviour. The staff are on the phone, but no one will approach the couple. I glance at Jamie; she rolls her eyes at me and moans because I dropped the biscuit.

"I wish he would shut up." Jamie exclaimed with a look of absolute contempt. I glance back over at the incident. Everyone else in the shop is trying to ignore what is going on. There is one barista kneeling by the couple now and he seems to have calmed the situation down a little, although the couple are still on the floor. Jamie and I get back to our coffees. I feel uneasy, not sure exactly what is going on but feeling like I should do something. The coffee shop door swings open and a police officer accompanied by two men enter.

We watch in horror as the policeman takes a step back and lets the two men who are dressed in suits, manhandle the woman off the floor. She begins to snarl and bite at them and before they manage to prise her from the man underneath, she takes a bite out of his forearm. His blood curdling scream fills the air. We all sit in horror as she is grabbed and pulled up to standing. Blood is running from her lips and down her chin, her eyes wild as she struggles. The man on the floor is still screaming, blood flowing freely from his wound. The two men remain stone faced and quiet as they simply carry the thrashing woman outside. Everyone glances around, looking at one another. The policeman talks into his radio and in seconds, two paramedics enter. I glance back to Jamie in shock.

"Brighton is full of nut jobs." She says without batting an eyelid. My eyes follow Jamie's. The man has been led out by the police officer and the paramedics. I just do not understand what happened here. Slowly the coffee shop returns to its usual hustle and bustle, I have gone completely off my coffee. Who were those two men and where did they take that woman?

Once back at the hotel I decide to do my weekly laundry and spend the early part of the evening battling with the industrial sized washing machine, just to take my mind of this afternoon. I had this strange feeling that I could have done something in that coffee shop, although what exactly, I didn't know. I was also antsy because I had heard nothing from Julian all day, no phone call or text messages.

By Monday morning I had still yet to hear from Julian but for now I am stuck in the office, working on next week's rotas, ordering stock, and catching up with my paperwork. At five I have finished for the day and head back over to the hotel feeling like I have had a good day work wise. I have still heard nothing from Julian and although his note didn't indicate that he would contact me, I kind of hoped that he would. I decide to join Nicky and Jamie in the staff room for dinner as I am absolutely starving and after having a peek to see what's on offer, decide to have a large helping of lasagne and salad.

"Have you heard from him today?" Nicky asks breaking his conversation with Jamie, to wait for my response. I shake my head as I swallow the warm mushy and satisfying goo.

"Nope, nothing since his little gift yesterday." I finally reply. Jamie gives me a sad look.

"If it helps, I haven't seen him around the hotel today, maybe he is off site?" Jamie stands, placing her hand lightly on my shoulder in a reassuring pat before air kissing me and rushing out, she is late for her shift on the reception desk again.

"I'm sorry darling, maybe he's working?" Nicky states trying to make me feel better.

"I'm sure I'll hear from him when he is ready." I manage to say as I take the last bite of my meal. Nicky gets up and puts his plate in the dishwasher, he looks smart in his work suit.

"I better get down there, a duty manager's job is never done."

"Don't work too hard." I snigger. I look at the Victoria sponge that sits in the middle of the table before glancing down at my empty plate, I'm tempted to cut myself a slice but decide against it. I put my crockery and cutlery in the dishwasher, along with two dirty mugs I find on the table and a pile of dirty plates that have been left in the sink before switching on the machine. I move around the staff room plumping cushions on the sofa and generally tidying up before leaving to go back to my room.

I walk out into the hall and up the stairs to my floor checking my phone again, no calls, no messages, nothing. The hair rises on the back of my neck as I turn, entering my hallway and look up. Julian is leaning casually against my door, dressed in blue slouch jeans and a dark hooded top. He looks different in his casual wear; his hair is all messy. Our eyes lock and he gives me a sad smile, he looks tired and then I notice the large bloody wound on his cheek.

CHAPTER EIGHT

Tantrums

"Julian." I run up the corridor towards him. My heart is in my mouth as I can plainly see that he is injured. My legs propel me forward while my brain tries to understand why he is leaning against my door, injured. From the few feet that separate us, I see the dried blood that has pooled and congealed around his dimple. His eyes search mine as I move, I watch him closely, looking him up and down as I get nearer. Julian looks tired but overall, he seems unharmed, although his face is a mess. I notice the odd shape of his left shoulder as I get closer and realise, he is not in as good a shape as I first thought. The hooded top he is wearing is dusty, with a dirty print on his chest, mud smears his cuffs, and he has scuff marks on his knees. I can't see blood anywhere else and for that I am grateful. Hurriedly I open my door and without thinking, take Julian's hand and pull him into my room behind me. Instinctively I reach for his face, he flinches and pulls away from my hand. I stop and give him a reassuring smile, my eyes searching his in understanding. I want to ask him what happened and then a memory of him finding me crying springs to mind. If he wants to tell me, he will in his own time.

"I need your help, Ellie." Julian states matter of fact as I stand looking at his sagging left arm.

"I have dislocated my shoulder and I need you to pop it back in for me." I swallow nervously.

"I have never done that before; I wouldn't know where to start. Let us get you to hospital." I exclaim, my voice rising slightly.

"I can't go to the hospital. Too many questions. You can do this;

I will talk you through it." Julian tries to smile but I can see he is in pain.

"Okay." I do not know what else to say, nodding my head in agreement.

"Good. I need you to take my wrist and forearm, just below my elbow. Rotate my arm slightly forwards until it all pops back into place, it is easy. Can you do that for me?" Julian does not wait for my reply, he moves and sits on the end of my bed.

"First I want you to hold my elbow with your right hand and my forearm just above my wrist with your left." I do as Julian instructs, placing my hands on his clothed arm. His eyes flutter closed for a second and he takes a deep breath.

"Now I want you to move my arm slowly towards you, slow and steady about 90 degrees." I watch him as I move his arm towards me carefully.

"Great now stop. I want you to keep my elbow still and supported while you move my forearm, raising my wrist in the air, ear height. Can you do that?" I nod in understanding and watch him take another deep breath.

"Are you ready?" I ask. Julian breathes deeply, his green eyes focused on mine.

"Absofuckinglutely." He replies through gritted teeth. I slowly move and lift his arm as instructed. Julian's face pales I am surprised just how heavy his arm is as I lift it, there is a slight bulge at his shoulder that I can see through his clothes. I feel a little resistance and then a pop. Julian releases the breath that he has been holding.

"Thank you." I look at him bewildered. Julian leans his head to his left shoulder, and I hear another pop as he works through the tension in his neck.

"That must of bloody hurt." Julian nods and uses his right hand to rub his left shoulder.

"I am used to it; it has happened before." I want to bombard him with questions about how this has all happened but don't.

"I am going to clean the wound on your face now." I state. I raise my hand slowly and place my fingertips on his jawline. Gently I inspect his cheek. The wound looks deep and fresh, his blood has only just begun to become sticky and clot. It makes me feel sick seeing him with injuries and this wound looks painful. I study his face, standing close enough to smell him, that subtle hint of citrus fills my nostrils as well as something else, the scent of the outdoors, woodlands, and fresh damp earth. The graze around the cut and under his eye looks nasty; full of grit and his skin is pink and inflamed. Julian looks like he has had a serious fight with the floor and the floor won. I do not speak and neither does he. He chooses to keep his head down and eyes firmly on the floor, he looks dark and brooding right now, anger is emanating from him as I listen to his heavy breathing. I want to ask him what happened, bombard him with questions but I just can't bring myself to. I have an unnerving feeling I won't like his explanation. Gently I reach for his chin and tilt his face up. His green eyes are bright and clear but there is fear in them. We are eye to eye and on closer inspection he looks like he has a bruise developing over his eyebrow too.

"I'm going to clean that for you." I say with authority. I walk to the bathroom and rummage around for my first aid kit, grabbing some cotton wool and my canister of Evian facial mist to use to wash out the wound.

"Okay this is going to sting a little, you're a big boy and can handle it." I place everything on the bed side table next to us. I go to move the objects to make some space and spot the daisy chains, gift box and his notes sitting by my bed. I momentarily look back at Julian and I am pleased to see a small smile, now he is aware that his gifts mean something to me.

I continue, swallowing my embarrassment and carefully pick everything up, moving them to the safety of the table at the other side of my room. I get back to my job and consider Julian for a moment, thankfully his nose doesn't appear to be broken. First things first, that wound needs cleaning. I angle my lamp so I can see better and pick up the Evian canister, holding down the nozzle with one hand and spraying the fine mist of water over the graze, whilst gently holding a wad of cotton wool against his jawline to collect the blood soaked, dirty runoff. Julian winces slightly as the cold pressurised water touches his inflamed, raw skin but he says nothing, choosing to close his eyes. I continue, letting the drizzle of water rinse away the grit, blood, and dirt from his face. Finally, when the water runs clear, I stop, dabbing around the graze with clean cotton wool and then head back to the bathroom to wash my hands. Julian studies me, raising an eyebrow when I return. I give him another reassuring smile and search through the first aid kit.

"Brilliant." I say aloud to myself as I find the tube of antiseptic cream. I check to make sure it is still in date and then break the seal. Applying a small blob to my finger and trying to be as gentle as I can, I smear it over the wound. Julian understandably winces and pulls away from me slightly.

"Hold still, this will help stop an infection." I continue dabbing the ointment onto his raw skin, making sure I have lightly covered the area before I head back to my bathroom to wash my hands again. Turning off the tap, I reach for the towel and spot Julian behind me through the mirror. My legs feel like jelly and my heart is thumping, he looks dark and menacing; a look that would scare others and should scare me. Humming between us is a connection, I feel like we have known each other forever, realising how odd that is. I stare back at him through the mirror, I could never be afraid of him not like I was before. That sensation has gone. I am aware that there is something more than a crush between us, I just can't put my finger on it. In this moment, my whole being feels like Julian belongs with me. I shake off my off thoughts and try to gain perspective all the while keeping my eyes on his. He continues to stare at me through the glass and in return I stare back, gripping the sink to steady myself. I find the strength to drag my eyes away from his reflection and turn to face him. I reach out and place my fingertips under his tender cheek, giving my handy work the once over.

"That looks much better." I whisper as his body moves closer, slowly he reaches for my chin. Julian's fingertips caress the skin on my neck and along my jawline, causing goosebumps to break-out over my arms. His hand brushes my ear before running his fingers through my hair, directing me closer to him. His lips finally brush mine, so gentle and soft that instantly my mind is lost in him. I can't control whatever this is between us, so I do the only thing I can, I reach up and run my fingers through his black hair, caressing the soft skin of his neck below his hairline with my thumb. His kiss is slow and gentle, his uninjured hand moves towards my back and with a little pressure he pulls me closer to him, my chest heaving against his. Slowly I move my tongue for-wards and swipe his lower lip, lightly brushing against his teeth. Julian's soft lips part slightly, his tongue finds mine.

Our movements are slow and tender as we continue to explore each other. A flush of heat sweeps through me from head to toe, I pull my hand free from his hair and run it down his strong muscular back. Soon both of my hands are caressing him, I want to feel his skin so much it hurts. I deepen the kiss and listen as he groans into my mouth, so I move forward slightly so that I can press my body as close to his as humanly possible. A soft moan leaves my mouth as I run my hands, down his hooded top, feeling the soft cotton of the dark material that covers his back. I move my hands under his top and find the waistband of Julian's jeans. My fingers move slowly, skimming over the skin of his hips and around his back, up and down his spine. Heat is radiating off his super soft skin, I feel his taut muscles tense at my touch, yet I continue completely caught in the moment and overwhelmed by lust. I take hold of a fistful of fabric and attempt to pull it upwards by the hem. Julian's nostrils flare, his brow furrows, and his breath hitches in his throat. He pulls away and steps back.

"Stop." He whispers. I instantly freeze. Julian's eyes search mine for understanding, he looks apologetic but serious, a brief thought flits across his face, he is wrestling with an inner demon. I stand rooted to the floor, dropping my hands back down to my sides, confused and trying to work out exactly why he is stepping backwards and away from me.

"To be continued..." He mutters breathing heavily. Him being as affected by what has just happened as much as I am. Julian plants one last kiss on my stunned lips before walking out of my bathroom, I hear my door open and then close, he has left me again without turning back. I run out of the bathroom. I am most definitely alone. What just happened here? I feel completely wound up like a tightly coiled spring. Why on earth did he leave? I grab my phone, anger coursing through my veins. I have nothing to lose. I'll phone him and leave a ranting voicemail if he doesn't answer. I find his number and consider my options quickly, deciding to send him a text message.

I am sorry you had to leave.

I type out the words, refusing to leave a kiss at the end and hit send, dropping my phone on the bed next to me in rage and pent-up frustration. I am angry that he left like that and what did he mean exactly by to be continued? Talk about leaving a girl needy, hanging, and confused. I've got to get out of this room, get away from the confines of these walls, I need some perspective, some air. I grab my keys and leave my room slamming the door behind me, and not caring about who I disturb. I feel angry and horny as hell, two ugly emotions I am rarely forced to deal with.

"Ellie. Hey Ellie, what's up?" Shouts Nicky over the reception desk. I ignore him and rush out of the reception entrance. I am not one for drama usually but tonight drama is emanating from my very soul. Who am I kidding, since Julian's arrival I have been stressed out, my behaviour over dramatic and now I am a ticking timebomb of emotion! This is not me, I'm calm, collected and pragmatic, but around him I feel every emotion that a human can all at once, it's exhausting but right now I am angry.

I walk down the stairs and out onto the hotel driveway and along to the main road. The fresh air is welcome because I did not realise how hot I was until I felt the cool breeze on my burning skin. The more I think about what just happened, the more ridiculously stupid I feel. What exactly is his agenda here? Why did he come to me tonight? There are too many questions floating around my head that I need answering. Julian Hunter is one frustrating man and if he thinks he can play around with me he can think again. Clarity and my common sense returning as I stomp angrily up the road.

I move onto the grassy verge as I walk, taking deep breaths in an attempt at calming myself down. There are no lamp posts, so I am being guided, purely by the headlights of the oncoming traffic. I rationalise everything that has happened. Julian is mysterious, sensitive, tender, romantic, thoughtful, sexy, anger inducing and most importantly, he is infuriating! And his stare is so intense. When I try and think of answers to his various behaviours, all I come up with are questions.

I walk aimlessly, no idea where I am heading, I just need to keep my distance from Julian and if it means I need to walk along an unlit road to maintain distance from that man, then so be it. Reaching into my pocket I find a five-pound note, folded into a neat square, I have enough to pay for the biggest bar of chocolate the petrol station a mile up ahead sells. The thought of chocolate gives me a fabulous reason to keep moving and my murderous mood lifts slightly. I walk at a faster pace, the sudden need of comfort food keeps me moving, giving my mind something other than anger to focus on. When a car slows down alongside me. I keep my eyes firmly ahead, ignoring the car and the passing traffic. The car pulls up just in front of me.

68

"Get in Ellie." I glance over my shoulder; cars are beeping their horns as they overtake Julian's car.

"Not a chance." I shout in defiance.

"Get in." he shouts in return, only louder.

"Go away Julian." I yell at the top of my lungs, so I am heard over the noise of the passing traffic. I hear a car door slam behind me and hope he has given up. I increase my pace, I can see the petrol station in the distance, when suddenly I'm swept off my feet and lifted into Julian's strong arms. He holds me like it is effortless, considering he has had a dislocated shoulder, I am suddenly furious again.

"Put me down!" I scream, pushing at his magnificent chest. The audacity of him to manhandle me in public. I hope someone calls the police as I am effectively being kidnapped!

"No." Is the stern reply I receive as he strolls in the dark and back to his car. I am gently placed on the passenger's seat; he puts my seatbelt on before slamming the car door shut. In seconds he is sat next to me with his key in the ignition, pulling off into the night.

"What in the actual fuck are you doing?" I ask through gritted teeth. Pure ugly rage is emanating from every pore, I cannot think. I just want to get out and run. I look at Julian, waiting for an answer, he keeps his eyes on the road.

"How dare you bundle me in your car. Kidnapping is a criminal offence in this country!" I yell, thumping my fist on the car door. being this close to him makes me want him so much, I hate myself for it. Julian's nostrils flare, he takes in a deep breath before speaking. He looks scary and angry in this light, I glance down at his hands, he is gripping the steering wheel tightly.

"We need to talk Ellie." I try to think for a moment, but it is difficult. We do not need to talk; Julian owes me no explanation. We do not actually know each other, and we are not in any kind of relationship. I am just a stupid woman who just so happens to like the most irritating man on the planet. Another wave of anger bubbles through me, I want to kick and scream for him to stop the car and to let me out. We drive in uncomfortable silence; I cannot think of a single thing to say to him. I glance over, he looks like he is starting to calm down, his grip on the wheel has loosened a little. He catches me looking at him, then turns his head and attention back to the road. Him and his challenging behaviour infuriates me.

"Where are we going?" I finally ask, still angry. It is dark and I have managed to miss every signpost we have driven past; I have no idea where we are.

"I'm taking you some place safe to talk."

"That doesn't answer my bloody..." Before I can finish my sentence, Julian reaches over and presses a button on the dashboard panel. I jump at the sound of the loud music filling my ears. Julian glances at my sudden movement. Whatever that music was, it finishes. I glance out of the window, completely unaware that the next song has started. Angry thoughts are replayed in my mind, Julian leaves me one minute and then throws me in his car the next, how is a girl supposed to understand constant mixed signals? I am suddenly aware of the loud repetitive beat. I can't concentrate on my thoughts, as the repetitive steady drum machine and the deep masculine voice emanating from the speakers penetrates my brain. The words capture my interest, each line of the song begins to sink in. The chorus hits me and a panicked flush, floods my cheeks. Eight words bounce around my head. What, no way! This song is currently singing my theme tune. Who is this? I look over at Julian who takes his eyes off the road for a moment to look back at me. I swallow and feel slightly faint, sick, embarrassed, and hugely turned on. Eight little words are being sung with what sounds like malice, they are directly responsible for causing me to feel like my very soul is on fire, I fidget on the seat, trying to compose myself.

"Switch that crap off." I yell with a hint of desperation. I am no prude but honestly you wouldn't hear those lyrics being played on Radio One. The music continues and this song is exactly how I feel at this moment in time, it is mocking me, teasing me and Julian knows it. Yes, the singer is most definitely singing what I thought he was singing. The melodic words "I want to fuck you like an animal." fill my head, wrapping themselves around my needy body and seriously confused mind. Julian's eyes leave the road once more and he looks back over.

"No!" This is too intense. The tension could be cut with a knife. I really want this angry man. The smell of him fills my nose and I am desperately in need of his touch. For a split second I think about opening the car door and jumping out, dramatic, but right now I would do anything to escape this torture. The music continues to play loudly, the haunting melody assaulting my ears and amplifying my need for Julian, I hate it.

The hypnotic beat is not helping my cause and if I am honest with myself, I am glad I am strapped to the car, as right now I just want to physically hurt him for putting me through this hell. I have never wanted to do anything violent to anyone. I move forward and start pressing various buttons on the dashboard, finally managing to switch the CD off myself to save my sanity. A snarl leaves Julian's lips, I flinch but not from fear. Julian notices my reaction but stays quiet. He keeps his eyes on the dark road, glancing over to me when he thinks I am not paying attention. I am angry at him. I am being taken to God knows where, he could be the next young Hannibal Lecter for all I know, let him do his worst. I mentally prepare myself to attack in self-defence If necessary. I need to keep my wits about me and not let these hormones and him get the better of me. We continue to drive in silence, neither of us speaking. I focus on the purr of the car while attempting to take calming breaths and plan my escape as soon as he slows down or pulls up. Julian drives me to a little town that I don't recognise, moving quietly through dark and empty streets. He slows down to a stop outside a pub, switches of the ignition and removes the keys. Julian unbuckles his seatbelt and gets out of the car; I hurriedly undo mine as my door opens.

"Do I need to carry you?" He barks.

"No." I reply through gritted teeth. I gracefully climb out of the car and stand stock still, weighing up my options; do I run? Julian tugs on my left hand like a naughty schoolboy, which just pushes all the wrong buttons and without thinking, my right hand reaches up and out as I feebly attempt to slap his face. Julian has the reflexes of a cheetah, he catches my wrist in mid-air, stopping me from striking him.

"I deserve that. But I warn you Ellie, don't ever attempt to strike me again." I am horrified that I tried to hit him, never in my life have I felt violent towards another person until tonight. Julian is clearly no good for me. He drops my wrist and walks forward, stopping a few feet in front of me before turning.

"I would like to talk to you. I will take you home afterwards." He holds his hand out and like the fool I am I take it. I am led into a pub, and it looks like rock night. Loud music is playing over the speakers, men dressed in jeans and band t-shirts, most of which I have never heard of. Long hair certainly is the fashion here, on the men as well as the women, while piercings and tattoos adorn various body parts of everyone present. Casually, Julian leads me to the bar.

"What would you like to drink?" I look at him, trying to judge his temperament. He seems a lot calmer, but his expression is stern and serious.

"A double vodka, neat. Please." I state. Julian raises an eyebrow but orders my drink and a black coffee for himself. Who orders coffee at this time of night? Our drinks are prepared and handed to us.

"Is the dark room free?" Julian leans over the bar and asks the barman who has long straight black hair tumbling down his back and dressed in a black T-shirt with Slipknot written on the front. The sleeves have been cut off, highlighting the exceptional muscles of his upper arms, his chest bulges through his T-shirt. This guy has got to be at least six foot two tall and built like a brick shithouse. The barman looks from me to Julian then back to me, before giving me a jaw dropping grin.

"It is always free for you Lion." He winks, not taking his hazel eyes from me.

"Thanks, Seb." Replies Julian with an arrogant air. The two men slap hands in an overly friendly way despite their lack of words. Julian moves away from the bar, he does not pay him which I find odd, I don't have time to dwell on that as I follow behind. I am led in the direction of the toilets at the back of the pub. As we walk by, people nod in acknowledgement to Julian, and he nods back. I can see that he is known around here. We walk through to a small hallway and up some stairs that finally lead us to a darkened room. Julian finds the light switch and suddenly we are standing in the doorway of a fair sized and completely under furnished room, two large black leather sofa's are the only pieces of furniture present and have been strategically placed to sit in the middle of the room facing one another. I have no idea what this room would be used for considering the music and crowd below.

"Sit." Julian commands. I knock back my double vodka in one gulp before sitting, my eyes never leaving his, I seriously need to settle these nerves. Julian sits on the sofa opposite and takes a sip of his coffee before placing the saucer on the carpeted floor below. He wraps both of his hands around his cup and stares back at me. His expression unreadable. I stay quiet, after all it was me who has been dragged to the arse end of nowhere.

"You didn't ask me how I ended up in the state I did. Why?" He takes another sip of the dark steaming liquid in his cup while waiting for my response.

"It is none of my business." I glance at Julian as I answer and then look at the door, it is not too late for me to make a run for it. I am not scared of Julian at all, but I am worried by the anger that is pulsing through my veins.

"Why didn't you answer your phone?" That question takes a second to sink in before patting my back pocket and realising it is still lying on my bed where I threw it earlier.

"I left it in my room." I reply thinking that I will need to let Nicky know that I am okay.

"Can I use your phone?" Julian raises his eyebrows but says nothing.

"Please." I continue. He stands, retrieving his phone from his pocket and hands it to me. I dial Nicky's number not caring how rude it is for me to make a call right now.

"Hey sweetie, it's me, I'm all right. I'll come by your room when I get back okay." I hang up and hand the phone back to Julian who is studying me closely. I sit back down, Julian follows suit, taking a last gulp of coffee before placing his cup on the saucer by his feet.

"I'm sorry I walked out."

"I'm sorry you walked out abruptly too." Julian sits forward, chewing on his bottom lip in concentration. I sit back waiting for him to tell me what is on his mind. Silently I will him to confess his sins.

"I am complicated. Everything about me is complicated." He says seriously. I wait a moment, expecting him to elaborate but he doesn't.

"Okay...complicated." I parrot. That does not give me much to go on. We stare into each other's eyes a little longer. Various scenarios begin to run through my head as I look at him. This is becoming intense and once again I am torn between running out of the door, down the stairs and out of the pub or moving across the room and onto his lap. I break the tension and silence with a completely stupid question.

"How old are you?"

"Twenty-eight." I nod considering what to ask next. I have goose pimples on my arms, I feel out of my depth here.

"What did you want to talk about?" I prompt not wanting to waste the rest of the night just staring at each other. Julian glances at the door before looking back at me. His expression sends a horrifying shiver down my spine.

"Death."

CHAPTER NINE

Twenty Questions

I can see unspeakable demons in those green eyes, along with pain and torment. Julian's haunted by something serious, pain is etched onto his skin, and oozes from within.

"Death." I repeat mulling over the word, conjuring up all manner of scenarios and wondering if he is trying to be dramatic?

"The question is where do I start?" He pauses, talking to himself. I sit here, am hanging on to his every word.

"There is so much that I need to tell you and I don't know how or where to begin." Julian's face lights up suddenly, I am a little taken aback by his sudden change in demeanour. He looks as though he has told a joke, only I have not understood the punchline. I feel at a complete disadvantage. He shrugs his shoulders, runs his fingers through his hair and shifts slightly on the sofa. His body language changes, a smile flits to a frown and then back again. I am confused by this curious situation that I currently find myself in.

"I have been waiting a very long time for you." He stops and blinks noticeably while shaking his head, looking like he is dislodging an ugly memory from his mind. I can't make out his expression, but it certainly isn't happiness.

"I have wanted you for so long. It is the reason I have come back to Hedge hill year on year." I shift uncomfortably as Julian begins running his hand along his denim clad thigh. My eyes are drawn to the scuff marks still present on his knees, watching his hand move in an almost hypnotic motion. I do not know what to say.

I open my mouth and then close it again. I must look like a goldfish gasping at the top of a polluted aquarium.

The hair rises on the back of my neck. There is more to what he is saying, I can hear another meaning in his soft yet husky voice, this goes beyond liking a woman and asking her out for a drink. If I did not know better, the way he is currently talking, almost borders on stalking territory, he is the hunter and I have been his prey. I keep quiet considering his words whilst studying his body language further. He sits back, almost nestling himself into the sofa. He runs his hand through his messy hair, sweeping it completely free from his injured face.

"I tried to come and see you sooner, but I physically couldn't get away. It's complicated" He stops again waiting for my response. I sit still, not moving, waiting for him to continue, we could be here like this all night if he doesn't get on with it.

"It is frustrating. I keep being called away to work, it appears that the powers that be are attempting to keep me busy and away from you." He looks away and laughs to himself. He really has my attention now. Julian has been working while here? My anger subsidies a little.

"Okay so what does all this actually mean? You have yet to say something that makes sense." I ask holding his gaze, willing him to continue and finish all of this.

"It is simple Ellie. I want you to be mine, but." He pauses and I hold my breath. Wow, I was not expecting him to be so blunt.

"You are meant to be mine; you feel it too. I know you are drawn to me as I am to you." I stare at him with wide eyes. He is right, I am.

"So, if you will have me kitten, I am all yours." He finishes, folding his arms over his chest. I flush, feeling hot from head to toe. I do want him, but I am not sure what that entails, I am frightfully scared by all of this. I am petrified that I could, despite myself like him more than I should and terrified that he will be gone in a few weeks. What do I do when he is gone? Alone. I will be alone and heartbroken. I sit and contemplate his strange proposition. It is oddly tempting. Nicky's advice on having fun rings in my ears.

"What happens in three weeks when you leave?" I ask. I can hear the quiver in my voice. I gaze at the floor, at my shoes and the carpet, noticing that the carpet is the same cream colour as the walls. I close my eyes tight momentarily as I try to order my thoughts.

"Ellie, what I want for us is huge. We should take one day at a time to begin with. Get to know each other while I am here. I want this, Ellie. I want you!" He throws me a cocky smirk which turns into a smile when his eyes find mine. His words echo in my head. It sounded like he has practised saying that for years. No point worrying about the future just yet when we are struggling with the present. He raises an eyebrow for an answer. One thing is for sure, this guy does not like to wait. I cross my arms across my chest, I have liked him for so long that for once my head and heart are in total agreement but there is more to this. More to him wanting me. No amount of awkwardness can gloss over that Julian has something else going on in his life that I am yet to find out about.

"Fine, you can have me." I have nothing to lose, except my sanity, my reply is definite, but I inwardly cringe at the way I worded my reply. Julian raises an eyebrow.

"Can I now?" I shake my head no, I'm still mad. I was man-handled here; I still have no idea what is going on with him.

"You are very much aware that came out wrong. What I mean is fine we can date." I force myself to shut up. Julian gives me the most amazing smile this time, pure happiness radiates from him, he looks like all his Christmases have come at once. I am amazed that I have agreed to be his, so to speak.

"One condition." I continue, holding one finger aloft. There is a pulling deep in my gut, I know there is more to him, more to his words then he is letting on, I can feel it, he is hiding something.

"You tell me the truth, no stories or lies, I won't pry into your life, but I want you to be truthful with me if I need to ask you a question." The words tumble out of my mouth and although I don't even know what I mean exactly, I just needed to say them. He needed to know I am not a pushover. Julian's smile becomes broader, drawing my attention back to the graze on his face. How did he get it? There is something about him that I can't quite put my finger on, there is more to him than meets the eye.

"How is your shoulder feeling?" I ask sternly. Since we arrived here, he has been acting like he didn't have a dislocation a couple of hours ago.

"My arm is fine. I heal quickly. And yes, I agree to your condition. I have every intention of telling you everything." He grins but the smile doesn't meet his eyes. Julian stands and moves, before kneeling on the floor in front of me in one swift motion. I take a short breath in. Okay this isn't going slowly. Julian presses his hips between my parting knees. We are practically face to face; I search his eyes for the secrets he is holding onto.

"Introductions are done. Now I want these". He runs his finger delicately across my lips. He continues, his voice deepening. He removes his finger from my lips and extends his hand, cupping my chin with his palm and running his thumb along my bottom lip. He leans in slowly, his lips brush mine and I can control myself no longer, I grab him and pull him towards me deepening our kiss. We are suddenly lost in each other, my hand grazes his jaw as he runs his fingers through my hair, pulling me closer.

I don't want to let go of this strange enigmatic man; he smells of citrus and tastes divine. Julian's lips are smooth, full, and plump and his tongue soft and delicious. He is gentle with me, showering me with small delicate kisses up my neck and along my jawline, his strong fingers gently glide up and down my spine, teasing my senses. It is simple and clear as day, I want him more than I have ever wanted anything in my life. I manage to gather my thoughts and pull away, getting some much-needed air into my burning lungs, I must look a sight, panting like a dog. A question flits across my mind and is out of my mouth before I have a chance to censor myself.

"What did you mean exactly about being complicated?" I whisper, not wanting to ruin the moment but not wanting to push things further with someone who has issues in life; what if he is married?

"I simply have been waiting a long time for you." I smile as his lips now ferocious, reach mine once more, silencing me. That didn't answer my question, but it is enough to shut up my enquiring mind. He moves closer so that we become a tangled mess on the sofa, I'm vaguely aware that someone could walk in on us at any moment, yet it doesn't faze me in the slightest. Julian's muscular body presses against mine, my legs wrapped around his and my fingers are gently playing with his messy hair, even though we are fully clothed this feels intense. I don't want it to stop, I do not want this to ever stop. I need him. We are interrupted by a loud noise. I pull away slightly to see where the continuous sound is coming from.

"Shit!" Julian jumps off me to standing and pulls his phone free from his pocket.

"Yes." He says flippantly as he answers, his eyes not leaving mine. He holds the phone out to me.

"It's for you." I take the phone, who in hell would be calling me on his number.

"Hello. Nicky, I'm fine. I'm a little busy .... Yes. I'll text you when I get in. I love you too." I hand the phone back and instantly realise that Julian is not happy with me, he looks angry, totally upset in fact. His nostrils flare, he is trying to control his temper.

"What is he to you?" He asks through gritted teeth. I give him a sheepish grin, realising how that must have sounded.

"Nicky is my family." Julian looks blankly at me, not understanding.

"He is my best friend, nothing more than the big brother I never had. Julian doesn't look any happier, so I begrudgingly elaborate.

"Nicky and I have known each other for years, I don't have any family, just him. I suppose now is a good time to tell you that he is a terrible flirt so watch yourself. But our relationship is nothing more than friendship." Julian says nothing so I continue because I don't want him to feel uncomfortable around the duty manager of Hedge Hill.

"Look you have nothing to worry about. Nicky has only ever looked after me." I finish, hoping that is enough to placate him whilst giving him my most reassuring smile.

"You should know, Nicky is not someone I am willing to give up. For you or for anyone else."

"We better go." Julian states matter of fact, while running his fingers through his unruly hair again. Clearly our precious moment is over and I'm getting the brush off yet again. Julian steps away from me, if he doesn't disappear when he gets uncomfortable, he just becomes mute I notice. I sigh in exasperation.

"You are probably right. Let's sulk and give each other the silent treatment" I say sarcastically, unable to conceal the disappointment in my voice. Just as we get things started, they stop just as quickly. Julian takes my hand firmly and leads me down the stairs, ignoring what I have just said. The bar is empty now, I completely lost track of time being upstairs with him.

"Night Seb." Julian says to the barman.

"Goodnight." Shouts Seb turning around with a tea towel thrown over one shoulder while beaming at us. Julian holds the door open for me.

"Am I going to see you any time this week Lion? It has been a while and I'm getting desperate; you know how I need you." Julian throws the barman a dirty look.

"Very funny Seb, hilarious." I am ushered through the door and out onto the dark street.

"Bye Ellie, it was lovely to see you again." I look over my shoulder, the barman stands at the bar laughing to himself.

"How does he know my name and what does he mean?" I ask as I am pulled towards the car. I have never met that man before tonight. And from the distinct look of him, he is not someone you forget in a hurry.

"Must have mentioned you in passing." Is Julian's uncomfortable reply. We drive silently for most of the journey back to Hedge Hill, my brain whirling from everything that has happened tonight. I'm perturbed by Julian and his unique confession that confesses absolutely nothing. I have more questions after seeing him with the barman, after hearing what the barman said. I cannot help but think Julian being complicated has other connotations. Am I getting myself involved with a bisexual man? Nicky will have a field day with this, I can see his face now. I want to ask Julian outright but feel I can't just yet. I don't want to make him uncomfortable and neither do I want to pry. Am I bothered if he is bisexual? No, no I'm not.

"You haven't asked me?" I look over at his profile in the dark, he wants to talk about something but I'm not sure what exactly he is referring to. So much and so little has been said tonight. Then an image of him and the barman together penetrates my brain. Julian let's out a loud guttural laugh at my expression.

"I see what you're thinking about, take your mind out of the gutter, Seb is of no importance." He stops waiting for my reaction, but I give him nothing, how on earth did he know that was what I was thinking about?

"Ellie, you never asked me about how I got this." He sounds almost sad as he points a finger to his cheek. I haven't enquired about his wounds despite doing the major clean up on him, truthfully, I am a little scared of the answer.

"I never questioned you because it is none of my business but as you have brought the subject up, feel free to tell me when you are ready." Julian glances at me then back to the road.

"Fine. Let's play twenty questions. Ask me anything and I will answer truthfully, I promise." I look over at him.

"Really. You want to play twenty questions?" I ask.

"Yep, you must have questions about me, I realise there is a lot you don't know. Fire away because in all honesty, I do not know how to tell you half of my shit!" I think for a moment, that really doesn't sound good.

"Okay I have one, have you ever been married?" I hold my breath and wait for his answer. "No, I have never been married and I am currently free and single." Well, that is one questioned answered.

"You have another nineteen questions." Julian states. I nod.

"I know, thank you, I understand how the game works. Is there a use by date or can I ask a question as and when I think of one?"

"As and when Ellie, as and when." A smile breaks across his face as he shakes his head. I try and not laugh at how preposterous this is. I am sitting next to someone who clearly has more issues than Vogue judging on his behaviour.

"I'm sorry that I walked out on you earlier, I wanted to, you know...I really want to get the timing right." I stare at him, that sounded so sweet that I can't help but smile to myself as my insides go a little gooey, although it doesn't change the fact that he did walk out. Julian shakes his head.

"I'm sorry I'm not good at this stuff." I raise my hand instinctively, the way he said that last sentence makes me feel a little uneasy.

"What do you mean you're not good at this stuff?" I ask, there is a nagging at the back of my head, instinct is telling me that something isn't what it seems although I can't quite put my finger on it.

"Is that question number two?" I consider this, is it? Do I want to know? Do I even care?

"No, that wasn't question number two, I need to find a good question to ask you." Julian glances my way and smiles.

"Nicky, what is he like?" I get the impression, that Julian has changed the subject for a reason. I have already given Julian a brief explanation of my friendship with Nicky and am not sure what else I can say about it.

"Nicky is the greatest guy. He is fun loving and cheeky. He is very protective of me and his family and despite his flamboyant lifestyle he is sensitive. We have known each other for years." A memory of Nicky getting into trouble springs to mind.

"When we were at university, Nicky had this party hard lifestyle which caused him to fall behind on his coursework. It was so serious that he was on the verge of getting kicked out of university during our second year. Somehow, he managed to sweet talk them into giving him a week to get all his course work done and sit an exam that he couldn't originally get out of bed for, and he pulled it off. Nicky stayed in our flat, we kept him topped up with coffee and snacks. I ran to the library and got books out for him while he studied and made sure he got sleep and decent meals. By Friday afternoon the following week, he handed in four completed essays, and he passed his exam with flying colours. The university agreed that he could stay. That week he moved in with my flatmate and I, we have been best friends since." I finish. I was not expecting to say so much. I glance over at Julian who remains quiet. I notice he is gripping the steering wheel tightly again and he doesn't look happy.

"Look Nicky really is one of the good guys." I finally finish, if Julian doesn't like my friendship with Nicky, then it is tough, he will have to get used to it.

"Did you love him?" I take a sharp intake of breath, talking about this makes me feel uncomfortable but this is clearly an issue for Julian, then again, I did ask him if he had been married and did fleetingly think he may have slept with that barman, maybe he just needs confirmation that I am single.

"I loved him like a brother back then and love him like a brother now. Sorry I thought we were playing twenty questions with you, not me?" I add trying to make a joke out of a suddenly cringe worthy conversation. Julian smiles for the first time in five minutes although I am not sure if it is because of my answer or my reaction to his question. I suddenly feel a mess. I am tired, over emotional and feel pangs of sadness, I really miss easy going Julian from last summer and I am growing tired of moody Julian of now, I am mostly angry with myself for wanting Julian so much.

CHAPTER TEN

Alone

Julian looks over at me intently. I do a double take not realising that we have arrived, until he is pulling up in the car park of Hedge Hill.

"Any other questions before we go in?" I have tons but I am not sure how to order them. I am going to have to jot them down as I am sure some questions will lead to others. One that is playing on my mind is how he knows my real name, I'm just not sure I want to hear that answer right now. I think hard and fast, what I really require is clarification on why he comes here to stay every summer.

"Question two Julian. Why do you come to Hedge Hill every year?" I put my hand on the car door while waiting for him to respond.

"Are you sure you are ready to hear my answer?" He speaks slowly, there is a serious tone to his voice. I stare wide eyed at him, of course I want to know the answer. I take a breath and let it out. I just hope I can understand whatever it is he is about to say.

"Yes. I would like to know." Julian nods his head once then runs his hand through his mop of black hair. He switches off the ignition and pulls the key out, holding it in his hand. His body shifts in his seat, so he is facing me. I study him, trying to read his expression, I suddenly feel sick. Julian takes a dramatic breath as I hold mine.

"I come back to Hedge Hill every year to see you and only you.

I come here because you belong to me... I can't fully explain that tonight. I know it sounds narcissistic and possessive. I have thought of a million ways to tell you. I guess being around you and needing you in my life Ellie, is important to me. We have a connection, again I will explain that soon." I stare at him, still not really understanding a word he has just said but I can see the pain he is carrying, can hear his pain when he speaks. Julian reaches over and takes my hand.

"Ellie, I have loved you for as long as I can remember and believe me when I say, it has been a very long time. We know one another Ellie and have done so forever." Julian's green eyes search my face, looking for understanding.

"How long exactly have you loved me?" A churning feeling hits the pit of my stomach, a memory from my childhood flits momentarily though my mind and I shake my head. He can't possibly be from my childhood.

"All of my life." I look away in an attempt at gathering my thoughts.

"Are you aware of how crazy you sound right now. We certainly haven't known each other long." I open the door and climb out of the car, scared by my own thoughts. I don't understand, if he has loved me for so long like he says he has then why has it taken him until now to declare it? I have, after all been here for years.

"I understand how this sounds. We have a shared history you and I; you just don't remember it." Julian closes his car door, the two of us standing face to face over the roof.

"Julian, sharing coffee over a four-week period doesn't count as history and I remember all of your visits." I reply keeping my voice low. The look I receive in return chills me, as does the angry intake of breath.

"That is where you are wrong Ellie, our history is from birth and our story is long and twisted." I stand opened mouthed; he is starting to sound deluded and quite frankly I wish I hadn't asked that stupid question in the first place. But there is a nagging feeling of recognition in my gut. I glance up at the hotel, glad to be home.

"I think I need a little time to process this." The words come out making me sound braver than I feel. Julian nods once.

"Take as much time as you need. I will be waiting for question three." He looks like he wants to say more but he doesn't. We stand looking at each other, I have nothing left to say so without looking back I walk away. I keep my head down as I enter reception, hoping I can just make my way up the stairs to my room without being stopped for a conversation, of course that doesn't happen. Nicky is by my side steering me up the stairs and in the direction of the staff room. We enter and thankfully at this hour the room is empty.

"You look like shit darling, what happened?" Nicky asks wrapping himself around me in his overly protective way, checking me over, his voice is calm and gentle. I can't keep it in any longer, my head hurts and I feel so damn bewildered by tonight's events. Nicky embraces me as I stand silently, bubbling with anger and confusion, not knowing where to start.

"It is so messed up." I finally answer, pushing Nicky away slightly.

"I've got you." Nicky says pulling me back towards him. The door flies open, hitting the wall behind it and Julian strides in finding me in Nicky's arms. Julian's face looks like thunder, he has one hand balled into a fist and his jaw is set tight as he glares at us. Nicky's expression turns into a scowl.

"Haven't you done enough tonight?" Nicky states protectively, holding me closer to him. Julian ignores him and slowly moves towards us.

"This has nothing to do with you." Julian growls, which makes me jump.

"Ellie let me explain?" His voice changes, reduced to a low sorrowful whisper. He sounds lost and his request for me to listen is a plea.

"Julian, I need to think, please give me a little time." I splutter as my eyes fill with confused tears. Truthfully, I don't even know why I am crying. Julian moves closer still, his face awash with hurt and pain.

"Please Ellie, there is so much you need to know, when I explain, it will all make sense." Julian pleads but Nicky steps in, letting go of me to stand face to face with the man I think I am in love with.

"Mr Hunter. I do not know what has happened with you both tonight. What I am aware of, is that you have managed to upset a member of my staff. You are in a private area of the hotel reserved for staff only, so I suggest that you leave, or I will be forced to have you removed from the premises." Julian's pleading eyes flick back to mine and like a coward, I move behind Nicky. Julian gives me one last pleading look and childishly I look away. He stomps out of the room, slamming the door behind him. I cry, feeling a sudden loss that only Julian can fill. Nicky holds me until I finish, handing me a tissue when I am all cried out.

"What did he do to you?" I truly don't know where to begin. How do I explain that I am upset because of Julian's declaration love and need for me in his life?

"I don't know where to start Nicky, I just need to process everything."

"Did he try something on with you?" He asks quietly, his face filled with concern. At his question I can't help but laugh.

"No. God no. He has been very gentlemanly. Julian has been very reserved despite my trying to get into his pants. That man has not laid a single finger on me."

Poor Nicky is worried that Julian has overstepped the mark and just as I am about to double over with the giggles, realisation slaps me around the face. I feel as though I have been hit by lightning. I feel alive, more so than any other time in my life. Julian has helped make this happen, regardless of how odd I find him, I can't but help be drawn to his energy, his body, his mind. I want to get to know him, I want him to know me. Fuck, I want to know myself and that will only happen if I let him into my life.

"I have got to go to bed Nicky, I am so tired." I say through a yawn. I really do need to be alone right now and despite being in the comfort and safety of Nicky's arms. I need to go and see Julian. Nicky nods in agreement.

"I'll walk you up." I thank Nicky and enter my room. I head to the bathroom and splash my face with cold water. I need to speak to Julian, I shouldn't have pushed him away like that, I should have let him explain further. My moment of confusion has been replaced by something I can't quite put my finger on but what I do know is I want to hear whatever it is that he has to say, I need to hear it. I grab my towel and pat my face dry, I need to go to him, apologise and hear him out. That's when I notice a familiar piece of cream paper sitting on the carpet as I exit the bathroom. I unfold it, my stomach in knots as I read Julian's note.

Dearest Ellie,

I am sorry I scared you, that was not my intention.

I am leaving Hedge Hill tonight and won't be back until the tenth of August. I want to give you the space you need to think freely and not be clouded by my proximity to you. I do have one request that I would like you to consider. I would like you to join me for dinner on the night of my return.

You have my number if you wish to contact me before then.

Forever yours

Julian x

I grab my phone from the bed where I left it earlier and scroll through to the main screen, I have had several missed calls from

Julian and one text from Nicky. Shit, shit, shit! Nausea washes over me. I have driven him away. I cup my head in my hands, I have no idea what to do now, my stupidity and fear has forced him to leave. I contemplate phoning him and asking him to come back as I crawl into bed and curl up into a ball. My mind is still racing, going over and over every conversation we have had since his arrival back at Hedge Hill, trying to make sense of my feelings and now I feel lost.

I switch off my lamp and lie in the dark, deciding against phoning him. He was angry when he left the staffroom, understandably so. Memories of Julian last summer force themselves into my mind. The first summer he came to Hedge Hill, he kept to himself, I have fond memories of watching him wander around the hotel grounds, he seemed so shy as he rarely spoke, but I watched him, I couldn't help it. This man comes here to stay, he was cute and there was something about him that intrigued me, so I found myself drawn to him. The second and third summers that he visited, he was polite and friendly, he would greet me if our paths crossed, ask how I was out of politeness.

Those moments made my day, made me feel alive. That was how my crush developed, it was silly, fun, and completely innocent, until Nicky found out about it one night while we were drinking, he tried to convince me to ask Julian out for a drink, of course I didn't have the guts to do something so brazen. But last summer things changed.

I was different, coming out of my period of mourning orphaned and alone. When Julian arrived, he was different too. No longer was he reserved, it was like he knew I was in pain and was silently suffering. He spent time with me, often doing nothing more than sitting on a bench reading a book as I worked outside, I felt comforted by his proximity and quietly supported.

Later we progressed to having lunch or drinks in the bar together. Even then when I think back, he never gave me any indication that he was interested in anything other than friendship, or I just didn't notice. Our relationship, to me was innocent, we got along, and I liked his sense of humour, it was the first time in a long time that someone had made me laugh. The time we spent together was comfortable, there is no point in denying how I thought it odd that, of all the places in the world he chose to spend his annual leave, he picked here.

Now it makes sense why he came. I just don't understand why it has taken him so long to tell me how he felt. It can't have been easy seeing someone but not acting on your feelings. Or was he unable to act on them? Was he in a relationship before? I dread to think. I roll onto my back and stretch out, something in me has changed drastically. I feel a need so deep in my bones that I simple don't understand it, I'm frightened by his admission. Yet on the other hand I have never been drawn to someone so fiercely before. Despite my initial gut instinct, I want to pursue time with Julian. Am I scared of what lies ahead, absolutely! But what I am terrified of the most is the unknown.

I awake to a soft knocking on my door. Instantly I think of Julian but it's Nicky with a breakfast tray.

"Room service." He calls sweetly, whilst unlocking my door and holding a breakfast tray.

"How did you sleep darling?" He asks trying to mask the concern on his face.

"Not great." It took me ages to fall asleep, spending most of the night deep in thought. Nicky places the tray with toast, orange juice and freshly brewed coffee down on the bed beside me. I smile up at him, he really is the best friend a girl could have.

"Just to let you know, Julian has had to leave... business. He came to see me before he left, he apologised for his behaviour, thanked me for looking after you for all these years. He also asked me to ask you to consider his dinner proposal on the tenth." "Thanks." I mumble, shocked that they talked.

"Did he say anything else?" I enquire desperate for information.

"He did. We had a long talk in my office and quite frankly despite my initial judgement, I really like him, Ellie. I think he would be good for you." Nicky stops and flashes me a pearly white smile. Nicky has always been quick to point out the faults in anyone I have ever dated so this is a real turn around. I sit up completely gob smacked. What on earth did Julian say to win Nicky over?

"Eat something darling and have a good day. Don't worry your little head, everything will work out. I really do need to get myself to bed, it's been a busy night with all the drama." Nicky plants a soft kiss on the top of my messy head and leaves. Well, that is a turn up for the books. I wonder what Julian and Nicky spoke about? I would have loved to have been a fly on the wall. I tuck into my breakfast, the toast and jam giving me a much-needed blood sugar boost, but it is most definitely the caffeine that really makes the difference. I sit and daydream while sipping my coffee and slowly I begin to feel human. Once again, I go over everything, driving myself crazy. What exactly did he say to Nicky? I lie back on the bed after breakfast feeling full and satisfied, my main concern now is how am I going to survive without seeing Julian for the next few days.

CHAPTER ELEVEN

Alone And Dancing

"Earth to Ellie. Can I get you a cup of tea or a shot of tequila?" Andy looks down at me with another worried look on his face.

"No thanks." I sigh, following up with a small smile. I shake my head, I didn't even hear him enter, which is strange for me, he is usually so noisy, and I am extra sensitive to his noise. Andy leaves the shed looking worried, I feel awful that he has had to put up with my quieter than usual self.

"Thanks Andy." I shout after him, he is just being kind and I need to remember that. Andy glances over his shoulder and smiles, whistling as he walks away. I busy myself with sweeping the last of the dirt up and disposing of it. With Julian gone, I managed to keep myself busy and had been productive, managing to throw myself fully into work by day and sorting out the mess that is my room by night.

Over the last couple of days, I had done so much thinking about my future and decided that things needed to change. I need to start living, with or without Julian in my life but preferably with and living starts now. I drag the last black bag of rubbish out of the door.

"You have done a really good job out here." I turn to find Nicky walking into the shed. I dump the bag of rubbish with the others, rubbing my dusty hands on my dustier trousers.

"Thank you. The junk Andy and I found was amazing. There is a pile of old rusty tools and I think a couple look like they could be worth some money. Seven mummified mice and two bottles of gardening chemicals that have been banned for quite some time. Andy was disappointed that we didn't find any World War two ammunition."

"I bet he was." Nicky replies running his finger along one of the shelves. I'm not offended by his actions; it is just one of his bad habits, but he is the night manager of a hotel, so I can forgive him for his actions.

"An unexploded bomb stored in the shed would really have made my working week." I sigh, blowing hair out of my face.

"You really have done an amazing job, but I haven't come to talk about work. What are your plans for the weekend?"

"Thanks. I am pretty sure I am going to ache like hell later, so not much planned."

"That is not an answer Ellie or an excuse."

"I hadn't really thought about the weekend to be honest." Nicky raises an eyebrow.

"Not even Sunday, I find that hard to believe"

I poke my tongue out, Nicky knows I have plans for Sunday.

"So, you have definitely decided to meet Julian then?"

"You will be happy to know that I have decided to suck it up and join Julian for dinner. I have thought a lot about the direction my life has been moving in and have decided to stop existing and start living. As for the rest of my weekend, it will involve me in my pyjamas, stuffing my face with Kettle chips and chocolate, why do you ask?" Nicky beams and I know that look. He has a plan brewing.

"That is what I like to hear, obviously not the binge eating part. Now that you have decided to start living, you're coming out to party with us tomorrow night darling. It's all organised, no need to thank me." Nicky smiles sweetly and flutters his long dark eyelashes to seal the deal.

"That's my weekend sorted then." I state dryly, leading Nicky out of the shed and locking the door behind us. We walk back to the hotel together, Nicky telling me very little about this event tomorrow, which worries me.

We say goodbye and I head up to my room to change into something that hasn't been thoroughly covered in dust, cobwebs and dead mice before meeting Nicky and Jamie for our Friday night feast, all the while thinking about what I want to say to Julian when I meet him on Sunday.

Nicky, Jamie, and I sit in the staff room pigging out on fish and chips, lemonade, and chocolate cake, all made fresh by the hotel kitchen. I've had two slices of cake already and am seriously considering a third, I simply live for Fridays.

"Where are you taking us tomorrow?" Jamie asks licking chocolate icing off her finger. I smile at Nicky as I raise an inquiring eyebrow.

"Well, what do you ladies fancy doing?"

"Like we have any choice in the matter, you said you have already made plans, now spill them." Mumbles Jamie with her finger in her mouth. I reach over and help myself to a third slice of cake. Nicky and Jamie stare at me as if I had sprouted a second head.

"What... I have worked hard for this." I take my fork and slowly sink it into the icing, before taking a bite.

"You are going to feel terrible after all that sugar and just think of the bloating." I look at Jamie and open my mouth wide like a child.

"That's disgusting Ellie, you are a pig." I snort into my cake, causing Nicky to laugh. Jamie crosses her arms in protest at my childish behaviour.

"Darlings, I have the perfect way to ward off the bloating. I suggest that tomorrow night we start the evening with a couple of glasses of water, to keep us hydrated. We enjoy a good meal of protein, carbohydrates, and lashings of vegetables right here in the staff room. And then we then go out, dance and get shit faced."

"That does sound marginally better than my Kettle chip and chocolate plan. But please Nicky can we not go to a gay club, Jamie wants to pull a straight male. Nicky reaches over and takes a second slice of chocolate cake.

"I took the liberty of getting us some tickets for an exclusive club night. The kind of place where anything goes darling. This event was advertised as dark with a distinctive fetish quality and pumping loud alternative music. I am positive there will be plenty of men to go around." Jamie shrieks with glee and claps her hands.

"What time do we need to leave?" Nicky considers the question for a moment between forkfuls of sponge.

"Is ten okay for you both? Does that give you enough time to get yourselves ready?" Nicky winks at me. Jamie nods with a smile and dumps her plate dreamily in the sink, completely missing that Nicky is taking the piss.

"I've got to get to work, or the boss will shout at me. I'll meet you guys in reception tomorrow night at ten on the dot, dressed and ready to party."

"I never shout at the staff for being late." States Nicky laughing as Jamie leaves the room, the door slamming behind her.

"Right, I'm off for an early night." Nicky looks at me in horror.

"It's only seven. The night is young."

"Hey, I have been busy all day in those sheds. If you want me to dance tomorrow, then I need to rest tonight." I rub my stomach lovingly, which is making horrid gurgling sounds, Nicky raises an eyebrow.

"I over did it with that third slice of cake."

"I hope you don't have stomach-ache all night. I better go and make sure Jamie is behind that desk. Sleep tight darling." Nicky kisses the top of my head before leaving me alone. I am ready to sleep, I tidy up the mess we have left after dinner and head up to my room for that early night.

* * *

I wake early, feeling refreshed although the guilt from last night's gluttony hits me. I decide to head out for a run. I dress quickly and brush my teeth, strap my small rucksack to my back with the intention of running into town to grab a few supplies and a decent coffee, then I'll walk back. I descend the stairs of the hotel two at a time and out into the open air, walking briskly to warm up my aching muscles before moving into a slow jog.

I take in the sights and sounds of the countryside, running alongside the road on the grassy verge, spotting a skylark soaring above me. I keep focused, taking the long route into town whilst, trying to keep my breathing even as I run past green and yellow fields growing rapeseed and maize. A little extra exercise and lots of fresh air will do me the world of good.

Once in town, I walk to the small supermarket hot, sweaty, and bright pink, grabbing myself a carton of juice and a large bottle of water. I peruse the shelves and fridges picking up an edamame salad for lunch and today's newspaper, a couple of rosy apples and a large punnet of mixed berries and a salted pretzel. Finally, I make a beeline for a well-earned coffee. This town has the quaintest little tea shop, small tables, cream teas and good homemade cake but goodness their little-known secret is their amazing coffee, to which I am addicted.

"Morning Ellie, latte?" I smile at the owner; the lovely Kate knows me too well.

"Yes please." Kate tells me about her busy week whilst making my latte in a cup and saucer and not the usual latte glass. I grab a table and sip my coffee whilst nibbling on a breakfast granola bar, reading the newspaper, and enjoying the morning. My mind wanders and I suddenly panic, I forgot to reply to Julian.

Dear Julian,
I graciously accept your offer of dinner tomorrow evening.
I look forward to it.

Ellie x

My afternoon was filled with crazy old ladies arranging flowers, checking my phone for text messages a million times and a leisurely nap. At ten I head down to reception, annoyed that I haven't heard from Julian at all but ready for my night out. I have gone for a sophisticated look tonight. My hair is brushed back and tied up in a bun and I am wearing a black, tight-fitting low-cut shirt that I borrowed from Jamie, which I have teamed with a black pencil skirt, black stockings, and black heels. I resemble a dominatrix or a funeral director, I can't decide which.

Nicky, Jamie, and I head into Hove in a cab. The club isn't what I was expecting, for one it is in a warehouse on an industrial estate and Nicky never purchased the tickets, this is an invitation only event and the drinks are free. The décor inside is dark and dangerous. Large sheets of black and burgundy velvet hang from the ceiling and cover the walls, giving the large space an intimate, womb like feel. Red candles in ornate black metal holders light the walls, black leather chesterfield sofas with matching armchairs around the bar. The dance floor is huge, with a massive DJ booth, which is already blaring loud heavy music. On entering the club, our phones were removed and stored for security reasons, each of us was handed a card with an individual number on it that gets us free drinks all night, it also has a map of the warehouse on the reverse. Jamie and I study our cards, on closer inspection we see there are areas of this place that cater for all manners of sexual tastes and appetites. That is when it dawns on me that Nicky has taken us to a kinky sex club.

"Drinks! What do you girls fancy?" Nicky asks as he looks around. I feel uncomfortable, I'm out of my depth here and feel self-conscious in my outfit. I shrug my shoulders.

"Girls, go grab a seat and leave the drinks to me." Jamie and I grab a sofa, Nicky arrives carrying a bottle of wine, two glasses and a coke for me.

"I've slipped in a single Tia Maria, I thought it might help relax you."

"You always do, and it always does." I smile, taking the glass and having a grateful sip. Nicky knows I don't like getting drunk, apparently it is because I am a control freak and he is right to a degree, I am not a fan of feeling out of control. We laugh, drink, and take in our surroundings. Jamie and Nicky are both on the prowl, hoping to catch the eye of the gorgeous. There is a real possibility I will be getting a cab home alone, in the early hours of tomorrow morning. I on the other hand am slightly shocked by the outfits on some of the guests, or lack thereof. There is a handful of people who are wearing nothing but nipple tassels and G-strings. I manage to get over the shock as one drink leads to another and soon the three of us find ourselves on the dance floor moving to the loud hypnotic music. By one in the morning, I realise I am having way too much fun and require a little more alcohol. Jamie has given up trying to pull the pretty boy barman she has had her eye on, and we resign ourselves to just dancing the night away.

Nicky goes in search of the toilets, and I am quite sure he really is scoping out what some of the other areas have to offer here to-night. Jamie and I continue to dance and move to all manners of heavy music until Jamie stops mid dance and points, she needs the bathroom and I need to go with her. We tipsily make our way through the moving mass of sweaty bodies, take the nearest staircase down to the lower floor which opens into a large seating area. Music is pumping and people are milling about with cups and saucers of tea and biscuits. Jamie and I glance at each other and laugh at just how surreal this area is, looking around the tea drinkers, we notice that there are at least 5 different doorways leading into other rooms and my curiosity gets the better of me.

The first room we enter is full of people watching a drag act on a small stage, I grab Jamie's hand and drag her back out. That looked cool but I want to explore further. We weave through the crowds of people and a door opens to my left, a familiar beat hits me and I turn as the door begins to close.

"Over there." I mouth and Jamie nods, following me. The hypnotic music gets louder as we approach, I hold onto Jamie's hand and together we enter the room. Recognising the music, I feel flushed as I remember hearing that song in Julian's car but what I don't expect as we make our way through a second doorway made of fabric is all the semi naked bodies. There are people everywhere, on sofas, armchairs and even a couple making use of the full-sized medieval stock in the middle of the room. Everyone here is engaged in sexual activity, and all seem to be moving to the beat of that damn song. Jamie stops in her tracks, mouth opened wide in surprise, I am stunned at seeing so many bodies having sex in public. I get Jamie's attention by clicking my fingers in front of her face, who for the first time looks as shocked as I am. Slowly we back out of the room and literally fall out of the door laughing.

"Shit, did you see that?" Jamie shouts over the music as I pull her in the direction of the stairs. I am still a little amazed by what we have just witnessed and in my head, I can still hear the words of that song being sung.

"Who sings that song?" Jamie gives me a funny look as we make our way through the crowd.

"We saw a room full of people fucking and all you can think about is the track that was playing. Seriously that was so hot, can we go back in?" I agree with Jamie, it was hot, but I feel a little weird witnessing it and there is no way on earth I am venturing back into that room tonight. After our bathroom visit, we finally make it to the stairs and as we walk up, we approach two people kissing. I instantly recognise Nicky and I rub his back gently as we pass by, Jamie just flicks him on the ear. It looks like we will be leaving without Nicky tonight.

"I need another drink." Jamie shouts and I know from her expression that she isn't happy that Nicky has pulled before her. So, we grab more drinks at the bar, Jamie has been spurred on by Nicky's good luck and tries to get the attention of a young man in a suit who clearly isn't interested. We stand and chat instead, I can feel myself getting steadily more drunk and I don't care. I down a glass of water before ordering shots of something I can no longer pronounce.

Jamie and I spend the next half hour laughing and giggling like naughty children. A couple of guys dressed head to toe in latex gimp suits come over and attempt to get our attention, but we are way past the chatting up stage now. They get the hint and don't waste their time on us for too long, which only makes us laugh harder and drink more.

I have no idea what time it is when Nicky finds us. He has ordered a cab which will be outside in ten minutes. Jamie and I are joined at the hip, partly because we are so very drunk and partly because we cannot trust ourselves not to get lost if we separate. We find the toilet, then grab our phones from the reception area before meeting Nicky and to our surprise his mystery partner outside. We travel back to Hedge Hill in relative silence, Jamie has fallen asleep in her corset and matching tutu outfit, her eyeliner all smudged, giving her panda eyes. Nicky's lips are locked with his guest who he is clearly taking home with him, and in my drunk and fuzzy state I can't figure out if it is a man or woman.

I elbow Jamie in the ribs when we arrive back at Hedge Hill, she wakes with a jolt, dribble running down her chin. I shout goodnight to the others as we enter the hotel via the fire exit around the back.

I feel dizzy and I'm not entirely sure I can make it to my room without being sick, so I walk carefully up the stairs. On entering my room, I strip off my clothes, pop two paracetamol into my mouth, gulping them down with a glass of water and climb into bed in my underwear, stockings, and a sweaty face of smeared make up. I grab my handbag and check my phone hoping to have heard from Julian by now, I glance at the withered daisy chains that are still sitting on my table, disappointed that I haven't. The room spins as I lie down and in seconds I am in a dreamless sleep.

CHAPTER TWELVE

Hunts And Meetings

The drive back to London was agonising, I barely managed to keep my focus on the road as I manoeuvred my way through the heavy traffic. So much going through my mind and having no idea how to handle it all. I was almost grateful for the annoying beep of my phone indicating that Seb required my services, or should I say, a rich landowner did. I pull my car over and sit in a lay by, phoning Seb back, traffic hurtling past. After a brief and curt conversation, I agree to take the next hunt and await the familiar text message of address details. I'm still annoyed, how can I turn what seems easy for others into a monumental task for myself, I wouldn't blame Ellie if she never wanted to see me again. My phone pings to life with a text message and I have an address.

I pull up to the gate of the manor just as the sun begins to rise, and am greeted by an elderly, flustered gentleman, a member of the security team who lets me in. I follow the driveway, slowly following the winding path and seeing the manor in all its glory in the distance. The sun rising behind the building casts an eerie glow around it. A man descends the staircase, frantically waving his arms and indicting for me to pull over, which I do.

"Mr Hunter, I'm Gerald. The butler for Manor Oak. Thank you for coming at short notice. We have an issue that requires immediate action and well there is another issue that has just occurred." I curtly nod at Gerald. It is common for me to deal with the staff until the job is done and I am thanked by the people who pay me.

"Please follow me." Gerald walks ahead, leading me along the front of the building and around towards the back. I notice movement, it is easy to see the new issue that has arisen.

"I'm so sorry, Bernard was looking after Master James, he was bitten you see. I managed to get him into the bathroom, so that I could look at the wound. I left him for a moment, to get help and the first aid kit. When I came back, he had jumped from the window." I look up and see a window on the fourth floor wide open. And look down at the squirming mess that this monster has become having been impaled on the small fence.

"The fence is there to keep the Pomeranians out of the flower beds." Says Gerald as he rubs the palm of his hand across the stubble on his chin. He looks exhausted and worried; I'm not surprised why, seeing a DROM up close is never easy. The flailing DROM on the ground is very much stuck to the foot and a half tall white fence. It is comical to see it thrash around, guttural, and gurgling sounds coming from its throat.

"Could you please, make it look like he died from the fall?" I watch the body, moving in its unnatural way.

"Yes of course." Although, it is not as easy as it sounds for this specimen. I only brought one death kit with me. I will have to re-use it. I pull out my open mouth gag, a black mask that covers the lower half of the face and nose, with an open gap that can be used to puncture the soft palate. I strap it to the DROMs face, it struggles and attempts to bite my fingers, thankfully it is not quick enough. I pull out my customised titanium guard father spike and push it through the gag hole, aiming the spike up at the soft palate of the mouth, at the right angle the brain is punctured quickly, death is imminent. One press of the release button and this poor soul ceases all movement. One down.

Removing the father spike, I drop that onto the grass below, undo the buckle on the gag and check it for gunk. I'm impressed with how clean this kill has been. Grabbing my equipment, I ask

Gerald to lead me to the next DROM. Gerald is a talker, on the way to the summer house, I have heard everything about the family and their little problem.

The family had locked their loved one away in a room for two days, hoping they would recover when he arrived home, violent and confused. It was how they had dealt with his heroin addiction some years earlier. In this instance, there was no recovery. Of course not, he had a bite on his wrist that the family hadn't noticed at first. The behaviour of their son became more violent and more animalistic, resulting in the butler having half of his arm chewed off when he attempted to feed it a bowl of soup, or so I was informed. That was when they decided to seek professional help, realising that there was nothing they could do to save their ex-addict of a son. Their only requirement was that they needed its death to look natural so they could have an open casket. This is what I specialise in; quiet, quick, and peaceful.

I am finally outside the summer house; it is a beautiful little building and under other circumstances, it would be a great place to socialise with friends. Gerald is still talking but I have him drowned out, needing to concentrate on this. I peer into one of the lower glass panels, I see bare feet, bare legs, and the back of two very naked knees. I tap on the glass to get its attention; I need to know how quick this beast is. It turns out this DROM is damn fast. The DROM is pounding on the glass in an attempt at getting to me. I laugh, I am going to enjoy this.

I instruct Gerald to swap places with me and stay there until I call his name. He is profusely sweating, and it is the first time since meeting him that he is quiet. I creep around the summerhouse and find the door, silently opening it and sliding in, closing the door behind me. The smell is putrid, there is dried blood on the floor, vomit too and mixed with the unmistakeable odour of human shit. The DROM is still pounding on the glass, trying to get to Gerald who is still standing outside. One thing I have learnt about DROMs is they have weak spots, the neck, the head, the soft palate, and the knees. DROMS run fast but they do not have the greatest balance. One knock to the knees has them down on the ground, giving the hunter a second to overcome the DROM and kill it.

I slowly walk behind the naked beast. Faeces, urine and intestinal fluids have been expelled. Faecal matter dried on the thighs and backs of the knees. I drop a couple of cable ties on to the ground, as I give one swift kick, hitting the DROM behind its right knee. Instantly it drops to the ground. Right knee, hip then shoulder hitting the floor. I hold this beast down by its head with my left hand and swipe a cable tie from the floor with my right. Pulling its blood-stained hands behind it's thrashing back; I tie its wrists together. Now that it is secure, I pull the face gag from my forearm and secure it around this monster's face. Happy that it is secure, I roll it over onto its back and it pains me to see that it has no penis. It is not unheard of for DROMS to pull off appendages; this one removed its own family jewels. I pull the father spike out of my pocket, insert it into the gap, the DROMs grey and cloudy eyes watching me as it thrashes its head. At the press of a button this beast is dead. I pull my spike out of its mouth and wipe it clean on the curtains. I head outside and call to Gerald who is still rooted to the spot.

"Completed." Gerald stands there, mouth open and silent.

"I'll be by my car." I turn and walk back around the manor and to my car. After wiping down my hands and adding hand sanitiser, I text Seb that the job is complete and make the call to the clean-up team who will stage the body in a manner the family feel acceptable. The father, walks down the grand steps of the manner and towards me, dressed in Harrods pyjamas. His face grey and gaunt.

"Thank you for dealing with our son." He is a peer; recognising him from the drug and orgy scandal his son was involved in years before. He extends his hand, and we shake.

"I have completed the bank transfer." I nod.

"In 15 minutes, the clean-up team will arrive, they will be happy to stage your son's body in a manner you see fit. I'm sorry for your loss." Without looking back, I climb into my car and head back to London.

I finally arrive home and Stanley, my assistant is nowhere to be seen. Everything is in place for the emergency meeting later. I run up the spiral staircase and rip my clothes off, leaving them on the floor in a heap. Glancing at the clock, my father will be arriving promptly in an hour, he is never late, so I jump in the shower. I'm not sure how much longer all of this can be contained and hidden from the public. DROM cases are increasing.

Questions have been asked, people are taking notice and it is only a matter of time before someone is forced or paid to speak out. The cover ups for the rich are increasingly becoming ridiculous while the missing posters for the lower classes line notice boards up and down the country. This is the worst I have seen it; we are on the edge of an epidemic of death, built on lies and cover ups. Life as we know it has changed, children no longer allowed to play outside, parks are void of early morning dog walkers and the streets are eerily quiet after dark.

The public know something is very wrong, life never fully returned to normal after the Covid pandemic back in early twenties. The public have had the wool pulled over their eyes for so long, that they no longer know what to believe and have just followed the ever-changing guidelines. There have been signs of an underground uprising. I shower and dress quickly in navy linen trousers and a white linen shirt. It is not exactly formal wear but smart enough to keep my father off my back. Hearing the front door slam, I head downstairs to the lounge where I find Stanley unpacking bags in the kitchen.

"Alright Lion." He shouts in his cockney accent.

"Hey Stan, how is it going?" I ask as I watch him pull open cupboards and fill serving dishes with small pastries.

"I'm good thanks mate. Seb gave me the heads up, I got here early to get everything ready." I raise my eyebrow and let out a frustrated sigh, bloody typical. I receive a message stating my father is coming for a chat, Stan is told it's a meeting, which means my father will not be alone.

"I'll be in my office, let me know when they arrive, please." Stan nods as he arranges fresh pastries on one platter and fruit on another.

"Will do. Can I bring you up anything? Tea? Coffee?" I shake my head no.

"No, I'm fine thanks." I leave Stan to it. Up in the safety of my office I open the draw of my desk and glance at the envelope. The white paper has yellowed slightly but it is safe. One day soon I hope to pass this onto its rightful owner, if she ever speaks to me again. I check my phone; another two messages have been left by Roth wanting to set up a meeting. The message rambles on, Roth has yet another tempting proposition for me that would be of interest financially apparently.

"Sorry not interested." I say aloud as I press delete. Why would I quit working with my family, to go work with him? He is a vulture determined to make money off the back of my reputation. I hear the arrival of the others downstairs and grimace, this should be fun. I leave Stan to it for a few minutes, letting him deal with my elders before I come down and face them all. I really am not sure what they are expecting from me. I am as much in the dark about all of this as they are. A second later my door bursts open, Seb bounces into my office, all suited and booted, with his long hair tied back.

"Seb, have I not told you before about knocking, do you need another reminder?" I say without looking up. Only my stupid cousin, who has no idea regarding the rules about privacy and personal space would enter my office without knocking first.

"I like to surprise, you know that. One day I'm going to barge in and catch you watching porn with your tiny dick in your hand." I shake my head in mock annoyance.

"That will never happen Seb, it will never happen." Seb walks across the room and sits on the edge of my antique mahogany desk. The dirty look I give him only makes him smile and briefly I contemplate pushing him off the desk and onto his arse.

"You look like shit. What happened?" I turn my chair around to face him, rubbing at my temples, I'm starting to feel the exhaustion and really, I could do without this meeting and head straight to bed.

"I told her Seb. Ellie completely freaked out and wouldn't speak to me, wouldn't let me explain." Seb claps me on the back, a rare look of sympathy graces his face.

"Well, no wonder. Telling her about us is bound to have freaked the poor girl out." I sigh in frustration.

"No, I didn't tell her about this." I gesture to all the books and paperwork on my desk.

"Just how I feel about her." Seb snorts loudly, any sympathy he had seconds early have vanished and have now been replaced by ridicule.

"Oh gotcha. Yes, I can see how that would freak her out too. Bring her over to the pub, I'll do the talking, she'll listen to me." Seb winks.

"About that, I didn't appreciate your comments the other night. Ellie now thinks there might be something going on between us." Seb laughs heartily, clapping me on the shoulder this time.

"Sorry Lion you are not my type." He continues laughing, standing up and moving away from the desk towards the door, he is right to do so, I feel like taking a punch at that smug face of his.

"Let us go and get this meeting over with. I have made plans for this afternoon."

"You always have plans Seb." I stay seated, I'm not quite ready to face my father and my uncles.

"Before you head down. Whose name do I need to use to address my thank you note?" Seb raises an eyebrow at me.

"Sorry you've lost me completely." He replies, confusion etched on his face. I can't help but smirk, knowing that he had to have something to do with it.

"The DROM I dealt with at the airport. Who came up with the cover story?" Seb smiles, finally catching on.

"Ah yes, well you know it wouldn't have looked good if the story reported had been about another religious fundamentalist loose at an airport, we can't keep using that excuse. The bottled water shortage idea was mine." I nod my head in approval and Seb takes a bow.

"That truly was a just a shit cover story, one of the worst you have come up with."

"My bank of press releases is running low, I'm happy it did the job." Seb sniggers, picking a paperweight up from my desk, throwing it into the air and catching it again.

"And the family of the deceased?" I enquire. As usual with these unusual stand-alone cases, the family debts were paid in full, with a little left over for the family, to help ease the financial burden of losing the main breadwinner. I nod again.

"And before you ask, the young chap you mentioned who dealt with the DROM. He was taking a year out to go backpacking with his sister. He miraculously won a competition that he didn't know he had entered; they are seeing the world via first class with spending money." He winks and I can't help but laugh.

"We better head down, father doesn't like to be kept waiting." Seb gives me a sad look. I know he despises my father almost as much as I do. I take a breath as I grab the handle and enter the room, Seb walking along behind me.

"Lion, I trust this morning's hunt went well?" I walk towards my father and shake his hand, followed by my uncle's Booth and Benjamin. It is typical that he greets me with talk of work.

"Hey uncle Brin." Seb shouts as he shakes my father's hand which somehow turns into a very awkward hug between the two men. I see Booth and Benjamin smile at each other. My father is a very serious and stuffy man and from a young age Seb has made it his mission to be the thorn in my father's, his uncles' side.

"Please take a seat." I wave my hand in the general direction of the twenty-seater oak table that separates my lounge from the kitchen. Stanley has done a stellar job in the short time I have been upstairs. The table is decorated with fresh fruit, cheese, an assortment of cold meats and pastries. We all sit, Stanley appears and begins offering coffee, pouring the steaming liquid into our cups.

"The hunt this morning?" My father prompts.

"It went well, quick and clean as requested. The family should have no problems with it looking like he died from natural causes, should anyone enquire." I reply.

"Uncle Brin, you know we were paid a hundred and fifty grand for that hunt." Seb states, sitting back with a satisfied smile on his face and folding his arms over his chest. My father looks less than pleased. He doesn't like to discuss money so openly, even in the company of family. My uncles on the other hand look over the moon at the amount paid for one hunt. Seb and I do all the work and they get to feather their nests from the safety of their armchairs.

"So why are we all here today?" I ask, stirring a brown sugar cube into my coffee.

"I thought you would like to know what your uncles and I have found out." My father stops to scratch his nose briefly, Seb looks over to me before adding sugar to his coffee.

"As you are aware our usual contact Muhammed has been ill for quite some time. Sadly, he has decided to retire from the police force which means he will be retiring from our duties too." Seb looks at me raising an eyebrow. Clearly, he wasn't aware of this.

"This means the force have kept on the chap who was covering Muhammad's position and he just so happens to be one of Roth's men. We all know it isn't working out very well, he is proving less than reliable when calling in a hunt and I expect it will only get worse, putting you both in danger."

"Fuck! I knew Roth was up to no good!" Shouts Seb, thumping his fist down on the table. Booth gives his son a stern look, Seb chooses to ignore his father's pleading eyes.

"Roth keeps contacting me, wanting me to come and work for him. I have now just stopped answering his calls altogether. He is the type of guy who doesn't understand the word no." We all look at Seb, I can see my uncles growing pale as they work out how much they would lose financially if Seb went to work for another team.

"Roth has been contacting me for exactly the same reason." I chip in. I can see my father is not happy hearing about this for the first time either. His face is stern, he is concerned that someone is trying to poach his son and nephew.

"Father, I have no intention of leaving." I state.

"Me either, not that I could possible fit in another job into my busy schedule." Shouts Seb finishing his coffee. My father rather audibly clears his throat.

"Are we under the impression that he and his men on the force are purposefully giving us wrong information regarding hunts?" Asks my father. Everyone nods in agreement, so much is going wrong, Roth being the root cause it would appear.

"Roth is our competitor. My fear is that he wants to be the one running the hunts down here. His main goal is profit. Whereas ours is..." My father doesn't get to finish his sentence.

"Profit!" Shouts Seb.

"Sebastian, control yourself." Chastises his father Booth. My father shakes his head at his nephew's outburst.

"It is the truth, as much as you three like to brush over what we do. We do it for profit, yes, we help in stopping mass panic. Yes, we hunt DROMs before they become public knowledge or do public damage but we do it for money." Seb stops when his father stands.

"A word outside please." He states. Seb rises and the two men leave the room.

"What I was saying is Roth is purely money oriented, always has been. He wants to play king here and I think it would be a big mistake to let him. Lion, if he contacts you again, would you feel comfortable arranging a meeting with him? Find out what exactly it is he wants or is offering?" I consider my father's idea for a moment.

"That would not be a problem." I too would like to know what he wants. Seb and Booth return and sit back down in silence.

"This meeting is over." My father states standing. Booth and Benjamin follow as my father makes his way through the room.

"Seb, Lion will fill you in." My father says flippantly as my uncles follow him out of the front door and into the small courtyard without a second glance or a goodbye.

"Did I ever tell you that your father is a monumental arsehole." States Seb, pulling out a chair, turning it around and sitting astride it, resting his arms on the back.

"You know he has threatened to sack me if I continue doing what I'm doing, dad just told me." He sits down and pulls his hair out of his ponytail. He doesn't like to conform.

"Really." I laugh, knowing full well my father could never sack him because he and I own the business. A family clause written many years ago. When the eldest son reaches the age of twenty five, the business is handed over to them. My brother wasn't interested, so signed the empire over to me. When Seb came of age, he joined me in the family business. What that means for our families is that ten percent of all profit each year go to each elder living male member. Stanley comes around the table and pours two more cups of coffee and places them in front of us. I watch him as he begins to tidy up the remnants of the untouched brunch, I stir my coffee.

"What do you think Stan, should Lion tell his father to back off?"

"He has a point; your father does have a tendency to treat you two like you are still boys." I glance from Stan to Seb, they are right. We need to distance ourselves from my father and uncles. Family politics never runs smoothly.

"What are you doing tonight?" Seb's eyes light up at my question.

"I'm off to a warehouse party as a plus one in Hove. I'm just going to check out the suitability of this warehouse for Club Flesh. But it should be fun. What about you?" I hear Stanley laugh to himself from the kitchen and I glare at him.

"What is so funny Stan?" Stanley laughs louder.

"Seb is going with Minnie as her plus one. Good luck mate." He walks over and claps Seb on the back who starts laughing, along with Stanley.

"One of Minnie's wild parties is it, why are you not going Stanley?

"Chicken pox." They both say together laughing.

"Huh?" My confusion is evident.

"The twins have chicken pox. I am on chicken pox duty while super mum takes Seb for a night on the town.

"I don't have the energy to figure out what is going on, I need to go to bed and sleep for a week."

"Yes, you need to sleep so you are bright eyed, and bushy tailed for tomorrow's date." Shouts Stanley. Seb raises an eyebrow.

"What are you up to Lion?"

"Absolutely bloody nothing, today I am just going to crash here and sleep the day away, tomorrow hopefully I will be taking Ellie to dinner." My phone beeps as if on cue and I thrust my hand in my pocket fishing it out. Seb glances at his watch then back to me.

"I am definitely taking Ellie to dinner tomorrow." I can't help but smile, even if the text message I have received from Ellie is brief.

"That's great mate. I will get that organised for you."

"Thanks Stan, that would be great." Seb grabs a pastry from the table and stands.

"Good luck with your date tomorrow. I better get going, got to get ready for my hot date with Minnie." Stan laughs again.

"Keep your hands off my wife's goods." He says swatting Seb with a tea towel.

"Will do, I only have eyes for you Stan." He replies, clapping Stan on the back as he passes.

"You know where I am if you need help with anything." I nod as my wayward cousin leaves.

"He is right you know." I look up, Stan is by my side, coffee pot in hand.

"I know but it's hard. I know I need to consider breaking away from my father and uncles but at least I have a date."

"More coffee?" I stand up and run my hand through my hair, exhaustion hitting me like a truck.

"No thanks. I have a couple of phone calls to make and then I really do need to go and get some sleep."

CHAPTER THIRTEEN

New Friends

I wake at ten on Sunday morning feeling sweaty and hot. I throw my duvet off and instantly have goose bumps as the sweat on my body begins to evaporate. My mouth is like sandpaper, my tongue dry and rough but it is only when I sit up and attempt to get out of bed, am I fully aware of the pounding in my head. I stand and carefully walk to the bathroom to fill my glass with cool water. I take small sips, expecting the nausea to kick in. With my glass of water in hand, I walk over to the window and open it, I need to take something that will alleviate this throbbing head of mine and the fuzziness that I feel this morning. I decide that I am not quite ready to stand on two feet and clumsily climb back into bed to recover, sloshing water all over my duvet as I move. I gulp down a couple of paracetamols before laying back down, trying to recollect the night before. I smile as memories pop into my head like bubbles, the two men in gimp suits made me laugh and our dancing towards the end of the night was seriously messy. Then I remember that room, the music and all the bodies. I rub my eyes suddenly remembering every sordid detail. I jump when my phones springs to life, alerting me to the incoming text message. Nicky is up and about; he thinks he has found the love of his life, and do I want to meet him for a post hangover lunch? I text back, yes. As sick as I feel now, lunch at the pub would be great and I am intrigued by Nicky's new love. I am assuming it is the person who came back with us last night.

I lounge in bed for another half an hour while the paracetamol does its magic, then finally find the strength to make myself a coffee, feeling much better now there is caffeine running through my veins. By eleven thirty I am showered and dressed in a denim skirt and a light blue and white gingham shirt and am looking forward to some proper food. As I apply a little mascara to my eyelashes, I notice a small sheet of cream coloured paper by my door. I know who this is from, my heart skips a beat.

Dearest Ellie,

I am looking forward to dinner tonight.

I shall be waiting in Reception at seven.

Forever yours

Julian x

I clutch the note to my breast and run to the door throwing it open, looking up and down the hallway for him. Julian has gone and I am very much alone. I close my door and stand with my back to it. I expected him to be standing there and can't help feeling disappointed that he was not. I receive two text messages simultaneously, one from Nicky who is already at the pub a mile and a half up the main road, he has got us a table and I am to meet him there. The other is from Jamie who is extremely hung-over, she sadly won't be joining us for lunch. I place Julian's note on my table before replying to my friends. Butterflies attack my stomach as I contemplate dinner with Julian tonight.

* * *

I arrive at the pub to find Nicky perusing the menu. I still feel peaky and could do with another nap. Food I am hoping will make me feel human again. That, and lots of water because I feel as dry as a bone. Last night was fun, but the dehydration alone will prematurely age me.

"Howdy cowgirl." He stands and meets me with a kiss on my cheek. He is smiling like the Cheshire cat as he sits back down.

I take the seat opposite him and only then do I notice the two empty glasses on the table.

"You had a good night?" I ask, knowing full well that Nicky wouldn't be smiling like this if he hadn't. He nods.

"It is probably up there as one of the best."

"Wow." I mouth, genuinely happy for him. He could really benefit from a stable love life. Nicky and I talk animatedly about the great night we had, when a tall and muscular man with long black hair, tied back in a ponytail approaches us. He's dressed in tight black jeans and a faded cut off t-shirt with the word Tool printed on the front. I'm hoping it is a band name unless Nicky has pulled a guy who works for Homebase. Either way that t-shirt looks like it has seen better days. I notice the muscles of this man's arms stretching the material of the t-shirt in a way that you just can't help but stare at in admiration. He smiles down at me, and I smile back politely, he seems vaguely familiar, but I can't figure out where I know him from. Nicky follows my gaze and looks up before breaking into an even bigger grin than I thought possible. Then it dawns on me, Nicky pulled this guy last night.

I study him as he pulls out a chair next to Nicky. I catch myself staring and not at his chest, yes, I know this guy from some-where. I watch as Nicky reaches out and gently brushes his arm. I have just witnessed a tender moment between Nicky and this un-named man, yet all I can think about is where do I know him from. A look of recognition flits across his handsome face as he cocks his head to one side making his neck click. I shudder slightly at the sound. Nicky is talking but for the life of me I haven't heard a single word he has said.

"Ellie, I'd like you to meet Sebastian. Sebastian this is my Ellie." At hearing his name, I snap out of my thoughts just as Sebastian extends his hand over the table.

"It is lovely to meet you again Elspeth." His face lights up and a grin spreads from ear to ear. I flush and pull my hand away. It clicks, I know exactly where I have seen this man before and I am a little taken aback. Sebastian was the barman from the pub Julian took me to the other night. The barman who was a little cheeky and led me to believe that he had something going on with Julian. Nicky smiles at me, clearly happy and lost in the moment, he hasn't even noticed that Sebastian called me by my full name, something I am grateful for.

"I'm starving." Nicky finally breaks the awkward silence. I glance towards the menus on the table, I don't feel quite so hungry now.

"Ellie, are you having your usual?" I nod. We always come to this pub for our post hangover lunch after a big night out which have been few and far between recently. Being a creature of habit, I always order the nut roast and a lemonade. I'm not sure I can eat at all now. My mind is running wild, and my stomach is churning. Exactly how well does this guy know Julian. I am guessing damn well; I think I have also been thoroughly researched and spoken about because it is too close a coincidence that they both called me by my full name. Nicky leaves the table to order at the bar.

"Please call me Ellie." I tell Sebastian, perhaps a little too sternly. Only my mother called me by my full name.

"Of course. Please call me Seb." He replies flashing me a perfect white toothed smile. I don't know what else to say. I sit quietly, mulling over how strange it is for Nicky to have hooked up with this guy of all people. I want to ask him how he knows Julian, but I just can't seem to get the words out of my mouth. The dull ache in my head has developed into a full-on throb and I really could do with some more pain relief and a very large coffee right about now. Nicky comes back to the table with our drinks, a lemonade with ice for me, a coke for Seb and a sparkling water, with a slice of lime for himself.

"Are you all ready for your date tonight, Ellie?" Nicky asks. I squirm in my seat. I really don't want to talk about this now, especially not in front of this guy. I nod my head as I swallow my sip of lemonade, trying to contain my smile.

"What are you two doing after lunch?" I ask in a vague attempt at changing the subject. Surprisingly it is Seb who answers.

"Actually, I thought we could go back to this Hotel of yours. Nicky can show me around the gardens that I've heard so much about." Nicky looks absolutely over the moon and completely smitten.

"Ellie plans the ground designs and works on the gardens. She does a fabulous job, one of these days she will be whisked away from us because of her talent."

"That might happen sooner than you think." Nicky and I both look at Seb who looks back at me.

"I saw the gardens from Nicky's window." He continues, Nicky smiles over at me warmly, but I can't help but think there is a double meaning to his words. Thankfully our food arrives, ending the conversation. We sit quietly the three of us as we eat. My meal is as tasty as ever, but I have lost my appetite. Nicky and Sebastian are tucking into the roast beef with all the trimmings. While we eat, my need for information begins to overwhelm me. Having someone close by who knows Julian in some capacity is just too tempting. Finally, I give in and decide to do a little harmless prodding.

"What do you do Seb?" I finally ask. He pops a greasy looking slab of beef covered in thick brown gravy into his mouth and chews it slowly before answering.

"Funny story that. I dabble in this and that but essentially I help run a couple of businesses and I own a pub." I look at him and then to Nicky who just raises an eyebrow but continues eating.

"That sounds interesting and hectic. Tell me about these businesses." The words simply fall out of my mouth. Sebastian looks thoughtful for a moment then a small smile creeps over his face, his dark brown eyes twinkle as they meet mine.

"One is really my baby and side project. A hobby so to speak and that is I organise club nights, like the one last night. My main headache is my family's, how shall I call it? Our hunting business. My role there is to check the finer details of information we receive about hunts. I make sure they are financially viable in the first instance and that they are as safe as they can be before I give the go ahead for a hunt to be completed." I'm taken aback, that was all as clear as mud. I look over at Nicky who is oblivious to what Sebastian is talking about. I nod my head not really understanding. I just don't like the idea of hunting!

"I'm essentially working with my cousin, we are a two-man unit, until he gets someone to replace me."

"What will you do when you are replaced and how does running a pub fit in?" Nicky asks, attempting to pile his fork with peas. Sebastian grins.

"I am going on a very long holiday when I am replaced. I will be so glad to get away from my cousin and his constant moaning about his love life. The pub, well that mainly runs itself thankfully, I just like hanging out there, which was why I bought it." Seb cuts a roast potato in half and pops it into his mouth. My stomach plummets, I have the distinct feeling that he is talking about Julian. Nicky seems impressed. I glance down at my plate of practically untouched food. When I look back up, the grin on Seb's face confirms that he is toying with me.

"So, the family business, is it stressful?" Nicky asks placing his cutlery down on his plate for a moment and wiping his mouth with his napkin.

"It can be at times. We can travel around a lot and that has its own problems. A lot of it is done on the phone and online. I am just a little fed up. All I hear lately is the constant talk about being with the one, or not being with her shall we say." Seb sighs and for a moment he looks sad before he smiles again and looks over at me.

"Sometimes it is like being around a teenager with a crush." Seb stops again and shoves a forkful of carrots into his mouth, he doesn't lose eye contact with me. I manage to pull my eyes away briefly; he is really dragging this out and I am stupidly hanging on his every word.

"It is horrible being lovesick." Nicky pipes up, gazing longingly at Sebastian.

"You see, Lion is deeply in love with this girl, it feels like he has been hung up on her forever."

Seb stops talking and winks at me. My attempt to finish my meal is now lost and I feel nauseous. He is talking about Julian and I'm now positive, the girl he is referring to is me. I find it hard to believe that Julian has had a thing for me for so long. My head is swimming with this information.

"That is so sweet, what is he going to do?" Gushes Nicky, always one for a good love story. I suddenly feel lightheaded, and it is not from the vast quantity of alcohol I consumed last night. I can't eat any more, I just want to get up and leave but know that I can't. Instead, I sit and push the peas around on my plate.

"He is taking her out to dinner to declare his love again tonight, in fact, I hope she doesn't freak out." I choke as I swallow and try to cough it out. Nicky and Sebastian look at me as I smile and turn purple. I try to take a sip of my lemonade, but the bubbles are not helping my cause. I cough into my napkin, desperately trying to compose myself as best I can while Nicky and Seb continue talking.

"I wish him luck. Love is never easy." Nicky states finishing his meal and putting his cutlery down on his empty plate, ignoring the fact that his best friend is choking to death. Finally, my coughing fit ceases. I have two choices; skirt around the conversation or call Seb's bluff and just come out and let him know he is talking about Julian and me. I decided to do the latter.

"I'm not sure if I will freak out. I'm only just getting to know your cousin." This time it is Nicky's turn to cough in surprise as his head turns to face me.

"What! Julian is your cousin?" Nicky's eyes jump to Seb, he looks disappointed and hurt. I reach over and put my hand on Nicky's as I try to clarify.

"I thought I recognized Seb when he sat down earlier. Julian took me to a pub the other evening and Seb was behind the bar. I didn't realise they were related until now."

Seb nods in agreement.

"It is a small world. That is my pub and funnily enough I wasn't supposed to be behind the bar that night. I somehow managed to leave a club last night, with the cutest guy who just so happens to be best friends with the love of my cousin's life. I'm guessing it was fate that we should all meet up like this." I stare at him open mouthed. Is it fate or is this all planned? Nicky is looking thoughtful, I can tell he is formulating a conclusion that may be like my own, that Seb is here to spy, report back. Either way Nicky doesn't look pleased.

"How did you come about tickets for the club last night Seb?" Seb looks from Nicky to me and then back at Nicky. He puts his hands up in mock alarm, his t-shirt looks like it is going to rip open in the Incredible Hulk kind of way.

"Ah I see where this is going. I know how this looks but it is entirely innocent and not planned, honestly. My mate Minnie designs and makes handmade corsets, she has worked for the promoters before, and they sent her a couple of complimentary tickets. I went along with her last minute because her husband had to stay and look after their sick twins, who have chicken pox. She left early to get back home to her boys. I met Nicky as I was heading out to collect my phone and leave. The rest is history." Seb stops, picks up his glass and gulps down the last of his coke. Nicky still doesn't look convinced and raises an eyebrow. I shrug lightly. I would like to hope this is all a crazy coincidence, otherwise this situation has just become creepy.

"I'm sorry I teased you Ellie, I know it was wrong of me." He looks tense, his expression serious and I must admit he does look sorry. Nicky looks at me with those big brown eyes of his, I can see he is attracted to him. I hope he is telling us both the truth. I give Nicky a reassuring smile, I want this to be innocent and I want my friend to be happy.

"Nicky, do you fancy coming back to mine after lunch?" Seb turns to Nicky in a bold move. I think I blush because from his expression I can tell Nicky is desperate to get him back into bed. Nicky looks longingly at me, but he is unsure whether to accept. I smile at him warmly and lower my voice in a conspiratorial manner.

"You go spend your afternoon together, try to get as much information from him on his cousin. I need all the help I can get." Seb laughs out loud but looks relieved.

"That sounds like a bloody good idea to me." Nicky replies with a beaming smile.

"I like you already Ellie and, in all seriousness, I am happy to spill the beans on Lion, any time." We sit and make small talk for the next hour, helped by a couple of shots of vanilla vodka, nothing like hair of the dog to make a girl feel better. I say my goodbyes to both men, and they wish me luck with my date tonight.

I take a very slow walk back to Hedge Hill. I haven't seen Julian in a few days, but my week has been so intense without him which has been good for me. I'm glad to know that Julian is really interested in me, that sends happy chills down my spine although I'm somewhat taken aback that he has thought about me for so long. I have already made up my mind and have decided to go with what feels right. Starting with our date tonight, I won't run or hold back. I want Julian.

CHAPTER FOURTEEN

Attention To Detail

I wake from my nap at five with a jolt, physically jumping when I hear another knock. My head is a little fuzzy from my post Sunday lunch nap and the vodka I dabbled in. I find Jamie at the door, looking worse for wear.

"Thought you might want to listen to this while you get ready tonight." The poor girl looks grey and pasty as she holds out a CD which I take, I look at the cover.

"The Downward Spiral." I read aloud, a little confused.

"You asked about track five last night." Jamie explains. I finally catch on and realise what I am holding.

"Thank you, sweetie." I squeal glancing at the CD.

"How are you feeling?" I enquire, although I probably shouldn't have bothered, the big black rings under her eyes give away the answer, no words are needed.

"Completely hungover but I will survive. I'm heading to the staff room for some food then back to bed."

"Another night with Patrick Swayze and Dirty Dancing?" I ask glancing down at the CD again and reading the song titles, finding track five and its title. I shall play this later.

"Yep, you got it in one."

"Why don't you come in and have a coffee with me first?" Jamie gives me a brief smile but shakes her head before wishing me luck with my date. I close the door and can't help feeling sorry for her, she always suffers from terrible hangovers, I feel guilty that I haven't suffered as badly as she has, although she did drink almost twice as much as me. I pad over to the bathroom and start thinking about getting ready but first water. I need to get rid of the dehydration.

* * *

I wait patiently in reception at seven on the dot; I have no idea what Julian's plans are but after our last date anything seems possible, daydreaming as I wait, my mind flitting to how Nicky met Seb: it is a small world indeed. At five past seven there is no sign of Julian. I glance around the large opulent room; a small group has arrived and are busy checking into their rooms. Their luggage is piled high as they try to organise rooms together on the same floor. I leave them to it; glad I never took the reception job I was originally offered. I decide to walk towards the entrance and wait outside on the steps of the hotel, some fresh air will help settle my nerves.

The sky is dark with grey clouds and the heavy taint of rain fills the air. If we are lucky, we may get a thunderstorm tonight. With that thought, I turn to nip back to my room and grab my jacket and umbrella but spot Julian instantly. Tall, dark, brooding and dressed in a navy-blue linen suit with a white linen shirt underneath. I smile, happy he is here, his dark hair swept messily back off his face. His eyes catch mine and he smiles. I swallow. He looks gorgeous standing mere inches away, watching me. I feel like my knees are going to buckle and give way.

"Good evening, Ellie." I virtually melt at the sound of his low deep voice; a bubbling mess of emotions flood my system.

"Good evening, Julian." I reply with a shy smile. He takes two steps forwards and stops, facing me. His hand reaches out and gently takes mine, raising it delicately up to his lips where he places a gentle kiss on my knuckles. I swoon a little, a flush sweeping over me as I feel my cheeks redden. I realise how much

I missed him over the last few days. Julian notices my reaction to him and smiles, his green eyes twinkling. I feel breathless. I hope he is feeling the same way.

"Shall we." He gestures to the door and as we walk, I spot his parked car which is sitting conveniently right outside.

We arrive in Brighton. I glance over at the pier as we walk, watching the bright colourful lights flashing from the fairground rides at the far end and listening to the faint sound of screaming and laughter drifting along the sea. Julian escorts me as we walk down the steps and onto the beach along the boardwalk. Despite it being a Sunday evening, it is still busy here. Families are out strolling and walking their dogs, groups of friends sit on benches, eating fish and chips out of newspaper while washing their food down with bottles of cold beer. Julian reaches down and grasps my hand, holding it firmly. I can barely contain the happiness I feel at this moment in time, the beaming smile on my face, proud for all to see. I am out walking in Brighton with Julian, moving together like a couple. I am busy revelling in the sensations of the skin-to-skin contact, something I have not done in so long, I have made the right decision to go with the flow, not overthink and enjoy the moment.

As we walk, a fight appears to break out amongst a group of men ahead of us, there is jeering and shouting, one guy swings a punch at the other but misses, the two involved stumbling all over the place. Julian stops dead in his tracks, holding me close, his hand tightens around mine. I look at him, his eyes are scanning the fight and the crowd, he has a strange expression. But as quickly as the fight started, it is over, the two men clearly drunk now clapping each other on the back and pulling each other into bear hugs. Their friends cheering and jeering them on. Julian says nothing, doesn't even mention what just happened but continues walking, taking me with him. He seems deep in thought, mulling over something which now has a bubble of worry settle in the pit of my stomach.

"This is us." Julian state's, mere meters from where the fight took place. We stop outside the door of a little cake shop that's nestled amongst the busy bars and cafés, the shop front decorated in pastel colours. Julian knocks lightly on the glass and a young woman unlocks it, letting us in.

"Ellie this is Jessica, she owns this little gem." Jessica reaches out her hand and we shake. She is a pretty woman with short blonde hair, wearing a bright pink apron decorated with colourful cupcakes and bright pink lipstick to match.

"Lovely to finally meet you. Okay Lion, everything is ready for the two of you. Have a lovely evening and don't forget to lock the door when you are finished." She smiles at both of us, takes off her apron and grabs her rucksack before waving to us both and lets herself out, locking the door behind her. I give Julian a curious glance, I guess Julian has told many people about me.

"This is a quaint little establishment." I say aloud. The shop is very sweet and extremely small, the walls are painted in pastel colours, which really brighten it up and give it a friendly feel. Little tables line the floor in rows with tablecloths that are colour coordinated, small stools surround each table. The counter is pastel pink, and I can imagine this place being a big hit with Brighton's yummy mummies and their darling children.

Behind the counter is a large chalk board offering various tea and coffee choices as well as different flavoured milkshakes. The wall opposite has shelves from floor to ceiling that contain jar upon jar of brightly coloured sweets of every size, shape, and colour you can think of and there is a massive scale behind the counter to weigh them on. This little gem must be a big hit with children and families alike. I spot a jar full of jellybeans and run my fingers over the glass. I loved Jellybeans as a child. Julian touches my elbow which brings me out of my reverie, I smile up at him.

"You have fond memories of eating jellybeans as a child." It isn't a question, but a statement and I nod.

"Me too. One of my earliest memories is eating them in my garden with my best friend when we were little." I smile at Julian, it is nice to hear about his life, he so rarely talks about himself.

"I think dinner is served." He says softly before I can ask a question. I realise as I am steered into the bright and spacious kitchen area that he has said very little tonight. Is he worried about tonight as much as I am?

I gaze at him, willing him to speak; he looks good in his suit, his hair swept back off his handsome face. Julian stands with his hands tucked into his trouser pockets, searching my face for a response as we enter the kitchen. I glance around with wide eyes. A smile dances on his lips as he absorbs my reaction, I find his smile simply adorable and return it with a grin.

"This is amazing." I grin up at him. The kitchen is huge and to the right is a big wooden table, all laid out for us. Julian pulls out a stool from under the table and gestures for me to take a seat which I do.

"If you haven't worked it out, this is a cupcake shop." I sit down, imagining the staff sitting here gossiping between cake batches, waiting for the lunchtime rush to start, whilst sipping on fruit teas. Julian comes around and sits opposite me. The table is lined with an oilskin tablecloth which is decorated with little daisies, I have no idea if this is mere coincidence or another personal touch of Julian's but either way, I love it. In front of us is a giant handmade vegetarian pizza and a big bowl of salad, a bottle sits to the side containing some sort of herb and garlic infused oil for drizzling. Julian places a slice of pizza on my plate and then one on his, before pouring us both a glass of sparking water.

"I hope you don't mind but I ordered for us." He says laughing at his own joke.

"This looks lovely, thank you. I love pizza. Did Jessica make this herself?" I ask smiling back at him.

"She did, Jessica is thinking of branching out and selling home-made pizza slices here at lunch. Tonight, we are her guinea pigs and are taste testing this vegan one. I hope she hasn't poisoned it." I smile at Julian.

"I hope so too, it would be a travesty to die at the beginning of our second date." Julian smiles at my reply. Suddenly filled with nerves, I reach out and help myself to some of the colourful salad, offering the bowl to Julian. He nods.

"Yes please." I place some on his plate. He has clearly gone to a lot of trouble organising for us to have dinner here alone and I want tonight to go well, it ended so horribly wrong last time. I mull over a question.

"How do you know Jessica?" Julian swallows his mouthful of pizza, putting his knife and fork down on his plate and rests his chin on his hands.

"Is that question number three?" Jeez this guy has a great memory. I laugh out loud.

"No, it is definitely not question number three, I'm still thinking of a proper question to ask you next. I just wondered how you managed to organise an intimate meal here for us tonight?"

"I know her father, Stanley." He replies picking up his cutlery and cutting into a juicy cherry tomato. I take a small bite of my pizza slice, holding it up to my mouth.

"This is lovely." I know it is very unladylike talking with a full mouth of food, but the pizza is divine. I chew quickly and swallow.

"Oops sorry." I say in way of an apology for my lack of manners. Julian shakes his head and reaches over wiping a smudge of passata from the corner of my mouth with his thumb before plunging his thumb in his mouth. With wide eyes, I slowly wipe the area he has just touched. We eat in silence for a moment, caught up in our own thoughts. I still feel a little nervous yet excited, I'm buzzing with electricity which has caused my appetite to completely disappear. I only manage to eat the one slice of pizza. I put down my knife and fork after emptying my plate.

"Are you not hungry?" Julian asks glancing at my plate and then to me.

"Sadly no. That pizza is delicious, but I have no appetite."

"Me too." He says pushing his plate away dramatically which makes me laugh.

"This place really is lovely, thank you for bringing me here."

"You are most welcome Ellie, although the best is yet to come." Julian stands and picks up our plates, taking them to the island in the middle of the room and placing them in one of the large white sinks that sits by the wall opposite. He returns, picking up the remainder of the pizza and the bowl of salad, popping them into one of the large catering fridges. Julian clearly has been here before because he knows his way around this kitchen.

I watch him walk with effortless grace. He walks over to another counter and comes back carrying a tiny three-tiered cake stand which he places delicately on the table between us. The offerings on the cake stand are beautifully decorated, being far too pretty to eat. Alongside them lie jewelled marshmallows and berries dipped in chocolate of various shades.

"Jessica is known around here for her mini cupcakes in crazy flavours, she makes them to sell here but also for parties and events." Julian gently spins the cake stand for me to see. We are talking Petit fours of the cupcake world. Tiny cupcakes that are beautiful, each no more than a mouthful and all decorated differently. They simply are too beautiful to eat. Julian reaches over and picks up one of two identical cupcakes that I didn't notice before and holds it out to me.

"Taste this one, it is my favourite." I feel completely self-conscious as I move towards his fingers. I open my mouth slowly and he gently pops the tiny cake onto my tongue. His finger brushes my bottom lip, leaving me a quivering wreck. I close my mouth as he picks up the second one and pops it into his own. Together we chew and wow! Delicate chocolate sponge, soft and springy invades my mouth. Flavour floods my taste buds, a very sweet layer of ultra-smooth and silky hazelnut butter with the delicate crunch of the ultra-thin crisp dark chocolate topping. These really are delicious and I'm truly surprised, I have never heard of these or had anything like them before.

"Good?" Julian enquires raising his eyebrows and waiting for my response. I nod, still deep in tiny cupcake heaven.

"I'm glad you like them." I take a sip of my sparkling water, the bubbles cleansing my palate ready for me to try the next one. Suddenly my appetite has reappeared at the thought of another of these little delights. Julian picks up another cake and holds it out to me, once again I open my mouth and he places it on my tongue. This tiny morsel is as good as the first. Vanilla sponge with a delicate fresh raspberry filling and topped with a light vanilla icing. This little gem is delicious and being fed by hand is an extremely sensual experience.

"You know Ellie, I have thought about you every day for a whole year." I stop chewing and look into Julian's green eyes. He is serious and looks like he is fighting with himself. I remember what Seb said earlier and what Julian had said to me before. I don't say a word, but my head is swimming, and my heart is pounding so hard that I'm afraid that he can hear it humming in my chest.

"Ellie I would really like for you to get to know me. I know we parted badly last time. When I came to your room, I was ready to confess all my sins. You took me in and took care of me without asking any questions. That only made my affection for you stronger. I know I upset you, I didn't mean to freak you out and for that I am truly sorry. Everything I said must have sounded so odd, unconventional." He sighs, reaching over and tucking my hair behind my ear.

"I just can't get you out of my mind." I sit stunned. Tonight, Julian isn't messing around. I open my mouth and then close it again deciding to choose my words carefully.

"I can't stop thinking about you either. I would very much like to get to know you better." My reply is truthful, my palms are sweating, and I feel incredibly warm.

"You don't know how happy I am to hear that." His expression changes, the tension clearly fading from his perfect features. I watch as his shoulders visibly relax, although I do notice his nostrils flaring.

"We better finish these cakes." He says, turning the cake stand slowly before choosing another delight. I open my mouth shyly and then laugh pulling my head back.

"No, actually I think it is your turn." I pick up a chocolate covered strawberry and hold it out by the stalk, waiting for Julian's lips to move closer to it. Julian moves towards me but for some unknown reason I pull my hand away and stand. Never taking my eyes from his, I tentatively walk around the table towards him. He smiles up at me and before I know it, I am in his lap, in his embrace, the strawberry has been forgotten, falling from my hand to the floor. Julian's soft warm lips find mine. I run my hands through his soft dark hair, his hands run over my back sending waves of pleasure through me, but as soon as I begin to deepen our kiss, he pulls away from me.

"What is it?" I ask breathless, frustration beginning to take over.

"We can't do this here." He kisses me on the tip of my nose, pulling me closer and effectively holding me against him to stand. He is right of course; a kitchen is not the place for this kind of activity. Brighton and Hove's environmental health department would have a field day. Suddenly Julian has me by the hand and is leading me out of the kitchen and into the main shop. I turn and glance around one last time as Julian unlocks the door and together, we head out into the night. We walk silently hand in hand. I am really confused; this is the third time he has pulled away from me. I know we were in the wrong place tonight; I just don't understand why he does it the way he does.

"What's wrong?" I ask as we walk. Julian shakes his head and snorts.

"Tell me what is wrong."

"Is that question number three?" Julian replies mocking me. I bite my tongue, fed up with this twenty questions game.

"Yes, it is if you give me an actual answer."

"Okay then, if you must know I am as horny as hell right now." He gives me a heartbreakingly apologetic smile. A giggle escapes my lips, I can't help but groan in amusement.

"I am glad to hear that, I think... But that was not really an answer. So, I'll ask again, what is wrong? Why do you constantly pull away from me?" I feel brave, licking my lips and waiting for his reply. Julian opens his mouth then shuts it again, this goldfish thing is contagious. His nostrils flare as he runs his hand through his messy hair sweeping its dark mass off his face.

"That is two questions." His expression tells me there is so much more to this then he is letting on, so I push further.

"Oh, for goodness' sake Julian, it is two questions linked by a common theme. Fine then, question three and question four." I don't like the feeling of being left hanging, a knot is forming in the pit of my stomach again, this could go badly wrong.

"Okay here goes Ellie. I have never been in a long-term relationship. I want us to work." He shrugs his shoulders apologetically and gazing down at his shoes. It is dark out now, but people are still mulling about the boardwalk. The sound of laughter and screams can be heard from the rides at the end of the pier, mingling with the waves crashing on the beach. I smile warmly up at Julian as he gazes at my face trying to read my expression.

"Wow, you are brave, saying that allowed." I state all matter of fact. I reach for his hand and squeeze it gently, then reach up onto my tippy toes and offer him my lips. He accepts them and we kiss, a gentle sweet kiss, lips lightly touching. Someone wolf whistles and I pull away to smile at a group of teenagers giggling

135

behind us.

"Let's go take a walk along the pier." I suggest as I look over and see the Helter-Skelter all lit up against the black night sky.

* * *

We arrive back at Hedge Hill after a lovely beach front walk. Julian walks me through the hotel and to my floor. We stop outside the door to my room.

"Goodnight, Ellie." He whispers, his lips briefly touching mine once more. Before I can answer, he turns away and begins walking down the hall and away from me, I panic. No not again.

"Julian." I cry out, adrenaline coursing through my veins. The thought of being on my own tonight fills me with dread.

"Come and have a cup of tea with me?" I plead.

"I don't think that is a good idea, Ellie." I shake my head not accepting his answer, this is not what I want to hear right now.

"Please come in" I shout, knowing that I will regret it, if I let him walk away again. Julian flashes me a nervous smile.

"Just for one cup of tea, nothing more." Julian studies me, looks down the corridor before looking back. His eyes hooded in contemplation.

"Do you have camomile tea by any chance?" He asks striding towards me. He has changed his mind and is staying, I am elated.

"I don't have camomile, will bog standard builder's tea do?" I reply sweetly.

"Bog standard will have to do" He replies as my door slams shut behind us.

CHAPTER FIFTEEN

Tea And Spooning

Julian takes off his jacket and hangs it on the back of my door.

"I wondered where I put that one." He comments, noticing the jacket he put around my shoulders on the night of our first date. I walk over and open my window looking sheepish, it was nice having something of his in my possession.

"Sorry I forgot about that." I reply realising that it's the worst lie ever. He blesses me with a knowing smile, I look away as I can feel my cheeks burning with embarrassment. I fill the kettle and switch it on, grabbing a couple of mugs and throwing tea bags in them.

"Interesting choice in music." Julian declares, holding up Jamie's CD.

"I would never have had you as a Nine Inch Nails fan." I feel my cheeks redden further and am reminded instantly by the lyrics of that one song and how it made me feel.

"Big fan me, I own all their stuff." I respond a little too quickly, realising that I am going to spend the rest of this evening lying.

"Milk? Sugar?" I ask splashing boiling water into the mugs.

"Black please." Julian puts the CD back down on the table and sits on my bed smiling to himself. I hand him two mugs full of steaming hot tea, then slip my ballet pumps off my feet, before I join him on the bed. I sit facing him with my legs crossed, my dress pulled over my knees and I rest a cushion on my lap, making sure I maintain my modesty. When I am suitably comfortable, I gesture, and he hands me a mug.

"What have you been doing over the last couple of days?" Initiating the conversation seems to be my domain, Julian looks like the kind of guy who is just happy to sit and watch me. He shifts uncomfortably on the bed, his expression darkens, and his pupils dilate, this I notice but I don't mention it.

"I have been called into work quite a bit. He stops and looks over my shoulder and out towards the window. I turn my head to see what it is that he is looking at and notice it has just started to rain.

"Thankfully the jobs I have been assigned, have been fairly local and very straightforward. However, it has been annoying having to rush off." Thinking back to my conversation with Seb earlier and about the kind of work they do, leaves me puzzled. Why is Julian being called into work? If I am to believe that he is involved in the family hunting business.

"What exactly is it you do?" I query, tilting my head slightly to get a better view of him. Julian attempts to take a sip of his tea but it is far too hot. Instead, he puts his mug down on the bedside table.

"Is that question five?" I raise my eyebrows at him in response.

"Must every question I ask be one of the so called twenty? Because I now have over sixteen questions all relating to you not being great at relationships statement from earlier. I can bombard you with them now if you so wish?" I smile sweetly and flutter my eyelids exactly in the same way Nicky does to me when he wants something. Julian is clearly amused by my outburst.

"Search and destroy." He replies. I sigh with fake exasperation.

"You're very frustrating." Clearly my attempt at trying to get to know him a little more, to understand him isn't working to my advantage.

"What?" he retorts. I shrug my shoulders and lean in closer to him.

"I want to get to know you better." I mutter under my breath just loud enough for him to hear, then I reach closer and kiss him on the tip of his nose. Julian sucks in his breath, his nostrils flare and he eye's me with something I have not seen before; need, want, lust or a mixture of all three. Julian moves slowly towards me, taking my cup of hot tea and putting it on the table next to his. Before I know it, I am in his arms, being lifted off the bed and onto his lap. We are face to face, my fingers running through his glorious dark hair, luxuriating at the feel of every strand. Our lips and tongues are moving, tasting one another. I feel euphoric, Julian is here with me, in an embrace that I never want to end. He shifts his body and lies back on the bed, his head and back leaning against my headboard. I am now astride him, my knees either side of his hips, my body is so close to his that it's intoxicating.

We continue kissing, exploring skin, nipping with lips and teeth. His hands are under my dress roaming up and down my back, his fingers dancing over my hips and waist. His hands move again and this time he wraps one hand around my hair, pulling roughly and causing my head to tilt right back. My neck is exposed, he kisses me with ferocity. It feels too good being on his lap like this, feeling his muscular body so close to mine.

What on earth am I doing! Reality kicks in or is it my guilty conscious. I stop moving and climb off Julian quickly. I move away from the bed on shaky legs, straightening my dress. My breathing is heavy as I run my hands through my mussed hair. I look down at Julian and hate my conscience, I feel flushed. He looks flushed. Julian sits up with confusion etched on his handsome face.

"What did I do wrong?" He asks confused.

"You haven't done anything wrong, nothing at all. Believe me that was so nice..." I stop. How on earth do I tell him what I really want to do with him right now. Tea was a very bad idea. Julian sits up, his nostrils flare as he runs his hand through his hair.

If anger, hurt, and confusion were combined and formed into human features, it would look like Julian right now. I realise my mistake.

"Oh my god Julian, you don't know how much I want you right now." I finally blurt out my thoughts in a panicked rush. I'm breathless and so worked up, I move towards the window where it is really pouring with rain outside. I need to cool down before I spontaneously combust. Julian's eyes follow me as I move. He mulls over what I have said and now looks like he is now at war with himself.

"You are absolutely right. Now isn't the time. I shouldn't be here." He adjusts his clothes. I want to go to him, embrace him but I don't because I am not sure I can stop myself again. I just stand here, a big bag of emotional hormones and fully turned on. I can only nod my head in agreement, oh how I hate myself for stopping and clearly not making my reason for stopping clearer. Julian stands, brushing his hands down his thighs, he looks lost, and it is heartbreakingly beautiful.

"I better go." He states, his tone quiet but matter of fact. He moves towards the door. I realise at that point that I do not want him to leave, I want to snuggle up to him, kiss him, let him know that I want him still and want to be in his arms forever.

"Please don't go!" I splutter in panic.

"Spend the night with me?" Julian stops, he looks down at the jacket in his hand and puts it back on the coat hanger on the back of my door. He walks two steps towards me, stopping and cocking his head slightly. I walk slowly towards him. I need him close to me and for the life of me I can't understand why. I feel right at this moment that I never want to be without him again. I take his hand in mine, locking my fingers in his.

"I want to get to know you and that doesn't need to involve sex right now. We can take things a little slower and save that for another time." I persevere, giving him a shy smile while hoping he will accept my offer of staying with me tonight. Julian's eyes never leave mine while I speak. I did half expect him to just keep going but after a moment he lets go of my hand and bends down taking off his shoes and socks. I watch him, overjoyed that he is going to stay with me. He stands back up and I place a gentle kiss on his lips. Taking his hand again, I lead him back to my bed.

A storm is brewing outside, my curtains are blowing and lightning flashes. I switch off the room light and turn on the lamp next to me. I move towards him and curl up as close to his body as I possibly can, he places his arm around me in an embrace that is so strong and yet so gentle at the same time. He plays with my hair, I feel safe. I breath in his subtle citrus scent, resting my head on the soft fabric of his shirt. I lay still listening to the thunder and the beating of his heart.

"We lie in comfortable silence for a while. Heavy rain pelting the glass of my window. A loud thunderclap makes me jump but Julian holds me closer to him. Another flash of lightning lights up the room momentarily.

"I have questions." I say smiling to myself. Julian sighs as if annoyed.

"This is my first time to date?" He volunteers before I have a chance to speak further. I turn towards him, lifting my head from his chest. My mouth is open in the most unladylike fashion. I am no prude, I consider myself a woman of the world and knowing Nicky for so long and having witnessed some of his escapades, I would say I was a very open-minded person. But this, I just don't get.

"You have never dated? Does that mean you are a virgin?" I clarify, more to myself then to him, maybe being a virgin is why he held back for so long.

"Correct and no."

"And you have never dated a single person, male or female?"

"Correct. I have never dated anyone and for your information I am strictly heterosexual." He states all matter of fact. Is his life-

141

style choice normal? This could quite possibly be the strangest conversation I have ever had.

"But you have had sex" I ask hesitantly, cringing at each word.

"Yes, I have had unfulfilling sex, it was unfulfilling because it was never with the right person." He replies looking deep into my eyes. I am grateful he has answered truthfully even if he is rather blunt. But I did ask him about his sex life. I nod, feeling foolish but a girl needs to know what she is up against.

"Have you anything else that you would like to ask?" Julian smiles, taking my hand, his strong fingers entwine with mine.

"Why have you been so gentlemanly?

"Just to clarify, I have spent my lifetime waiting for you, I didn't want to rush this."

* * *

A cream-coloured note lies beside me on my pillow when I wake the following morning.

Dearest Ellie,

Thank you for the perfect evening.

I'm sorry, I have been called away by work. I would have liked nothing more than to have woken up with you this morning.

I expect to be back late this evening and I would very much like to call on you at midnight to be the first to wish you a Happy Birthday.

Stay awake for me.

Forever yours

Julian x

I feel empty like a part of me is missing. I wanted to wake up with him, feel his arms around me and his lips on mine. I place the note on the bed and notice the tiny, jewelled box tucked away just under the pillow. I pull it out and thank the gods that the box isn't damaged. I open it carefully and break out into a huge smile, the box contains a tiny chocolate covered cupcake, complete with a tiny message written on a sliver of white chocolate which reads.

Forever yours

Julian x

Is there nothing this man doesn't think of. This is the sweetest gift to wake up to and I finally understand his message, if I want him, he is mine. Our heart-to-heart last night has me convinced that his feelings for me run deep. I can now forgive him for leaving me to wake on my own. I close the box put it next to my biscuit jar, I will have that later.

My Monday flies by in a blur, all tasks completed, calls made, orders submitted, and roses deadheaded. I finish work at five and head back to my room hot and sweaty, I feel dismayed that I haven't heard from Julian all day but decide to take my mind off that fact and give my room a bloody good pre birthday tidy up.

I meet with Nicky for an early dinner in the staffroom before he starts his night shift. I'm glad to hear that his Sunday evening went well with Seb. Nicky is absolutely glowing, and he looks happy, clearly all the sex he is bragging about agrees with him.

"How was your date?" He finally asks after telling me about his extremely hot evening with Seb.

"It was lovely, thoughtful and romantic. Julian took me to this little place in Brighton and then we came back here, he spent the night." A shiver runs down my spine remembering how I fell asleep in Julian's arms but woke up to an empty bed.

"He finally got into your knickers, good for him!" Nicky winks and I elbow him in the ribs.

"No actually, he didn't. He stayed in my room, we were fully clothed, and we didn't have sex of any sort, I wasn't quite ready."

Nicky smiles at me.

"Darling, I'm proud that you are not rushing into anything with him." I laugh out loud.

"I wanted to, but felt I needed to wait and not rush that side of things?" Nicky gives me a reproachful look.

"I'm glad you are taking things slowly." Nicky reaches over and holds my hand.

"What has dear old Ellen made for pudding tonight?" Pulling the lid off a giant catering cake tin and peeking inside.

"Ooh my favourite." He cuts himself a giant slice of jam sponge and then notices the jug of custard on the side. He reaches over grabbing the jug and pours the viscous yellow liquid over his cake, then bungs the lot in the microwave.

"Do you want some?" He asks cutting a second slice before I even answer.

"Just a small bit but no custard thanks." I reply salivating at the smell wafting from the noisy microwave. We tuck into our pudding, the vanilla sponge with its thick layer of jam is sickly sweet but is delicious and satisfying.

"What are your plans for your birthday?" Nicky asks with his mouth full of cake.

"I haven't any plans as such, I've got my birthday and the rest of the week booked off on annual leave. I'll probably do some shopping, get my haircut. Basically, just chill out and read a book on that gadget you and Jamie bought me for Christmas.

"Darling it is called a Kindle." Nicky shoves another spoonful of cake and custard into his mouth.

"Julian wants to see me at midnight to be the first to wish me a happy birthday." I answer smiling. Nicky grins as he finishes the last of his pudding.

"I like his way of thinking, maybe you'll get lucky tonight instead and have a birthday shag." He says with a wink. I choose to ignore his last comment but hope Nicky is right.

"We should go out Saturday night and celebrate your birthday in style." Nicky will use any excuse to go out and party.

"That would be great." I answer finishing my own slice of cake, happy to be having a birthday celebration this year.

"Leave it to me and I'll get it all sorted." Nicky stands and kisses me on the head.

"Thank you." I reply blissfully happy to have him as my best friend.

CHAPTER SIXTEEN

The Quickening

I'm on edge which isn't all that surprising. Julian is coming over in just under 5 hours and although I am excited to see him, I can't help feeling that I need to be careful around him, guarded even, it is a weird notion because I cannot put my finger on why. My heart feels like I cannot live without him, my body is craving him. This is not normal at all. These are not normal feelings and therefore to protect myself I need to be careful. It's frightening, it's amazing and most definitely perplexing.

After dinner, I go for a walk in the woodland behind the hotel grounds. I have so much to think about. I want him in my life more than I thought I could want anyone, ever. An owl hoots high above me as I walk the small loop back to the hotel. If I had to try and explain my feelings, I simply couldn't put them into words. All I know is that I crave Julian when he is away from me. Every cell in my body yearns for him, which is ridiculous, I know it's ridiculous; yet it is the only way to describe it. I can't stop thinking about him. I can't stop myself wanting to be around him. My developing need for him scares me but there is nothing I can do about it.

* * *

I climb out of the shower, dry off and slowly get ready for bed, I even spray myself with a little vanilla perfume before running my brush through my damp hair. Lowering the volume on the radio and climbing under the duvet, it is best I get some sleep before he arrives. My thoughts are all over the place tonight. It has been eighteen months since she passed away from a brain tumour. Not having my mum around this last year and a half has been difficult. I would have loved for my mum to have met Julian. I roll over onto my side hugging my pillow and let the tears fall, remembering all the happiest of birthdays spent with my mother.

"Coming." I shout in a sleepy daze as I jump out of bed completely disoriented. Fumbling madly with the lamp in an attempt at switching it on, I pull on my robe while throwing a mint in my mouth, before running the hairbrush through my wild mane and fixing the bed. Julian stands in my doorway, resting his shoulder against the door frame, a purple balloon with Happy Birthday written on the front is floating behind him. He looks tired but takes one sweeping look at me before breaking into a wide grin. "Happy Birthday kitten."

"Thank you." I step aside to give him access to my room.

"Did I wake you." He enquires, looking at my hastily made bed.

"Yes sorry, I got comfy and dozed off." I smile to myself, closing the door feeling every cell of my body buzz to life. My melancholy from an hour ago dissipates and is replaced by happiness.

"So how does it feel to be twenty-eight?" Julian asks as he starts to go through the bags, he had brought with him.

"Same as being twenty-seven." I reply deadpan, rubbing the sleep from my eyes. Julian stops what he is doing and moves closer to me, giving me his full attention. He looks me in the eyes, his expression is serious as he scans my face.

"Your eyes are puffy." I look away briefly, I have no excuse to give. His fingertips lightly brush my arm, getting my attention and my eyes meet his. Julian moves closer and leans in to kiss me. I move closer still, just for the comfort that his strong arms offer and I am blanketed in his embrace. Having him here makes me feel better, feel safe. I am grateful that I don't have to deal with my birthday alone. I kiss him back, gently at first but the taste of him has me wanting to devour him with a ferocity that frightens me. We eventually separate gasping for air, I give Julian a shy smile.

"I think it is time for presents. I want you to close your eyes." I oblige, feeling a little giddy, excitement chasing away my earlier melancholic mood. I hear Julian's movements around my room, mixed with the sound of Edvard Grieg's In the Hall of the mountain King playing on the radio. I hear the tap in the bathroom followed by the click of the kettle. What on earth is he doing?

"Can I open my eyes yet?" I ask. Julian's laughter fills the room as he mooches about.

"I did think you would have peeped by now but as you haven't, no you can't." I continue to stand still for what feels like forever, with a big smile plastered across my face, my arms wrapped around myself in anticipation.

"Okay, all done." He finally whispers as he moves around the back of me. Julian gently places his large, soft hands over my eyes. I can smell him and feel his breath on the nape of my neck causing a shiver to run down my spine. Very quietly Julian sings his own rendition of happy birthday to the thumping of my heart.

I am overwhelmed with emotion when he removes his hands. In the short time I have had my eyes closed, he has dotted at least 20 daisy shaped tea lights around my room, they look so pretty, their light collectively illuminates my bed, bouncing soft flickering shadows off the walls. The balloon, tied to the back of my chair and sitting on my table is a cake; a small delicate Victoria sponge with a single lit candle perched on the top.

"This is perfect." I sigh feeling tearful again but for different reasons.

"I'm glad you like it. First things first, you must blow out the candle and make a wish." Which is exactly what I do, bending over the table and blowing gently. Sitting next to the cake are two porcelain plates, two cake forks and a knife. Julian proceeds to cut us both a slice, handing one plate to me. I take a nibble as I watch him pour boiling water into two mugs and leaving them on the table to cool.

"I think a special occasion such as your birthday deserves tea and cake, I hope you don't mind camomile." I watch him amused, he looks happy as he pours sparking water into a champagne flute and hands it to me. I cannot believe he has gone to so much trouble. Again!

"Thank you, Julian." I smile feeling overwhelmed by this thoughtfulness. After a sip of water, Julian takes my glass and puts it on the bedside table with his, we sit eating the cake, listening to the classical music playing on the radio.

"How did you know Victoria sponge was my favourite?" I ask between mouthfuls. Julian just taps his head and winks. I suppose a man can't divulge all his secrets. I am amazed by how attentive he is, I have never met another individual who thinks of absolutely everything for every occasion.

"How was work today?" He asks, taking my plate. I shift slightly on the bed.

"Productive." I answer, gazing at him in the candlelight. I don't really want to talk about work, gardening can be mundane. I can think of a million other things we could be doing right now and talking about my job isn't one of them. Julian is wearing dark trousers and a black linen shirt, the graze on his face has almost healed and I am trying hard, not to reach out and run my hand through his dark hair.

"How was your day?" I finally respond, hoping he will give me some insight into what he really does for living.

"It was busy." Julian takes my hand in his and kisses my palm.

"I'm sorry I woke you."

"Don't be, I'm glad that you did." I feel breathless with him being so close.

"I now think it is probably time for your present. Or would you prefer to open it tomorrow during daylight hours?" I glance over at the bags before answering.

"You can't ask me that, of course I want to open up presents, I have absolutely no self-control." Julian is clearly pleased that I want to open his gift now.

"I can't have you thinking about a gift all night when I want you to concentrate on me. And as for having no self-control, I quite like that Idea." Julian presents me with a large red satin box with a white bow on the top. It is only then, that I notice he is standing with bare feet.

"Open it." He encourages and I don't need to be asked twice. I untie the ribbon and prise the lid off. Inside is a mass of red tissue paper. Reaching in, I rummage around and find another box. The second is smaller, blue with a blue-ribbon trim. Once again, I undo the ribbon and remove the lid. Inside is a third box, smaller and wrapped in red tissue paper. I look up at Julian and raise an eyebrow. I unwrap the paper and am left holding a square black velvet box. I look back up and into Julian's eyes.

"Open it." He whispers and I do. The box is beautifully lined with white satin fabric and sitting in the middle is a delicate and ornate daisy chain bracelet. It is beautiful.

"May I?" He asks, taking it out of the box and carefully placing it on my wrist.

"I had this made for you and I hope you will think of me when you wear it." He closes the clasp, his fingers skimming my trembling wrist. I look at the bracelet, the attention to detail on each daisy is astounding. I stand and pick up the boxes, feeling overwhelmed and just needing to take a second. Julian is by my side, his hand resting on my arm admiring the exquisite piece of jewellery in the candlelight.

"Thank you." I breathe as I reach up and place both of my hands on either side of Julian's face, my fingers brush his hair as my thumbs caress his cheekbones. I tug his hair gently towards me, guiding his lips closer.

"Happy birthday." He whispers and then I kiss him. Julian's lips are soft and warm, the taste of him intoxicating. I run my fingers through his hair, pulling him closer to me, feeling the heat radiating off his body. Whether because of the romantic candlelight, my birthday or simply down to animal instinct, my need for Julian is overwhelming. I can't help but take control, I move slowly towards my bed nudging him backwards with every step. He stops and in one motion I place my hands on his chest and push him gently.

"Sit." He watches me intently as I very slowly untie my robe, pushing it down my shoulders and letting it fall to the floor revealing the black chemise underneath. Julian's nostrils flare as I move closer to him, I know he can see my heaving breasts underneath the lace of the fabric. Placing my hands on his shoulders, I climb onto his lap, my thighs astride his, my knees resting on the bed. Julian's breath catches in his throat as I lower myself onto his waiting lap. I tilt his head up towards me, searching his face, looking for a sign for me to stop. I find nothing but a sexy smirk dancing on his lips, Julian is perfectly aware of what is going to happen next. I continue, slowly allowing my lips to meet his again, his tongue caresses mine, his fingers are feather light as they run down my back, dancing over skin and lace. I run little kisses along Julian's muscular jaw and nip his ear.

"Tell me to stop and I will." I whisper. Julian nods once in answer, then visibly swallows. I pull away, so we are eye to eye and smile.

"Please by all means continue, I'm beginning to enjoy this." I run my fingers down his sides and across his back, feeling every taut muscle and rib beneath his soft linen shirt. His hands skim over my hips and down to my bottom where he gently massages my buttocks. I feel braver than I would ever have thought possible and in one motion I grab the hem of my chemise and pull it over my head. Julian's eyes widen as his hands move over my naked skin, before finally stopping to rest on my waist.

"Is this, okay?" I ask barely able to breathe, the feel of his hands on my body is making me dizzy. Julian nods, he moves slightly to adjust himself and suddenly I can feel his arousal through his trousers. I guide his hands up from my waist and leave them just under my arms, his thumbs instinctively reach out and brush my breasts gently. I leave his hands there to play and kiss him again, pushing him slowly down onto the bed but I hear no complaints. With my lips nipping his, my hands move to the top button of his shirt, as I attempt to undo it, Julian grabs my hands and pulls them down towards his thighs, holding my wrists tightly.

"Leave the shirt on." His voice is heavy with need, I do as he asks, not wanting to take any chances. His expression darkens as he looks away from me. I pull my hands away from his and guide his chin back to centre so that we can look into each other's eyes. I lift myself up on my knees a little, giving me room to move.

"Don't stop." He whispers. His nostrils flare and he gives me a lust filled look before taking my hair and wrapping it around his wrist and takes control, lust overcoming both of us.

We lie together, me wrapped in his arms, spent and gloriously happy. His eyes are closed and there is a small smile dancing on his lips.

"Hey" I whisper feeling a little shy, naked, and completely exposed, my self-confidence from minutes earlier begins to falter. Julian says nothing, his arms are tightly wrapped around me, holding me close, my nipples are hard and pressed against his shirt, but I'm beginning to feel a little uneasy because he is so quiet. I will him to speak, to open his eyes but he doesn't. I move my hips, hoping to get a response but nothing.

"Hey." I say again but he is still unresponsive. I'm not sure what the etiquette is in this situation.

"I'm going to go use the bathroom." I mutter, feeling incredibly warm and flushed with embarrassment by my soiled, naked state. Julian finally opens his eyes; his green pools bore into mine; he doesn't let go of me. The expression on his face is horrendous, causing my heart to beat erratically. I can't stand the silence any longer and pull myself up onto my hands and knees, moving my sticky self from the bed. I reach down and swipe my robe from the floor, hastily putting it on, needing to cover up my nakedness.

"Can I get you anything?" I ask, needing to break the frostiness that has settled in the room, I am way past the point of trying to impress him with my hostess skills. Wiping away the sweat that has formed on my forehead with the back of my hand. I bend down and pick up my chemise off the floor and instantly feel dizzy as I stand. Julian reaches out, catching me by the arm and steadies me. I feel hurt, stupid and a little nauseous.

I wasn't expecting the silent treatment straight after sex and I really don't know what to do now that it is happening. Out of nowhere, a dull throb begins at my temple; a migraine is not what I need right now. I move to get some water, finishing what was left in my glass. Could this get any more awkward, I don't know where to look, Julian sits up and adjusts his trousers and zips himself up. He stands, moving towards me. His eyes search my face.

"You are pale and feel hot." He says concerned, resting his hand on my forehead, and moving it down to my cheek, tutting to himself. I look at him quizzically trying to understand what went wrong and not sure what to say, the last two minutes have been awful. A shiver runs down my spine and I suddenly feel cold to the bone.

"I need to go. I will be back in a few minutes." I open my mouth in silent protest as a tear runs down my cheek. Julian glances at his watch, leaving me to stand stock still and dumbfounded.

"There are two mugs of camomile tea, they will be cool by now, drink them both, I'll be back." I look at him confused but feel too weak to protest at his odd request.

"Damn that curse! If my mother is correct, that tea will help you recover quickly, so drink it." He places a chaste kiss on my temple, ignoring my distress completely as I double over in pain. Opens the door and strides out leaving me behind. I am horrified and heartbroken as the dam finally breaks. I sob into my hands, upset that my romantic birthday is shattered. The man I have just slept with has deserted me and on top of everything else I am really starting to feel unwell. Ugly thoughts fill my head as anger begins to bubble through my veins. Another wave of dizziness hits me, I feel sick to my stomach, whilst the cramping in my abdomen gets stronger.

"Shit!" I shout aloud. The realisation hits me that I have just had unprotected sex too. This only fuels my anger, confusion, and nausea.

"Shit. Shit. Shit!" How stupid could I be! Cramps grip my stomach in a horrible churning sensation that I run to the toilet and vomit violently into the bowl. What the hell is going on? I vomit again and just about manage to wipe my mouth before collapsing onto the cold tiled floor. I am on fire, sweat is dripping from me, yet I am freezing cold. Panic takes over, I clearly have got a bug. My head is pounding and the cramping in my abdomen is getting increasingly worse. On hands and knees, I will myself back into the other room. I need to get my phone and call for help. I double over, searing pain is ripping through me now, If I didn't know better, I would say it is emanating from my uterus but period pain this is not. My increasing agony is a thousand times worse than any pain I have ever experienced. The cramping intensifies, followed by pain shooting up my spine, up my back and down my legs. I can't move, I lie immobilised by it on the carpet of my bedroom.

When the current wave subsides, I slowly unfurl myself and attempt to move again. I feel a trickle of something warm run over my lips and onto the carpet below. Looking down, I see deep red blood dripping from my nose. I stare in disbelief as drop, after drop, hits the carpet. I wipe at my lips with the back of my hand as another wave of pain floods my body. I can't scream, my throat is dry and sore, completely burnt out from the vomiting.

I ride out this wave of pure agony, biting the back of my bloodied hand. I don't know what to do, my head feels like it is ready to explode, I can't think clearly as thirst overwhelms me. All I know is I need to get my phone. I move as quickly as I can and just about manage to pull myself up to a kneeling position by the table. I see my phone and reach out for it just as I notice the two mugs of warm camomile tea. The last words from Julian flood my confused brain, something about camomile tea. Without thinking, I grab the first mug, sloshing its contents with my trembling hands but I drink what I can. Without hesitation I do the same with the second cup. Before I can grab my phone another wave of excruciating pain floods my body, the room spins into darkness.

CHAPTER SEVENTEEN

Superstitions

Shutting Ellie's door behind me and use all my willpower to keep my legs moving. Christ, I feel like a complete fucker walking out on her like that. Seeing the horror on her face and the look of sadness and confusion, which no doubt will have turned to anger the second I closed that door. I stride down the corridor and up the stairs to my room, kicking myself for leaving her. The heat emanating from her body, freaked me out. We were both hot, but Ellie was burning with fever.

I never wanted to believe my mother's superstitions yet deep down I did. Its why I have been so careful, physically around her. Ellie's body temperature was not right, her smell changed after her orgasm, she smelt sweeter. I am afraid to accept that the quickening has begun. She is going to hate me for leaving her to deal with it on her own. Fuck this stupid old wife's tale.

I stop and turn around, ready to go back to Ellie. My body feels a gravitational pull towards her which is far stronger now than it has ever been before. My body is willing me to go back, my brain ready to apologise for walking out. My mother always joked that if I got this far with Ellie to expect the quickening. I, in all honesty didn't think it happened at all. I figured it was just a stupid story to scare her teenage sons into keeping our cocks in our pants. Yet there is a tiny part of me that believes that myth now. What I have just experienced with Ellie was not normal and that is why I am walking away momentarily; I want to give Ellie the grace she deserves to deal with the quickening if that is what is happening. I accept that I will probably have a great deal of sucking up to do if it wasn't the quickening, which I hope it isn't.

I hit play on my phone and Up in the air by 30 seconds to Mars screams from the speakers as I move towards the couch in the darkened room. I stand and stare out of the window, it is completely still and silent outside and here I am, a freak of nature whose sole goal is to hunt and kill the innocent. There isn't a single thing I do that can be considered normal. I jump from the vibration of my phone in my pocket, no doubt Ellie has messaged me in anger, I would too if the tables were turned. I root around for it, she probably thinks this is just a game to me. Absolute fear fills my chest, I hope she will let me explain why I had to leave her.

I wipe at my mouth, I still can taste Ellie on my lips, smell her skin on my shirt. I look at the screen, which lights up the whole window with its brightness. The message is not from Ellie at all, but from my older brother Charlie. I don't even bother to read it, instead I glance at the clock on the screen, it's been fifteen minutes since I walked out and left the woman, I love to deal with God knows what.

I can't believe I have waited ten years for tonight, I have had meaningless sex before, never had I felt satisfied. Christ, working with Seb I have seen everything a person can imagine and then some, yet being with Ellie was perfect. For so long it felt like I have been poisoned and Ellie was my own personal antidote to it. I am a fool for being up here alone while she is down there.

Fuck the old wife's tale, I can't wait any longer, I was stupid to have left her without explanation in the first place. I only hope her mother had the good grace to fill her in on the delicate details of hunters mating for life. I move to the office area of my room, switching on the desk lamp before grabbing a bottle of Whisky and a glass, I need to settle my nerves and a shot of this should do the trick. I pour and then down the measure without thinking about it, luxuriating in the burn as it makes its way to my stomach.

I switch off the music and quietly leave my room, praying that my lame arse apology will be good enough and Ellie will at least let me spend the rest of the night with her. I knock softly on Ellie's door but get no response. I knock again, mindful that it is late and there will be people sleeping in the room next door, nothing. She must seriously be angry and really, I don't blame her. Fishing my phone out of my pocket, I find her number and hit dial. I stand, waiting for it to connect, finally I hear her phone from the other side of the door, but I hear no movement, Ellie's phone goes straight to voicemail. I rest my forehead on her door in frustration. I know I am a prize idiot for walking out, I know it, I just want the chance to explain. I knock again. Nothing. I hit redial and nothing.

A sinking feeling hits my stomach and I feel shaky. Shit what if she is ill. Some of the old wife's tales regarding the quickening have been frightening and downright ridiculous but surely, they are just tales. A bead of sweat forms on my top lip which I brush off with my forearm. Wildly I begin patting myself down until I find my wallet and pull out a credit card. I slip it in the crack of the door, using an old trick I was taught in my younger days, I manage to unlock it and quietly slip in. My eyes frantically scan the dimly lit room, it is eerily quiet and there is no sign of movement. In three strides I'm at her empty bathroom. I turn around and finally spot her, slumped over on the floor on the other side of her bed.

"Ellie!" I shout moving towards her. My heart is thumping madly in my chest, she doesn't look good. I notice the drying, sticky blood from her nose, staining her pretty face and neck. My first thought is she must have fallen, but she wouldn't have landed in this position. I run my hand over her forehead and cheek, she is pale and clammy, her breathing slow and slightly raspy but what worries me most is she is completely unconscious. Gently I move her body away from the table and put her in the recovery position before pulling out my phone and dialling my brother.

"Charlie, I need your help." With Charlie on his way, I decide to move Ellie onto the bed where she is likely to be more comfortable. I clean the blood off her face and find a t-shirt and some underwear, stripping her out of her ruined robe and dress her before repositioning her lifeless limbs back into the recovery position. I cover her with a blanket that I find at the foot of the bed and go about cleaning up the mess, blood, and vomit in her room, while I wait.

"What on earth happened?" Charlie whispers as I close the door to Ellie's room behind us. Charlie doesn't give me a second to answer. He puts his bag down and pulls out a thermometer, taking her temperature and notes everything down in a little notebook that he retrieves from his bag.

"She has a fever." He states while taking her pulse. I stand helplessly watching him, as he checks her pupils and does everything a good doctor should.

"What's the diagnosis?" I ask rubbing at the stubble on my chin nervously.

"What did she take Lion?" I'm completely floored by my brother's question. Charlie finally looks up at me. His eyes searching mine for answers.

"What did she take?" He asks again firmly. I open my mouth horrified at what my brother is insinuating and am faced with his steely glare.

"For fucks sake Charlie, she hasn't taken anything. She was with me and was fine. I left her for less than half an hour and when I came back this was how I found her." Charlie looks from Ellie's now shivering body to me and then back to her again.

"Well, it looks like she has had a reaction to something." Charlie lifts Ellie's wrist and takes her pulse again.

"Could she have overdosed on medication that has been prescribed? Has she taken anything illegal?" Charlie stops, he begins feeling Ellie's lymph nodes before carefully opening her mouth and looking inside.

"There isn't a sign of an allergic reaction as such, no swelling in or around her mouth that I can see." He checks her arms and pulls up her t-shirt, checking her torso for rashes, finally pulling the blanket back over her shivering body. Charlie stands and scratches his chin.

"We need to get her admitted to hospital for monitoring because I have no idea what has caused her current state." He looks at me again, clearly seeing my shock.

"Just to be on the safe side, Lion." I run both hands through my hair in panic.

"Fuck I don't think we can explain it to the hospital, I mean how do we explain the quickening?" Charlie's jaw drops. He turns to Ellie and checks her pupils before retaking her obs.

"Are you telling me that she is having a reaction to you?" He says incredulously. I will never forget the look of pure horror on his face as I nod, feeling mortified.

"Yes, we had sex tonight. She was fine beforehand, and during, but she felt warm when I left her." I watch as Charlie places his hand on her forehead, his brow furrows as he sits back down on the side of the bed and takes her pulse for the third time.

"I'm completely at a loss for words Lion, you have heard of safe sex, have you not!" Charlie shakes his head in disbelief and then I see the realisation of what I have just said hit him.

"I have always thought they were stories to make sure we practised safe sex." He strokes his chin as he looks down at Ellie's shivering frame. I run my hand through my hair before pointing at her, my voice rising in panic.

"Clearly fucking not! Look at her Charlie. This has got to be caused by the quickening, she was fine an hour and a half ago." I begin pacing the room, my mother's words ringing in my ears. It must be the quickening; it must be. I walk over to the table and notice the two cups of camomile tea that I had made earlier have gone, two teacups sit side by side devoid of their contents and there are small puddles on the tables surface from where the tea has spilt. She did what I said and attempted to drink the tea that I had left for her.

"So, what do we do then?" Expecting Charlie to insist on taking Ellie to Accident and Emergency, he checks her over again.

"We stay here and keep her comfortable, if there are any changes then we will take her straight to hospital. But right now, we wait it out." I nod in agreement and take my place next to Ellie on the bed. She is really shivering, so I lie down next to her with my chest to her back under the blanket, using my body temperature to help stabilise hers.

"Was it worth the wait?" I look over to Charlie who has just sat down at the table, he looks down as he makes notes in that pad of his. I smile and plant a kiss on the back of Ellie's head.

"Was it worth waiting a lifetime for...Yes it was worth it."

"You know Lion, I never could understand why you chose to wait for her, hoping for a chance to be with her. Our parents were so worried about you. The way her mother kept you away like she did. I guess her death changed all that. I shake my head knowing full well that he can't see me, his face will be stuck in that note-book of his.

"She wanted me to look after Ellie after her death, she asked me to. She gave me her blessing to pursue her daughter. She wanted to die knowing that Ellie would be looked after." Charlie lets out a sigh and I hear his pen drop to the table.

"That is creepy Lion, if I do say so myself. What would you have done if she wasn't interested in you romantically? I mean you spent years hunting that poor girl down. You were obsessed with her. What if she doesn't want you the same way? Especially after tonight." I kiss Ellie's hair before I answer, hoping that doesn't happen.

"I made a promise to her mother that I wouldn't make myself a nuisance if she rejected me. I just hoped that she would grow to love me as much as I love her." Charlie snorts.

"Lion you are crazy, you really are. And I thought our mother crazy too. Knowing the human body, the quickening isn't natural. Humans have the ability to make monogamous decisions, the human body and behaviour doesn't change, like this." Ellie's shivering begins to subside slightly, she doesn't feel as cold as she did half an hour ago. I sit up slightly as Charlie comes over and takes her temperature and observations again.

"That is a good sign. Her temperature is dropping, her oxygen saturation is back to 100 percent." He reaches over and lifts her wrist again, taking her pulse while looking at his watch the entire time. He frowns as he places her hand carefully back down on the bed.

"Amazing, her racing pulse has slowed and seems to have returned to normal. This is crazy, if her symptoms are truly caused by the quickening, I mean." Charlie shakes his head in disbelief.

"As a doctor, I thought that the stories of the quickening were bullshit. When I questioned mum about it, she swore it happened to her but what she described was period pains, plain and simple." I lie back down beside Ellie, moving as close to her as I possibly can.

"And it's never happened to any of the women I have been with." Charlie looks thoughtful for a moment.

"You can't deny our mother is a fierce hunter, Charlie. She is stronger and faster than father was, and you have seen the pictures of her before she married father. Chubby is putting it mildly. In under a year of marriage she physically changed, from someone who couldn't run for a bus to someone who could outrun one at 40mph." Charlie laughs at my statement.

"Yes, well a change in diet and a decent exercise regime could have had a lot to do with it, Lion, you know that. I think I am going to have words with mother tomorrow. Find out if she is aware of anyone else this has happened to in the last thirty years." Ellie stirs, mumbling something in her sleep. Charlie is back, checking her pupils, pulse, and temperature. Thankfully all appear to be back to normal. Ellie groans, paws his hand away from her face and then falls back into deep slumber.

Charlie sits back down at the table and adds the latest data into his notebook. After another hour, Ellie is looking much better, colour has returned to her cheeks. I run my fingers through her hair, de-tangling the red strands as best I can, adjusting the blanket around her small frame and covering her back. I walk around the bed, sit down on its edge and face Charlie.

"You know if what mother said is true, you two will be joined at the hip. The whole quickening thing keeps hunters together. Ball and chain fashion." Charlie states matter of fact.

"Really? I don't remember mother ever mentioning that." I reply as I study Charlie removing his glasses and watching him rubs his eyes, before putting them back on.

"Mother told me she wanted to leave him years ago and who could blame her, but the quickening stopped her from doing so, or so she said. If there is an element of truth in that, then you're stuck with Ellie for the rest of your life."

I am a little taken aback by the uncomfortable information regarding my parents' marriage, yet I can't help but smile. Being with Ellie forever is all I have wanted for as long as I can remember. The room falls quiet as we both look at Ellie both lost in our own thoughts. Charlie looks perplexed.

"Have you spoken to mother recently?" I shake my head at my brother's question.

"Mother is always busy with her work, so I tend not to bother her. She phones me when she wants to check in." I momentarily think about my screwed-up family. I am a skilled hunter, have an excellent reputation and get the job done quickly and cleanly.

Seb keeps tabs on hunts, chases up payments, checks out safety and makes reputable contacts. On occasion stepping into help hunt, he is an accomplished hunter himself. All the while my father sits on his high horse, at the head of the family business, reaping the financial benefits yet being next to useless. Having clung onto the family name and reputation for as long as I can remember.

Charlie is the only one who escaped, becoming a well-respected doctor and GP. And my mother, well, she gave up parenting in favour of her research. Research that has got us no further on why we became hunters in the first place, she found a gene that we all have, that Ellie and her family all have as do a dozen or so hunting families across the globe but has been unable to unlock it. I rub my eyes; it has been one hell of a day and a seriously hellish night. I need coffee to help keep my focus.

"They love you; you know." I snap my head up and face Charlie.

"Are you getting sentimental in your old age?" Charlie laughs.

"Not at all, I see our parents more than you do, you are focused on hunting and Ellie and that is good. You need to share all of this with someone. I hope things work out between you and she doesn't blame you for what has happened here tonight. I think her mother kept her completely in the dark." Charlie stops and nervously fidgets with his hands, something he has done since he was a child and why he is a GP and not a surgeon.

"What I am trying to say Lion is we all love you, just be careful. When Ellie finds out exactly what we do, she may not be as interested in you like you hope." I shrug, I have a terrible feeling that he could be right, she may not want any part of this, any part of me or my world when I tell her what we are. I only hope her heart will help guide her to me.

"Water." Ellie moans and rolls over. Charlie and I are by her side in seconds. She is stirring and her eyes flutter open.

"Water." She mumbles again, I look to Charlie who nods his head.

Walking to the bathroom I fill a glass that I swiped from the table and fill it halfway. I watch Charlie check her over again before I am allowed to give her a sip. Tipping her head back slightly, I drizzle the water into Ellie's dry mouth. She swallows keeping her eyes firmly closed. I lie her back down where she falls back to sleep.

"It looks like everything is back to normal here. She will have a major headache and muscle fatigue when she wakes up. Encourage her to drink plenty of water and give her paracetamol should the headache persist. I'm going to shoot if that is, okay? Any problems, call me and I'll come straight back." I smile and extend my hand to my brother. Charlie grins and pulls me into a bear hug instead.

"Take care of yourself Lion and take care of her. She is precious." I look down at Ellie and nod in agreement.

CHAPTER EIGHTEEN

Confessions Of A Sort

My tired eyes try to focus on the dimly lit room, the pounding in my head makes it difficult to think and I ache from head to toe.

"Hey kitten, how are you feeling?" I move my head with difficulty towards the sound of the whisper and look over to the right of me. There lies Julian, his big green eyes staring back, waiting patiently for my response. He gives me a weak smile, he looks worried. I'm confused. Madly my mind flips through memory after memory. I remember Julian coming here. I remember what we did. Oh Shit! I remember the searing pain ripping through me. I swallow or at least attempt to; my throat is dry and sore.

"You came back." I say huskily. Bits of the puzzle starts fitting together, I remember being with him, I remember him being quiet and cold after we slept together and then him leaving. I remember the vomiting and the pain. I was alone. I rub my eyes and mentally check myself over, I seem to be in one piece, yet my muscles are sore. Julian raises an eyebrow at me before frowning.

"You gave me a real fright." I continue to stare at him not knowing what to say. I move slightly, trying to alleviate the pounding in my head, did I dream what happened after he left last night? I am lying in my bed with Julian lying next to me and something just isn't adding up. I'm clearly missing a huge chunk of the night.

"What time is it? I finally ask.

"It is just after ten." He answers placing his hand on my forehead.

"How do you feel?"

"My head is throbbing and I'm really thirsty. What happened?" The last thing I really remember is feeling like I was dying. Now I am lying in bed with a dry mouth, aching muscles, and a head-ache, If I didn't know better, I would say I was recovering from one hell of a hangover after being violently beaten. The question on the tip of my tongue is how I got here. Julian sweeps his dark hair back and away from his face, never taking his eyes from mine.

"I am so sorry for leaving you Ellie. I never would have guessed it would have affected you like it did, when I came back and you didn't open the door, I thought you were just pissed at me for leaving. When I finally managed to get in, I found you un-conscious on the floor." I focus my eyes on his green penetrative stare, trying to piece together what happened last night.

"What affected me?" I feel myself starting to panic, bile hits the sensitive spot at the back of my throat and instinct tells me to try to sit up. Was I drugged? I eye Julian with suspicion as he takes my hand whilst trying to settle me back down.

"I'm so sorry for leaving you."

"What happened to me?" I demand, my voice deep and men-acing. Julian takes a deep breath.

"Ellie, there is a lot I need to explain to you but first you need to eat. I'm going to help you get dressed and take you out for break-fast." I stare at him dumbfounded.

"How on earth am I supposed to get dressed and eat when a huge chunk of my memory is missing. My body aches like I have been hit by a bus and you want to go for breakfast. I am going nowhere until you tell me what is going on!" I wince as I sit up, seething with fury and defiance. In an instant Julian is off the bed and begins pacing the room. A sick feeling settles in the pit of my stomach as I watch him move.

"Why was I ill Julian?" I shout, my body trembling with anger.

"I want you to know this first. Last night with you was perfect. I have wanted nothing more than to be with you and I waited so long for it to be so." My mind switches off, I'm watching him move, I can hear his voice, I have no idea what he is on about, I have no interest in his feelings, I want the facts.

"Look, this is going to sound absolutely crazy, this is my life and now it is yours too if you choose to join me in it." My ears prick up, these words get my attention and I snap my head towards him, I open my mouth to speak but Julian's dark look silences me.

"You won't remember this, but you used to play naked in my garden, we ate jellybeans together."

I don't remember doing any such thing as my foggy brain tries to rifle through old memories and then it dawns on me, fuck, I do! There was one summer where I spent my days playing in a big garden. I must have been five or six, we stayed with a family who were friends of my mother, we saw the family a lot, they had a dark-haired son who I called Lion.

"No, you can't be." I scramble backwards toward the headboard. No, Julian just can't be the Lion from my childhood.

"You remember don't you." I pull my knees up to my chest and wrap my arms around myself, this is freaking me out. I remember playing with a boy who had long dark hair, long dark eyelashes and piercing green eyes, he always carried a lion toy under his arm, he rarely spoke, unless it was about jellybeans.

"Why haven't you told me this before?" I don't know whether I should be angry with him for keeping it from me or happy to have my childhood playmate back.

"Let's get you dressed; I will tell you about the rest on the way to brunch." Julian glances at his watch, I reach over and pick up my phone from the bedside table, it has just turned eleven. The volume has been muted, the screen shows I have two missed calls and three text messages to read. I put my phone back down, I'll deal with them later, when I get my sanity back. I make my move to get out of bed.

"Drink this first." Julian hands me a glass of apple juice which I gulp greedily. He pulls the duvet off my lower body, I do nothing but watch as he swiftly picks me off the bed, cradling me in his strong arms. I am carried into the bathroom; Julian pulls the toilet seat down and places me gently on the lid while he turns to switch the shower on. Only then do I realise that I am wearing my baggy t-shirt and knickers.

"What's wrong?" He asks concern etched on his handsome features.

"I don't remember getting dressed or getting into bed. What happened Julian or would you prefer I call you Lion?" Julian thrusts his hands under the shower stream, checking the temperature, completely ignoring my question again, but I notice his mouth turn up in a small smile at the mention of Lion.

"Let's get you out of those clothes." He drops to his knees in front of me. Gently he reaches under my t-shirt, and I watch as his hands move slightly as he tugs my knickers down my legs and tosses them to the floor.

"Arms up." I do as I am told and raise my hands into the air as he slowly pulls my t-shirt over my head, throwing it to the floor to lie with my knickers, he is doing all of this on purpose, I am sure. Julian is smart, he is diverting my attention, so he doesn't have to answer my questions. I sit perched on the toilet seat completely nude, yet I feel no embarrassment being alone and naked with him, only a strange feeling of contentment and some nausea. Julian is here and is looking after me. I am scooped up once again and placed upright in the shower. He grabs my washcloth and the shower gel. I take both from his hands, being undressed by him is one thing but I will not allow the indignity of being washed by him also.

"I am perfectly able to take it from here." Julian merely nods, taking a step back. I watch him as I pour vanilla gel and start to massage my aching shoulders.

"Would you like to join me?" I ask glancing over my shoulder; he looks rougher than I do.

"I would love to, but I didn't bring any clean clothes to change into." He shrugs.

"I'll wait for you in the other room." I'm left alone in the shower with my thoughts and without a single answer. The warm water feels good on my skin, soothing the aches. I shampoo and condition my hair quickly, wash my body and switch off the taps. Holding onto the wall I carefully step out of the shower.

Julian is suddenly by my side with a towel. He wraps me up snug and carries me back into my room, placing me on my bed. I sit in uncomfortable silence; Julian has made himself at home going through my wardrobe and selecting an outfit. He throws a dress on my bed and heads to my small chest of drawers pulling out red bra and matching knickers. I watch him closely.

"What?" He asks without looking at me.

"Look at us. We hardly know each other and here you are looking after me, getting me dressed and ready for the day." Julian finally turns around, looking at me with pleading eyes, guilt etched all over his face.

"It is my fault you were sick, Ellie. "

"Don't be silly, you were not responsible for that, unless you poisoned that cake!" Julian scoffs at my way off accusation, he ate a slice of the cake too.

"As I said I'll explain later but first I need to feed you." Julian drops to his knees, tapping each of my calves to get me to lift my foot as he pulls my knickers up my ankles, my knees and towards my hips. He grabs my bra next and hands it to me.

"This, I will leave to you." His statement making me giggle, breaking the tension between us ever so slightly. I take it from him and let my towel drop to the bed, I see his nostrils flare, clearly, he is still affected by my semi nudity. I'm thankful that my being ill hasn't put him off. I pull the bra straps over my arms and do the clasp while Julian grabs my blue summer dress, carefully placing it over my head.

"Ready?" He asks glancing at the door.

"No, I have to run a comb through my hair first." Julian has that in hand too, grabbing my brush off the table and throwing it to me.

* * *

We drive with the windows down, the fresh air blowing on my face, I'm lost in the moment, thinking about how I can phrase my question.

"So how exactly did you make me ill? Don't tell me the cream in the sponge was off?" I mock, laughing lightly to myself.

"No, it wasn't the cake, more what I put inside you?" I look at Julian who is keeping his eyes on the road, he is being serious, there is no hint of a smile on his face. A feeling of dread washes over me.

"What do you mean exactly? Julian keeps his eyes focused on the road.

"To be perfectly honest, I don't really know where to start. It's all so weird and kind of complicated." I look away, he is going to tell me he is riddled with some nasty sexually transmitted disease. As if he knows what I am thinking, he reaches out and squeezes my thigh.

"I don't have any STI's; I have never used needles for recreational purposes and until last night, I have never had unprotected sex. What I do have to tell you will sound odd, it is all completely true. I would never lie to you Ellie." Julian stops and takes another deep breath while I hold mine.

"What happened last night was supposed to happen, destined to in a way. I waited for years for you, always knowing that you were the one for me. I waited for so long, it drove me crazy, but I am happy that I did wait. The fever, cramping and nausea you experienced last night was normal for you, it was your body's reaction to me or specifically a gene I carry. Your reaction means that you carry the gene too."

"Are you trying to tell me that I had some sort of allergic reaction to you?" I ask, while wondering how he knew what my symptoms were.

"No, it was definitely not an allergy. In a nutshell, your body reacted to mine, it seems that your reaction was a genetic compatibility test if you will." I blink hard, I really am none the wiser, I do not understand what he means, I frown, confused.

"Genetically speaking I have a unique ability you could say, it is something that until recently, I didn't realise was in your genes too. When we had sex last night your body had a reaction to mine. The reaction that took place, works a little like the way a vaccination works. Now that you have had the reaction you will be immune to my genetic information in the future so no more sickness. That's a good thing, right?" Julian studies me briefly then moves his head and eyes back to the road. I raise my eyebrows as I consider the nonsense he has just babbled on about, I mull over every single stupid word, while trying to find the words to speak.

"What you're trying to tell me is that you have inoculated me using your own semen. You have done this intentionally and I now have immunity to what exactly? What disease or specifically, what virus did I need protecting from?" I shake my head. I can't believe I am even having this conversation. But I continue.

"When you say immune, what specifically do you mean?" I manage to get the last words out of my mouth while keeping my rising temper under control. What he is saying is utter nonsense, I can feel my blood sugar dropping and I am in desperate need of caffeine.

"You are aware that is not how the human reproductive system works!" Julian mulls this over for a second.

"Okay, I didn't explain that very well, scrap what I just said. Sorry, this is hard to explain. Look my genetic information unlocked a specific ability in you and as crazy as this all sounds, you had a reaction to it. It means that we are genetically compatible as a couple in both the romantic sense and in another way. Until last night, I genuinely thought it was an old wives' tale, utter nonsense and from your expression, this is something you have never heard of." I rub at my throbbing head which is desperately dehydrated. Julian keeps talking but I only hear his last sentence.

"So, this ability of yours has been lying dormant in you and now you will be able to use it so to speak, utilise it when you need to." Julian stops talking and rubs his chin. I can see he is exhausted, he has been up all night, after all. I can't help but laugh in disbelief and wonder if Julian has succumbed to the bug that I had last night, then a scary thought occurs to be.

"Are you trying you tell me that you have super sperm and have just got me pregnant?" Julian's face looks like thunder.

"I really hope I have not got you pregnant, at least not yet."

"Me too, I need to stop at a pharmacy today for the morning after pill." Julian nods his head, and I am thankful that he doesn't argue about that decision.

"Okay, so your super sperm has given me a superpower?" Julian clears his throat, me saying super sperm makes him uncomfortable.

"For all intents and purposes, yes a type of superpower." I gawp at him; I wasn't expecting him to agree. I think I'm going to stop asking questions because I truly don't know if he is joking with me or not. I take a glance over at him and his expression is still deadly serious. Julian sighs and flips the left indicator on, turning us off the road and into a pub car park.

"Where are we?" I ask gazing out of the window. The pub is quaint, an old coach inn.

"We're just outside Newhaven." We get out of the car and Julian steers me through the pub and out into the lovely beer garden, this place is breath-taking. The garden is a fair size, buzzing with flowers, the design although simple, looks stunning, a real English country garden. Julian leads me over to a picnic bench that is situated away from the other tables, a beautiful lavender shrub bustling with bees adds an element of seclusion, partially hidden from view.

"What do you fancy?" I pick up a menu and glance at it, this place serves the usual pub grub, nothing stands out but that could be from being ill last night and the strange conversation we have just had.

"Anything that you recommend?" I ask not looking up.

"The veggie bunch is good."

"I'll have that then, a large black coffee and some tap water please." He gets up and heads inside to order. I sit under the sun, watching the bees and ladybirds buzz around next to me while I think about the last 12 hours. Regardless of what Julian has said, the last few days have been utter madness. I am intrigued by him and a little freaked out that he knew we were playmates as children. I wish he had told me before, that he was my Lion. I am starting to think that he is a Hunter in more than just name, but have I always been his prey? My conversation with Seb springs to mind. I think Julian has kept his eyes on me for quite some time. Julian comes back with the drinks, placing them and our cutlery, complete with a bucket of various condiments on the table.

"Ellie are you alright?" His strong arms lift me clean off the bench.

"What is the matter?" I shake my head.

"Tell me why I called you Lion because I don't remember?" Julian smiles at me, and for a fraction of a second, I think I catch his green eyes twinkle.

"My father told me this because I don't remember it myself, when we were really very young, I carried a stuffed lion around, actually I still have him somewhere. When you used to come and play, you couldn't say my name properly only emphasising the end of my name. So naturally because of my toy lion, you began calling me Lion instead and it stuck. My father still calls me it now, actually all of my family do, it is their little joke."

"I remember your toy lion; you were never without it." I look around and realise I am still in his strong arms, upon his lap.

"Would you mind putting me down now." I command. Julian sets me down on my feet and I scramble back to my seat, glancing around to see how many people have spotted our moment. I take a sip of my coffee. Julian's eyes focus on me as he sips his own. He has gone quiet again, I notice that he has periods where he becomes silent, almost withdrawn. I put my cup down, my eyes meeting his.

"Tell me about this ability I now have thanks to you." I slightly shudder at the thought of something so ridiculous. Julian rests both elbows on the table while clutching his cup between his palms.

"You remember the clay pigeon shooting?" I nod. Yes, I remember that night fondly.

"Well, you were really good. That confirmed to me that you were the Ellie I was looking for, I knew you were, but I needed the confirmation. Someone with no shooting experience being able to grasp the concept and technique, then be able to hit so many clay pigeons on their first attempt are unheard of. From now on and with thanks to the quickening, I would hazard a guess and bet that you would be able to accurately hit every clay pigeon that flew into the air above you. If I gave you a bow and arrow you would be able to hit the target perfectly and without any practice, no doubt if I gave you a basketball you would be able to get it in the basket with no issues at all. You will run faster than you did before, and for longer periods of time. Your physical and athletic ability has increased, as has your common sense and your sense of danger." He stops and smiles.

"And probably your sexual appetite too."

"Phew not much of a change to my life then. Why has this happened? I mean why am I now blessed with these new abilities?" Julian glances around.

"We were born to hunt Ellie." He says simply, his voice low, as if this one sentence will make perfect sense to me, fleeting overheard conversations rattle around my head. My brain on overdrive trying to piece the jigsaw that is my life together.

"We hunt what?" I push a mental image of Godzilla out of my head.

"I really would like you to just tell me what you have got to tell me Julian. Everything you say is in code and I really don't have the brain capacity to work out the message." The handsome man sitting casually opposite me with his messy black hair, days old stubble and still in yesterday's clothes, rolls his coffee cup between his palms, he watches me as I study him.

"This is where it becomes difficult and hard to explain. I was born a hunter, my parents are both hunters, their parents before them and it goes back many generations. Ellie you were also born a hunter, to parents who were also hunters, from a long line of hunters. What we hunt is something so abhorrent that the world has hidden it away." Julian glances at me and holds my gaze.

"What we hunt are called DROMs."

CHAPTER NINETEEN

Choices

Julian is waiting for my reaction and all I can do is take another sip of my coffee. We are no different to anyone else here, a young couple out simply for lunch. Yet my world seems to be on the verge of crashing down around me. I am desperately trying to piece together everything Julian has told me thus far, whilst battling with my emotions and my common sense. What Julian has discussed seems to be in code, because it is so farfetched that it sounds fantastical. I like to think I have a logical brain; I can problem solve. Yet, what he has described so far is biologically and physically impossible and all this nonsense about hunting being in our blood is simply preposterous.

I stifle a nervous laugh as our food arrives, the very thought of me being born to fight is ridiculous and that Julian somehow triggered that reaction in me, borders on insanity. The waitress puts our plates down on the wooden bench then leaves us to our meal. I lock my eyes with Julian. His mood has shifted, something dark lurks under his skin. I pick a mushroom off my plate and pop it into my mouth, chewing slowly, trying to read his body language whilst battling with my lack of appetite. My gut instinct is telling me he is being truthful or at least he believes everything that he has told me so far. I have no idea what he hunts, and I am beginning to feel completely lost and drowning in secrets that never reveal themselves. Yet the pain I experienced last night, that was very real, I have no logical explanation for. Following my lead, Julian picks up his knife and folk and attacks his beef tomato, slicing it in half and half again. He pops a chunk into his mouth, chews before swallowing, placing his cutlery carefully back on his plate.

"What can you tell me here?" The words slip out in a hurried whisper. The last few days my big decision was deciding whether I wanted to be with this man, did I want to meander into a relationship with him. Today I'm trying to figure out what he isn't telling me, I am reading between the lines and getting lost, he is carrying around something ugly and I need to know what it is. This is no longer a game of twenty questions, this goes far deeper, I feel the dread creeping over me.

"I'll tell you a little about me." He says glancing around us then learning towards me and lowering his voice further.

"I was born with the ability to hunt; it comes as a sixth sense to me. My work requires me to be physically fit one hundred percent of the time, others like us are quick but I am quicker. I research, I track, I hunt. If it makes you feel any better, feel free to call it bounty hunting. I search and destroy quickly and cleanly. I am so good in fact that I am constantly called away to handle the more delicate aspects of the job and I'm paid handsomely for my effort. I am very much in demand and that is something you need to understand, if you decide to join me." Julian stops. He considers my stunned expression for a second, choosing to pick up his cutlery and continues to eat. I stare at him; he has a scary side that has just completely put me off my food. Julian's strange explanation is serious, and I don't doubt a single word. I have seen him shoot. I think back to the night he took me on our first date, remembering how accurately he was able to shoot the gun, he did it with such ease, like he has been shooting his whole life.

Then I remember how perfect the gun felt in my hands, how I found it easy to hold, to aim and fire. I do not understand this at all.

I push my plate away, not being able to finish my meal. I place my knife and fork down noisily which gets Julian's attention. Our eyes meet again as I look up and study him for a moment, half expecting him to laugh and tell me this is all a joke and I am a fool who has fallen for it hook, line and sinker but he doesn't. I feel like I am suffocating, I need some breathing space, air, or a slap to the cheek to wake me up. What is a DROM anyway?

"I am going to go and get some cake; do you want some?" I ask, standing and grabbing my bag from the bench next to me and pulling it over my shoulder. I need a few moments away from the table, away from him to make the most important decision of my life.

"Just another coffee, please." I smile sweetly at him as I walk away and head to the toilets.

I stare into the mirror, dabbing at my damp skin with a paper towel. Am I an idiot? No, I am not. I want to bombard him with questions almost as much as I want to run and hide. I dry my hands before rummaging around my bag for my phone. I need to call Nicky; he will know what to do. Reality hits me, I can't possibly turn to Nicky for help with this. What could he do except demand that I leave the pub at once and return to Hedge Hill! I cannot make any sense from what is going on with Julian, how on earth would I expect Nicky to.

I grasp the sink and gaze at myself in the mirror, I look closer at myself. What I do know is that Julian has been in my thoughts and dreams for years, in one way or another. I played with him when we were young, he didn't speak then, not much has changed now. I have the overwhelming urge to run back to that table, to him. The distance between us feels like an ocean and I can't help wondering if what he says is true, is us being together ordained by the stars? Reaching into my bag for my lip balm, my fingers brush against a rogue coin. I grasp it is if holding the key to my fate and am instantly reminded of my favourite play by Tom Stoppard; Rosencrantz and Guildenstern Are Dead.

I understand the difficulty in the ability of making meaningful choices. I am compelled to make a life changing decision right now, yet am being forced into doing so blindly, simply because I am not aware of all the facts. Does it matter? Deep in my heart I know I want Julian, my body feels it too, being merely a few feet away has me yearning for him. Only my common sense tells me to be weary. I look down at the coin in my hand, look at the ornate bracelet I was given for my birthday. Today is my birthday and I need to now let the fates decide. I flip the coin into the air and watch it, as it falls to the floor; heads I leave Julian, tails I stay with him forever.

I return to the bench in the beer garden fifteen minutes later with a tray, one large slice of a vegan chocolate cake, two forks and two more coffees. I put the tray on the cleared table and sit back down opposite Julian.

"I was starting to think you were not coming back." Julian states calmly looking at the cake. I give him a warm smile as I choose my words.

"I flipped a coin while I was in the queue. Tails won so here I am." Julian grins picking up a fork and digs into the cake.

"I thank the laws of probability that tails won." Julian pops the cake into his mouth.

"I have questions and I am not playing games. Tell me about this life you expect me to lead." I watch as he digs into the cake with gusto, as if we are having a perfectly normal conversation.

"For the sake of argument, let's call my profession bounty hunting. If you wanted to, you could join me. I would very much like for you to partner with me. It is dangerous work but easier if there are two of us. We would, could work as a team. If that doesn't appeal to you, we can just continue to be lovers, I promise not to push you into my world if you don't want to. Either way we can stay together, we can marry, have children. We can do whatever you want to do and are comfortable with." I deliberate over his words picking up my coffee cup and blowing on the hot black liquid before taking a welcoming sip. He has it all worked out.

"How long have you been bounty hunting?" I scrutinize his handsome features while waiting for his response. His brow furrows as he peers at me, his jaw set tight. He briefly glances around us then his eyes are back and boring into mine. I have chosen to ignore his speech on being lovers, a wife, and a mother, choosing to focus on his so-called profession. I want to know what it is he hunts. What a DROM is.

"I beheaded my first DROM when I was eighteen years of age." I gasp, beheaded is a strong term.

"Beheaded." I whisper letting the word sink in. These DROMs he hunts, he beheads them. Can this get any worse? I am strangely calm. In the last hour I have realised the sweet, thoughtful, and romantic man I have been getting to know is a killer of DROMs. I am sitting with someone who is dangerous.

"Ellie whether you like it or not, you have always been a part of this, a part of my life. I have always known you were the same as me, last night proved that." Julian's voice is low and husky, he reaches over the bench, extending his hand and gently rubs my check. He tilts my chin up and smiles, I see that dimple, the tiny groove in his skin to the right of his lips that make him look so human, masking the monster hiding inside.

"When we were kids, you were all I talked about. When we stopped seeing you, I felt like a piece of me was missing. At eighteen I came looking for you. You had been whisked away on a, around the world trip by your mother. I got caught up with my degree and starting a new life when one evening during my Christmas break, I was forced to kill my first DROM. I won't go into details now, but I had been trained. It was a matter of putting my training in practice. I know how all of this must sound to you. How you must feel hearing this. I grew up knowing what I was to become, it didn't make it any easier that night."

"Wow!" I breathe. I remember Lion, the shy little boy, always so quiet. I had on occasion wondered what happened to him but nothing like Julian's obvious obsession for me. But there is that word again; beheaded. Whatever he hunts, he kills them by be-heading them.

"What exactly is a DROM?" Julian looks around the pub garden, we are very much alone.

"Have you finished? Let's go and I'll explain in the car." I nod in silence; my head isn't doing well with all this new information. I rub my tummy, hoping the mild nausea will subside soon. We both stand and Julian holds his hand out for me to take.

"As it is your birthday, I want to take you to the beach. I'll explain about the lie we live and what DROMs actually are on the way."

CHAPTER TWENTY

Surprises

"What did you behead Julian? What is a DROM?" We pull out of the car park and onto the main road, Julian puts his foot down and we zoom off.

"DROM stands for. Deceased. Revenant. Onus. Monstrosity." He enunciates each word as I look blankly at him.

"Damn it! I forgot my dictionary today, silly me."

"Sarcasm doesn't suit you kitten." Julian retorts, keeping his eyes on the road as he switches gear. I am sick to the back teeth of him talking in code.

"If you want us to work together. If you want me in your life. If you want this to ever work between us. You need to start explaining yourself fully. I am over the beating around the bush bullshit. Spit it out. What the hell is a deceased monstrosity or whatever?" Julian laughs out loud.

"I am fucking in love with you." I stare gob smacked, and for the very first time I recognise Lion, my childhood friend sitting next to me.

"You love me. Great. I get that bit. Now tell me what a DROM is!" I recognise the Royal Pavilion in the distance as we reach Brighton. Julian finds a spot to park the car and switches off the ignition. He gets out and comes around to me, opening the door, sweeping me into his arms. I reach up and wrap my arms around him as he holds me tightly, burying my face in his neck.

"I'm so sorry Ellie, my life is madness and I've dragged you into it."

"I mean it Ellie. I am in love with you." He kisses me on the top of my head as he pronounces each word carefully. Julian places me back firmly on the ground, I'm hesitant about letting him go but still need answers.

"I get it, I do. You love me. I love you." The words are out of my mouth before I can think. Julian beams. It wasn't the way I wanted to tell him how I felt, I know this is another stall tactic and I can only guess that DROMs are something horrific, it is why he is taking his sweet time in explaining to me.

Julian pulls me by the hand, we stroll along Brighton beach in silence, crunching the pebbles underfoot. I stop and pick up an interesting one and skim it into the choppy sea. I decide that for the rest of the day I don't want to hear any more talk of secret powers, beheadings, or shared childhoods. As much as I know his declaration of love was another diversion tactic, I am grateful for it. Before I find out exactly what it is I have become and what exactly a monstrosity whatever is. I just want a few more hours of a normal existence.

I flipped that coin and promised myself to stick with the outcome. In the pit of my stomach, I know that whatever it is that Julian has left to divulge; it is going to change my life forever and I am okay with that. But for the rest of my birthday, I just want to focus on the connection Julian and I share, no more drama.

"I could really do with a birthday ice cream." I declare heading towards the closest ice cream and gelato parlour and pulling Julian with me by the hand. The sun is high in the sky and beaming down on us, the pebbles beneath us glint and twinkle under the hazy sunshine.

"What would you like birthday girl?" I peruse the menu of pictures on the glass window.

"I want a large vegan soft serve with hundreds and thousands on top please." Julian rolls his eyes.

"You are a big child." He retorts, tickling me in the ribs before he orders. The ice cream man hands Julian a double cone, each cup filled high with soft white deliciousness, colourful sprinkles scattered over the top. I grin when he hands me the cone.

"Thank you." I am impressed at the sheer size of the ice cream.

"You know it's doubtful that I can eat it all by myself, so you are welcome to share it with me."

"I'm a mint choc chip kind of guy." He replies with a smile, I get a glimpse of carefree Julian as he orders his gelato and pays. It is easy to forget that me being here with him is all new to him too. I walk along with my ice cream, scanning the beach. I feel settled for now in a strange place that is not happy but no longer scared.

"Let's sit over there." I point to a spot which is secluded. We sit together side by side, our thighs touching, watching the waves crash along the beach. I glance at Julian out of the corner of my eye. He loves me, he kills monsters and has somehow heightened my sympathetic nervous system. I take a big lick of the stupidly large and colourful cone; it tastes good, yet I can't help but think about everything that has happened over the last 24 hours. I have made my decision. My life has been mundane at best, I survive each day and have done for as long as I can remember, a life with no real purpose, like millions of others. Now it is time to take a chance, a risk that will change my life forever. And if Julian turns out to be a nut job, I won't hesitate to haul his arse in the direction of the police. Nibbling on my cone, watching the waves hit the shore, Julian lies back on the beach. Two brazen seagulls, get closer to me, I toss the remnants of the cone in their direction, one grabbing it and takes flight.

"You shouldn't feed them you know; they are pests." I smile at Julian and roll my eyes.

"I like feeding the birds, pests or not." I reply with a mouth full of chocolate, feeling like we are headed back onto the right path. Julian leans back, propping himself up on one elbow.

"You have some sprinkles there." He wipes them from the corner of my mouth, before licking his thumb.

"I like you. You can buy me ice cream again." I state matter of fact. Julian sits up and leans closer to me, his lips barely touch my ear.

"I love you. I think I might have mentioned that before." I turn my head to face him and feel his soft lips brush mine. We become lost in each other in seconds. I run my hands through his hair pulling roughly. He moans into my mouth and pushes me back, his torso on mine. I want him now, every synapse is firing, a sensation that is setting me ablaze. The word DROM flashes and I manage to pull away, taking a breath, he opens his eyes lazily.

"I think we should head back to Hedge Hill. The traffic will be murder if we leave it any later." I state. I am desperate to feel Julian's body against mine again, suddenly needing to relieve my primal urges.

It is just after five by the time we arrive back at the hotel, I sneak Julian in the back way, I really can't face anyone now. We run up the fire exit stairs and down the hall hand in hand to my room. I feel like a teenager doing something I shouldn't. I push my key in the door and walk, pulling Julian in behind me. I gasp, my entire room is filled with colourful balloons and bouquets of flowers of every type. I turn around, taking in all three hundred and sixty degrees of bricks and mortar that comprises my personal space, every surface is covered.

"Happy birthday." Julian whispers in my ear, then kisses my temple. Tears well in my eyes.

"This is beautiful and surprising." I reply with an overwhelmed smile. Julian wraps me in his arms, he lifts my chin up so our eyes meet.

"I have been waiting for you for so long Ellie." I reach up on my tiptoes and really kiss him with everything I have. Despite all that we have talked about, this crazy new world I'm now involved in. All that angst has finally melted away, it doesn't bother me anymore. My brain, body and heart are finally in agreement. Julian and I were somehow meant to be. Julian picks me up effortlessly, I wrap my legs around his waist. He moves towards my bed and puts me down, kneeling on the floor in front of me.

"We definitely don't need this." He pulls my dress over my head and gently throws it to the ground. He kisses my left shoulder and then the right.

"Ellie, you are so beautiful." He whispers as he tugs the straps of my bra down my arms then reaches behind me to undo the clasp.

"I can do that." I say huskily, he has beaten me to it, sliding the straps along my arms and throws it over to where my dress now lies. I'm naked except for my knickers. He moves closer and takes my left nipple in his mouth. My eyes flutter closed, and I groan in unadulterated pleasure. The sensation of his mouth on me is doing terrible things, I feel like I may explode any minute. He stops, as if reading my mind.

"You're doing terrible things to me." I utter breathlessly. His lips brush mine as I reach out and attempt to undo the top button on his shirt.

"Leave the shirt on." He growls, his nostrils flaring. I remove my hands from his neck and raise my eyebrow. I don't say anything, I will ask him about his shirt issues later. Julian runs his hands up my thighs stopping at my knickers.

"These need to come off. Now." He slides his thumbs under the fabric then pulls them down with force. Julian slides them down my legs and throws them behind him. I sit there holding my breath, He takes his time, studying my body. A small smile dancing on his lips.

"You are the most breath-taking women on this planet and most definitely worth the wait." He trails off as I grab his face and pull it close. I reach down and undo the button on his trousers with fumbling fingers, he helps by standing and pulling his trousers down, quickly stepping out of them. I pull Julian onto me, kissing and caressing his muscles through his shirt.

"I need you." I whisper positioning my body closer. Seconds turn to minutes and minutes feel like hours until we are both spent, lying in a heap on my bed. Julian rests his head on my stomach, his shirt buttons tickling my hip.

"Wow."

"Wow indeed, where did you learn to do that." I tease.

"Porn actually, I've had a lot of time on my hands over the years." I feel his grin as he kisses my hip bone, I can't help but grin too. We lie in a comfortable and cosy silence, after a time, Julian slides off me and lies on his side. I move my exhausted body slightly so I can gaze at him.

"I want to do that again." The words are out of my mouth which makes him smile.

"What now? He enquires, I peep at him through tired eyes. Julian laughs heartily.

"No, not right this minute." I reply, planting a gentle kiss on his nose.

"That is a shame." He grins as he attempts to wink at me lazily. I kiss him, stroking the stubble on his jaw. I like him with stubble. His green eyes flash, he looks completely blissed out, lying here beside me, his dark, handsome features are soft and relaxed. I'm blissed out too and can't stop myself from moving forward and kissing him on the end of his nose again.

"Sorry about the mess, I figured pulling out although not the safest against pregnancy may stop the quickening from happening again. If it were to happen again." I'm puzzled.

"What's the quickening?" Forgetting about any bodily fluids that may be on my body. Julian reaches out and tucks my hair behind my ear in a tender manner.

"It was the reaction you had to me. The cramping is supposed to resemble the feeling of those first gentle, foetal movements in pregnancy. I can't confirm or deny this, as I have never experienced either." I think about this and how I currently feel. I mentally check myself over, we have been lying here for half an hour and I feel fine.

"I think we need condoms." I state.

"Just so the quickening thing doesn't happen again. I hope you have a book or manual explaining all of this to me. There is a hell of a lot I need to know." Julian and I are disturbed by a loud knock on my door.

"Open up Ellie." Nicky is outside, pounding on the wood. I put my finger up to my lips. Julian copies me while trying to stifle his laugh.

"I know you're in there. If you don't open, I'm letting myself in." I hear a key rattle outside.

I jump off the bed and grab my robe, throwing it on and opening the door.

"Finally, Ellie. I have been trying to call you all day. You had me worried darling." Nicky pushes past me and into my room.

"Lovely flowers." He stops dead, his eyes focused on my bed.

"Hi Julian." Nicky's demeanour instantly changes, he is in his element looking from Julian to me. Julian on the other hand has an embarrassed smile and a pillow covering his well-endowed modesty.

"I'm taking you out for a birthday drink. You of course are more than welcome to join us, Julian. I'll meet you in the bar in an hour. And wear something nice, it is your birthday." Nicky kisses me on the cheek before walking out. I close the door.

"Right then, we have our orders, up you get and let's go shower." Julian watches me, the pillow still placed over his groin.

"I'll go get changed in my room." He stands dropping the pillow, revealing his arousal.

"If you come shower with me, I can do something about that." I raise my eyebrow willing him to join me. Julian looks torn, not sure what to do. I drop my robe on the floor and casually walk naked into the bathroom, switching the shower on, getting under the water. I hear Julian enter behind me, he walks over and presses his naked chest into my back. I turn around and smile, finally I get to see this gorgeous man naked.

CHAPTER TWENTY-ONE

Inky Confessions

I fully see why Julian was hesitant to let me remove his shirt. I had simply wondered whether Julian had a third nipple or an offensive scar of some description on his body, I was wrong on both fronts. Julian studies my face as my eyes wander over his upper torso, moving from nipple to nipple, shoulder to shoulder and down to the top of his hip bones. I look down his arms to his wrists and must stop myself from asking him to turn around. Julian eyes me wearily.

"Now you know why I kept my shirt on." My eyes flutter up to his. How long did he think he could hide this from me?

"Yes." I reply concentrating on his masculine features, with my initial shock over, my eyes rove over his body, noticing the muscle definition that lies beneath his skin, water from the shower trickling over us.

"I think I may have figured out what your hobby is. You are into knitting right." I reach out and run my hand down his smooth chest, feeling every hard muscle from his pectorals down to his beautifully defined abs. Julian laughs nervously and flinches at my touch.

"I have a thing for needles." He says as I smile up at him. My hands continue to explore his soft skin. Black ink covers the top half of Julian's body.

"Why were you embarrassed to show me?" I query as I place my hand over my heart. One pattern stands out and catches my eye, it is larger than some of the others, situated above his heart. The tattoo is of a perfect circle containing an hourglass. I kiss Julian there, placing my lips on the centre of the hourglass, his heartbeat increases beneath his breastbone.

"I like what I see so far but I love this one. What is it?" Julian smiles and releases his breath.

"This is the extinction symbol. The circle represents the world while the hourglass serves as a distinct warning that time is running out. I'm glad these don't freak you out." He says pointing to his chest with his thumb.

"You were worried I would freak out about seeing your tattoos and these." I run my fingers over the two balls of metal that protrude from each of his nipples.

"Yet you tell me you behead DROMs and what not. I am still waiting for you to tell me what these DROMs are?" I stop for a moment, my finger tracing the circle of the extinction symbol, I can no longer keep quiet. I have asked questions; I have been disappointed and have been treated like a princess and now I must let it all out.

"You know that your way of thinking is warped, there is so much you have yet to explain, so much I need to know about you and your life, so much you have held back over the last year. Then you arrive, sweep me off my feet with romance, kidnap me, romance me again then you fuck me, fuck up my birthday, fuck up my insides, fuck with my mind and then fuck me again. And through all of this, it was a few tattoos that worried you. You are funny, in a funny peculiar kind of way." Julian takes a step back from me, rivulets of water running down his body, I think I may have upset him.

"You are right. I have given absolutely no thought about how you are dealing with this. I really have piled it all on you and expected you to just accept what I have said and done. I am touched that you trust me this much when you know so little." I move toward the stream of water, allowing the heat to clear my mind and sooth my skin. I trust him in ways I cannot explain, any other relationship and this would boarder on narcissism and gaslighting. There is a pulling in my gut, a knowing that he hasn't lied to me. Julian has only tried to keep me safe. Eureka! Maybe when he tells me the full story, I will finally feel like I have been drawn out of the dark and into the light.

"Julian, I want you to tell me everything. Starting at the beginning. I want to know what you are. I need to know what I am and most importantly what on earth a bloody DROM is, because all I know about them is you remove their heads." I move deeper into the stream of warm water, my hair getting wet.

"But first, you need to join me." I reach my hand out of the shower beckoning him towards me, dripping water everywhere. He hesitates before accepting, wrapping his fingers around mine. I pull him back into the shower with me.

"I have a problem." Julian state's rubbing the towel over his naked body. I sit on my bed in my underwear with my towel wrapped around my head.

"You have a lot of problems, just saying." I state calmly taking in his gloriously muscular and decorated torso.

"I have no clean clothes here. I would just chuck on what I was wearing earlier but my shirt is covered in, well you know." He holds his stained shirt out to me; I wrinkle my nose in disgust.

"I don't want those thanks." I knock the stained shirt away from my face, causing it to fall on the floor much to Julian's amusement.

"What do you want to do? I have dresses you could wear?" Julian gives me a seriously sexy hooded grin, we could just stay in, no clothes necessary.

"We haven't done it on your floor yet and I am sure we can put your table to good use too!" I pull the wet towel off my head and hurl it at him.

"I have created a monster." I snipe while attempting to run a comb through my matted hair.

"Now that I have had a taste of you, I don't want to ever stop." Julian grins and I can't help returning it.

"Well, romantic as that is, I'm almost dressed, would you like me to go to your room and get you some clean clothes?" I realise as I say the words out loud that I have never been to Julian's room, I don't even know what floor he is on.

"Would you mind? It doesn't bother me about popping up to my room in just my trousers, but I don't want to frighten anyone. Knowing my luck, I would run straight into one of your ultra conservative old dears." He looks down at his chest and smiles.

"I don't think you would frighten anyone to be honest, but I understand you not wanting to turn the old dears on. They are man eaters here; Nicky constantly gets his bottom pinched." Julian laughs to himself.

"Do you always cover up your body?" I ask hoping he doesn't.

"No, I don't. I only cover up when I am here. I didn't want to freak you out, with what I had and still have to tell you. I figured these may have been the last straw." I'm genuinely happy to hear this, I've never thought about tattoos before but seeing them on Julian, I have concluded that they are nice to look at but on him they are damn right sexy.

"You are right though, you still have a lot to explain Julian, I am placing my trust in you so don't forget that." He nods in understanding.

"And I will explain. I promise" I walk to my wardrobe smiling, hoping to hear his story soon.

"Thank you for all the beautiful flowers dotted around the room. And thank you for looking after me last night. I'm guessing you cleaned me up?" I grab my cream dress off the hanger and put it on.

"When you didn't open your door, I got worried and broke in. When I found you, you were sweating and so pale, it scared the hell out of me. You were unconscious and bleeding on the floor. I picked you up, cleaned you and got you dressed, putting you to bed. I cleaned up the blood and tidied up the candles. Then I spent the night monitoring you until you woke." I stand horrified. I hadn't realized how bad it must have looked. I remember the searing pain and nausea, but it must have looked frightful to him.

"Thank you, where did the blood come from?" I hear the panic in my own voice, haunted that he had to do all of that when I have no recollection of it and now fearing I was bleeding from somewhere I shouldn't be bleeding from.

"You had a nosebleed." He states matter of fact, rubbing his towel through his hair, I look up my nose in the mirror, all seems fine. I have never had a nosebleed.

"Okay, I'm ready. What is your room number?" I enquire as Julian who is still completely naked tries vainly to paw at me. The look of him is doing serious things to my libido, his lovely hips, chest and his beautifully sculptured shoulders have me practically drooling.

"I'm tucked away in room four twenty-five." He picks up his trousers and pulls out a black wallet, opening it and handing me his key card. I suck in my breath, room four twenty-five. That suite is nicknamed the penthouse.

"Thanks, is there anything in particular you want me to grab?" Julian thinks for a minute.

"You'll find everything in the wardrobe. Could I please have a pair of jeans, a t-shirt and a jacket." I smirk, no undies. Lovely, he is a commando kind of guy. I slip on a pair of black flip flops.

"I'll be back in a minute. make yourself comfortable" I head out into the hall. I had absolutely no idea Julian was in the penthouse. I have been up there once with Nicky when it was being renovated and it is a seriously plush space. The room is not officially called the penthouse, it is just our nickname for the largest and most expensive suite in the hotel. I walk quickly to the stairs and up to the fourth floor.

I reach his door and put the card in its reader, the green light flashes as the door clicks open. I walk into the vast room, with its big, beautiful windows that overlook the hotel gardens. The room is huge, divided into sections, the bedroom area is on the right-hand side of the room, it houses a dark bed that is made from solid oak and is the centrepiece of the room. The bed itself is a four poster and is tastefully decorated with dark brown linen and cream cushions.

I turn around and notice the sofa has been moved from the lounge area, it now sits directly in front of the largest window. I stand behind it, looking out to the grounds of the hotel below. From up here Julian has the perfect view of the entire gardens and me when I'm out there working.

The suite houses a massive bathroom, with a large walk-in shower complete with four shower heads and a giant oval shaped bathtub that could easily fit two people, three at a squeeze. I walk back into the main suite and glance at the large office area, Julian's desk is piled high with books, papers, his laptop, and a tablet. The shelves behind the desk stacked high with more books and box files. This area is most definitely in use, he clearly has been working whilst here. As much as I have his permission to be in his room, I feel like I am snooping just by glancing around. I notice no television at all, just two speakers in the living room section, that he must play music through his phone with.

I head to the giant walk in wardrobe and locate his clothes. I pull out a pair of button-fly, stonewashed Levi's, and a navy linen jacket. I walk to the other end and find his t-shirts all folded neatly. I grab the first that sits at the top of the pile and close the wardrobe doors. Spotting the large oak chest of drawers, I start to rummage, he does indeed have underwear, so I grab a pair of jockey shorts and some socks too just in case. I notice his shoes all lined up against one wall. I pick up a pair of Vans trainers and leave the room with my arms full. I take a last glance around Julian's room and notice the novel sitting by his bed, it is battered and well-read and instantly I gravitate towards it. I pick the book up and am surprised to see it is a very old copy of Les Trois Mousquetaire by Alexandre Dumas. I flip the book over and read the back, remembering how I had read the translated English version years ago.

"You were quick." Julian says as he rushes over to me when I enter the room, sweeping me off my feet and swinging me around. I giggle like a teenager. I am loving all this touchy-feely attention from him. I hand him his clothes when he finally lets me go, which he throws down onto the floor casually, choosing to pick me up again instead. I am nuzzled and caressed, he inhales deeply before showering me with kisses. His display of affection does wonderful things to me. I like this carefree side and I like how it makes me feel happy. I pull away and laugh.

"Nicky will come and knock this door down if we are not in the bar on time." Julian groans as he puts me back down and picks his clothes up. I watch him as he pulls his jeans on without the jockey shorts. He slips the t-shirt over his head.

"Good choice kitten, this is one of my favourites." I unknowingly chose a shirt with Iron Maiden written across the front and a scary looking monster across the back. I raise an eyebrow. I have heard of them. Julian pulls his socks on and then sinks his feet into his trainers.

"Good choice with the shoes too." He flashes me a heart melting grin revealing his perfect white teeth. Shrugging on his jacket, he puts his wallet and phone in his back pocket and holds his hand out to me.

"Ready to go birthday girl?" I'm pulled out of my reverie, I got completely lost watching him dress.

"Ah no not yet." I blurt out as I dash to the bathroom and close the door. I take a moment to calm down. I'm going out with Julian tonight as one half of a couple and I'm fine with that, I will just have to ignore Nicky's big brother routine and teasing. I glance at the mirror; my skin is glowing; my hair is under control, but I need a little something extra. I grab my makeup bag and apply some mascara and lip gloss. Now I am good to go.

Julian is sitting on my bed waiting, he looks laid back, his messy hair damp and swept off his face, his dark stubble clearly visible, accentuating his jaw and outlining the cupid bow of his top lip.

"All done?" Julian smirks revealing that sexy dimple of his. It is now my turn to grin as I nod my head and grab my handbag. Holding my hand out to him, he clasps it, and we leave to face Nicky down in the bar.

CHAPTER TWENTY-TWO

Like Buses, Two Come Along At Once

"Finally, the birthday girl has decided to join us." Nicky is out of his seat and wrapping his arms around me, squeezing me hard. I elbow him in the ribs and Nicky feigns injury with mock winces. I smile up at him and squeeze him back, resting my head on his chest. Happy to be back in the comfort and safety of my very best friend, it feels like forever since I saw him last. Jamie, Andy, and Alice are all seated around the table. Julian pulls out a chair for me and I sit down. He plonks himself next to me with Nicky sitting on my other side. I introduce everyone to Julian and Jamie gives me the thumbs up from across the table when she thinks Julian isn't looking. Everyone makes small talk; I feel a little giddy having my friends here to celebrate the final hours of my birthday with me. Nicky, Jamie, and Andy are all more than aware of how I retreated into myself when my mother died. I feel blessed that they have taken time out of their evening to see me tonight. Of course, having Julian by my side completes my evening. I am beginning to feel like my old self, which has been a distant memory for so long, I'm getting my life back as each day passes.

The hotel bar is busy, people are milling about, drinking, and chatting. I look round our table as a tray with glasses and a bottle of sparkling water arrives. Nicky, forever the host, begins doing the honours, pouring, adding a slice of lime and a cube of ice to each glass before handing them out. I take a sip as Nicky raises his into the air.

"To Ellie." I flush red as everyone raises their glasses before Nicky leads our friends into a rendition of happy birthday. Having happy birthday sung to you although sweet, is highly embarrassing when you reach adulthood. As soon as Nicky's booming voice begins singing, everyone in the bar stopped what they were doing, looked over at us and began to join in. I felt myself flush even more than I thought possible from embarrassment, and I really didn't know where to look. Julian noticed my unease, raising an eyebrow at me. I shake my head at him and smile, I'm just a little uncomfortable is all, but very touched. He reaches for my hand under the table, squeezing my fingers gently. I gaze longingly at him, guiltily wishing we were anywhere but here right now.

"Thank you, that was really sweet." I squeak, stifling my nervous giggle, taking a quick sip of water, and standing to give a brief curtsy to the whole room who jovially whoop and laugh. Alice and Jamie find that hilarious and clap at my feeble attempt. Jamie knowing full well I do not like being the centre of attention. Alice hands me an envelope as I give her a brief thank you hug as she stands and says goodbye to everyone at the table. Jamie hands me a small present before kissing me on both cheeks.

"I'll see you tomorrow for breakfast." She says patting me on the shoulder. The girls are off to work the night shift and I really appreciate that they stopped by before work. It's just me and the three boys left.

"A round of drinks is in order, what can I get you all?" Asks Julian before he wanders off to the bar with Nicky. I am left alone with Andy, who takes the opportunity to move closer to me by swapping seats. Andy and I have always got along and have worked well together for absolutely ages, yet I am a little surprised he is here tonight as we have never been out together socially.

He rarely joins social occasions, come to think of it, he always misses the Christmas party too. Reaching under the table he pulls out a gift, wrapped in gold paper and hands it to me.

"Andy, you didn't have to buy me anything but thank you." I reach over to kiss him on the cheek, but he turns his head and I catch his lips ever so briefly instead. I am deeply embarrassed and then realize that he moved his head on purpose.

"Sorry." I murmur more to myself for feeling so stupid. Andy sits back in his chair, a small smile playing on his lips.

"No problem, I've always wondered what your lips felt like." I give him a flustered smile. Oh goodness this is awkward, I feel highly uncomfortable right now. Bugger. Andy tried to kiss me and practically succeeded. Although my back is to Julian, I can feel his stare.

"Thanks for the gift." I say putting it on the table next to Jamie's unopened package.

"Anytime birthday girl." I smile again politely, hoping the boys will return with the drinks soon. I try and not stare at Andy; he has made the effort to be here tonight. His usual sandy blonde hair has been cut and waxed off his face and he isn't wearing shorts and a t-shirt, which is his usual attire. Andy when he is not working likes to surf, having spent many summers as a surfing instructor to the tourists who frequent Newquay. My thoughts are disturbed when Andy shifts slightly and moves closer, clearing his throat.

"I might be a little out of line here, but do you think it is a good idea being seen out with a high-profile patron from the hotel?" I'm taken aback, what exactly does he mean? I don't want to know what he means. I feel my cheeks redden slightly.

"Have you booked your annual leave this summer?" My feeble attempt at changing the subject is not very well thought out, knowing full well Andrew hasn't, because I organize the work rota.

"Ellie, you are aware that Julian is from "The Hunter family"." He uses his fingers in quotation marks in the air, I give him a quizzical look and frown.

"You didn't know. His mother is the famous scientist. The one who got a lot of flak in the press for experimenting on people back in the late eighties." I shake my head no. I was not aware of what Julian's parents, did or who they are and right now I don't care either. What his mother does for a living is none of my business. I glance behind me to see what the hold-up is, Andy's eyes follow mine and he changes tack.

"Do you fancy going for a drink sometime?" My jaw practically hits the table. I can't believe he is asking me out. We have been working together for over two years and he has never shown any interest in me before. He is sweet and cute, but I have never felt anything remotely romantic towards him. My mind races trying to think of something to say, I don't want to hurt his feelings, because we work together but I don't want to give him the wrong impression either, so I opt for the truth and hope he understands.

"Andy, thank you." I smile warmly and turn to fully face him. "To be honest I am seeing Julian and I know it is early days, but I am happy. To answer your earlier question, being seen with him doesn't bother me, despite what his parents do. I don't have anything to do with him professionally, I work here in the gardens and like you, we don't have the same restraints and code of conduct as the actual hotel staff do regarding patrons. But thank you for your concern, you are a good friend." I reach over and pat his hand like a true friend would do, while taking a deep breath. I wonder why it is taking the boys so long to get the drinks.

Andy is not happy with my rebuff but that is not my concern. We sit in an uncomfortable silence for a moment, I turn and see Nicky talking to the barman, Julian standing next to him. His face contorted in what looks like rage. My eyes widen and I shake my head at him willing him to stay calm. I'm guessing he has witnessed what has happened over the last few minutes.

Nicky and Julian return from the bar with the drinks, a pint of lager for Andy, a strawberry daiquiri for Nicky, now I know why it took them so bloody long and two sparkling waters for Julian and I. Andy doesn't move, he is alert, body angled towards me, watching. Julian sits on my right side, I can sense he is not happy despite the polite smile plastered on his face, Nicky is totally oblivious to what is going on. Julian sizes up Andy before reaching over and kissing me. I see his she is mine look on Julian's face as he places both hands gently on either side of my head. I hesitate for a fraction of a second because we are sitting in the hotel bar, but I soon melt, kissing him back. Nicky makes a vomiting sound and then laughs which brings us up for air.

"Save that for later you two, you have the rest of the night for that and more." Nicky winks and I can see Andy's tanned face begin to pale.

"I've got to work in a bit, I haven't seen you all day Ellie. I have missed you." Nicky continues, looking at me with his big puppy dog eyes.

"Sorry." Julian and I blurt out together and I can't help but giggle, Andy has an expression that I cannot read. He sits sipping his lager watching us all quietly. I can't help feeling a little sorry for him.

"What is your plan for the rest of the week? I am so jealous that you are off when I'm not. We could have had so much fun together Ellie." Say Nicky picking up his drink and taking a sip.

"Nicky, why are you drinking if you're working tonight?" Nicky laughs at my question.

"A certain young man has introduced me to virgin daiquiris, all of the flavour and none of the hangover." I snort, Julian looks puzzled, and Andy is now completely lost.

"So, you are basically drinking a strawberry smoothie?" Nicky takes another sip.

"In essence darling, yes I am." I feel Julian's hand stroke my thigh lightly.

"So, how are things going with you two?" I can tell Nicky is just desperate to talk about his new relationship, trouble is he can go into a little too much detail. Although on the plus side it could move Andy along, I'm sure he doesn't want to hear about Nicky's colourful sex life.

"It is going really well thank you for asking. I'm surprised you haven't seen him about the hotel, he's been shadowing me around here today." Nicky stops, looking thoughtful. It is so lovely to see him happy. I just hope Seb doesn't hurt him.

"He is taking us all out to a club in Brighton on Saturday night, Julian you are more than welcome to join us, you too Andy."

"Where are we going?" I ask rolling my eyes.

"Well, the tickets have been obtained for a fetish place. I don't know exactly where it is, and I've forgotten the name of it." Julian who has been sitting quietly up until now sits forwards listening.

"Please dress for debauchery darling, you too Julian. I'm sure you can pull that kind of look off now that you are exposing ink." Nicky gives Julian a sweeping look from head to toe and I realise I am going to have to have words with him.

"The club, please tell me it's not called Club Flesh?" Asks Julian. All eyes fall on him as Nicky laughs and points his finger, clicking it in mid-air.

"Yes, that's it. You would think I would remember a name like that wouldn't you." Julian groans whilst looking at me.

"That isn't a club for you." He states firmly.

"Or you Nicky for that matter, it's pretty hardcore."

"I think Seb will look after us, he knows the owner or something." Replies Nicky all sheepish. The penny finally drops, I can see Julian putting the pieces of the puzzle together. He is all wide eyed and gorgeous.

"Are you friends with Sebastian Hunter?" He asks looking from

Nicky to me. Nicky has the gall to flash his toothy smile while acting all innocent, knowing full well that Seb and Julian are related.

"Oh yes darling, I'm friends with him, having seen every last inch of him and a little bit more." It's my turn to produce an audible groan as Julian shakes his head and looks at me.

"Did you know?" I nod in reply. Andy stands up looking confusedly at the three of us.

"I've got to go. Thanks for the drink. Ellie, enjoy your annual leave and the rest of your birthday." He bends down and kisses me on the cheek before striding out of the bar.

"Bye Andy, thank you for the present." I shout after him. My stomach sinks a little. I had no idea he was interested in me at all but at least I know why he follows me around at work. I'm not looking forward to dealing with that next week.

"What, don't I get a goodbye?" Chirps Nicky affronted; his comment causes me to chuckle a little under my breath but Andy either didn't hear Nicky or is ignoring him completely. Julian sits stone faced and deep in thought. He doesn't look happy and I'm not sure if it is because of Andy, the club or Nicky seeing Seb.

"I really should be heading down to reception. I'll speak to your lovely cousin Julian and sort out Saturday. You are both going to come out and celebrate Ellie's birthday and we are going to have a marvellous night." Nicky is serious and is all matter of fact as I groan inwardly. I'm starting to feel a little selfish just wanting Julian to myself.

"As I have already said yes to Nicky." I mumble turning to Julian.

"And as it looks like it is all organised, will you come with us?" Julian rolls his eyes.

"Look, if you insist on going to Flesh, I am going to have to come with you Ellie. I really don't think it will be your scene and I don't want you going without a chaperone." Nicky claps his hands.

"Brilliant I am glad that is all sorted." Nicky replies animatedly. I think we have just made his year.

"Has Seb said where it is going to be held?" Nicky shakes his head no.

"Seb said, to keep the club exclusive it moves about to different venues, but you probably know that already." Julian nods in agreement.

"But as soon as I find out, I'll let the two of you know." Nicky finishes the last of his drink, air kisses me on both cheeks and shakes Julian's hand before leaving.

"That was an interesting hour, sorry I forgot to tell you that Seb and Nicky had hooked up." I say as I turn my body towards Julian. He doesn't seem too fazed now that the initial shock has worn off.

"Seb is a complete whore. I hope Nicky knows what he is getting himself into." Julian's words hit a nerve.

"Nicky is a slut too. I caught the look he gave Seb on Sunday. He really likes him. So, this club what is it like and why so secret?" Julian shakes his head.

"Seriously Ellie, Flesh isn't a place for you." I raise my eyebrow at him, I've been clubbing, I know what goes on in the toilets. Hell, I went to that place with Nicky and Jamie a few days ago.

"I know what goes on in the world." I reply indignantly. He must really think I'm square. Julian reaches out and tenderly tucks a loose lock of hair behind my ear.

"Flesh is just a place for sex Ellie." I look up at him batting my eyelids.

"I love sex but only with you." Julian merely grins.

"Club Flesh is not your usual club, if the name hasn't given it away then maybe you needed to take heed of what Nicky called it. It is a fetish club where anything goes. There are a couple of rooms for dancing, but the main attractions are the traveling dungeon and in particular Master Brutus or Sir as he likes to be called and of course the Playpen." I giggle.

"The playpen, men in nappies?"

"Exactly kitten, it is not your usual club where people meet and leave together. People go there specifically to have sex in public, to be flogged in public or both; It is that kind of club." I sit and stare at Julian.

"People have kinks, it sounds like a safe space for consulting adults to indulge." I stop to ponder on a question; how does Julian know so much about it? But I continue.

"Brighton is home to loads of cool conventional clubs, why is Seb taking Nicky and us there?" Julian flashes me a smile.

"Seb is the king of the mindfuck pure and simple. My guess he is just showing off. Seb owns Club Flesh, it's his baby and he is proud of the reputation he built regarding his club." I reach for my glass and take another sip of water before finally having the gall to ask my last question.

"So, how do you know so much about it?" Julian studies my face and grins before he answers.

"That would be because I have worked with Seb there."

CHAPTER TWENTY-THREE

Noodles And Zombies

"Shall we head on to somewhere else?" I ask changing the subject. I have a million questions. It seems the longer I am in Julian's company, the list of questions grows. I could really do with sitting down and grilling him on his life story, in fact I'm going to start jotting all my questions down and ticking them off when they are answered, if they are ever answered.

"It is your birthday kitten, what would you like to do?" I haven't a clue.

"Why do you call me kitten?" I ask wearily, expecting a long arsed historical explanation.

"I don't know" Julian replies, running his hand over his stubble.

"Just so you know, I hate cats." I reply dryly, standing up and stretching. I know I just need to get out of here and fill my lungs with clean, fresh air.

"Do you want to go and get something to eat?" I ask, knowing that I didn't eat much for lunch. And as if on cue Julian's stomach growls loudly. He grins like a child.

"Come on let's go and stuff ourselves."

"Where to Lion?" I clasp my hand over my mouth.

"Shit. I'm sorry that just slipped out." I mumble through my fingers. I haven't called Julian that in twenty-three or so years, as odd as it sounded out loud, calling him Lion felt right but he might not appreciate it. Julian turns to face me in the car.

"Ellie, hearing you call me that, brings back so many memories.

Happy ones, when my life and yours were relatively uncompli-
cated and ugly." He stops, his eyes glazing over, a melancholic fog
descending upon us again.

"I like that you called me Lion, I would like it if you continued
to do so, but just so you know, I do like cats, all animals in fact.
That includes spiders, maggots, snails." I blink stifling a laugh.
We drive with Julian's car playing music in the background. I
have no idea what we are listening to or where we are going, and
I don't ask. Julian is quiet, lost in his thoughts and for the moment I am happy to leave him there, giving me time to dissect
mine. It is beginning to look like our budding relationship will
be haunted by our collective past, present and possible future together and I'm okay with that.

We eventually end up at a very small Vietnamese restaurant. I
have never had Vietnamese food before and really have no idea
what I would like or to expect. We are walked to a table in the
darkened restaurant, despite the time it is quiet here with just
a handful of people seated in shadow. The decor has me surprised and suppressing a smile; bamboo poles hang from the
ceiling with plastic vines entwined around them. One wall of the
restaurant is mirrored which would make the restaurant look
bigger except it comes complete with smudges and fingerprints
which someone clearly forgot to polish away today. We're seated
by the window and are handed our menus by the waiter.

"I don't know what to order?" I look at each dish and its description, everything sounds so different and tempting.

"How hungry are you?" Julian asks and I consider this for a
moment.

"Actually, not hungry at all." I answer honestly. I have completely lost my appetite, not sure if it is caused by our earlier
conversation or because I'm tired and overwhelmed by the day's
events.

"The portions here are big." He states looking over to me.

"You really should try to eat something. You will need something to line your stomach for what I'm about to tell you." My eyes meet his, my ears alert, not sure if I heard him correctly. "You can share with me if you don't mind." I smile in agreement. Finally, he is going to talk.

Our food arrives. It all looks lovely. A big bowl of thin white rice noodles with crunchy colourful vegetables, lemongrass, coriander and mint, chunks of tofu with a sweet chili dressing arrives first followed by a plate of steaming rice with crispy tofu, decorated with garlic slivers and fiery chopped chilies. Finally, the waiter brings over the last dish, a plate of stir-fried Pak choi, choi sum and various other vegetables, the smell alone is amazing. The food looks vibrant, and the flavours are simply divine. My taste buds think they are being spoilt rotten as do I, but then Julian is feeding me with his chopsticks from across the table.

"Are you vegetarian?" I ask wiping a dribble of sweet dressing from my chin.

"No, I'm vegan. Why do you ask?"

"I just wondered." I reply shrugging, in truth I'm not sure why I asked at all. Julian watches me closely before he continues

"I have issues with what I do. I feel that I take enough life so much so that I can't bare the idea of eating the flesh of an animal." His logic is understandable if only I understood what exactly it was, he took life from. A thought pops into my head.

"The night you were outside my room with the wound on your cheek. How did you do it?" Julian finishes chewing, I watch his Adam's apple bob as he swallows.

"I was surprised when you didn't ask me at the time." His nostrils flare. Clearly the thought of that night ingrained on his memory as it is on mine.

"I was called out to a hunt where there was a manifestation of DROMs." I stop chewing, there is that word again.

"Sorry, you never did explain what a DROM is to me, I would

understand a whole lot better if I actually knew what a DROM is?" Julian looks up, chopsticks mid-air. He glances around the restaurant and then stares at me.

"What I am about to tell you is going to shock you. It will sound unbelievable and horrific, but it is the absolute truth." He stops, putting the chopsticks down on their little porcelain holder. Julian reaches over the table and cups my hand in his.

"I am a hunter, Ellie; I hunt and kill DROMs, you know them from folklore as zombies." He stops and watches my reaction. I put my chopsticks down on my plate, he continues.

"That night there were seven of them in total, a whole family of DROMs. Zombies. I was on the move; one was close and was faster than I was expecting. I lost my footing and fell forward cheek first. I was lucky, the damn beast tripped over me, which gave me enough time to roll over, jump up and away from it before it did any lasting damage." He stops, his eyes darting around the room. He doesn't look at me. I gaze out of the window absentmindedly as an old man walks past with an elderly Jack Russell. Julian hunts zombies. Now it is my turn to study Julian, he looks uneasy. I pull my hand away from his and pick up my chopsticks, popping another chunk of tofu into my mouth, feeling it crunch as I chew. It is the only thing I can think of to do while I absorb this new information.

"You are paid to hunt zombies. Like zombies as in reanimated dead folk, The Walking Dead, World War Z. Humans who get bitten and die but don't die, becoming flesh eating monsters, that kind of zombie?" Julian nods his head ever so slowly, trying to figure out where I am going with this. I mull over his words for a moment.

"You kill them by beheading them?" I whisper, trying to make sense of this new piece of information. Julian looks uneasy and I can see a bead of sweat begin to form on his forehead, he is nervous.

"That is an extreme way of doing it. I rarely behead DROMs, my

211

preferred method is with a gun, a single shot to the head." I nod, that makes perfect sense.

"Who pays you to do this?" I remember Julian telling he was paid handsomely for his efforts. Julian looks up shocked by my question.

"Private landowners, the government, rich families. Whoever needs the infestation removed pays me." I resume eating, thinking while I chew.

"Ellie, are you alright? You are very calm and for someone who wasn't hungry, you are still eating." Julian reaches over the table and tries to hold my hand again, but I pull it away. Not out of malice but confusion.

"I'm fine. I never knew we as a nation had a problem with zombies. I genuinely thought zombies were from fiction. But...It doesn't surprise me." I continue to eat; my brain trying to rationalize and make sense of everything I have just heard.

"Do you want me to kill these DROMs too?" I ask finally meeting Julian's eyes and holding his gaze. He nods again.

"Ellie you were born into a family of DROM hunters, the same as I. This has been the career path of our families for generations. That is why I couldn't give up until I found you. You are the only woman I can and have wanted to share this life with."

"Do you do this on your own?" I query, he hasn't mentioned working with anyone but surely there must be others out there doing it too if it is such a problem that he must kill seven in one night.

"Yes, I do this on my own. There are various teams around the country who do this also. Unlike me, they were not born into this. They do it for money and I guess you could say they are true bounty hunters. Mostly hired by government agencies to remove what is considered vermin DROMs. There are teams and companies around the world who do it also because sadly, this is not a British problem, it is a worldwide problem with frequent breakouts these are covered up and concealed. It has always been the case. I work alone when it comes to the hunting part mostly. My cousin Sebastian has on occasion joined me in a hunt. There are disposal teams, who clean up and dispose of the remains where necessary. Seb is the first point of call, he passes the details on to me and handles the financial transactions. We work as a team." I mull this over, it must be horrible, fighting and killing dead folk by yourself, it sounds morbid and creepy, something straight out of a horror movie.

"Is it not lonely doing it on your own or dangerous even?" My stupid question is out of my mouth before I have had time to think about it. Julian looks thoughtful, thinking about his answer carefully.

"I am not going to lie to you. Yes, it is a very dangerous job, some DROMs are incredibly strong and surprisingly fast. Yes. It is lonely, but it is what it is. Although after today, it no longer has to be lonely."

The room spins momentarily as the magnitude of Julian's words penetrate my brain.

"Sorry." I whisper more to myself then to Julian. Despite what he said before about it being my choice, it isn't really. He is hoping that I will make the decision to choose his life. I would be doing it blindly because I have never seen a DROM before. I do not know how to fight, the idea of killing something other than greenfly or weeds, I find wholeheartedly repugnant. Yet remembering that evening, the wound on his face and considering his explanation, I have a fear of him going out and doing his hunting alone. I have an overwhelming urge deep inside to keep him safe. Julian's eyes glow deep green against the backlight of the restaurant.

"Look, I didn't want to discuss this so soon but as the topic of conversation has arisen, now I guess is as good a time as any." I can't possibly make a life changing decision on this over tofu. I am tired, I am still achy from last night and I simply have had information overload. I can't trust myself to make the right choice right now, although it is becoming blazingly clear that the only choice I have if I want to be with him, is to do what he does and hunt. My heart is beating fast in my chest, and I can feel my palms begin to sweat with nerves. I just want to go home, curl up and go to sleep. Give my tired brain time to assimilate what I thought I knew to be the truth about the world in which I live. Fucking real life, living zombies.

"Julian I can't make a decision like this right now. This doesn't feel right, I don't know all the facts and implications. I need to think. I need to discuss what all of this means for my life, what it would mean for us as a couple." My words come out in a mumbled rush, adrenaline spiking and fear taking over. I stop and try to compose myself. Julian cocks his head to one side, hearing the satisfying click of his neck.

"I understand kitten. You have been kept from all of this, for your entire adult life. It must be a shock to you. I'm so sorry. You have taken everything so well that I thought I'd push my luck and go a little further. But you are right. It is your decision, and it can wait. I promise I won't pressure you into hunting. It really is a decision that you need to make on you own."

"I am full. I can't eat another mouthful." I put my chopsticks down and push the small white plate away from me. The change in conversation has dramatically reduced my appetite again.

"Me too." Julian replies picking up his bowl and placing it on top of my plate. He indicates to the waiter who brings the bill over to us, Julian pays, and we leave. I finally allow Julian to take my hand and together we walk back to the car.

I can feel the tension radiating off Julian as we move along dark winding roads. My common-sense kicks in. As much as I don't want to hear what he has to say right now, it is completely unfair to deny him the chance to get all of this off his chest. If I am to believe what he has said, he has been waiting his entire adult life to have this chance and he has been carrying around all this emotional baggage for years. I finally break the silence.

"Tell me what you mean when you say that you would like me to join you, you know, in the family business." I adjust my seat belt, moving so my body is facing his.

"Are you sure you want to know what it means?"

"Yes, I have questions and we will get to those. I want to know what it is you want or expect from me." I study his silhouette, the gentle shadows of light and dark wash over his strong features as the car hurtles back to Hedge Hill. Julian shifts in the driver's seat. It occurs to me he looks torn and is fighting with himself, which is something he does a lot.

"I need to know everything. I'm pragmatic, I always look at both sides of the story before I make any decision. This will be treated no differently." I want to reach out to him, stroke his thigh and run my fingers through his hair but know that if I do, he would be under the impression that I will have made my decision already. The car indicates left then turning off this road and on to the next.

"It is not uncommon for us to hunt in pairs. My parents and my grandparents did this for a living as couples. They were all married hunters and for them it was the norm. Although my parents have retired from actual hunting some years ago, they still play their part if needed. When I finally tracked you down, I kind of hoped that you would join me." His voice is low and soft, and I hear the quiver of nervousness as he speaks.

"Why me specifically?" I simply don't get why he looked for me, what it is about me that he is attracted to and why it is me that he wants to share all of this with.

"We have this link, Ellie; we were playmates from an early age for this very reason. Our families for the want of a better explanation threw us together as children with this solely in mind. They hoped that as we grew older, we would develop a bond that would stay with us forever. We were separated, unexpectedly and even though we were pulled apart, I never forgot you." He stops and I can feel him looking over at me. I keep my eyes downcast, listening to his words and absorbing their meaning.

"Look, I know this all sounds crazy, hell my family thought I was absolutely mad. The long and short of it is we were meant to stay together, at least that is how I felt deep down. I grew up never feeling quite whole, there was always something missing. I never managed to meet anyone who I could look at, in the way that I see you.

When I eventually tracked you down at Hedge Hill. I was in shock not quite believing that I had finally traced you. Seb warned me to take my time and not frighten you off with our crazy history. He was right. But Christ, seeing you, just being close by you kitten, made me feel different. I felt happy for the first time in a lifetime. That first year I came, I couldn't keep away from you." Julian shakes his head and smiles at the memory.

"I thought you would have called security to tell them that a weirdo was following you around the grounds. Then you surprised me and said hello. Our first conversation was about lavender, do you remember." I smile at the memory. when I first met Julian, I certainly thought he was an oddball eccentric. He constantly walked around the grounds come rain or shine for the entire four weeks he spent at Hedge Hill during that first year. Twice a day he would take his walks, he was so prompt that I started to time him, just to keep myself amused while I worked. He rarely said a word to anyone. I noticed how he never stopped to talk choosing instead to walk with his head bowed, deep in thought. Wild stories filled my head, was he a religious man; deep in prayer, or a writer coming up with his next masterpiece or someone heartbroken and in mourning. Thinking back Julian had always looked so forlorn and serious, like he had the world on his shoulders. Odd really because in a very sick way, he does.

"Just so you know, I never thought you were weird, just eccentric. I liked watching you walk around the grounds." I stop, not sure how to phrase the words that were pooling on the tip of my tongue.

"And I'm not going anywhere. Whether I decide to hunt or not, I will still be here by your side."

CHAPTER TWENTY-FOUR

Watched

Julian smiles at me. He looks happy again as we hurtle along the dark roads.

"You know, I was unhappy and overjoyed at the same time when I first saw you. I was happy that I had finally found you, despite you not knowing who I was. And I was ecstatic to just be in your presence. I wanted to approach you but knew it would have been wrong to do so. I held myself back which was incredibly difficult for me, but it needed to be done and it was a good lesson in self-control. The second year I came back to Hedge Hill, ready to get to know you, but I was forever called away, that was one crazy summer; DROM infestations were everywhere that year. I was being sent on hunt after hunt, so that interrupted my plans to get to know you. I must tell you; I was not happy about it."

"Your mother announced that she was dying during the third year, my parents were in shock." My head snaps up and I look at over at him.

"You knew my mother was ill?" I find myself holding my breath. I don't know if I want to hear this.

"Ellie your mother contacted my father and uncles and informed them that her brain tumour was terminal." He stops and glances at me as a single tear runs down my cheek. Julian continues.

"My family and I were at her funeral. I watched you from afar, believe me when I say this, I felt like I was grieving too, I could feel you, sense your pain. It was like I was in your head reading your thoughts, aware of your emotions. It freaked me out. During the wake I couldn't keep my eyes off you, that was when I knew we were meant to be together. I wanted so much to be able to comfort you and help you deal with your pain; it was killing me that I couldn't." Julian laughs lightly as I stare at the floor.

"My father actually made me leave early that day. He knew that I wanted to approach you and more importantly, that I had finally been granted permission to do so." I sit quietly not knowing what to say. This is all news to me, I'm sure I would have recognized Julian at the funeral if I had seen him. I simply do not recall him being there at all and I greeted each guest. I don't know how I feel about all of this. Just as I begin to think I am getting my head around what Julian confesses, he hits me with something new that I need to consider, explore, and deal with.

"After that, I was compelled to come and see you, I was here that third summer, you were dealing with your mothers' diagnosis, so I watched you from afar, not daring to make myself known. I returned for a fourth year, last summer. It was six months after your mother's death that I decided to come back. I had kept an eye on you from afar, ready to step in. I'm ashamed to admit it but I wanted to sweep you off your feet but knew I needed to do this slowly. You are so lovely Ellie, you humoured me, we chatted in the bar, laughed together over the rose bushes and I felt elated that I was able to help alleviate your pain a little just by bringing you coffee. I took a step back, forgetting about me and tried to become a friend instead."

Julian changes gear and indicates right, pulling us over onto a secluded back road. He stops the car, undoes his seatbelt, and turns to me, reaching over and carefully taking my hand. "Last summer was when I fell in love with you. Up until that point I was a man obsessed, I didn't know you as a person, yet I hunted you down like an animal. I followed you, watched you and hoped that it was you who could fill the void in my life." Julian squeezes warmth into my cold fingers and slowly at his words I begin to feel subtle heat, warm blood again flowing through every vein and artery.

"I couldn't stop thinking about you after I left you. Seb called me an idiot for talking about you constantly, you were in my dreams and every wakeful thought. I made two bookings to comeback this year and then chickened out, cancelling them both. I was driving myself crazy. I decided that I would come back to Hedge Hill one last time. I wanted to start where we left off last year, but it didn't work out that way." He smiles apologetically. I finally find my voice, still reeling for his confession, his obsession.

"Thank you for your honesty." I hold onto his hand and pull it towards me. His beautiful green eyes search mine in the dark. His hooded expression sets my body on fire, the warmth from moments ago tuning to flame. I need to feel him, I want his hands on me, his mouth on mine. I need him to make me feel alive. I hold his hand up and kiss his palm.

"Please take me home Lion."

We don't speak for the rest of our journey. I am lost in my thoughts; he is lost in his. Julian parks the car and I get out as soon as it is safe to do so. I walk around to the driver's side and watch Julian as he opens his door. My heart breaks when I see his face, illuminated by the lamp above us. Julian looks crestfallen, he is dark and brooding, his shoulders hunched slightly a haunted look in those perfect green eyes of his. Clearly, he is under the wrong impression. I take his hand.

"Take me to your room." Julian studies my face, he is serious and a little taken aback by my request, but I notice a fleeting look of hope. I don't need to ask twice. Julian sweeps me up into his arms and carries me into the hotel. Nicky is at the front desk with Jamie. They watch us as we enter but say nothing. As Julian walks up the stairs with me still cradled close to his chest, I turn my head and look at Nicky. I see happiness and love on his face. He winks and I smile. Nicky approves.

Julian carries me effortlessly all the way up to room four twenty-five. He holds me tightly to him like he is scared to let me go but says nothing. The only tell-tale sign I have is he is flaring his nostrils. Somehow, he manages to extract his wallet from his pocket, using one hand and pulling his key card out with his teeth, my arms tightly wrapped around his neck, I release one hand, take the key card, and slip it in the card reader, opening the door. We walk into the dark room, the only light coming from outside the window.

"Put me down on the couch." I ask breathlessly. Julian does as I ask.

"You moved this couch here to the window?"

"Yes, I always have it moved when I'm here." He answers in a low, deep voice.

"Why do you stay in this room?" I ask, I know the answer, yet I need to hear it from him.

"I think you know why I stay in this room and why I move the couch to the window with its perfect view of the grounds." His answer is confirming my suspicions.

"I want you to tell me." I stand and walk slowly around the large couch to face the window, observing the dark shadowy grounds below. I'm on fire and I'm not sure how much longer I can be apart from Julian. My body aches for him. Julian silently walks behind me, he rests his hands on my shoulders, his chest is close to my back. I can smell his citrus scent, feel the tingle emanating from his fingertips, causing jolts of electricity to course through my body, it feels downright delicious. The air surrounding us charged with emotion. Julian is still and continues to say nothing.

"Tell me Lion." I demand. His fingers grip my shoulders lightly.

"You feel it too?" He asks huskily, emotion catching in his throat. A shiver runs down my spine. Julian's breathing has increased, as has mine.

"Yes, I feel it." I whisper. I stop and close my eyes before I speak again.

"I want you to tell me why you move the couch. I need to hear it." Julian spins me around to face him, his thumb tentatively tips my chin up, so we are eye to eye.

"I move the couch so I can watch you. I come here and torture myself by watching you. Every single day that I am here, I sit and watch you come and go, watch who you talk to, who you laugh with. I can't help myself. I have loved you for so long kitten." He stops abruptly and I take in a deep steadying breath. I should be horrified that I have been the prey to this hunter for so long. I should be shocked that he has tortured himself like this but I'm not. I push his jacket off his shoulders and down his arms where it drops to the floor. I move closer and then stop. Standing in the light from the window I reach down and grab my dress pulling it up and over my head. I drop it to the floor. Julian stands quietly, considering my actions. I remove my bra, brushing the straps down my arms and tossing the garment away, quickly followed by my knickers, shimmying them down my legs and stepping out of them.

Julian's breath hitches but his eyes do not leave mine, I grab the bottom of his t-shirt and pull it over his head, adding it to the pile of clothes already discarded. Julian picks me up and walks us to the window. Looking into Julian's eyes I feel nothing but love, no fear, no hate, just overwhelming peace. My head spins at the realization that I mirror Julian's feelings. I have never felt whole, but I do now, I understand his obsession. Having him this close feels like I have found the missing part of a puzzle I had been searching for. Being joined to him in this tender way, has re-inforced the feeling of love that has been missing from my adult life. Julian picks up on my mood.

"What's wrong?" He asks raising an eyebrow, concern etched on his masculine features. I smile and for the first time in my life I feel overwhelmed with happiness. I am here with the man I love, a man who is my past, present and now my future.

"I love you." I whisper. Julian smiles broadly and kisses me.

"I love you back." An overwhelming feeling of completeness fills me deep to my soul. I'm overcome with emotion and silent tears trickle down my cheeks, Julian tenderly kisses each one away. I feel safe in his warm embrace watching the full moon together. We find ourselves on the couch, a tangle of limbs, content and happy. In some sick way my life feels like it has purpose. I don't know what the future holds for me exactly, but I know I'm no longer alone. I now have Julian to share it with. Thirst gets the better of me. My head is resting on Julian's muscular chest while he plays with my hair. I push myself up from him.

"I need some water; can I get you something?"

"Some water would be good, then a shower and bed. You need a good night's sleep. Time to process all the information you have taken in." He kisses me on the nose, I smile back at him. I don't want to get up because it means I must let him go. I manage to pull myself away from his arms and off his lap, instantly missing him. My logical mind screams at me to stop being silly, he is just mere inches away from me. Julian stands up too and sweeps me into his arms, he rubs noses with mine while grinning like the Cheshire cat.

"Put me down." I ask.

"Please." I continue as Julian shakes his head no and carries me across the room.

"Sadly, I can't do that, I missed you while you were gone." I wriggle and attempt to smack him on the bum as we stop at the small fridge, he reaches down and with one hand opening the door and pulls out a bottle of San Pellegrino while still managing to carry me.

"I missed you when you left." He continues carrying me back to the couch. He puts the bottle of water down on the table and then takes me back to collect two glasses.

"I didn't actually get very far, so you couldn't possibly have missed me." I retort, secretly loving the banter between us. I smile, happy that I felt our ridiculously stupid separation too.

"I simply felt that you were out of reach. So, I'm keeping you close to me. Well at least for a little while." Julian places me on the sofa and sits next to me pulling me close to him. He opens the water and fills both glasses, handing me one and taking a sip from the other. I am so thirsty that I down mine, the bubbles and the temperature burning the back of my throat and giving me brain freeze. I put the glass down and grip my temples.

"Ouch." Is the only sound that leaves my lips. I grimace in agony; my eyes feel like they are about to explode and pop out of their sockets. Julian picks me up and places me on his lap rubbing my head and laughing.

"We need to warm you up." I am lifted and carried to the bathroom.

"A girl could get used to this." I state slowly while planting a kiss on Julian's shoulder. Julian's smugness is evident, he reaches over and switches on the taps, testing the water before gingerly placing me under the warm stream.

"I'll be back in a sec and with that he is gone." I submerge myself, wetting my hair and getting carried away under the crazy amount of shower heads this bathroom contains.

Music starts to play, I have no idea where it's coming from, I glance around the room and then spot the speakers, very cool. I've not heard this before; the singer has a slight accent and an incredibly deep voice. Julian is back and joins me under the water reaching for the shower gel and squirting a large dollop onto his hand.

"I want to wash you, Is that okay?"

"Of course, but I know it's really because you can't keep your hands off me." Julian nods in agreement his nostrils flaring as he begins working the liquid soap into my shoulders and down my body. I send a small prayer to the gods, thanking them for reuniting me with this man who is so attentive and caring.

When Julian finished washing me, I grab a little shower gel.

"It is your turn." I start massaging his shoulders and work my hands down, moving my bubble covered fingers in slow circles. I look at each of his tattoos, there are too many to count. I am amazed by the detail; they are all beautiful and no two are the same.

"Who does these for you?" I ask as I turn Julian around to wash his strong smooth back.

"A friend of Sebastian's, she is amazing at what she does, a true artist." I continue washing his back, down towards his hips, buttocks and thighs, the backs of his knees, calves, and ankles. Julian looks down at me as I wash his feet, I can feel his watchful eyes on me in my almost submissive pose.

"Do they have any particular significance?" I ask. Julian sighs as he looks down at me.

"Yes. They do." I am all finished, and I stand slowly, rinsing the soap suds of his skin, waiting for him to elaborate. I grab the bottle of shampoo and apply some.

"What do they mean?" Julian speaks in low tones, the water from the shower almost drowning him out.

"They are my own private memorial to the lives I have taken." I move closer to him, wrapping my arms around his decorated torso, offering myself as his support. I can't imagine how he must feel, knowing that he has killed so many for the greater good.

"I never want to forget what I do and have done."

We are both rinsed clean, and I shut the water off. Forever the gentleman, Julian gets out first and holds a towel out for me while he stands in a puddle on the floor. I'm wrapped up snug in a giant cream coloured fluffy towel while Julian finally wraps one around his waist. We dry off, I realize I have nothing up here, no toothbrush, hairbrush, or moisturizer. Julian seems to pick up on my thoughts.

"Here you might need this." He hands me a toothbrush. I smile opening the wrapper and pulling it out by its pink handle. We stand side by side at the sink brushing our teeth together. After sharing Julian's comb and attempting to detangle my unruly hair, I'm dressed in Julian's black Anthrax t-shirt; another band I have never heard of.

"Who were we listening to in the shower?" I ask as I climb into Julian's rather large four poster bed.

"HIM. They are a band from Finland. Did you like it?" I nod.

"Actually, I did. I wasn't listening to the words, but the guy has a lovely voice." Julian smiles, picks up his phone, switching the music back on.

"I guess we can listen to them again." I turn over to face Julian as he climbs into bed with me. I scoot over and snuggle up to his naked body, resting my head on his chest. I feel exhausted, it has been a crazy twenty-four hours and a birthday I will never forget.

"It is almost midnight. Happy birthday one last time." HIM's Heaven Tonight is playing in the background as Julian kisses me on the top of my head, I hold onto him tightly as I drift off into a deep and dreamless sleep.

CHAPTER TWENTY-FIVE

Hunt With The Hunter

I couldn't tell where I ended and where Julian began. Lying as one being with two beating hearts in his bed. I lazily gaze out of the window up at the moon lit sky. Sleepily and with my head resting on his chest, we dozed, warm and cosy in a state of contentment. I smile blissfully to myself, if this is happiness, then I have finally found it. Julian's phone disturbs our perfect silence, lighting up the table with its shrill cry for attention and breaking me away from my thoughts. Sitting up, I scan the room for the phone. Julian sits up next to me and rubs his eyes before pulling me closer and resting his forehead against mine.

"I'm so sorry. Duty calls." Begrudgingly, Julian detangles himself from me and instantly I feel lost.

"You rang?" I hear Seb reply on the phone. Julian switches on the bedside lamp as he talks to Seb, rubbing his hand over his eyes to wake himself.

"Yes, has it been checked out?" Julian sounds tired and that is my fault entirely.

"Yes, we are here, I'll go. I'm not happy but under the circumstances." Julian hangs up and sits on the edge of the bed. He reaches for his glass and takes a gulp of water before speaking.

"That was Seb. A hunt has been called. Should be easy. A DROM has been found on a private golf course that needs dealing with." Julian looks over at me.

"Sorry kitten I am going to have to go." I sit quietly and wait; Julian says nothing more as he begins to get himself dressed.

"Can I come with you?" I ask sounding braver than I feel, an overwhelming feeling of dread washes over me. I don't want him out there on his own tonight.

"It is probably not the best idea. Too much too soon." He replies pulling on his jeans. I take a deep breath, frustrated by Julian's response. This gets Julian's attention, and he looks at me, raising an eyebrow.

"You have thrust me into your world tonight, now, the opportunity has arisen for me to finally see these DROMs you have been talking about for the first time. I don't want to point out the obvious, but it appears that this is a good opportunity to see what a DROM is for myself and more importantly what you do with them. I will not wholeheartedly believe the existence of zombies until I see one." Julian looks sternly at me.

"I mean DROM. Sorry, if it is okay with you, I'm going to call them zombies, DROM sounds ridiculous. I digress, I can't believe of their existence until I see one. I am ready for this Lion; I'm not a delicate little flower that needs protecting. My life, body and world has been turned upside down and inside out this week with a massive bombshell that life as I knew it was a lie. I think I am owed this." Julian mulls over my request while pulling his t-shirt over his head.

"I don't want you freaking out on me."

"I won't. I can stay in the car and just watch. I don't want you out there on your own. You have had so little sleep over the last couple days. You would be putting your life at risk, going out alone and tired." Julian rubs his hand over his stubble.

"Okay I guess there is no time like the present. You need to get dressed." I find my knickers and bra and hastily put them on. I pad across the room and grab one of Julian's t-shirts and throw that over me.

"On the way out, we need to stop off at my room so I can grab some trousers and trainers." Julian nods, I can see he is in the zone. He does the dark and brooding silence while he grabs what he needs. Lost in work mode. This is how the hunter prepares for the hunt. Julian is ready and stands by the door. All the hotel patrons will be in their rooms asleep at this hour, so I'm not worried about running into anyone just wearing a t-shirt.

I leave the room and walk down the hallway to the stairs. Julian's long strides match mine as we descend the staircase and walk to my room. I open the door, Julian stands in the doorway, holding the door open while I pull a pair of jeans out of a drawer, pull them on and slip my feet into a pair of trainers. I grab a small bag, throw in my phone, purse, and a bottle of water. Grabbing a hair bobble and tying my hair up as I duck under Julian's arm and head back out into the hallway. Julian pulls my door shut and together we step out into the night. We drive in silence for five minutes or so. Julian's phone bleeps to a life flashing an address and post code.

"Where are we heading?" I ask studying Julian's face in the dark. The road is empty, so wherever we are going, we will arrive there fast.

"The golf course is in Lewes; twenty-five minutes and we will be there. Some rules. One. You stay in the car, no exceptions. Two. You stay in the car. Three. Just watch. DROMs move fast when they spot the living. Keep your eye on them when you spot it. Four. You will be fine. I have done this one too many times to count. Seb said it was just one reported. So only one kill. Are you okay with all of that?" I watch the road signs as we change lanes.

"Yes, I'm fine, all seems sensible. I will stay inside the car and watch." Adrenaline is coursing through my veins right now. I swallow, feeling wide awake and full of curiosity. The existence of zombies being a little over the top, I still don't quite believe.

"What causes people to change. I mean how does one simply become a DROM?"

"That is the million-dollar question. No one truly knows. It has happened through the ages, all over the world. There are theories, many theories but no solid scientific proof of a specific known cause or trigger. What is known is it appears to come in waves, there will be years of nothing and suddenly there are DROMs being reported." Julian stops talking, the windows of the car open a little, blasting us both with the cool night air.

"I don't remember ever reading about DROMs in the history books?" I say to myself more then to Julian.

"As like now, they have always been cleverly hidden or covered up. Why on earth do you think King Henry VIII beheaded wives? Then there is the plague, that was one of the worst DROM infestations in British history. Although there have been numerous outbreaks over the centuries, far too many to mention." Julian replies, his answer matter of fact and dead pan. And there he is, back to himself, a glimmer of the man I have fallen in love with. I guess he has figured out his plan for the DROM we are heading to and is beginning to relax.

"DROMs are fast or so you have said. Is there anything else I need to know about them?" Julian takes the second exit off the roundabout, and I spot the sign for the golf course.

"They are super-fast. It doesn't matter the size of the DROM. When they smell us, they move at speed, and nothing stops them. DROMs are strong, again like the whole speed thing, they can easily hold down an average sized human male. Their bite is strong enough to rip skin and muscle tissue clean off the bone and their strength allow them to easily rip limbs off their victims." I audibly gulp. I wasn't expecting that level of gory detail.

"Never underestimate a DROM. You can't talk to them, can't reason with them. They no longer understand common language, appear to have no memory and move solely on instinct, they are fighting machines whose instinct is to kill and consume." I nod my head in acknowledgement, despite the horror story I have just been told. I still don't know what to expect. As we drive closer to reaching our destination, my heart rate increases in anticipation.

"The plan is always to deal with this as quickly as possible. I don't play games; I don't do anything I don't have to. When we arrive, I will switch off the engine but keep the headlights on. DROMs are attracted to any type of movement, sound, and smell. Very much like a starving, rabid dog. I will only get out of the car when I can see the DROM and have accessed that the risk of danger is low. When I get out and slam the door, the noise and my scent will announce our arrival, this will cause the DROM to run in our direction to get to me. It will move fast. Expect that. Don't get out of the car or make a sound. Just observe it."

"Okay." I respond, as we pull into the grand driveway of the golf course. This is a very large area of land. It is pitch black out here and I can't help but think this will be like finding a needle in a haystack. Julian follows the drive around to the club house and bypasses the car park. He finally parks behind another smaller building. Reversing so the windscreen of the car is facing the grand expanse of the golf course. Julian switches off the headlights and we sit in darkness. It takes a few moments for my eyes to adjust to the dark, the full moon shadowed by passing clouds. Silence. I see no movement at all. Julian scans left to right, nothing, he checks his phone briefly but says nothing to me as he reads his message.

"Are you ready?"

"Yes. Ready as I will ever be." After a couple of minutes, he switches on the headlights of his car, illuminating the grass in front of us. We sit in a long dark silence, Julian repeating his lookout, scanning left to right. Then over to my left in the distance I see movement. I blink hard to make sure it isn't a trick of my eyes. I turn my head slightly to keep my eye on them, on it and point.

"Well spotted Kitten, we will make a hunter of you yet." I keep my eye on the target. It ambles forwards, towards the light. Its movements are slow and wobbly. It is now a good two hundred metres away from us. From its outfit, it was or is male. Its movements are simply bizarre, jerky, and wobbly. This doesn't look like something that will suddenly sprint at Usain Bolt's speed. The DROM has registered the light but appears confused, walking slowly, tripping over its own feet. Its head jerks to the left and right, up, and down. I can't figure out what it is doing or why. It is moving in such an odd way. If this wasn't so serious, it could be considered funny. Julian studies the DROM before reaching under his seat and pulling out a small case. He opens it to reveal a handgun and silencer.

Shit, he has had that under there this whole time. I swallow, seeing the gun has suddenly made this very real. Julian keeps his eyes on the target. While my eyes flit between what Julian is doing and the moving creature before us. The DROM is now one hundred and fifty metres from us, sniffing the air very much like a dog, when it picks up the scent of another dog on a long walk.

The DROM continues to follow the headlights and its upright movements are consistently odd. It walks with its hips and pelvis jutting out, attempting to maintain its upright stance and keep itself balanced but it doesn't look like this is a conscious decision. As it weaves along the grass, I notice that its clothes that it is wearing are heavily soiled and tatty. I don't know if this person was homeless to begin with or if its turning has created the look. Julian squeezes my hand but remains alert. I don't speak. I physically can't. I'm awestruck watching the DROM attempt to sniff us out.

"Stay in the car". Julian opens the car door and gets out quickly, gun in hand. He slams the door shut loudly. The sound echo's and instantly gets the DROMs attention. It sniffs the air wildly, catching the scent it so desperately craves. In seconds it begins to run, moving faster than the average man. Faster than I have seen a man of that size move ever. I hold on to the seat, my nails dig into the material beneath me as the DROM charges forward. This creature is now no more than twenty-five metres away from us. It is male; I find it hard to read the expression on its face in this light. There is no thought process, it's not planning on how to get to Julian, it just runs straight for him.

Julian stands quietly in front of the car. He doesn't say or do any-thing, he just waits for the DROM to get closer. Twenty meters, fifteen meters. It keeps moving, Julian raises his hand, finger firmly on the trigger. The DROM is less than ten meters away now. I can feel myself begin to break out into a sweat. Seven meters and bang. The sound of the gun echoes into the night. The DROM stands motionless, stopped in its tracks for a split second before collapsing onto the floor. Julian stands still. Main-taining his vigil over the golf course. I stare down at the body on the floor a couple of meters away from where I sit. This once was a stocky, well-built man. Average height but had packed on the pounds over the last year or two. Although lying face up on the ground. There is no movement, only a sizeable hole in his forehead that is trickling oozing mush. His trousers stained and soiled. I'm assuming the cause of death emptied both his bladder and bowels long before he spotted us. Julian takes one last look around before getting back in the car. He places his gun back under his seat. Reaches over and kisses me on the forehead. I'm in shock, I can't keep my eyes of the body on the grass in front of us.

"Taken care of, send clean up." Julian hangs up his phone, switches the engine on and off we drive in silence.

* * *

We pull back into the hotel car park. It is still dark, but I can hear the stirrings of the early morning birds and the start of the dawn chorus. Julian and I drove back to the hotel in twenty minutes flat. The roads were empty and the night quiet. Neither of us speak. Repeatedly my mind replays the DROM running at speed. It ran with only one goal. I can't help but wonder exactly how long can they run for, when would it stop if its prey got away? So many questions. Julian's hand rubbing mine.

"We're back." I look at him for the first time. Seeing him in this light, Julian looks no different to the man I was cuddling a couple of hours ago. There was no malice in him, he didn't brag about the shot afterwards, no derogatory remarks about the beast he slaughtered. He just did what he needed to quietly and as humanely as possible. I nod. Acknowledging our return. Julian is by my side of the car opening the door, and once I have released myself from the seat belt, Julian sweeps me up into his arms and carries me to his room.

CHAPTER TWENTY-SIX

The Morning After The Night Before

Julian and I sleep all afternoon, comfortably cuddled up and spooning in his big bed. My eyes flutter open and I feel like I am cooking under the heat of Julian's strong tattooed arm that is draped over me. I lie still, enjoying the silence that is only punctuated by Julian's deep and steady breathing. His face buried in the crook of my neck; my eyes study each delicate design that has been tattooed onto his skin. My mind is hurtling through the memories of the last couple of weeks and of course last night. The existence of zombies or DROMs as Julian calls them doesn't shock me as much as it should. That I find weird. I realise I am aware that life never got back to normal after Covid from a few years ago. People continued to work remotely, families kept their young one's home and the homeless who had lived in disused buildings, shop doorways and alleyways have simply disappeared. I hadn't thought about any of this in any detail, living and working at a hotel, kept me sheltered. Well, until now. I look over at the sleeping beauty, lying next to me. How did I get here? How can one person believe that he was destined to be with someone he didn't know. It goes far beyond love at first sight. And the zombies, he has killed so many. I lie still and think about what Julian does, how I have walked into a life of governmental secrets, cover ups and lies. There is a whole world out there that I was oblivious to, one that is shrouded in darkness. It worries me that the existence of zombies has been kept hidden for the greater good.

I used to dream of having an exciting life, the kind that gets posted on social media, all sun kissed skin, beaches, cocktails, and smiles. My life until the last couple of weeks was mundane, the highlight of my working week was the manure delivery. Things have changed in a way I could never have expected. I never imagined that I could feel so blissfully happy quite so quickly whilst knowing that the human body as I know it, doesn't always die.

I can hold on no longer; I am desperate for the bathroom but don't want Julian to wake. He is a man who survives on little sleep with him being called out to work through the night. I can only imagine how many nights a week he does this. Gently I push his strong hand away from my hips and quietly climb out of the bed, creeping over to his bathroom and closing the door silently behind me, I want him to stay asleep for as long as possible. I head to the loo, looking around the spacious room.

I think of Julian as I glance at the shower. His passion is astounding. Memories of last night drip through the sleepy haze. I can only hope I live up to his expectations and despite my confusion earlier, I'm head strong, I hope he can deal with that. I splash water on my face and stare into the mirror looking back at my freckled and flushed skin. My naked form looks no different to yesterday and my thoughts grow darker. If I were to die right now, would I become a DROM? Do I need to be bitten by one to turn? So many questions flood my brain that it is hard to focus on them all. The cooling feeling of evaporation from the water droplets moving down my neck and chest brings me back to reality. I knew relatively little about my family. For years my own mother kept being a hunter from me. Knowing that both of my parents were zombie killers sends a shiver down my spine. I must hand it to my mother, for her ability to keep me in the dark until her last breath is astonishing. I head back towards the bed; Julian is awake and has a small sketchbook and pencil on his lap, I wonder what it is he has been drawing? Julian follows me with his eyes.

"What have you got there?" I ask walking towards him, my

messy hair cascading down one shoulder.

"Just new tattoo designs." I nod in understanding as he lowers the pad and pencil onto the bedside table. Remembering our previous conversation on the meaning behind his tattoos, I don't question him further. I crawl back onto the bed instead, first planting a kiss on his lips before resting my head on his hard chest, listening to his heart beating as he wraps his arms around me.

"Good morning." I can sense his smile as he kisses the top of my head. I look up and place my lips on his stubbly jaw, causing him to grin and our lips meet kissing long and deep.

"Good afternoon or possibly even evening." I reply smirking. I have absolutely no idea what time it is, but it must be late afternoon as Julian's tummy rumbles with his tell-tale sign that he is hungry.

"How are you feeling?" He enquires. I look up at him. I really don't think I have fully processed last night. I was there, I watched. I observed. I saw a DROM, and I saw Julian shoot it dead. It was quick and over in minutes. The rational side of my brain noticed it didn't move like the living. But it was in human form. That I cannot forget. I still have so much to understand. To learn.

"I think we should probably get up and get the blood pumping. I'm not used to being horizontal all day, although it has been lovely to just snuggle the day away with you." I say playing with my hair.

"I have no problem with that kitten." He replies, not pushing me to answer his question. Instead, he does what any hot-blooded male does, makes a suggestive thrust of his hips in my direction. Laughing, I pat him on the head.

"Down boy." I command, much to Julian's amusement.

"You are shocking." I climb back out of the bed and open the heavy curtains.

"It's definitely afternoon." I state, heading back to the bathroom.

"Are you going to join me in the shower?" I ask stopping to turn and face him. Julian is still on the bed, his hands behind his head with a big and stupid smile on his face.

"What?" I ask amused, he really can't go at it again, surely.

"I simply love it when you call me Lion." He replies with complete sincerity.

* * *

We are both up and dressed. Well, Julian is dressed. I am proud that I could exert some self-control and kept my legs tightly shut, much to Julian's amusement. Although he is finding it difficult to keep his hands off me while I'm tightly wrapped in his fluffy white robe. After giving him a long list, Julian manages to drag himself away from me, to go and hunt around my room for clean clothes and my much-needed toiletries. This gives me a few minutes to think, and I do this as I snoop around his office area, looking at the books and papers on DROMs, zombies and all the folklore and biology in between.

Book upon book sit in tall piles on the desk; anatomical, physiological, biological, medical, historical. So many different genres all linked by a common theme; the undead or at least what could cause the human body to shut down, die then get up and move again. I shake my head at the memory of last night. Goosebumps cover my forearms at the thought, this is something that is going to take a lot of getting used to. Thankfully it was dark, and I couldn't make out the features of the DROM. I need Julian to give me a crash course on the history of DROMs. A crash course on DROMs in general would be much appreciated right now. How does a person change? Why would a body be clinically dead but can continue to move?

My mind flips through various biological scenarios that could possibly cause such an occurrence. None of them making any sense. A mobile phone rings and my eyes sweep the room looking for it. Do I answer? I find Julian's phone and glance at the screen. It displays a number only, probably one of those dodgy payment protection insurance companies? I make the decision to answer it.

"Hello." When I realise it isn't a dodgy company, I dash across to Julian's desk.

"He isn't available at the moment; can I take a message?" I pick up a pen and write down the name and number before hanging up. I continue to look through Julian's books. He really has quite a collection. I notice he has coloured post it notes stuck between pages. There are handwritten notes stuffed in various chapters acting as bookmarks. He has made notes, underlined sentences, highlighted entire paragraphs and scribbled in margins. This is a recurrent theme with every book here and gosh there must be at least twenty. I can't help but smile. My man is certainly dedicated to his job.

"You look hot in that outfit." Julian interrupts my thoughts. I didn't hear him enter the room.

"I'm not hot, I am bloody boiling in this thing." I state, walking towards him and taking my clothes from his outstretched arm.

"Thank you." I blow him a kiss. He is all gorgeously handsome, complete with stubble at my request and is dressed in a plain black fitted T-shirt and a clean pair of Levi 501's in black, his tattooed arms are exposed, and his dark hair swept back off his face, revealing his dark eyebrows and deep green eyes. My heart sinks a little. How did someone so incredibly clever become caught up in something so sinister?

"I could do with a walk, stretch my legs and get a little fresh air." I say grabbing my bag and throwing my purse, keys, and my phone inside.

"Are you okay Ellie, you seem a little distant?" I turn slowly and face Julian. Before I can censor myself, the words are out of my mouth and rolling off my tongue.

"I know nothing on how a human can become biologically declared dead, yet carry on moving, it worries me. There is much I need to know." There I've said it, I managed to get swept away with Julian's romantic gestures, his temper, and his career but there was something eating at me, and I finally figured it out after witnessing my first DROM. Julian says nothing, shocked by my statement understandably.

"I simply don't know much about you as a person either, your family life, your likes or dislikes. I know you hunt. I have gotten my head around that. But back to the fundamentals of DROMs biologically, I don't understand how they exist or how you have developed the mentality to euthanise them." Julian takes my hand, pulling my palm up to his lips and kissing the soft pads of my fingers.

"What would you like to know?" He asks quizzically. Although I am positive that I saw a fleeting look of fear flit across his face. I have no plans to run from him, I have seen the worst of his secret and I am still here with him. I shrug my shoulders and gaze into his eyes.

"Can we start at the beginning? What did you study at university? Where did you study?" I shrug again, pulling on my bra and knickers as he watches.

"I want to know everything about DROMs and believe me, I want to bombard you with a hundred and one questions. I need time to process last night, so my DROM questions will come. But for the rest of today, I want to know about you, your life. I want to know the small things that make you who you are." I stop to pull the dress that Julian has chosen for me to wear, over my head

"I know this usually takes time in a relationship and that is great and all, the problem I have is that all I know about you, is the scary stuff." I stop, trying to think of a better way to put it.

"We have started all of this in reverse order, I'm sure I'm supposed to find out about the secrets in your closet in years to come, not at the very beginning of our relationship. I'm sure you were supposed to hide all the DROM stuff from me for at least two years." I laugh nervously as Julian listens. I can see his expression change as he mulls over what I am saying.

"I simply don't know who you are in here and I need to understand that, so I can understand the killing." I finish with a whisper as I place my hand over his steadily beating heart. All the while kicking myself because I know I shouldn't be worrying about this right now. I have forever to find this information out. Julian's green eyes search mine.

"I understand. My life to an outsider is horrific at best. I want you to feel that you can ask me anything." I smile to myself, glad that we are on the same page.

"And we are back to your game of twenty questions again?" I grin, nudging him with my elbow.

"If that is what makes you happy kitten then sure. But if I remember rightly, you were not very good at it." He moves to his desk to get his car keys, wallet, and phone, stuffing them in his pockets. Julian pulls me towards the door.

"We never did get to question twenty. Let's start again." I stop, remembering suddenly the phone call Julian had minutes earlier.

"You had a call when you went to get my clothes, here is the message. The guy just asked that you call him back. He didn't say what it was about." I pull Julian towards his desk and hand the slip of paper to him. He looks at it and frowns.

"I am going to have to call him back and arrange a meeting with him." He says holding his hand out to me.

"But not until after we have eaten, I'm starving." We step out into the hallway and head to the stairs.

"Question one where did I study? I went to Kings college London." Julian states as we descend the stairs and out past reception where Nicky is at the desk. He looks tired, either someone has called in sick, or he has been called to deal with a problem. He spots us and waves, I wave back followed by a gesture that I will phone him soon. It feels like I haven't seen him in weeks.

"Question two; I studied Medicine." He says as he holds opens the door and I climb in. I sit gobsmacked. The car purrs as we pull out of the hotel grounds. Julian looks over at me and grins.

"My father is called Brinley. Or Brin to his friends, he is a monumental arse. My mother is called Rosemary, but everyone calls her Rosie, she has spent the last twenty years in research. DROM research and research on the Hunter gene. I have an older brother called Charles, or Charlie as he prefers to be called. We don't get along, he too studied medicine and is a GP." He slows the car down as we begin to stop at a red light.

"I beheaded my first DROM at eighteen, but you already know that. I have never had a long-term relationship but know that too. I love chocolate, my favourite book is I Am Legend by Richard Matheson and I love you, but I may have mentioned that before." He smiles over at me.

"I play piano well. I play guitar too but not so well. I'll leave Seb to tell you that tale one day. I hate cricket but love watching tennis. I watch the men's finals at Wimbledon every year." He glances over at me and winks.

"I don't like to wear underwear, but I suspect that you're already aware of that. I love movies but don't get a chance to watch them very often. I love music, heavy music, metal, punk, industrial, opera and classical too. I detest Jazz. Most importantly, I love you, Ellie. My heart belongs to you and hopefully you know too." I start to giggle out loud and I know I shouldn't.

"What's so funny?" Julian asks all indignant and rightly so. I really shouldn't laugh at him.

"You sound like such a girl. All I love you, Ellie." I say in a high pitch voice. Julian keeps his eyes on the road as the tone of his voice changes. I can tell that I have hurt his feelings, which I now feel guilty about.

"I cannot help how I feel about you. Really if I could have controlled and ignored my feelings, we really wouldn't be here now, and I would probably be in the bed with another of Seb's girls." He stops, taking a deep breath in exasperation while shaking his head.

"I. Love. You." He pronounces each word slowly, tapping his fingers on the steering wheel with each word. I feel thoroughly ashamed of myself and realise I have hurt him.

"I'm sorry Julian, I didn't mean to tease, but it is just so easy." I laugh again and run my hand along his denim clad thigh.

"You do realise that now I have loads of questions for you." I say, trying to lighten his mood. Julian just nods. He really is not happy with me but I'm past caring.

"Shall we go somewhere for a coffee?" I ask in an attempt at changing the subject. A good shot of caffeine would really help right now.

I find a vacant table with two armchairs in Starbucks. Julian comes back with a tray.

"One vanilla latte in a soup bowl, extra shot for the lady." He puts the big mug down on the table in front of me.

"What are you having for future reference?" I'm curious, wanting to know as much as I can about him.

"I am treating myself to a small oat, caramel latte with three shots." I wrinkle my nose at the thought of the oat milk. Julian smiles at the face I'm making.

"I have been drinking it for a while now. Try it" He places a skinny blueberry muffin on a white plate in front of me and a ginger biscuit next to his mug. I tuck in suddenly ravenous. It is just before five in the afternoon, and we ate breakfast at nine this morning, it is safe to say we are both starving.

"Where did you grow up?" I ask between mouthfuls of muffin and steaming hot coffee. Julian mulls over the question while chewing. He swallows. I can't keep my eyes off him as I sit mesmerized watching his Adam's apple bob in his throat, there is something about his Adams apple, a sign of his masculinity and I am captivated by it.

"We moved twice when I was a kid, we lived next door to my father's best friend and his family in Brighton. When I was six, we moved to the Lake district. Before we moved my father's best friend died and my father didn't cope well with his death, I guess it is one of the reasons he is so bitter. We moved as far away from the south as we could for a year in a period of mourning. We moved back down South to London a year later when I was seven and that is where I grew up." I take another sip of my coffee; I feel the much-needed buzz from the caffeine and sugar awakening my brain.

"What was your life like growing up?" Julian has wolfed down his ginger biscuit, I observe him closely as he turns his head, his eyes light up with glee when he spots the counter and the goodies displayed behind the glass. He hasn't heard my question at all, feeding his stomach was far more an important task. I smile to myself as I stand up wordlessly and walk over to the counter. I can feel Julian's eyes following me, no doubt checking out my arse and wondering what I am doing. I purchase two vegan chocolate and raspberry cakes and return to the table.

"Here, eat these." I place both plates down on the table in front of him. He thanks me with a glorious smile, the way to this man's heart is truly through his stomach.

"Chocolate cake is my favourite cake, except for those little hazelnut cupcakes." He chuckles as he takes the wrapper off the first cake, offering me some first before he tucks in. I ask Julian my question again and this time he hears me.

"It was pretty lonely to be perfectly honest. My parents worked hard building up the business and then dad got into politics for a while but that was short lived. I didn't see my parents an awful lot, they were busy. Thankfully my grandmother was around to help out and she became our main carer as kids." Julian stops and laughs to himself clearly remembering a memory from his youth.

"My brother and I hated each other, so I stayed out of his way, locked myself in my bedroom and studied hard instead. I didn't have friends as such, girls at school showed too much interest in me. The guys thought I was weird, gay or both and stayed away. Seb was in the same boat as me growing up, he was an outsider, so we became close. We hung out as we reached our teens. He built up his business from scratch and worked hard on his little empire. I helped him out when I could, and he now helps me with my work." Julian stops to take another bite as I finish my coffee, placing my white mug on the table.

"It sounds lonely, a little like my childhood." Julian nods in agreement.

"What was yours like?" He casually enquires whilst picking up his folk from the white plate.

"I don't really remember much of my father sadly. Mum and I were incredibly close, but she was overprotective which became stifling as I got older. I wasn't allowed to go to parties, go to friends' houses or go out in general. When I was seventeen and finished my A 'Level's mum took me back packing for nine months. We had fun, saw a lot of the world." I stop, tears begin to sting my eyes as I desperately try and blink them away.

"I went off to the university of Portsmouth and studied biology, finally escaping home and tasting real freedom for the first time." I stop again and use my napkin to dab away the tear that is threatening to spill. Julian watches but says nothing.

"Whilst studying for my degree, I met Nicky and we became best friends. I got lost a little afterwards not sure what to do when I graduated, so I got a job as an assistant to an old gardener.

More of a summer job really, while I figured out what to do next. Found that I loved the job and was a natural. I am blessed with green fingers if I do say so myself." Julian grins and I give a mock bow from my chair.

"There isn't a plant I can't get to grow. I stayed on with John and after a year and another harsh winter he retired. He was kind enough to pull a few strings and I found myself with a job at Hedge Hill. The rest you know." I give Julian an uneasy smile. He stands up and extends his hand.

"Let's go for that walk."

When we get back to the car Julian returns his phone call from earlier. I politely try and not listen while I strap myself in. He is setting up a meeting for later tonight which is a shame as I was looking forward to having him all to myself again. I guess this is what he meant by being busy. I am sure it is something that I will grow used to.

"Sorry about that." He says hanging up. I am rewarded with his beaming smile which leaves my centre all gooey.

"I need to go and speak to this guy later tonight."

"That is fine." I know it can't be helped. I know it is work related and Julian doesn't work the conventional nine to five. I understand and I will get used to this. Julian's phone rings once. "Seb. Yes, spoke to Roth. I have a meeting with him at ten tonight. Yes, in Brighton. Okay, that sounds great. Fine. See you then." I raise my eyebrow at him, what was that about.

"I have this meeting. Seb is on his to way to collect Nicky and is taking him to the attic. As they will be in Brighton tonight and my meeting later is in Brighton, I am going to take us for a little walk first, then I am going to feed you and drop you off at Seb's with him and Nicky, if that is okay? I will meet you back at Seb's when I am all done.

"Okay that sounds like a plan, thank you. Oh, Seb lives in an attic?" I smile, heaving an overly dramatic sigh of relief. I'm glad he isn't leaving me on my own like I was expecting. Julian laughs at my question but doesn't answer. Less than twenty-four hours after witnessing my first DROM and then being left on my own would cause me to freak out. I don't want to lose it and have some sort of panic induced meltdown when the sun goes down. I am grateful that I won't be alone. Julian reaches over and grasps my hand in his.

"I won't be long with Roth, then we can make up for lost time." I don't know who this Roth is and from Julian's body language, I can't help but feel anxious.

CHAPTER TWENTY-SEVEN

Set Up

Sitting in the car contemplating this crazy idea of my father's. I'm going to go and speak informally with Roth Addison, our competition, and the guy who we think is trying to poach me and Seb. I have no idea what he is going to offer, although I expect it to involve obscene amounts of money, which by all accounts is how he works, if I am to believe his reputation. Vast sums of money are not required as I already have that. There isn't anything he can possibly offer me that I would want except maybe a way out, to stop doing what I do and attempt to live a normal life. Funny how my life has changed in mere days.

I was beginning to think I was never going to find a way into Ellie's Life. She is the most perfect person I have ever had the privilege to meet, I can't be any happier knowing that she somehow wants me and my screwed-up life. I am just overwhelmed that she is so accepting of who I am and what I do. She is intelligent and strong both emotionally and physically. I love her strength and courage and I always have. Scrolling through my phone I find Seb's number and hit it sending him a text.

Hey I am here. Is there anything that you want me to ask? How is Ellie? Make sure you and Nicky keep her busy. This won't take long.

I have five more minutes before my meeting with Roth. Here goes nothing. I walk around the block having checked out the lay of the land before heading up the steps to the entrance. I tilt my head back to get a view of the roof. This is an incredibly impressive block of council flats in Brighton and architecturally speaking, it is one hell of a building. It stands twenty-four floors high. it wouldn't surprise me if this was one of the tallest council blocks in the country. One thing is for sure, I wouldn't want to climb to the top floor when the piss ridden lift is out of order.

I whistle at the thought of the view. It would certainly give the London Eye a run for its money. I press the button of the flat number I want, glancing around me. No one is about tonight, no teenagers, no dog walkers. Which doesn't surprise me. People don't hang around in the dark like they used to. Parents who love their offspring, certainly don't let them walk the streets and congregate in groups of their friends on dark stair wells at night anymore. I am thankful that this place is well lit and there are CCTV cameras, so someone is keeping an eye on things.

The door buzzes and I let myself in, stepping over the pile of pizza delivery fliers and the local free newspaper. I look left then right. Accessing the surroundings, figuring out all escape routes if I should need them. There are two fire exits down here that lead out to the back of the building as well as the main entrance. I count six windows that I could break if I needed to make a hasty escape. I ignore the lift completely and walk up the thirteen flights of stairs, glancing for possible exit routes on the way. This staircase is cleaner than I expected, the windows too. Walls could do with a lick of paint but overall, they are clean and graffiti free. I continue to scope out the place for escape routes, hoping I won't need them tonight.

I reach the thirteenth floor and walk along the corridor searching for the flat number I was given. I knock twice and the door opens. A tall, broad set man dressed in black, with terrible acne scarring steps back and gestures for me to enter. I thrust my hand out once he has closed the door.

"Julian Hunter."

"Dave. I'll take you to Roth." He says shaking my hand first before leading me down the hall. I follow Dave and am led to a large room where I am offered a seat. This looks like the lounge judging on the furniture. The television is on but on mute, a lamp is lit in the corner of the room casting eerie shadows on the walls. I walk to the window, as Dave leaves me alone presumably to alert Roth of my arrival. This all seems to be for dramatic effect because I rang a fucking doorbell, they knew I was coming up. I glance out to lovely views of Brighton, moonlight providing the perfect backdrop to a constantly bustling City.

"Julian, thank you for coming." I turn to find a small squat man, bald and dressed in jeans and a navy shirt. He can't be more than forty. He is certainly not what I was expecting. I walk towards him with my outstretched hand, and we shake.

"Thank you for the invitation." Roth gestures for me to sit and I do, he joins me on the cream leather sofa.

"Before we start can I get you anything to drink?"

"No thanks, I'm good." I reply politely, sizing him up. His jeans are tight, and he has his shirt tucked in. No sign of a concealed weapon on his person. Unlike Dave, who I'm guessing is wearing a gun under that jacket of his.

"Thank you again for agreeing to see me. Look, I am going to cut to the chase. We have a problem and I'm guessing you will be aware of it." I raise an eyebrow. I wasn't aware that I came here on a problem-solving mission.

"I'm listening." Prompting him to continue but not acting too interested.

"I'm sure you are aware that there has been a distinct increase in the amount of DROM calls. A dramatic increase in the last three months, particularly here in the south, southeast and southwest." I nod, fully aware.

"We are swamped, I cannot get enough men trained in time to deal with the volume that we are getting. I'm sure you are the same." I nod again, noticing that Dave is standing outside in the hall, why doesn't he just come in and join us.

"I have one of my men, who has replaced your chap on the force. He is trustworthy and I have known him for years. I just wanted to get that straight. But through him, we have been getting the wrong information so to speak. I know that you have too. I have spoken at length with him, have listened to the tapes of the calls. They are legit! Yet when my men arrive, the information is dangerously wrong."

"Please clarify what you mean by the wrong information." I ask, I do not want to tell him what we have been getting, although I'm aware that he probably already knows.

"I like your style Julian, its why I contacted you and that cousin of yours. We have been getting the wrong coordinates, wrong locations. Always close enough to where the DROMs are, but the information is rarely correct. The DROM estimates have been wrong too. I send one guy out to hunt one DROM, only to find there were two, or three or seven. We have run into some large pods of DROMs, putting my men at risk. That kind of wrong information. I am having to send two guys out each time as a safety precaution." Roth looks earnestly at me; he is calm but frustrated. I thought he and his men were behind the wrong information being called in. I was wrong.

"We have been experiencing similar issues too, of late." I confirm. Roth shakes his head angrily, frown lines marring his tanned face. I am getting the feeling that he might know more than he is letting on. Dave is pacing around outside; his presence is making me nervous.

"I am glad we are on the same page. I have no idea who is behind it. My man on the force has had the original calls traced and found nothing unusual. The original callers are genuine people, who when questioned had not faltered in their information, the payments are always on time and in full. I just don't understand why we are both getting the wrong information?" I consider what he is saying, my mind thinking fast. We knew we had a problem. Seb and his father have been looking into it over the last three months but have so far come up with very little.

"What about the other teams? The ones in Wales, the Midlands, Scotland. Are they having similar issues?" Dave stops his pacing and looks at me, at the room and at Roth before continuing. He moves silently for a man of his size.

"No. That is the peculiar thing, they haven't had a single dodgy call out and I have contacted every team in the country. You were the last to get back to me."

"We have a problem then don't we." I reply. My throat feeling dry.

"Yes, that we do. I have my men on it but have found nothing. It is not good for business, it looks unprofessional turning up and not being prepared for a hunt and as much as I hate to discuss it, it is beginning to cut into our profit margin, my men want double for every hunt they attend, and they are working in pairs for safety." I could understand how that was becoming a problem, particularly when he hunts purely for profit, Roth and I presume all these men do not posse the hunter gene. This is pseudo government work.

"What I am proposing at this stage is that we cover each other. If you find anything, I would appreciate it if you would let me know and vice versa. I don't want to partner up, like your cousin accused me of. I am certainly not interested in stealing you or your cousin from the family. There is more than enough work for all of us out there now." I nod in acknowledgement, thankful for his honesty.

"I just want to find out who is responsible and why." Roth stands abruptly. Dave enters the room and manoeuvres himself to stand by the door. Roth extends his hand out to me, and we shake again.

"I really do appreciate you coming." Roth gestures to Dave and holds his hand out, Dave walks forwards, thrusting a card into Roth's waiting palm who then hands it to me.

"Look Julian, here is my business card, contact me day or night if you find out anything that might need looking into." I thank him and slip his card in my back pocket. Dave is like a whippet leading me out of the lounge and into the hallway.

"Something big is happening and we need to find out what it is and why. I am worried this could get out of control." Roth shakes my hand once more. Dave opens the door and I leave.

I text Seb to say I'm done and am informed that they're about to leave the attic and are returning to Hedge Hill. Roth had confirmed Seb's suspicions, this is looking more and more like sabotage. Is someone releasing DROMs? It is only a matter of time before this kind of problem becomes public knowledge, something all involved have tried to keep hidden for quite some time. Most DROM attacks have been blamed on terrorists, religious fanatics or manufactured disasters and new viral diseases. Not sure what other excuses and cover ups the government can come up with next.

"Damn it!" I shout hitting the steering wheel as I power along. I have just found Ellie and she is going to get caught up in all this shit. My mind is contemplating options, I have a few I could consider. My first thought is we could run. Now that I have found her, I could just take her away from this hell. I have enough money that neither of us would ever have to work again and to purchase our own island to see out the rest of our days. We could set up a new life somewhere, enjoy each other, grow old together. Nope. Who am I kidding, that will never happen, I would always be looking over my shoulder! These DROM infestations are getting worse worldwide, I didn't mention it to Roth but teams in Barcelona, Berlin and Paris are having similar problems. It's not just us and I would hedge my bets that if I were to contact one of the Edinburgh or Northern Ireland teams, I would find it was the same for them.

I just don't understand who it is that is behind the misinformation. I am good at what I do, but that is because it has been my life for the last ten years. Roth's men would find it difficult; they are nothing but hounds. Men who are all brawn, trained like nightclub bouncers, sent on a couple of courses, and taught the bare minimum, before being allowed to begin hunting. Many of his men do it for the money, it is a well-paid profession but a few of them do it to feed their ex-con, aggressive, murderous needs, and nothing more.

"It is looking like Seb, and I are going to have to work harder, if I am lucky maybe Ellie will join us and become my partner. She is strong minded, strong willed and I have seen her work, lifting bags and boxes around the gardens with ease, even that gardener guy she works with uses a wheelbarrow to transport compost and tools. Not Ellie, she carries it all with ease and without batting an eyelid. She is stronger than she realises. I want to train her, if for nothing else but her own safety, but dragging her into this doesn't sit well with me. My gut instinct is to protect her and not to put her in harm's way. I pull out my mobile to phone father and let him know how the meeting went. He will be happy that Seb and I are not being poached but he won't like that Roth wants to work together to find out who is messing up the hunts. I really don't think we have much choice. If Roth can provide information that helps us, then so be it. The last thing we need is for this situation to get out of hand and we have a DROM epidemic on our hands.

CHAPTER TWENTY-EIGHT

The Fight

I let myself into Julian's room, only to find a muscular and very topless man stalk towards me. I am grabbed into a bear hug that makes me grin, causing me to drop my bag on the floor.

"Hey, you beat us to it." Julian begins to man handle me, attempting to get my dress over my head while kissing any area of my body he can plaster his lips to.

"Stop, stop, Nicky and Seb are on the way up. How was your meeting?" Julian shrugs, letting me go. His brow furrows in a look of annoyance which he follows with a tired smile.

"It just confirmed what we thought." He continues to paw at me and in the heat of the moment I let him. His hands move over my skin, under the fabric, before grabbing the hem of my dress and pulling it over my head where he tosses it to the floor. My partially clothed body pressed to his, Julian's strong hands move around to my back fumbling with my bra strap when there is a knock at the door. I scramble for my dress, pulling it back over my head as Julian sighs and goes to answer it.

"Seb you really do have the worst timing." Julian steps back letting the boys in. Seb notices my flushed state and winks.

"Just be grateful Lion that I don't have a key. You know what happened last time." The four of us settle on the large sofa, looking out over the dark hotel grounds. I am nestled comfortably on Julian's lap while he plays with my hair. Seb and Nicky sit as close as humanly possible to one another. The boys arrived with refreshments which are welcomed. Julian and I stick to water while they drink gin and tonics out of cans, we all nibble and crunch on a bag of kettle chips and a share bag of vegan chocolates as we chat.

"How was the meeting?" Seb asks, trailing his finger up Nicky's leg from knee to thigh and back down again. Julian tells us all how it went, He speaks mostly in code, Nicky looks lost but listens without interruption. I now have confirmation that Seb has not mentioned the hunts at all to Nicky.

"What did Uncle Brin say?" My ears prick up at the mention of Julian's father's name.

"The usual, keep family business, family business. Don't trust Roth. Continue what we are doing, he'll look into it." Seb's face changes, contorted into pure rage. I hope you are not going to follow your father's advice! I agree with Roth, we should work together, at least until we find out who the bastard is that is behind this shit show."

"Not here Seb." Julian remails calm, in an attempt at keeping the peace. Clearly this is an ongoing family issue that they don't or can't agree on and it is probably something that should be discussed when Seb is a little calmer. Seb fumes, changes tact and turns to me, looking me straight in the eye. Instinctively Julian holds me closer, trying to use his body to shield me from Seb.

"Ellie needs to know just how dangerous all of this is becoming; all these problems are beyond our control. And you are going to drag her into it, Lion, I know you are. Your fucked up father puts profit before his own son's life, don't do the same. Not with your own life. Not with hers." Nicky puts his hand on Seb's thigh. Seb stops his rant for a second, looking at Nicky who has worry etched all over his face.

"Lion, he will do the same to her if you train her. You know that right. He has done it before."

"For fucks sake. Enough Seb!" Julian shouts making me jump. Nicky looks sternly at him, keeping his hand firmly on Seb's leg and then looks over to me. His eyes plead for an explanation that I barely understand myself. I don't know what to do. I can't tell Nicky what Julian does and I only have an inkling about what Seb is talking about myself. I simply shrug at Nicky and hope he doesn't get a moment to question me about it tonight.

"Fine Julian. I just don't want one of your father's decisions to get you killed." I move off Julian's lap which is enough to change the subject. I feel on the spot, as all eyes are on me.

"Where are you going?" Julian asks as I walk over to the sound system, ignoring the three men behind me.

"We need some music; can you help me switch this thing on please." Julian gets the hint, leaving the sofa and walking over. Seb and Nicky whisper in hushed tones, Nicky attempting to calm Seb down. I get the distinct impression that Seb is not very fond of his uncle, Julian's father. Great, drama for me to get involved in and family drama at that, the worst kind.

It's just before three in the morning, the music helped diffuse the tension earlier and conversations were changed to future nights out in Brighton together, our childhoods and some of the colourful characters who stay at the hotel and keep Nicky on his toes. I can't stop yawning and neither can Julian, we are both exhausted and I for one, am looking forward to going to bed at some point tonight, having assumed that I will be sleeping up here with Julian tonight. Today has been tiring. All the thinking, talking and decision making, and it has really taken its toll on me. Nicky nibbles on Seb's ear, he is a little tipsy and that always leaves him feeling horny. They won't be sleeping anytime soon and are ready to leave when Seb's phone rings. He reaches into his pocket, pulling it out and reading the screen. He looks over to Julian who simply nods back.

"Ellie, would you mind making us a coffee, we are going to need a little caffeine." Asks Seb as he strides over to Julian's desk and fires up his laptop. I raise an eyebrow in response, knowing they have received a call about a hunt. Silently I walk across the room, like a robot to the coffee machine, popping a pod in and pressing a button. Nicky looks over at me puzzled but says nothing at all and I know he is dying to ask what is going on. Seb is in deep conversation on the phone, busy typing co-ordinates into Julian's laptop. Julian is in the bathroom splashing cold water onto his face. With two espressos in hand, I walk back to the desk and pop a mug down next to Seb, who takes a sip. I hand Julian his coffee, he takes a tentative sip, swirling it around the cup a couple of times before he downs it in one go. Seb is furiously typing while talking animatedly on the phone. Nicky watches from the sofa as Julian pulls me close to him waiting for the information.

"Okay, two spotted on Littlehampton beach. A dog walker out half an hour ago reported two men's odd behaviour and called the police." Nicky snorts and we all look at him.

"That place is still a gay cruising site, there is no way that guy was walking a dog at this time of night." Nicky laughs while Julian just rolls his eyes. Seb rubs at his chin, looking worried.

"Lion, you need to be careful with this one. If two DROMs are sighted, how on earth did the witness live to call it in, that seems nonsensical. This just doesn't feel right." Seb looks at the map on the laptop again, shaking his head.

"We could let Roth's team deal with it." Seb's hopeful look doesn't sway Julian.

"It's fine, I'll deal with it." He shrugs on a black hoodie.

"Do you want to come with me?" Momentarily all eyes are on me. Nicky looks really confused, while Seb looks truly uncomfortable. Seb shoots Julian a look that is full of warning. I nod yes instantly. I don't want Julian going out on his own tonight, or ever again if I can help it.

"We better go." Seb says to Nicky who is still observing our collectively odd behaviour. Seb catches a hold of my elbow gently as he passes.

"Are you sure you want this? You don't have to go if you are not ready." I look blankly at him, there is warning in his voice but concern too.

"I will be okay; I'll just observe again." I reply, this time ignoring Nicky altogether.

"You have a choice, Ellie. Make sure this is what you want." Seb sighs, kisses me on the cheek before pulling me into a fierce bear hug.

"Keep her safe." He grabs a hold of Nicky, dragging him to the door by the hand. We whisper our goodbyes, and the boys leave.

"Seb is right. Are you sure you want to come tonight? Because you don't have to."

"Yes. I want to. I really do. I don't want you out there on your own." I reply grabbing my handbag. I down the rest of my espresso which is now almost cold and pull my trainers on. Julian does the same and we head out before the sun begins to rise.

* * *

We arrive in Littlehampton just after four in the morning. The town is quiet and still. Julian follows the signs for West Beach Local nature reserve, and we drive along looking out for signs of movement. I can barely see the beach or the sea as we drive along, my view blocked by the sand dunes as we study the area for signs of movement. Julian pulls over and parks at an angle behind the visitor's centre, out in the distance along the boardwalk, he thinks he sees someone or something moving. Everything happens quickly, Julian reaches under his seat for his handgun. He checks and fills the barrel of the gun and attaches the silencer.

"Under your seat is a case, can you get it for me." I unbuckle myself and reach under my seat, feeling around until I have the requested case in my hands, pulling it out and handing it to Julian.

"Same drill kitten. Stay in the car. Do not get out under any circumstance." He opens the case; it contains another handgun. One gun in his possession I understand but two. My heart is beating heavily in my chest.

"I am leaving this gun on the dashboard to be used in an emergency only." I nod, taking it all in while looking out of the window. I can see the figure moving now, its silhouette wandering around aimlessly in the dark. Julian reaches over and kisses my cheek.

"This looks like it should be fairly easy. I'll do what I did before, put the headlamps on and we should see both move towards the light." I nod again, checking all the mirrors. I can still only see one DROM. The other is out there somewhere, the only question is where?

"Have you got your phone?" I pull it out of my bag and hold it up.

"If there is a problem phone Nicky and speak to Seb." I nod again. I really am not prepared for this. When tonight is over, I want all the training. Julian takes a good look around before turning on the headlights. Brilliant light floods the beach and out towards the boardwalk, illuminating the side of the visitor's centre and instantly DROM number one begins ambling towards the car. We wait, watching it move towards the light. The first DROM is close to us, when I spot the second, I silently point so Julian can see it too. Both DROMs are clean looking and appear well dressed, considering. In unison they head towards the source of light, ignoring each other, which I find curious. I watch them closely, their movements are jerky as they take each step, very much like the DROM from last night. It really is the strangest sight, adults walking like toddlers.

Without a word of warning, Julian opens the car door, climbs out and slams the door closed behind him, leaving me in the car alone. The handgun on the dashboard mocks me sitting there cold and metallic, although it is strangely comforting to have it so close. Julian stands quietly watching both DROMs move towards him.

He slowly walks towards the front of the car. Stopping to the left-hand side of the building and me, sitting directly behind him in the passenger seat. The DROMs speed increase, having heard the car door slam and smelt Julian as they both head in his direction. They run, ignoring each other completely as they sniff the air with every other footstep. I hold my breath in anticipation, adrenaline coursing through my veins as I wait to hear the first bang of the gun.

I hear screaming, loud and high pitched, it takes me a second to realise the sound is coming from me. I sit paralysed with fear watching the scene that has begun to play out before me, the window acting like a cinema screen. In a matter of seconds, one DROM lies dead on the floor with a perfectly aimed hole to its forehead. The second DROM with his hands outstretched and dried blood and dirt smeared around its mouth, is mere meters away from Julian. This DROM moved with such lightning speed that he has knocked into Julian, which has thrown his balance off course. I glance to the right only to see a third DROM hurtling towards us; there was only supposed to be two infesting here.

"Shit. Shit. Shit!" I shout to myself in panic, bile stinging the back of my throat as my stomach heaves. I glance down at the handgun on the dashboard in front of me and then back out to the head lamped lit beach. Julian said under no circumstances to get out of the car. To only use the gun in an emergency. I look back at the gun now, truly scared. There is a problem out there. In the split second that I glanced at the handgun on the dashboard; Julian has managed to drop his own gun onto the sand. It is a miracle that it didn't go off.

I watch as Julian begins to struggle, his gun out of reach. Julian moves, ducks, and dives the outstretched hands of the DROM closest to him, while desperately trying to locate his gun. The DROM lurches forward, his mouth open, ready to bite, but Julian is quicker and moves out of his grasp, before kicking the DROM in the chest sending it hurtling backwards, on to the sandy floor below. I honestly don't know what to do. I sit helplessly and watch. Hoping Julian can retrieve his gun and get back into a position to kick arse.

Julian punches DROM two in the face causing it to stagger backwards, Julian scan's the ground, his gun is a meter or so away from his feet, covered in sand from the scuffle. I can see DROM three moving forwards relentlessly. The punch to its face, not making a blind bit of difference to its behaviour. Straight away it is back, arms out in front of him trying to grab at Julian again. Julian manages to swing around and lands a flying kick to DROM two's chest. I sit wide eyed watching DROM two, it only has attack mode. That kick caused it to hurtle backwards but in a split second, it regains its balance, righting itself and lurches forward to continue its attack.

I sit stock still in horrified amazement, despite the odd jerky way these DROMs walk when moving, when they sense their prey is close, their posture and positioning are faultless, they move with ease, having speed and agility to match. Julian was right, they do seem to have in incredible strength too. How is this physically possible. My eyes flit to DROM three who is getting closer, running fast towards the sound of the fight and the streaming light. This DROM, like the other two is wearing clothes that seem to be in good condition. Physically speaking, this DROM is unlike the other two, DROM three has a much smaller frame, its hair is tied messily back in a low ponytail. It is moving super-fast.

I look back to the fight, Julian is silent as he takes a step and reaches down to grab his gun with his right hand, while holding DROM two by the scruff of its neck with his left. He is successful, finally managing to bend and scoop up the gun but just as he lifts his arm to aim, the DROM shifts position and is out of Julian's grip, attempting to bite Julian's arm. I hear myself scream again, Julian looks towards me in the car, DROM two moves effortlessly, grabbing Julian, picking him clean off the ground and pulling him towards his open mouth. If I had kept my stupid mouth shut Julian wouldn't have momentarily been distracted. A loud guttural sound resonates from deep within DROM two's throat as he attempts to bite at Julian's neck. Julian manages to twist himself, stopping DROM two from sinking his putrid teeth into him by delivering a single punch to its head, grabbing its arm, and twisting it. There is an audible click I can hear from the safety of the car and the DROMs arm hangs limply by its side.

The way this monster is fighting, reminds me of a drunk at a pub I saw brawling once, alcohol numbing the pain, so he absorbs every punch without the common sense to stop throwing punches himself. Julian is now rolling around on the ground with DROM two. I make out the glint of metal from the gun and I breathe out, not realising I was holding my breath. Silent tears run down my face from the shock of seeing Julian attacked and there is not a single thing I can do to help him.

Julian looks up at DROM two, judging the distance between the DROM and himself. He rolls onto his stomach and jumps to his feet, pushing himself off the ground. DROM two takes the opportunity to grab Julian again but loses its balance. Stumbling forwards and falling over. Julian grabs at the DROM awkwardly, causing the DROM to land with a horrible thud and a crack on the floor below, from the angle that he is lying in and the way he is moving, it looks like DROM two's other arm has been broken, but he doesn't seem affected by that.

in a split-second Julian is on his feet. He points his gun and pulls the trigger, the gunshot making me jump. Before Julian has the chance to move, DROM three reaches him and knocks him back down to the ground from behind using all its force. I scream again, DROM three looks around for the sound that emanated from my soul, that one second diversion gives Julian time to attempt to push it away, but it doesn't budge, its teeth gnashing wildly looking to bite. This DROM throws itself down on top of Julian and although it doesn't look heavy, the force of it landing on Julian's torso knocks the wind out of him for a moment and Julian hits his head on the ground.

I sit stock still, a hundred thoughts rushing through my head as my eyes attempt to rationalise what is happening. I watch as if in slow motion, DROM three shifts its bodyweight, it is sitting astride Julian's chest. It places both hands on either side of Julian's head and with ease picks up and pulls Julian's head backward towards its open mouth. Julian's hands desperately try to push and pull the DROM off him but to no avail.
I glance at the handgun on the dashboard. Picking it up, feeling it's weight and heftiness for something so small.

I open the car door and move silently behind the DROM, my eyes wide in concentration and fear. I shift slightly and force the barrel of the gun to the DROMs head. I notice the tell-tale sniff as DROM three registers my arrival. It looks up and back at me with big, cold, grey, and cloudy eyes and it drops Julian's head hard to the ground to study me. I glance down at her lifeless face, her lips curled into a snarl, dried blood staining her chin and neck, I now have become its prey.

The DROM stops moving and slumps to the right, falling to the floor, half slumped over Julian's shoulder and head. My ears ring from the sound of the gun firing and I stumble backwards from the force of the shot. I sink to my knees, my hands numb, dropping the gun. It feels like hours have past but, it has been mere seconds that I have knelt on the sand. I catch my breath quickly and shakily stand, using all the force I can muster to pull the bloody remains of the DROM off and away from Julian. Reality kicks in when I see Julian's bloodied face, he is still alive and breathing, thankfully.

I attempt to rouse him, but he is out cold. I pat Julian down searching for his phone, removing it, and popping it under my bra strap before rolling him into the recovery position. Finding a large rock under Julian's head, jutting out from the sand. Clearly him knocking his head on that rock is the cause of his unconsciousness. I run back to the car and find my phone, scrolling quickly to find Nicky's number and hit dial. I hold my breath while I wait for him to answer.

CHAPTER TWENTY-NINE

Panic

The phone is picked up on the first ring.

"Ellie, are you okay?"

"Sebastian, I need your help!" I relay what has happened to Seb who curses loudly. I explain where we are, how Julian is unconscious and how the sun is beginning to rise making us and the three dead bodies around us very noticeable.

"Has Julian been bitten?" This I am not sure of, I check Julian over, no scratches or bite marks to his body, only a head wound caused by a protruding rock.

"No, no he hasn't. No bite marks. No scratches." Julian groans and I am instantly by his side as he opens his eyes and rolls onto his back.

"Seb, he is coming around." I rub Julian's shoulder and comfort him as he slowly sits up.

"That is good news Ellie. I have alerted clean up, they are on the way. Are you able to get Julian into the car and get him back here? We can check him over when you arrive. I will have Charlie come to access him."

"Sure, I can do that". I hang up the phone and see to Julian. He sits rubbing his head and checking himself over, he looks dazed, is squinting and is pale.

"Take it easy, you have hit your head." Julian attempts to stand, but I stop him. Indicating that he needs to sit for a few minutes.

"What happened?" Julian asks as I check him over, he has no broken bones, but does have a small head wound, atop a large bump. That is going to be sore.

"There were three DROMs, not two. You killed one and the second kicked your arse and you dropped the gun. Do you remember that much?" Julian nods. I help him up after I have finished checking him over. He has no bites or scratches, I'm assuming that just like the movies, this is how the disease, if that is what it is can be spread.

I manage to walk Julian over to the car carefully, guiding his head, assisting him to sit in the passenger's seat of his car. I check his arms, hands and feel around the back of his neck. I reach over him and attach the seat belt before reaching into my bra, pulling out his phone and handing it to him to hold. Julian sits silently, only wincing as I manoeuvre around him.

"The third came running out from behind that sand dune, I don't think you saw her. You killed the second DROM as she pounced on you, knocking you out. I had to..." I stop, reality kicking in, rationalising what I had just done.

"You killed it." Julian looks pale as he confirms what I was about to say.

"Yes. I killed it. I took the gun off the dash and shot her. It was a woman, the last DROM, the other two are male. Not that it matters that she was a woman." Julian rubs his face before reaching out and grabbing my hand.

"You did what you had to. Don't feel guilty. You saved my life."

"I don't feel guilty, whatever the fuck that was, she was going to kill you. I needed to stop her." I am resolute in my answer, I have no remorse. It was simple, right now it was a matter of killing or be killed. I did what I had to, what was necessary.

"Seb is aware of what happened. I am going to drive us back to Hedge Hill where you can get checked out. Is that okay with you?" Julian nods, awkwardly patting himself down.

"You were not bitten or scratched. I have already checked." He stops all movement and sighs a breath of relief.

"Seb told me to check for bites. Why did I need to do that?" Julian sighs again.

"DROM bites and scratches can lead to the formation of another DROM. Have you got any water; I have sand in my mouth?" Rummaging through my bag, I pull out a bottle of water, open the lid and hand it to him, instructing him to only take small sips.

"How does that work exactly?" Julian looks very pale, and I am worried he has a concussion.

"Whatever is in their bite can be transmitted to their victim, poisoning them and causing them to become a DROM". Julian gulps at the water and I steady the bottle. Small sips or you will vomit.

"My head hurts, I feel slightly nauseous, but I'll be fine." Julian attempts to glug at the water again.

"Take it easy, I don't want you vomiting on the upholstery. Are you okay for us to leave?" It is getting lighter; it is much easier to see the three bodies that are lying in front of the car.

"Sure, let's get going." Turning the key in the ignition, I put the car into reverse.

"In that case I am glad you were not bitten. Don't want you turning on me."

"Wait, where are the guns." Julian asks hurriedly, looking towards the back seat of the car.

"Shit. I forgot about them." I stop the car. And open the door. Grimacing whilst looking down at the bodies lying prostrate on the floor, the mush that used to be their brains soaking into the sand around their heads as the car door slams shut behind me. All three DROMs lie still, a nasty odour emanating from their corpses as I search for the two dropped guns. I find mine with ease but must look closer for Julian's. There is a taint of blood and decay rolling on top of the saltiness of the sea breeze, assaulting my nose and making me gag as I swoop down and pick Julian's gun from under the leg of DROM two.

The sound of footsteps alerts me that we are not alone, I turn to see two men dressed in black, walking towards me. This must be the clean-up team. Turning back to the car, I put my hand on the door and leave them to get on with whatever it is they do. One of the men, shouts over to the other and then shouts over to me, I stop and look over at them both. Do the clean-up guys usually make so much noise and where is their vehicle?

"Great job." He waves, his statement a little creepy considering, and I'm left with an uneasy feeling in the pit of my stomach. Julian shouts at me to get into the car, which I do.

"Drive. Now." Julian shouts as he undoes his seatbelt. I toss the guns onto the floor beneath my feet as I start the engine of the car and release the hand break, but my car door is wrenched open, and I am pulled off the seat and out of the car backwards by my hair. Julian reaches over, trying to pull me back in as I'm cleanly lifted out of the car and dropped onto the sand below.

"Lion." I scream fighting off my attacker, jumping to my feet and pushing the man away. Julian Jumps out of the car and runs around to me, punching the man closest to me in the head repeatedly.

"The car." He growls just as the second man, reaches us. The two men close in on us and with the car directly behind us, Julian and I have been forced to fight. Julian throws punches, landing two before being punched back. I kick out at the man closest to me, aiming for his groin but catching his thigh instead, he lashes out and punches my face, the shock of his fist has me crashing against the car. The other pulls a gun out.

"Don't be a hero. And get that pretty bitch to stop fucking around, she isn't no fighter." He says cocking the gun and aiming it at my head then to Julian. The assailant who just punched me in the face, takes a step closer to me, the rage I feel unleashed. I run at him with every ounce of energy I have. I kick him success-fully in the groin and follow it up with a kick to his left shoulder, pummelling him to the ground where I stamp on his chest.

"Tell her to stop or I shoot you." I turn back around and the man with the gun has it inches away from Julian's forehead. I stop for a second, figuring out how to stop him when a black gloved hand with a wad of strong-smelling material covers my face, I elbow him in the chest, and sidestep him trying to turn around so I can really hurt him. A punch to my left side momentarily winds me and I collapse to my knees on the floor. The gloved hand is back pressing the ball of wadding into my face.

CHAPTER THIRTY

Taken

"I don't like this. Neither of them are answering their phones and they are not back yet." Seb paces the room attempting to locate Julian using an app on his phone.

"Shall we drive to them? Maybe Julian passed out and Ellie has had to pull over?" Nicky tries to reassure Seb, but it isn't working.

"No, Julian's phone is still registering that they are on the beach. They haven't left. I just don't understand why they haven't left. Seb's phone rings and he answers it instantly and listens intently. Nicky watches Seb for a sign that Ellie and Julian are okay. He hangs up the phone.

"We need to go."

Seb and Nicky reach Littlehampton beach. All four of Julian's car tires have been slashed. Seb parks and jumps out running towards the black van, parked on the other side of the car. Julian's back rests against the passenger seat door, talking heatedly on the phone, until he sees Seb.

"What happened. Are you okay?" Seb shouts over to Julian.

"No. Not okay, they took Ellie. Those bastards took her." Nicky glances around the beach, notices the blood-stained sand and what looks like a body stored in the van.

"Where is Ellie? Who took her?" He shouts, running at Julian. One of the clean-up guys grabs Nicky.

"You need to calm the fuck down." He hisses, letting him go. Seb looks at Nicky and then back at Julian.

"Who took her, Julian?"

"An activist group called TRUTH! One of them held a gun to my head as the other carried her away. He said he had a message for me. I was told I needed to reveal the truth, or I would never see Ellie again. Then the fucker hit me with the gun and when I came around, Barry was cutting through the cable ties."

"Julian was left behind with a nasty wound to his head and his wrists cable tied when we got here." Confirms Barry.

"Fuck." Julian and Seb say in unison.

"Who are they and what the fuck do they want with Ellie?" Nicky asks, panic flooding his body.

"TRUTH! Are an activist group who want to put the truth out there in the public domain. They have been around for a while." Says Barry, busy shovelling the blood-stained sand to hide the evidence of what had happened there earlier that morning.

"They are the kind of protest group that out dodgy politicians, whistle blow on corrupt police. Hang judges. Christ, they know what we do, are doing." Says Seb shaking his head.

"What do they want with Ellie?" Shouts Nicky, none of what the others are saying, makes any sense. Ellie is a gardener, who would want to kidnap a gardener.

"We are ready to go, you know where we are if you need us." Says Barry. Seb shakes his hand.

"We need to get you back to the attic, get you cleaned up and get you checked out. Nicky, do you want to come with us or, they can drop you back to the hotel."

"What kind of question is that, of course I am coming with you. We need to find Ellie."

Seb organises for the vandalised car to be collected by the closest garage and replace the tires, once it is collected, Julian, Seb and Nicky all pile into Seb's car and head back to Brighton.

* * *

The fifty-five-minute car ride back to Brighton was fraught with phone calls and heated conversations. Charlie, Julian's brother has been called and told to meet them at the attic. Seb made numerous calls trying to find out if the group TRUTH! Had been in contact, where they were currently situated and who they are working for? He also put a reward out for information on their whereabouts. So little was known about this group that the calls ended with no decent leads to follow.

"I need to phone Roth, see what he knows. He can alert the other teams that there is a mole." Julian says making the phone call only to hang up when he gets voice mail. Nicky sits sullenly in the back of the car while Seb and Julian continue to make calls. He keeps his phone in his hand, dialling Ellie's number repeatedly in the hope that she will answer. Nothing. Seb watches him through the rear-view mirror.

"Nicky, when we get back to the attic, I will explain everything." Julian looks over to Seb nodding in agreement.

"He needs to know what he is now involved with." Charlie meets the car as it pulls into the small car park, worry etched on his faces as he looks in the window and sees the damage his brother has sustained in the attacks of that morning.

"Christ Julian, you look like shit. Let's get you inside for a thorough check up." Charlie leads Julian off, while Seb parks the car.

"What in the actual fuck is going on Seb? What are you all involved in?" Nicky is in panic mode, not used to being kept in the dark and the last twelve hours have been a little surreal. He knew something was going on, he just didn't know it would lead the kidnapping of his best friend,

"What I'm going to tell you, is going to freak you out. You will need to keep an open mind because not everything you know about life is true. I suggest, we go up, make coffee and discuss this, because you really will need to sit down with what I am about to say." Seb heads to the door and holds it open for Nicky. They get into the lift contained inside a warehouse and get out on the top floor.

Seb leads Nicky through a large hall, draped in dark red velvet walls. To a large airy kitchen, with a massive black table.

"Sit." Says Seb as he strides over to the window. Silently he grinds coffee beans before putting them through an expensive coffee maker. He comes back with two espresso cups of freshly made coffee. Nicky watches him, realising he knows absolutely nothing about Seb or Julian. Glancing around the huge kitchen he feels completely out of his comfort zone and completely in the dark.

"Julian is a hunter; our family are hunters. Up until Ellie was five or six, her family were hunters too. Although she wasn't aware of that until recently." Seb stops to take a sip of his coffee. Nicky says nothing, he just watches Seb, patiently waiting for him to continue.

"TRUTH! Are a group of activists who like to expose the truth, or I should say force the truth into the public eye. They are a group who believe that the public have a right to know everything and had lobbied for what we now call the freedom of information act. The way they do things are usually over the top and in your face. It appears they have figured out what our family hunt, what specifically Julian hunts. And they have taken Ellie to force us to declare what we hunt and reveal the truth publicly."

"Which is?" Nicky prompts, not yet touching his coffee but unable to keep his eyes from Seb's.

"We hunt DROMS. You know them as zombies. Julian and Ellie went out to kill two zombies that were spotted at the beach early this morning." Seb finishes his coffee. Nicky glances at his.

"Zombies as in dead people who walk... like the movies?"

"Yes, exactly".

"Fuck! All the missing people posters everywhere, all the reports of loved ones who have disappeared, did they all die and turn into zombies? Then they were killed?" Seb nods his head once, attempting to read how Nicky is processing this news.

"That makes sense. It was weird how all the homeless just disappeared from the streets overnight. Did Julian kill them all?" As Nicky says this statement out loud, he realises how stupid it sounded. There are hundreds of missing people, there is no way that they could all have turned into zombies or that would have been killed by Julian alone.

"No, Julian didn't kill them all. But you are right. Many of the homeless turned into DROMS and had to be killed. The streets became unsafe, many of the homeless went home, some stayed with friends or moved on, thinking other cities would be safer. Sadly, and just like the movies, DROM bites and scratches are contagious and can turn healthy people in to DROMs. If a person turns, then they need to be euthanised. There are other teams of DROM hunters, here in Brighton as well as located all around the UK."

"How is Ellie involved in all of this?" Seb taps the table with his finger, angry at himself for letting her go with Julian. He should have gone instead. There was something not right that a dog walker had survived to make the call about a sighting.

"It appears that, TRUTH! Have infiltrated the police and have been tampering with the DROM reports. For a while now we had been receiving the wrong information about hunts. I suspected that someone was trying to set up the hunters, cause senseless deaths to publicly out us. Push our hand to publicly reveal all. Instead, they changed tact and saw an opportunity. Ellie was that opportunity and they have taken her. They are hoping it will spur us on to report to the world what we have been hiding for years, in exchange for Ellie's life." Nicky swirls his coffee in his hand before drinking it.

"Will you do what they want?"

"Hell no. If we have the public knowing what is happening here, there will be mass panic. The NHS will go under, there will be stockpiling which will lead to looting and unnecessary violence. There will be attempts to overthrow the government and this effects the economy. It would cause chaos, we as a nation would not cope. Think back to the beginning of the Covid crisis a few years ago. The country ran out of toilet paper for fucks sake. The public cannot be trusted with this information. We do what we do to keep the public safe."

"You can't possibly know that is what is going to happen if you go public."

"But I am. I know exactly what will happen. How do I know? It is on the news because it is happening all the time. War is the result of DROM infestations. They are a great example of when a government loses control. Most of the wars or the overthrowing of governments that has occurred over the last fifteen years are due to DROM infestations. The governments cover up the problem but are unable to do a decent enough job. The public find out and all hell breaks loose. Next come the reports of ethnic cleansing, innocents killed in protests and riots. These are excuses used to cover up the truth because the real issue were DROMs to begin with. Zombies set on mindlessly causing havoc. In doing so they spread their pestilence." Seb stops and watches Nicky closely. This is a lot of information to have to hear in a short period of time and he is truly sorry that he must break it to him like this, under these horrific circumstances.

"For example, Ebola became the most troublesome excuse for DROM infestations in recent times. Ebola is a nasty viral disease, leads to horrific illness and death. But it also triggered severe DROM activity, in many of the population who were unfortunate to become infected with Ebola. Teams from around the globe went to destroy the DROMs, this led to the local people fighting them and the army becoming involved. War is declared and is used to convince the rest of the world. Poverty and a corrupt government lead to civil war. The evening news reports a short segment on what is happening on the other side of the world. But we, here in the west don't care and we lose interest fast." Charlie enters the room.

"Julian is asleep, I have given him a sedative as he was attempting to rally the troops to go in search for Ellie. He has no DROM bites or scratches thankfully, nothing was broken but he is very bruised and will be tender for a few days." Seb nods, still looking at Nicky.

"What is the plan?" Charlie enquires, pulling open the fridge and pouring himself a glass of orange juice before pulling up a chair and joining them at the table.

"I have informed the government of the breach. For the moment they are happy for us to deal with this internally. Mainly because we have before. I have put a bounty on the head of TRUTH! Someone will want that two million more then they want to keep TRUTH! A secret. The press is aware, and we have journalists ready to hide or get rid of any DROM related stories should they arise, at least for the time being." Nicky is stunned at what he is hearing, the whole establishment is involved in a monumental zombie cover up.

"Julian will be asleep for a couple of hours but when he wakes, he will be ready to hunt for Ellie, you may want to restrain him." Seb rolls his eyes.

"I think he has had enough restraining today, don't you?" Seb's phone rings.

"Roth. What. Shit. I'm sorry to hear that. Yes, we believe it is TRUTH! Yes, they have taken one of ours. My people are searching, will keep you updated; you need to do the same." Seb hangs up and shakes his head.

"Roth has had two of his men killed last night in a DROM attack in Kent. Two DROMs were reported, turned out to be seven. They tore his men apart and TRUTH! Had drone photographs sent to Roth with cryptic instructions on informing the public or more would die."

"This is going to get ugly, and it is going to happen very quickly." States Charlie more to himself then to the other men in the room.

"And Ellie, how do we find her?" Asks Nicky.

"We wait. From what I know about TRUTH! They are likely to maintain the moral high ground. Which means that Ellie will be kept safe. It is only a matter of time before we find out their location and we shut them down and get Ellie back.

* * *

Julian wakes with a sore head and a dry mouth. At first, he is confused by his surroundings. Before realising where he is and remembering what had happened and how he got here. He gets up and heads to the kitchen. Finding Nicky on a laptop and Seb on the phone. Both look up when he walks in.

"Update." Seb passes Julian a bottle of water and a packet of paracetamol, with his phone still glued to his ear he leaves the table to make coffee. Julian pops a couple of tablets into his mouth and finishes the entire bottle of water.

"How long have I been asleep?" Seb places a coffee in front of Julian and one in front of Nicky. Before placing a third cup on the table in front of himself. Julian pours soya milk into his cup and two spoonsful of sugar before stirring.

"Is no one going to answer me?" Seb points to the phone, which he is still holding to his ear. Nicky looks at Julian, feeling mixed emotions. He knows it is not Julian's fault that Ellie was taken but he can't help but blame him, nonetheless. Seb hangs up.

"You have been asleep for three and a half hours; you have Charlie to thank for that. As for updates, Roth had two hunters die last night in Kent. A set up. Two other teams have had close calls. One in Edinburgh had nine DROMs roaming around Edinburgh castle. Twelve DROMs running riot in York cathedral. All three had video footage and photographs of the hunts and footage of the DROM killings shot via drones, CCTV and in the case of York cathedral, live video footage. All three teams were contacted by TRUTH! Advising them to make a press release and tell the world about the existence of DROMs and the continuous governmental cover up that they are involved in or more people will die."

"What about us? What about Ellie?"

"That is the thing. We have received nothing. Nothing at all. Only what those who took Ellie told you this morning, when they had that gun to your head. I have spoken to everyone, everywhere. There is a two-million-pound bounty for information that leads us to Ellie. Everyone is looking, the police, the army. Everyone." Julian finishes his coffee, pushing his cup away from him.

"What are we doing now?"

"I'm searching CCTV footage from this morning. We found the car, but the registration number used is fake. I'm now checking road footage and have tapped into highway England's CCTV, attempting to find the car and follow it to its destination." Nicky answers as Seb stands and places his hand on Nicky's shoulder.

"What are you doing Seb?" Right now, I am waiting for the pizzas to arrive. We need to eat before we continue the search. Nicky found the car was heading into Hampshire. We are guessing that they may transfer Ellie and move her to the Isle of Wright. We have the boats and ferries on lookout. The car hasn't gotten further then Portsmouth." Julian gets up, he puts his cup by the sink and runs the tap, filling a glass and gulping down the cold water.

Seb's phone rings, Nicky and Julian look at him as he answers it.

"It's just the pizza."

Seb walks to the door and waits for the delivery, the delivery boy couldn't have been more then nineteen, acne ridden and completely gormless. Seb accepts the three pizzas, hands the delivery boy a fiver as a tip and closes the door.

"This one is yours Nicky, mushroom and pepperoni." Seb opens the box to check the toppings before handing it to Nicky.

"This one is mine." He puts his down on the table in front of him and hands the last box to Julian.

"What did you order me?"

"Your usual, scotch bonnets, red peppers, capers and vegan cheese." Julian opens the lid of his box, and his eyes widen in horror.

"What's the matter, did they use cow tit cheese again?" Julian turns the box around. Attached to the inside of the box is a photograph of Ellie, bound and gagged. The message below the photo reads:

**You have 48 hours to tell the world about
the existence of DROMs.**

If you fail to comply, she will be turned into one,

live on air and broadcasted around the world.

Your 48 hours start now

#TRUTH!

To be continued

ACKNOWLEDGEMENT

I would like to thank all of those wonderful peeps who have championed my crazy dream and encouraged me to actually publish this book, you know who you are.

Thank you to my daughters Voirrey and Freya, who put up with my endless zombie talks, zombie walks and
zombie movie marathons over the years, although they love it really.

Lastly, thank you to my partner Paul who has been encouraging this project from day one.

ABOUT THE AUTHOR

Zom Lee

Zom is a biologist who currently resides in London
with her two daughters, Four pet Giant African Land
snails and numerous plants, but dreams of living by
the sea in Brighton.

This is Zom's first novel, based on an endless zombie night-mare that lasted 11 years.

When Zom is not writing and drinking coffee, she can
often be found walking the streets of London
looking for graffiti.

You can find Zom on Instagram:

@zom.lee or @zomsonsta

Printed in Poland
by Amazon Fulfillment
Poland Sp. z o.o., Wrocław

85546421R00168